THE SIGNAL
OUT OF SPACE

BOOK ONE OF
THIS FINE CREW

Mike Jack Stoumbos

Theogony Books
Coinjock, NC

Chris Kennedy/Theogony Books
1097 Waterlily Rd.
Coinjock, NC 27923
https://chriskennedypublishing.com/

Publisher's Note: This is a work of fiction. Names, characters, places, and incidents are a product of the author's imagination. Locales and public names are sometimes used for atmospheric purposes. Any resemblance to actual people, living or dead, or to businesses, companies, events, institutions, or locales is completely coincidental.

Cover Design by Shezaad Sudar.

Ordering Information:
Quantity sales. Special discounts are available on quantity purchases by corporations, associations, and others. For details, contact the "Special Sales Department" at the address above.

The Signal Out of Space/Mike Jack Stoumbos -- 1st ed.
ISBN: 978-1648552533

To my wife, Morrigen, who never doubted my dream.

Prologue:
Lidstrom

Day 4 of Training, Olympus Mons Academy

I want to make something clear from square one: we were winning.

More importantly, *I* was winning. Sure, the whole thing was meant to be a "team effort," and I'd never say this to an academy instructor, but the fact of the matter is this: it was a race and I was in the driver's seat. Like hell I was going to let any other team beat us, experimental squad or not.

At our velocity, even the low planetary grav didn't temper the impact of each ice mogul on the glistening red terrain. We rocketed up, plummeted down, and cut new trails in the geo-formations, spraying orange ice and surface rust in our wake. So much of the red planet was still like a fresh sheet of snow, and I was eager to carve every inch of it.

Checking on the rest of the crew, I thought our tactical cadet was going to lose her lunch. I had no idea how the rest of the group was managing, different species being what they are.

Of our complement of five souls, sans AI-assist or anything else that cadets should learn to live without, Shin and I were the only Humans. The communications cadet was a Teek—all exoskeleton and antennae, but the closest to familiar. He sat in the copilot seat, ready to take the controls if I had to tap out. His two primary arms were busy with the scanning equipment, but one of his secondary hands hovered over the E-brake, which made me more anxious than assured.

I could hear the reptile humming in the seat behind me, in what I registered as "thrill," each time I overcame a terrain obstacle with even greater speed, rather than erring on the side of caution.

Rushing along the ice hills of Mars on six beautifully balanced wheels was a giant step up from the simulator. The design of the Red Terrain Vehicle was pristine, but academy-contrived obstacles mixed with natural formations bumped up the challenge factor. The dummy fire sounds from our sensors and our mounted cannon only added to the sense of adventure. The whole thing was like fulfilling a fantasy, greater than my first jet around good ol' Luna. If the camera evidence had survived, I bet I would have been grinning like an idiot right up until the Teek got the bogey signal.

"Cadet Lidstrom," the Teek said, fast but formal through his clicking mandibles, "unidentified signal fifteen degrees right of heading." His large eyes pulsed with green luminescence, bright enough for me to see in the corner of my vision. It was an eerie way to express emotion, which I imagined would make them terrible at poker.

I hardly had a chance to look at the data while maintaining breakneck KPH, but in the distance, it appeared to be one of our surface vehicles, all six wheels turned up to the stars.

The lizard hummed a different note and spoke in strongly accented English, "Do we have time to check?"

The big furry one at the rear gruffed in reply, but not in any language I could understand.

"Maybe it's part of the test," I suggested. "Like a bonus. Paul, was it hard to find?"

The Teek, who went by Paul, clicked to himself and considered the question. His exoskeletal fingers worked furiously for maybe a second before he informed us, "It is obscured by interference."

"Sounds like a bonus to me," Shin said. Then she asked me just the right question: "Lidstrom, can you get us close without losing our lead?"

The Arteevee would have answered for me if it could, casting an arc of red debris as I swerved. I admit, I did not run any mental calculations, but a quick glance at my rear sensors assured me. "Hell yeah! I got this."

In the mirror, I saw our large, hairy squadmate, the P'rukktah, transitioning to the grappler interface, in case we needed to pick something up when we got there. Shin, on tactical, laid down some cannon fire behind us—tiny, non-lethal silicon scattershot—to kick up enough dust that even the closest pursuer would lose our visual heading for a few seconds at least. I did not get a chance to find out what the reptile was doing as we neared the overturned vehicle.

I had maybe another half-k to go when Paul's eyes suddenly shifted to shallow blue and his jaw clicked wildly. He only managed one English word: "Peculiar!"

Before I could ask, I was overcome with a sound, a voice, a shrill screech. I shut my eyes for an instant, then opened them to see where I was driving and the rest of my squad, but everything was awash in some kind of blue light. If I thought it would do any good, I might have tried to plug my ears.

Paul didn't have the luxury of closing his compound eyes, but his primary arms tried to block them. His hands instinctively guarded his antennae.

Shin half fell from the pivoting cannon rig, both palms cupping her ears, which told me the sound wasn't just in my head.

The reptile bared teeth in a manner too predatory to be a smile and a rattling hum escaped her throat, dissonant to the sound.

Only the P'rukktah weathered this unexpected cacophony with grace. She stretched out clearly muscled arms and grabbed anchor points on either side of the vehicle. In blocky computer-generated words, her translator pulsed out, "What—Is—That?"

Facing forward again, I was able to see the signs of wreckage ahead and of distressed ground. I think I was about to ask if I should turn away when the choice was taken from me.

An explosion beneath our vehicle heaved us upward, nose first. Though nearly bucked out of my seat, I was prepared to recover our heading or even to stop and assess what had felt like a bomb.

A second blast, larger than the first, pushed us from behind, probably just off my right rear wheel, spraying more particulates and lifting us again.

One screech was replaced with another. Where the first had been almost organic, this new one was clearly the sound of tearing metal.

The safety belt caught my collarbone hard as my body tried to torque out of the seat. Keeping my eyes open, I saw one of our tires—maybe two thirds of a tire—whip off into the distance on a strange trajectory, made even stranger by the fact that the horizon was spinning.

The red planet came at the windshield and the vehicle was wrenched enough to break a seal. I barely noticed the sudden escape of air; I was too busy trying, futilely, to drive the now upside-down craft...

* * * * *

Chapter One:
Paul Newman

Mother's gaze filled the cavern; the sweep and scope of what she could feel, hear, and smell radiated along each of the tunnels. She scented of the planet's native *tch'thi* flower as well as the protective fluids that surround the blind larvae, a scent I have often found comforting.

"*Jaiku,*" she began, addressing me with the word she would use for any of her children, but with a mental connection that meant it was certain she was speaking to me. "Do you know why I have summoned you?"

Both my mind and the color shift around my eyes responded before my mandibles and vocal cords. Mother already knew my excitement, but still I said, "I perceive I will be selected to join the Interstellar Initiative."

Mother's upper thorax thrummed in adoration and pride. "You have been selected," she softly corrected. "You have grown and learned beyond your imprinting. Your Human is excellent, and your pronunciation is clear. Furthermore, I am told you are understanding their nuances better than any other child of mine."

I felt my chest vibrate to receive the compliment. "Yes, Eminence." I resisted the urge to say "thank you" as a Human would, or to commend my tutors. Instead, I said, "I will positively represent the family."

Mother's eye chromae shifted, not to scolding, but something serious, nonetheless. "No, *jaiku*, you represent our species, as does every other worker selected for the Interstellar Initiative."

I understood and did not question this. First duty was, after all, first duty.

Although I was bred and incubated as a free-mind, Mother could naturally hear my moods and my thoughts, and she sought to educate me. I felt the gravity of one final lesson before I would travel incalculables away.

"When you ride to the Human system," she said, "to their academy and then to any stars beyond, you will have to see yourself as two people, as two minds—much like your queen is herself *and* her family. You must be one of *them*, without forgetting that you are one of us. Your imprinting has helped you to learn their language, to appreciate their scent, to handle their environmental tolerances. Your training has taken you further."

I agreed. I interpreted all as positive.

"Everyone has a role, *jaiku*, because everyone has different abilities and can hone different skills. You are of me, but you can do something I cannot."

I felt my eyes grow colder in wonder; my antennae arched in expectation.

Mother did not "keep me in suspense," as the Humans say. "You have demonstrated an ability to love the Human people. Not mere intrigue, but a love, similar to that you have for your own family. This is a great asset, and you shall nurture it. But do not forget that you are one of us. Your first duty is to the safety of our people, to this hive, to your queen."

I warbled a little, not in disrespect or disagreement, but confusion.

Mother sensed, and invited me to, "Speak."

"Eminence," I said warily, "Humans are our allies because they saved us from the enemy." I shuddered at the thought and felt my face grow colder at the mere memory, even if the memory was not firsthand. "Why would an ally, who saves and protects, betray the safety of our people?"

Mother's eyes shifted color again, but she also conveyed warmth. "The whys and hows are not for you to worry about, *jaiku*. That is not your role. Simply be aware that Humans, for everything else they are, are mighty and that might is dangerous to anyone they call their enemy."

I believed I understood. My tutors were never particularly mighty individually, but I knew how Humans had saved us before I was a larva and that they had vanquished an *enemy* whom we could not.

Having given her final lesson, Mother relaxed further. She asked me, "Have you chosen a Human name yet?"

"Yes, Eminence," I said. Tensing all four fists and hoping for approval, I told her, "I am called Paul Newman."

* * *

"*Jiki*," I said, verbally and without the use of a hind-brain connection, "you are supposed to say 'congratulations.'"

My winged companion, who stood a few Human centimeters taller than me, regarded me with green eye chromae: minor annoyance. "Paul Newman, I do not understand why I should congratulate that you are fulfilling the expectations of your imprinting."

I could not argue with her on that point. In many ways, my path to the Interstellar Initiative and the academy on the planet Mars-Human was preselected by my incubation imprint. I could also acknowledge that she, the more medically trained of us, had both of her hands occupied while all four of mine remained idle, and was working on an urgent schedule.

Still, I prompted her, saying, "It is a common Human convention, and we are practicing speaking Human." My antennae lowered in subservience, I added, "Also, I congratulated you."

She paused to regard me, and I could feel her tamping down the annoyance. "Then congratulations, Paul Newman, soon to be Green Cadet Paul Newman of the Interstellar Initiative. How was my inflection for compliments?"

"Very well done," I said, grateful for her efforts, but wondering how closely our interactions would be mirrored by real Human cadets.

"Good," she began, but was cut off by a surge of ambient noise.

The thrum of engines had been low enough that we'd not needed to shout or resort to non-verbal signaling, but now the volume increased and gained additional pitches. Nearby drones, the largest and least independently minded molts, began moaning in collective anxious energy, received from workers of several hives. The travel pod behind me lit green to receive.

My *jiki* adjusted the pitch of her voice to be heard precisely between the other chaotic frequencies. "Do you have anything else to address before we begin our journey?" She inspected the device on my forearm, on the hard shell just above the pivotable wrist, which would relay my life signs and, more importantly, identify me as a cadet.

I considered taking one last look in the direction of hive and home. Instead, I said, "No."

"Good. Please step into your pod."

She indicated, and I complied, walking both feet backward into the open shell, a semi-organic casing perfected for my people and my particular molt, which would soon jet up to the interstellar liner. I filled one of two cells.

The outside din muted as I settled into the semi-flexible grooves that would protect my inflexible limbs in the event of unexpected inertial interference. "Are you frightened of what we will encounter?"

She paused, giving the matter due consideration. "Not yet. Lift your head."

I complied, stretching my mandibles so she could apply the feed-tube for deep space. It was a comfortable apparatus, modeled after the natural structures the drones used to feed the young semi-sentient nymphs.

She ensured everything was connected and reading properly. With two hands and steady eyes, she demonstrated how effectively she too had surpassed her imprint through formal training. I was proud of my kinsmolt, one of my closest connections, who was both hatched and incubated in the same generation as I. Humans would say we were technically siblings, like brother and sister, but that is not a fair comparison.

For one, my primary *jiki* was not actually a "she," having neither reproductive organs nor societal gender, but after assessing the voices and relative shape of our Human tutors, we determined that I would be *he* and she *she*. *Jiki*, like *jaiku*, is a hard term to translate directly, but it is easy enough for us to use alongside our modern Human speech—also called Transnational English by some groups on Terra-Human. The inside of our travel pod, like our recent dwellings, used only this Human writing, which Mother hoped would give us "an edge," so we might better represent our hive. Even partially encased, I could see other pods from other on-planet hives, each of whose representatives could be just as prepared as we.

My *jiki* had started placing electrodes on the soft tissue of my torso just below my thorax shell, and noted, "Your chromae are turning blue. You are frightened."

There was certainly a buzzing in my core, and my extremities tingled with the cool sensation of near hibernation, but it was not for fear of takeoff or the trip. Drones were on stand-by to interpret and soothe that kind of fear. This was harder to explain, for more reasons than the device in my mouth.

"I am…anxious about working with Humans. They are said to be skilled and clever and aggressive." I trailed from there and tried to communicate the general feelings telepathically. Even though I had been selected for this prestigious honor, I had trouble believing I could compete with someone from the species who had advanced so quickly in military standing and galactic position.

"You neglect to mention, they are also flawed. Less-precise, incapable of imprinting knowledge. And the fellow cadets are not experienced warrior Humans. Neither were our Human tutors."

Her statements were accurate. The Humans had a special term for what I felt that was not present in Jyikj'tch'tyeek, the formal name for both our language and species, abbreviated to "Teek." Their term was "imposter syndrome."

My *jiki* continued her work on our pod, much faster, I noticed than some of the other hive representatives. She also practiced her bedside manner. "You ought to relax. The transition into a space fold will be easier. Tell me what you are most excited about."

"I am excited to meet more home-system Humans." Which was true, but optimistic. Mine was an anxiety borne out of a desire to form true friendships, as was depicted in Human-style long literature.

She gave me a mental nudge to continue.

"I am excited to see a formal cooperation between Tsangharee and the P'rukktah species, especially far away from either of their contested territories."

"So am I," she agreed.

"And I am *very* interested in the alliance's new hybrid ships. To be able to walk around while traveling between systems."

"That is just a rumor," she reminded me. "What is the phrase? Do not get your hopes up. *Hyi, jiki?*"

"Yes, *jiki*," I agreed.

"Good." She modified her voice again and turned it into something lower and more soothing, akin to Mother's. "I am about to activate your hibernation. Sleep well, Paul Newman."

I knew she would be going into the pod beside me, so I reciprocated, using her chosen Human name. "Goodnight, Ella Fitzgerald."

She leaned forward and touched one antenna to mine as a familial comfort before inducing sleep.

The electrode on my lower torso buzzed. My parasympathetic nervous system reacted to the signal as if it were a drone indicating winter. My exterior soft tissue began to grow rigid and fibrous, closing me from danger during sleep—an evolution that made more sense on the ground than in the dead of space.

As my compound eyes stopped registering the visual, I focused instead on a mental recollection, a simulation shown to all prospective cadets. It portrayed a crew, composed of bipedal Humans, large and furry P'rukktah, and long-tailed Tsangharee. The next time I woke, I would be among them, more species than I had ever encountered in one place.

* * * * *

Chapter Two:
Lidstrom

"Wake up, Greenies!"

The trainer's brassy, masculine voice echoed through the cylindrical hull of the transplanetary vessel. The words distorted unnaturally through my earpiece, even though I could hear it in person as he floated between the many rows of highly secure and disoriented passengers.

My eyelids felt heavy, which was weird in the zero-grav environment. I checked my seat partner, a Greek kid named Yiorgos, whom I'd known for only a couple hours of conscious time but had been sitting beside for days. He had these mighty, dark brows and an islander's tan, even though he too had grown up in the northern States. Right now, those brows drooped, and he looked quite a bit greener than I felt. A quick glance to the left and right told me he wasn't the only one. Maybe that's why they called us "Green Cadets."

While I didn't consider myself prone to nausea, the sum of the factors climbed above and beyond the usual. I could smell that faint acrid scent of a stimulant being pumped into the atmo, something to bring us out of a mild space sleep. Chemical stabilizers for both physiological and psychological effects traveled through my veins and some of them pressed on my bladder. I knew I was hooked up to a seat with "evacuation properties," but I still wasn't space-savvy enough to pee whenever the spirit struck me, especially when sharing a room with a couple hundred other prospective cadets, as well as former TSF officers who could become direct supervisors.

"Are we there yet?" Yiorgos asked, his lips forming a weak smile that did not budge the upper half of his face.

"Must be," I replied—or, more accurately, rasped. My throat was so raw, they could have served it for sushi. "System, water?"

The round light above my head pulsed red, but instead of delivering requested hydration, the blasted AI asked me to, "Confirm seat number."

I gawked, but didn't remember so simple and stupid a detail. My mind went into a kind of freefall, trying to catalog the facts of my life in seconds, from where I'd been when they announced first-contact and the Human-Teek Alliance to beating the prelim thresholds on Luna, somewhere between a few minutes and a few weeks ago. But my mind was too scrambled by chemicals, both natural and imported, to spit out a number.

"E-84," Yiorgos supplied, clearly handling the mental side of the disorientation better than me. "Got you, brother."

"Right. E-84," I repeated, finally noticing that the number was printed in the overhead space, just beyond the blue circle that indicated the system's voice-assist intelligence.

Whirring came from the shoulder of my seat and a straw extended to where I could catch it with my lips and absorb the steady stream of liquid refreshment. My arms were still securely constricted, and I couldn't even fully turn my head, but I could have water delivered to me on command if I had the wherewithal to name my ID number. Yes, this was the life, pressed into a temporary full body cast with dozens of rows of other cadets, one of whom was still trying to help me adjust to the most mundane detail of this entire experience.

"E-84," he went on, seeming to gain energy and focus by the second, "just think seven by twelve. Or like *Nineteen Eighty-Four*—pretty good novel, terrible VR game."

That particular piece of Virtual Reality had always sounded too bleak for my tastes, and, although I had always been good at math, I saw no reason to take number theory as philosophy. He might have dug deeper into number theory and tried to rewrite the cosmos, but I let go of the straw and cut in, "Yiorgos, there's no real need to memorize my seat number, right?"

I think he tried to shrug in response, but when that didn't work, he remarked, "You never know."

In fact, I only had an inkling of what I was in for, but I was determined to listen and learn.

Several rows behind me, the trainer who had woken us was yelling something else, sans headset, about how much we were each costing the allied governments of the Sol-Human System and how we'd better be worth it. The monitor screens, which looked about a century old, showed a computer generated, or CG, rendition of this metal tube's approach to Phobos Station, displayed on a weird enough angle and delay to make me even more dizzy.

I willed my eyes to accept the upside-downness of my point of view, and I knew I shouldn't complain. After all, the shuttles from our Lunar pre-training out to Mars were supposed to be the safest Human vessels ever constructed, with the smoothest known wake-up procedures for in-system flight—or so they told us. The Transnat

Space Force veterans would tell us they'd never been afforded our current luxury, let alone that of the cooperative *Command*-class ships we'd crew in the Initiative; those poor souls were barred from becoming cadets *because* of their military training.

Every single Human cadet in this first wave had to be under twenty-four, non-military, and "non-dynasty"—whatever the hell that meant—in order to keep things fair between the varying species. Watching the squirming, swinging feet of rows of peers and competitors sharing this pristine space cylinder, I had to wonder how many of them might have cheated just a little to get where they now were.

Everything in me wanted to burst out of the restraints and charge to the front of the line, to prove that I belonged and deserved to be here, but I also knew to keep my cool and try to make a good impression on the staff.

It only took a few minutes of idle nausea before the intake officer arrived to inspect my row, to see if any of us were dying and needed to be redirected. She was wearing the standard-issue full-body flight-suit with the sleeves rolled up and no uniform jacket or EVA-prep kit. Her skin was genetically dark but muted from what I assumed was low, direct sunlight. She also sported a TSF-regulation buzzed head and apparently felt no disorientation in a moving but otherwise null grav environment.

"Morning, cadets," she said, communicating little warmth, but sounding more procedural than mean. "Addressing E-section cadets, numbers eighty-one through eighty-four. Can you all acknowledge you can hear and understand me?"

I said, "Acknowledged," in practiced chorus with three other young cadets, like I'd been doing for months on Luna.

"Excellent." She made her way to the end of the row with one hand on the rungs and an occasional push.

Periodically glancing at her tablet, she went through our vital stats and personal info. It was weird to hear everyone's name, birth year, and point of origin in a read-off dossier. The last of the group, I used the downtime to check out the progress map and try to ignore the sounds of a bad wake up from a couple rows behind.

After finishing with Green Cadet Yiorgos Stratis, at least a year my senior, she planted in front of me.

Now that she faced me squarely, I could clearly read "Staff Sergeant Clancy, I.I." across her collarbone, which meant she most likely came from the Transnat Space Marines and would probably be involved in ground training and nothing related to piloting. Clancy gauged my eyes for dilation and tracking. She scanned the status bar above my head, the kind that tracks blood pressure and respiration rates, like a simulator's HUD.

"Green Cadet Darren Lidstrom," she said. "Born 2089, from Detroit, Michigan, Incorporated States, Terra. Please confirm."

She turned the tablet toward me, commenting "Spring chicken" in a low voice. With pinned forearms, I reached out a fingerprint authorization. A yellow banner flashed with the word, REVIEW. I stiffened awkwardly in my restraints and heard my heart monitor ping, but the banner self-cleared. Clancy hadn't reacted, so I decided to hope the displayed alert was standard operating procedure and not a sign the Initiative had reconsidered my former infractions and subsequent recruitment.

"Lidstrom, can you confirm you are of sound mind and are joining the Initiative of your own volition?"

"Come on, Sarge, are any of us really of sound mind?" I didn't mean it to sound disrespectful, more an attempt at levity to hide my nerves. Maybe I could blame my poor word choice on having just woken from a several-thousand-kilometer induced nap. There were a couple of chortles from the others in my row, including Yiorgos, whose laugh sounded exhausted and dizzy, but in no way muffled.

Lucky me, Staff Sergeant Clancy's expression turned up in amusement, suggesting she had heard this kind of response many times before and held no grudges about the reused quip.

Still, I didn't want to chance good graces, so I changed tack. "Yes, Sergeant. I am of sound mind and joining the Initiative of my own free will. And I'd show more excitement if I weren't bolted in place."

"Ask and you shall receive," Clancy remarked, quietly enough that I had a feeling the comment was just for me, and she disabled the comprehensive safety restraints. Decoupling and whooshing sounds accompanied the disappearance of forearm and shin stabilizers. The staff sergeant's overall demeanor softened, and she said, "Though it's a little premature, welcome to Mars."

Soon, we'd disconnected everything other than the basic straps across our chests, and Clancy was off to check some boxes for another row.

Instinctively, I started massaging my wrists. Beside me, Yiorgos was doing the same. Our feet floated freely, swaying beneath us, casually pressed this way or that by the soft waves of the shuttle's vector adjustments.

"You know," Yiorgos said, "they say on the new hybrid interstellar vessels they'll counter internal inertia, so you don't need to be strapped in all the time."

"That's the dream."

Sergeant Wake-Up clicked in over the earpiece. He was also making his way forward along the rows while he gave his intro speech, the time disconnect very slight between the electronically relayed and the real version of the sound. In person, his manner was even more military, but I couldn't tell if he was Transnat or States-Local, like my folks had been. Either way, he conferred a level of discipline and rigor to this supposedly non-military operation, effectively separating it from the classroom style of Luna.

"Greenies," he said, climbing hand over hand past dozens of waking cadets. "As your safeties are removed, you may feel the urge to get up and stretch your legs. Do not give in to this urge during unauthorized windows. The transition from thrust grav to zero grav to station rotational grav will serve you up to the Initiative on a stretcher."

I was hyper-aware of our shuttle's torque, the change in rotational momentum pressing me up from my seat and against the chest belt. My mind tried to map the docking angles, even using windows to supply real-time visuals.

"To give you something to focus on other than your own nausea," he went on, "you are going to provide your fingerprint and John Hancock to a very important document, the kind that you are not authorized to sign while in Terran local space."

A semi-holographic touch display extended from under my arm rest. It populated with the I.I. emblem and then my info. I did feel compelled to scan for the red flag I was told would *not* carry onto any permanent record or anywhere out of the state of Michigan. Fortunately, anything prior to Luna training had been left out of the otherwise thorough dossier, complete with standard-frame portrait.

The computer had generated an approximation devoid of makeup, digitally erased my sandy hair, but produced a likeness that was distinctly me. Swedish chin, wide nose, and an expression so smug, they probably should have retaken the picture. But you can't really blame me, it was snapped right after the recruiter said I was the youngest person to earn a spot in the first wave. Among a bunch of other eighteen- to twenty-four-year-old hopefuls, a couple of days' edge felt like years of bragging rights.

The trainer was within spitting distance when he said, "Please read and respond to every item on your screens and acknowledge that all our information on you is correct. This is absolutely mandatory before you enter Phobos Orbiting Station and breathe one breath of its valuable air. If there's an accident, you wouldn't want the wrong blood type from the wrong species just because someone goofed the records."

A ripple of laughter came from patches of the recruits, but I had the queasy feeling that the remark referenced a real anecdote. Sure, our ship was an Earth vessel, transporting only Human recruits, but I truly could not guess how many different sentients would be on Phobos Station or on Mars' surface. I'd never even been up close to a Teek, and there were rumors we'd be working with many more people than our four-foot-tall insect allies who were helping us make a huge leap forward in travel technology.

A little buzzer pulsed three times, warning us to expect reorientation and docking turbulence. The trainer started telling everyone how they "might be feeling the urge to vomit" and where they should point that urge if they couldn't suppress it.

I tuned him out to read the print on my screen, and in so doing confirmed all the rumors of the scariest comprehensive waiver I'd ever seen, which would be unheard of in what we Terrans liked to call "civilized society." The death-and-dismemberment policy alone could kill anyone's appetite, and the less said about the "Missing in Service" protocols, the better. Sure, the tech was climbing and the training stellar, but the bottom line was this: once we were in the Initiative, everything was an unknown risk. Terra and Mars weren't prepared to take that kind of responsibility for citizens, so we'd be citizens of the galaxy. Thank my lucky stars my folks were sturdy.

The echoing, shuddering sound of docking interrupted my focus. I looked up to see our progress on the viewer, the CG representation of hatches lining up, on the other side of which was a new life filled with new lifeforms. My heart rocketed in anticipation, and I was really glad I'd already passed any pulse and blood pressure tests. When the awesome ambience was shattered by someone vomiting in the next row, I turned back to my form.

The truth was, I didn't need to read it in full, and I certainly wasn't going to hesitate to sign. Legally, my path had been set at fifteen, when pre-service pilot training became the best option for curtailing a juvie. Even beyond that, I'd been dead set on flying between planets since I'd learned about the Teek Alliance in primary school, whispered about the classified W-Wars on the playground, and memorized the *Spacegirl Stella* theme song. My family had always known I was a lifer and not one of them bothered to object when I jetted up to Luna just shy of my eighteenth birthday.

Out of thousands of people in classes on Luna, only about a tenth of us were chosen for the first wave. I couldn't imagine any would get cold feet and back out now.

I acknowledged, signed, and submitted. Quietly enough that no one else could hear, I said, "Green Cadet Darren Lidstrom, reporting for adventure."

* * * * *

Chapter Three:
Arrksh

Day 0 - The Stellar VII Docking Transfer,
Human-Teek Alliance Station

I kneel with great precision and politeness. I bow my head low toward the Belbeh ambassador, who has also been my safe-passage captain for several legs of my interstellar journey. It is difficult for one of my people to be lower than the eye level of a Belbeh, who stand less than one third our height and less than one twentieth our mass.

The ambassador paws at his own neck with one of his thumbless hands and squeaks gratitude through twitching whiskers. They may have provided the long-range vessel, but I have been instrumental in their surviving each docking. This port is my final transfer before going to Human space. By reputation, Stellar VII is among the safest for spacefaring folk, especially now that the Human-Teek Alliance positions suppression weapons at the most trafficked transit platforms.

The Belbeh vessel is attached to an airlock among the lower, smaller platforms of the transit station, and we are grouped close to that entrance. Although it is proper and right to receive well wishes from one's host, I am acutely aware my back is exposed to a major walkway. Perhaps my unease is less about tactical safety than a desire to rendezvous with my connecting vessel, for which I have secured a rare invitation.

The ambassador commends my family's fur and praises their breeding stock; his two wives echo the sentiment. Then, he wishes me safe and well-fed travels; the wives chitter approvingly. One shuffles forward, her bootless feet and little claws making a *shh-tik* sound, which, yes, I will miss. She hands me a spherical bundle of food in a satchel. She carries it in both arms, but the weight would not burden my smallest finger.

I reciprocate the positive sentiments, adding ridiculous terms like "tenfold" and "infinitely more," without rushing. It is their manner, and I am accustomed. Truthfully, I have grown fond of some of their rituals. I hope this journey will prepare me for life among even stranger species, as well as sparing me from the skirmishes on my home planet.

This particular rodent ambassador likes to bestow physical gifts as well, trinkets of nominal sentimental value rather than trade power, one of which is already sheathed in my belt. He leans his head to one side to twist free a corkscrewing earring from his comparably fan-like ear, which he hands to me. Despite his regularly groomed fur coat and appearance of cleanliness, he also has no concept of communicable disease. Perhaps general precautions are less important for creatures with such brief lifespans.

Still, I trust in my immune system and ongoing favorable relationships between the P'rukktah and the Belbehan peoples. I accept the gift graciously. The coiled and hardened bone jewelry looks tiny in my hand, but the point is effectively sharp.

"Gratitude," I reply, but more importantly, I demonstrate. I take the tip of the earring and start it through one of my current piercings, creating new punctures as I coil it down. The Belbahan do not have as many nerves in their ears as my people do, but I endure the pain without a flinch. I do not say this to express superiority; after all, the Belbehan ambassador wears two nostril piercings, and I know from personal dissection work that their noses are intensely nerve-mapped.

"You will always be welcome in our vessel, sister Arrksh," the ambassador says, dropping some of the ceremonial tone and concluding this parting. "Our children shall know your name and call you friend."

"Gratitude," I say again, growling out their language in a way we can both understand, but with a much deeper voice. Beyond the transportation alone, my time with this Belbehan crew has done more for my family's name than this small-statured, short-lived ambassador can comprehend. Finally, I straighten and place the back of my wrist against my forehead, their form of salute, which looks much more fitting with their small, thumbless hands. "Safe travels."

I about-face, a new bit of polished bone hanging from my ear, a lunch satchel in one hand, and my gear on my back.

I start toward a station display board to confirm platform number and departing time. As I suspected, I am behind schedule but not in danger of losing my seat.

However, I pause when I register a deep murmur: completely organic, too low-pitched for Belbehan ears. My fur mats down on instinct; self-smoothing for swift movement. I catch the brief rush of scales in my peripheral vision, dark-hued in my eyes, but probably appearing camouflaged against the drab metal walls to a Belbeh's vision.

Now occupied by onboarding cargo, the ambassador has not noticed the reptile looking to slip in and stow away.

"Ambassador," I call, my own voice filling the range of my middle eardrums.

He twitches in fright, his tail alert. Two other Belbeh have dropped to all fours to start running.

The scales have vanished as well, either invisible to me or hiding behind one of many cargo crates.

So certain am I that I say, "I smell lizard."

Whether or not the camouflaged Tsanghar understands, she leaps into view, eliciting squeaks and shrieks from the crew.

The ambassador draws a precision pistol, appropriate for duels against similarly sized foes, but not for a Tsanghar.

I close the distance in two leaping steps and physically threaten the lizard, whose camouflage is now erratic and ineffective. She seems to consider: harming a Belbeh, running, or attacking me directly. I am apparently the least appealing option.

The lizard intruder and would-be stowaway flicks her tongue at me, then tries to wager. "*I take one rat. We all walk away.*"

She speaks in a dialect of Tsanghar I assume to be Segranee, a now disbanded nation and the defeated enemy of the P'rukktah. Scattered and unmanaged, they are less mighty but still dangerous to the poorly defended.

This Belbeh crew is not defenseless right now; they have me.

The fur around my head and neck changes from flattened to raised. This physiological posturing is not comfortable under the restrictive travel vest and the straps of my backpack. My discomfort will be brief; this lizard's will not. I have not been trained in negotiation of this kind, but I have excellent aim and a strong arm.

Before the Tsanghar can lash at any of the retreating Belbeh, I throw the satchel of food, appreciating how the Belbeh prefer to compress their nutrients into spheres. It connects just below her ribcage, not lethal, but one of the three most sensitive areas of a Tsanghar's body. This also gives me time to charge her. She looks up from her distress just in time for me to barrel into her neck, getting my armored shoulder under her chin.

With my sensitive lower eardrums, I pick out the wheeze of a deflated sac in her throat cavity beneath the high screech of pain. Second of three target spots. Her pain intensifies as my momentum carries her into a wall, putting pressure on her other throat sacs. She foolishly tries to claw at my eyes, an instinctual counter of the unstudied. I've already closed my eyes and tensed my brow, the muscle and skin tissue pulling tight and acting as armor.

I headbutt, which does no damage but disorients my foe. She is upright enough for me to aim a knee between her legs just before her tail's connection. Third target spot. Her neck collapses over my shoulder, and the scales grow pale, apart from the dark diamond pattern on the center of her face. Her tail is no longer in this fight.

Have I broken her will? No, she tries a final ploy, sinking her retractable claws into my upper arm.

I ignore that arm and pull my blade with another. The blade is thin, curved, single-edged, and not even as long as my forearm; a bejeweled Belbehan sword, which I had never expected to draw in combat. Its point is sharp and now presses against her neck. The bruised organs in her long throat will heal, unless she gives me cause to slash.

She spits out an insult, something about interspecies relations and our potential mutant children, a fate I would prefer to their single-sex existence. Neither the Belbehan nor any of the gathering onlookers react to her disparaging remark.

In my best attempt at Tsanghar, poor though my pronunciation is, I say, *"No dinner for you tonight."* I try to ignore feelings of foolishness; I have no idea what the relative "time" of day is in this station.

I quickly survey my surroundings, confirming no other noticeable aggressors. In addition to the Belbehan crews and tradesmen, there stands the odd arthropod whom I have been told do not even register violence if they have not been programmed to understand it. I also notice a primate, armored, most likely a renegade or a drifter. Their kind are becoming much more common among the reaches. The pinkish primate lifts its chin and flashes its dull, unimpressive teeth. Perhaps it is a bounty hunter who respects my physical prowess. Every time I see one of the Humankind, I am shocked by how unintimidating they look in person, given their powerful reputation. They are becoming a more frequent sight throughout the sector, and soon will be as common in the ports as the scurrying Belbehan. They will also be a majority where I plan to spend the next span of my life, and one toothish expression from the witness to a fight should not give me pause.

I give a grunt and a jut of my chin to the onlookers, attempting to convey that the situation is in hand.

To the ambassador, who is still breathing very quickly in excitement and fear, I say, "Gratitude manyfold for the sword. I cherish it."

* * *

I waste no time dragging the bound but writhing Tsanghar. Upon reaching a security sign, I drop her roughly before the very different boots of the primate and arthropod forms standing before me. The sign reads Port Authority in so many languages, it is more distracting than helpful.

"Whoa!" intones the primate: Human, but in a uniform that matches the arthropod's and is not originally designed for the Human body shape. He speaks Human to me, whose terms I cannot make out, even though I understand the intent from the tone.

With both hands free, I take my mobile translator out of my pack and put it around my neck. As soon as I have the piece in my ear, I can interpret a blocky approximation of phrases in the databank on slight delay.

It now speaks with its Jyikj'tch'tyeek partner "—I tell the P'rukktah—Not bounty office."

The arthropod is less animated, less emotional. As they always do, this one smells wonderful and inspires hunger, arousal, and nostalgia. Humans are either quite strong of composure or weak of nose if they do not notice. This arthropod has only four limbs—two arms and two legs—and long wings. A scout type, as we label them.

"Hello," it greets, its eyes a warm orange, its more recognizable language forming full sentences in my translator. "Do you have a crime to report?"

"Crime prevented," I say, in my own language. The device clicks back a translation. "Lone Tsanghar attempted harm against Belbehan crew." Jerking my thumb behind me, I say, "Witnessed," and give the platform number where it occurred.

The Human speaks with a language so cadenced that it might as well be a dialect of Tsanghar. My translator relays, "File report?"

"No," I reply. "Meeting my ship."

I hope that is all, but I feel I should formally exit the conversation. Though the gesture is Belbehan, and the Human is only a head shorter than I, a salute seems appropriate. I place the back of my wrist against my forehead, fingers curling forward slightly.

The Human's bald cheek twitches. The corner of its mouth draws to one side and a little up, perhaps a smile. It mirrors the gesture, but with the right hand held stiffly, just in front of its own brow at a slight upward angle. After receiving the Human interpretation of a Belbehan salute, I take my leave.

Within a few steps, the Tsanghar protests wildly, but that is not my concern. Whether they throw criminals in holding cells or declaw them does not impact me. I will soon be on another ship, and as I near the platform, my excitement resumes.

My foreseeable future is with the Human-Teek Alliance, in something that best translates as the "Interstellar Initiative." I have been told this program is one where citizens will not have to worry about hungry Tsangharee. However, I can see from the line of other late-arriving passengers that the Tsangharee from other factions or moons will still be present. Very few of my people, the P'rukktah, are among the waiting passengers, and they are close enough to the vessel's loading doors that they will not have a chance to speak with me in queue. Their bulk and spread postures appear foreign to me after so much time among the Belbehan.

This platform is massive compared to the single hatch docking points for cramped Belbehan ships. Here, the ceiling is vaulted enough to inspire dizziness in the cave-dwelling arthropods—or "Teek" as I should get used to calling them; the light is bright enough that some groups of Tsangharee wear tinted lenses to protect their eyes. A huge cylindrical tank is being connected to a specialized cargo hatch. Most likely for pumping water into the vessel's hold or transporting an amorphous aquatic species I've heard about but never met.

I take a spot at the back of the line and increase my translator's sensitivity to pick up as many conversations as I can. The translator is arthropod tech, as are most modern items, adapted to fit around my neck and with earpieces that only go into one of my three sets of ear canals on either side. This translator is probably several updates behind, as are most pieces of arthropod tech traded by the Belbehan, such that it is hardly calibrated for the Human language. Given the range of syllables from the surrounding Human folk, I can't help but wonder if there is more than one dialect of Human; perhaps they even have multiple languages, despite being emergent space sentients who reside on only one planet.

Of all of the species waiting, the Tsanghar are the most vocal. They hum and warble their words, through wide mouths with tiny, pointed teeth. Several colors, representing several moons and bloodlines, even a few different dialects. No one speaks directly to me, but more than a few speak about me, then hush as they notice my translator or catch my eye. Shortly, behind me in the winding line, joins one particular green-faced Tsanghar with bright gold eyes who says nothing and does not look away. Her spread lips form the illusion of a pleasant smile, and I remind myself that it is better for Tsanghar to talk about you than silently plot against you.

I remind myself of the truces between all recognized factions of Tsangharee people and the P'rukktah Confederation, even though our people have been literally at each other's throats for generations. I wonder if I will have difficulty explaining idioms like "at another's throat" when among the Humans.

When I am near enough to the front of the queue, I hear translated remarks from the Human security, discussing whether or not a rare form of perfume can be allowed on the vessel when it is clearly poisonous to one or more species.

As I carry no poisons or explosives, I am not worried about these security persons scanning my belongings. Furthermore, I have been prepared for the idea of a new life on a new planet and therefore would not be particularly troubled if anything of mine were confiscated. I have been given a new sphere of food—rodent food, unpleasant to eat—which might raise some fur to the unknowing, but I would part with the nutrients if I could not explain that it was safe for myself and passengers.

When the Human with facial fur ululates at me, I present my identification and ticket authorization. My translator does not register, *"Have a kind day,"* until I am past him and to the bag inspectors, and I find myself doubting the accuracy of this phrase. I do not imagine Humans would consider a period of time capable of being kind, but perhaps they are more prone to figurative language than even the Tsangharee.

The Human with goggles recalibrates his sensor to see through the exterior of my pack. He indicates *up* with his thumb, so I look up. Then, with a laugh, he says something that feeds into my ear as, "Cleared. No chemical—power signature—Flags." I need to speak with an arthropod about upgrading my translator.

"Whoa!" intones another, without goggles. She points at my waist, a rude gesture to be sure, but I do not smell or hear either sexual intent or mockery. The sounds she forms are *"Is that a sword?"* before my translator asks me, "Sword?"

I begin to pull out the tiny blade, which only seems to agitate them. I am not presenting aggressive postures; perhaps they are jealous of the gift. Are these gems particularly valuable to Humans?

The din progresses. People in queue behind me step back, creating a crowding effect, as there is nowhere to go. I attempt to gesture that the sword is not a threat unless I have cause to use it, but my commentary generates no results.

An arthropod with four arms intercedes. I had been so tense, I had closed my inner nostrils and had not even noticed her scent when she approached, stepping in from behind the two Human security officers.

She gestures to me with fists against the thorax and then open palm, or claw, to me. Finally, she says in my language, "Greeting."

My agitated height reduces by fractions as I exhale relief. "Greeting received."

Continuing in slow but practiced P'rukktah, the arthropod's mandibles push out, "Forgive their reaction. They worry about weapon."

I pulse forward, nodding my understanding. "Receive this sword from a Belbeh. It could not damage the vessel's hull."

The arthropod's eyes go yellow orange, like a midday sea on the homeworld. "Please, show me your identification. I will sort."

Not knowing the arthropod's aim, but trusting the scent and eyes of goodwill, I once again show my dossier, including my ticket and invitation. I brace for disqualifying reaction. I have been told that my employment as muscle for a Belbehan ship will not bar me from the Initiative, as it does not constitute formal military enrollment. My family name might raise other questions to well-informed observers. It would mean little to most Humans, but possibly more to an arthropod on Stellar VII.

The orange parts of her eyes go white. Then, as she turns to the Human security, I can see them tint green in irritation. She lectures them in their language. Though arthropods are far less tonally inclined than most other sentient speakers, I can tell she is faulting their judgment and expects better treatment for one such as me.

The scent of both Humans change, one to contrition, another to, I believe, resentment. After a few terse comments, a compromise is reached. The contrite security Human indicates the sword.

I need no translation to sheathe and hand it over.

Contrite security Human sprays my "weapon" with fast-hardening foam from a suppressor gun.

Carefully, using two of her four hands, the arthropod returns the cocooned sword. "We will dissolve the compound once we dock in Sol-Station Phobos. Apology, Princess Arrksh."

I do not completely lose composure, but I am glad that my eyes do not change color like those of the arthropods. Fortunately, only she and I seem to understand my language.

I collect my belongings without expressing gratitude. I deactivate the identification holo on my forearm, hoping no one else had time to see or hear the exchange. Perhaps few enough people can speak enough P'rukktah to decipher the old terms for royalty. Perhaps no one else en route to the Human system for the Initiative will assume I am given special treatment.

I enter the vessel and am directed toward my seat. I realize I am most grateful no one opened my pack. If they reacted so strongly to a tiny sword made for rodents, perhaps they would have tried to jail me for carrying surgical instruments. My scalpels are far more adept at dealing precision damage, and the bladeless devices could be far more intimidating for creatures with poor constitutions and vivid imaginations.

I still have not yet seen the destructive evidence of the Human military prowess, but I have heard enough stories to have a healthy respect for their imaginations.

* * * * *

Chapter Four:
Kesiel

Day 0 - The Stellar VII Docking Transfer,
Human-Teek Alliance Station

The atmosphere of the Stellar VII Orbiting Station was simply magical.

I experienced a symphony of different voices, the screeches and clangs of moving metal, and disparate bodily functions of more spacefaring species than I knew how to name. Naturally, as I had never before visited an interstellar hub, I had the luxury of bright-eyed fascination about everything I saw.

To think that most of my litter-kin had never even left the home burrow for more than a day, and yet I was shipping off to the edge of this galaxy, to rendezvous with the fiercest warriors to ever reach out across the stars before destroying themselves entirely!

But I am getting ahead of myself. From the moment I exited the route-liner, I wasn't thinking about interstellar politics and the greater forces who wrested for control. No, I was being delighted by the little furry numbers who flinched at the sight of me and would have blanched if only they could change their color. I had not studied more than a few phrases of Belbeh and might have even gotten these wrong.

"Greetings!" I said, trying to sound exuberant but not hungry. *"Which way to Upper Platform 24?"*

From behind me, an unpleasant digit pushed up against my scales. I refrained from trying to trip the owner with my tail; it was another Tsanghar. *Not* from my home burrow or even my native moon, but with faction camaraderie that I was not to disrupt.

She said in our language, "Stop talking to the prey, Kesiel. Turn instead to the display board."

Some of my travel companions had already done so and picked a heading, but I was determined not to leave the interaction without a tail to balance.

I turned to the diminutive creature who had begun biting the hair off the back of its wrist in worry. Giving a sweeping flourish with my own hand, complete with a friendly tail arch, I said, *"Thank you. Safe travels,"* or something close in pronunciation.

"Kesiel!" she hissed. "Your conduct is most embarrassing. Do not forget that we are ambassadors not only for the Yavamee—" our cluster of moons and therefore our primary faction, "—but the Tsangharee!" My species. That was how we chastise each other; dreadfully polite, if you ask me. How charming to think that I would soon learn Human insults, which would put those to shame.

Now, before you grow cross with your narrator over any confusion, I shall clarify: I am not in fact a Human. I am a member of the sprawling Tsangharee people, who inhabit a network of moons and the occasional planet—and who apparently developed airtight bubbles for space hopping before anyone had thought of a written language to describe the feat. To Humankind, we are referred to as lizards—though to be zoologically accurate, we are physically much closer to their endangered *tuatara*, who have a nicer-sounding name.

As I would tell the checkpoint officers, my name is Kesiel of the Yavamee moons and the Tsangharee people. I had an appointment in the Human home system that was more important than arguing with a stubborn, nextmoon toad named Liesarn—clarification, Liesarn is not literally a toad, but another Tsanghar; toad is merely a close translation for small, warty non-sentients from our home moons.

"Very well, Liesarn," I said, in as regal and stately a manner as I could stand to fake. "Please do lead on."

Liesarn snarled and revealed the sharp, triangular teeth of one side of her mouth, the blackened lips framing her jaw within the burnt orange face. Then, she turned and led as instructed, meeting up with the other Tsangharee.

Upon moving closer, I could see that we were not the only ones experiencing tension and trying to mask it. Though we wore little to impede movement—the thermocoils around our torsos as the only absolute requirement—every one of us lizardly folk also wore at least one band of colored symbols to signify home moon or high matriarch, and it was clear that almost every one of them wished to assert or display some measure of superiority and physical dominance. There are obvious reasons the rest of the galaxy perceives us as snarling predators, given how much infighting there is among our people.

I was traveling among a group of thirteen—which I have been told is an unlucky number for Humans, though I do not know why. Each of us came from a different clan or faction of Tsangharee, but from the same cluster of inhabitable moons. I wasn't sure if I'd see them, but supposedly there would be several more groups in representation riding in on the same final leg of the journey as we.

Clans beyond the counting, each vying for representation, and yet I do not need to name any of them, for names are only important for those who recognize, and I fear that no Human folk would recognize any clan names, except the most dastardly, who would not be allowed to enroll in the I.I. Yes, the most infamous becomes the most famed: the violet-faced Segranee.

It is a shame that—given everything else to notice along the main walkway of the station—I should spot and become fixated on one such purple-facer. As they are known for active camouflage, the common nickname for the Segranee is not always accurate, but it is hard to miss the dark diamond pattern along the snout when their color-shift abilities are not employed. This one was twenty strides away, cuffed and mewling, standing between two security folk who were unsure of how to interact with the prisoner.

"How peculiar," I mused.

Once again, Liesarn thumbed up one of my shoulder scales, an irritating action to be sure. "*Don't get involved!*" she hissed, or rather ordered in an angered whisper.

"I did not know there would be any Segranee on this station."

As I spoke such, the purple-facer stopped her mournful cry and raised her nose toward our group passing along the platform. I doubt that she could have heard my mild voice with so many other noises around, but whether smell, sound, or that strange instinct for like people, the Segranee looked directly at me.

"*Free me!*" she cried in a near language to my native one, but with some changes in pronunciation and conjugation. "I am captive of terrible uniforms for no crime. Free me, sister!"

I must admit, I paused, and a toady digit probing my shoulder scale would not move me as quickly. I also admit that I had no intention of saving the individual who gave no sign of innocence, but I wished to watch. Liesarn was insistent, reminding me that we were already late for boarding time and that not many large liners traveled as far as the Human system—even fewer could support highly varied species. It would be a shame to not board...

"I'll follow shortly!" I told Liesarn, inflating my neck and increasing my height. The show of dominance was more for the purple-facer than Liesarn, but she reacted as if intimidated, or, more likely, just surprised at my audacity. "And if I miss, then I miss."

Without waiting for a response, I left her and approached the Human security. This individual held what I perceived to be a rifle, albeit with a compression canister rather than a sleeve of slugs or darts. The shape of the nozzle was geared for maximum aeration. It was a foam gun, apt for immobilizing, but only at relatively short range.

"*Hello*," I said, in my best impression of their typical intonation and in their language. "What was the nature of—"

"Stay back," the Human said, a little too brusquely, but this approach seemed in fear more than any animosity toward me personally.

I opened both my hands and let my tail fall against the floor—which was unsanitary but unthreatening. I could wash or shed later.

"My apologies," I sang, but sensed from his expression that I should have used a less lyrical approach. "I do not intend to free the prisoner, but I am curious how you found a Segranee so far outside of their territory. I had thought they were not permitted to travel here."

The Segranee in question was looking between us wildly, clearly unable to comprehend any of the Human language. This amused me.

The Human security agreed, "They're not. Your kind affiliated with the Say-Graw-Nay are not allowed on this station, but we don't have an insignia or banner in reference, only the nose markings. She's already being detained for attacking some rat-kind." He indicated a direction, then amended, "Sorry, Bel-Bays. We've got her on that even if she's not Say-Graw-Nay."

Having heard her clan name several times, the Segranee hissed in our tongue, "*Sister! You can help me. What do they say?*"

The strategy amused me so much I almost broke composure, but I refrained from smiling when I asked, "*Sister, are you Segranee?*"

Her neck oscillated forward and back. Yes.

"Good. Simply tell this soldier you are a Segranee refugee and needed to eat a Belbeh because you were starving, and you will be shown sympathy."

The skin around the diamonds went to a muted purple-gray, the camouflage completely abandoned. She craned to face the security *Human*.

In Human I said, "Record. You might catch a confession."

The Human only missed the first word before clicking on the device at the shoulder, catching most of the confession. Even if his translator was not calibrated to handle it, someone would be able to interpret.

This time, I let myself smile. I picked up my tail—which I would refrain from touching to my hands or neck until sanitized—and said, "One is happy to serve the Initiative."

As I turned away, I heard the Segranee cursing after me. She might not have noticed my ploy in a timely manner, but some credit is due for even a late realization.

"You declawed groundworm!" I heard her yell. *"How dare you turn tail against your own people to ally with the scaleless! Who is your clan leader? Curse your mother's throat! May the* hridan *destroy you!"*

I saw no need to respond to insults against my parentage or wishes of ghostly visitations. After all, I had done my duty already. More importantly, I had spoken with a real Human, rather than a language-teaching simulation or a Deyelyan-clan tutor, for the first time. I had very much enjoyed it, almost as much as tricking a treacherous Segranee.

I quickened my pace, not as much as I might while evading a predator, but enough that Belbehan in my path darted away as if *I* were a predator. I clearly need not have worried, for, when I arrived, I found that my companions were only a few spots further ahead in the serpentining line to the airlock, which featured even more security personnel.

The wraparound queue largely consisted of Humans and arthropods, with the few Belbehan, a few fewer Tsangharee, and the very rare smatterings of other species. I had the poor fortune of standing behind a drone-type arthropod. Not only were they effective at blocking views, they were not capable of being conversationalists. I remember being intrigued when I learned that the bulky drones were all living computers of record for the hive, then considerably less intrigued when I further learned they could only interface with other Teek. This one did not even smell particularly inviting and seemed to sleep between each step forward.

When the line shifted far enough, however, I spotted a very intriguing person, a P'rukktah without any house markings or much armor. She—I assumed "she," given her height—did not appear nervous, but there was something different in her manner. As if she could sense me staring, she glanced back over one of her shoulder plates toward me. I attempted to put on a smile that would be more recognizable than the subtle sort my folk give each other, but I might have revealed too many teeth.

I also had to recognize that I was not wearing any clan markings either. My torso was wrapped in a thermocoil suit, but I had left my arms, legs, and tail bare. Most of my travel group had signified both their clan and home moon with symbols and colors. I wore the natural green of my people on my scales but had otherwise opted against showing loyalty to a Tsangharee clan in favor of becoming part of the new Initiative and my powerful Human hosts.

I waited, on display and not distracted by local Tsanghar songs, and I occasioned to notice one more oddity: the craft's loading process appeared significantly delayed compared to typical galactic passage. Not just in terms of the passenger queue—there was no accounting for late passengers—but also the large loadings in the bay to my left were still in progress.

At that moment, one significantly sized container paused before being wheeled the rest of the way onto our connecting vessel. Prior to the pause, it had traveled very slowly, as if all movers, including the animatronic, were afraid of jostling it. It *looked* like a water tank, but even from a distance of about ten lengths I could see that it did not have the right kind of coupling for this ship. Perhaps the coupling was on a side I could not see, or maybe they had an adapter within the vessel itself, and yet…

I asked the broad drone-type Teek to hold my place in line, knowing that it could not understand or apply any of my commands.

I slipped away, willing my skin as gray as it would go to blend a little with the walls of the station. My people were much more acquainted with lush greenery on our moon, Yavamee-3, and as such we do not camouflage as adeptly. The fins on the top of my head cannot change color in the slightest, but I did not let my lack of natural stealth deter me.

I spied a window, a circular transparency on the side of the tank facing my direction, small and mounted about twice my resting height above me.

Before, you ask, I had no concerns about getting caught; I would have lost respect for the Humans if they did not catch me, but I was curious, curious enough to climb the side and look in. Without any claws to retract, I used the full articulation power of my fingers to grip and pull my way up. I managed to get one golden eye to the opening!

All I saw was a shiny metal mesh, reflecting and filtering a muted white light with traces of orange. And, for a second, I felt as if I heard a sound—

"Hey!" the Human said, a second time, for I had ignored the first. "You can't be up there. Get down!"

I removed myself from the side of the tank, and I began my prepared excuse. "Apologies, I did not see a sign about climbing on this apparatus."

This Human was tall and closed his eyelids a couple of times. He had dark brown skin, like a cave-dwelling Tsanghar blending with the earth. There was also fur around his lips in a pattern that I did not believe to be natural. He was wearing not a station security uniform, but a sleeveless jacket over what I perceived to be a Human flightsuit. It had an I.I. insignia, partially blocked by his folded arms. He waited until I had both feet on the floor again to say, "Okay, there's no sign, but it's off limits. Do you make a habit of climbing other people's property?"

"Not at all!" I countered. "I saw the tank size and wondered if perhaps there was an Avowol inside. I have never seen one in person, and I had heard—"

"No, there's no Avowol on this ship today. Just a lot of bipedal passengers and supplies." This Human managed to pronounce the name Avowol, the most common term for the gelatinous aquatic sentients, without needing to pause or employ flat, overenunciated computer-trained phonetics, which impressed me. He drew a device from a clip on his hip and moved his fingers as if on a holographic representation that I couldn't see. "That tank carries a radioactive isotope. Safely contained and necessary for these engine systems."

"How wonderful!" I exclaimed. This was completely sincere. "I am an engineer—or, rather, an engineer candidate for the Interstellar Initiative."

This seemed to surprise him, or at least that was how I interpreted his raised brow-fur. "Really? A Song-Har?" I was no longer impressed. "You have passage on this ship?"

A part of me wished to question whether he was surprised by my species, my intended profession, or my questionable first impression actions. However, now was the time for positive interactions. "Yes, indeed. I noticed this tank while I was in line."

"Let me see your ticket," he said in a way that did not feel like a polite request.

I obliged, making every show of being happy to do so. I showed my display on my personal wrist device, which apparently he could corroborate with his handheld one. I even managed not to laugh when I saw the so-called helpful pronunciation guide populate on his screen.

"Keh-Seal?" he asked, a little clunky, but acceptable. However, when he stumbled over my clan name and moon of origin, I attempted to help him.

"And as for my clan, you may call me green fin. That is as close a translation as you'll ever find by approximation." Was that a rhyme? It sounded like a good one to me.

"Kesiel, of green fin," he said again. This time he smiled. He put out a hand toward me, his right one. "I'm Gordon. Don't worry, my surname is hard for a lot of species to say."

"Gordon!" I repeated, hoping that I was more adept at saying his name than he was for mine. "Nice to meet you. Well, I shall return to the line."

"Here, I'll go with you. I'm taking the trip too, and I'd like to get to know you a little better."

"Splendid!" I said. Naturally, this Gordon of hard-to-say family name, Human, was staying with me in order to monitor appropriate behavior. I respected this and would have done the same.

Gordon had apparently thought one step ahead and took the opportunity to walk me down the personnel route, bypassing the winding line. I saw my travel group still waiting. Liesarn spotted me, and plainly showed frustration with a minor flare of her orange shoulder and head scales.

I managed admission onto the ship right after the P'rukktah I'd smiled at earlier, which only shows the advantage of talking to everyone.

* * *

Even among the green fin, I was considered special. The kind of special they needed to put toward an important task, so I was selected as a representative for the I.I. As had been the case in so many areas of my life, I would go into the academy and make it my own in a manner many of my people would envy.

One of my most special qualities was highlighted when I was fingerprinted and inspected by the vessel's chief medical officer. It was also an aspect which others might erroneously call "tamed."

This doctor remarked on my lack of claws as if he was worried I did not realize. I assured him that I knew Tsangharee naturally matured with claws, dangerous, hazardous, terrible claws. I, however, did not.

"This was not a miraculous birth," I said. "This was a chosen removal. Yes, I am a declawed reptile, incapable of scrawling my name on the side of any clay wall."

"There's no notable scarring," the doctor said. "Either your species has an extreme capacity to heal, or this happened a long time ago."

"Both," I explained, a little eager to do so. "They were surgically removed by choice before they had fully developed. Pardon me for denying any sordid theories, but I never had a chance to be punished for attacking anyone."

The doctor laughed, and I echoed him.

"Why would you have this done?" he wondered.

I waggled my eight digits. "Articulation."

Yes, my claws were removed so I would have greater articulation with my fingers and full suction capability. The kind that you only find in the very young, the very old, and the very chosen—those who have made the choice to sacrifice.

The doctor, however qualified, was not in a position to ascertain the second reason why I am so special.

Amusingly, this second but less noticeable reason is actually the cause for the first, for why would there be a need to remove the claws unless someone wanted to do something even more brilliant with one's hands? I am, as some would say, a genius. Measures of such a standard vary greatly among the species. For some, the most intelligent creatures who may ever live are the unnamable tree folk of Uua Prime. They maintain such great wisdom, but they take so long to articulate and add to any of it, that they might as well not be seen as intelligent at all. Others—though I can't imagine why—have cited the underfoot rodents, the Belbeh, as reasonable candidates. As the smallest and quickest sentient creatures, their nerves apparently send faster signals. They reportedly are more populous and present throughout the galaxy, and so, collectively, they might have the most knowledge—not that there is ever a way to collect them or get them to agree on any course of action for longer than a day.

For my part, I am brilliant at both the collecting and the using of knowledge. I can acquire it, adapt it, manipulate it. I have quite a handle on patterns. I can change and rearrange them to make them work better for me and, of course, to benefit any team I join.

For this reason, the Interstellar Initiative would want me as an ally and not an enemy; they just didn't know to articulate it.

My genius had been most thoroughly applied to technology. Assembling, disassembling, rearranging, repurposing, and, best of all, reverse engineering.

For generations upon generations, my people have been at the mercy of the technologies traded by the Teek. They use us for expanding planetary claims, and we use them for their propulsion. When we can, we collect morsels of advancement from the Belbeh, who are so widespread and fruitful with their multiplication that they go everywhere and interact with everyone, and occasionally will have ripe nuggets of information that other species will put to better use. It's not that they are smarter, simply that probability eventually catches up to them. The Belbeh do blow themselves up as often as not, which makes it a wonder why any fair-minded people would dare risk sailing on one of their vessels when there are so many other options to choose from, even if they are slightly slower or more inconvenient. The odds of catching your connecting voyage a little late are not nearly as distressing as the odds of being disintegrated. Without knowing the original passenger manifest, I had no way of knowing how many poor travelers did not rendezvous with this Human-system-bound vessel due to unplanned delays or Belbeh incompetence.

There did seem to be a high number of empty travel pods, but then, I admit, I had never been on so large and impressive a ship. Perhaps they were typically empty. I suspected, however, that these kinds of ships were gradually filling as the Human presence in shared space increased, and more kinds of species trusted their hybrid passenger liners.

Either way, there was lots of room at the viewers when we took off. Apparently, the Teek-Human innovations had cracked the code to prevent inertial kick on takeoff, *and* they had gravity. So, like many others, I stood as I watched the Stellar VII station shrink against the backdrop of a lovely red sun, a rocky planet, and its two moons. I checked the time; I didn't have long before I'd have to strap into my pod for the space fold. That part was reportedly quite taxing on the organic frame.

Before you wonder, no, I did not rejoin my fellow scale-skins, though I did keep an informal mental tally, and I only had to catch Liesarn's glare once. I was on the search for meaningful interaction with new people.

While the launch and space fold safety instructions played out on the speakers—in every language imaginable—many groups clustered by species or even tighter social clusters within species. Some, like myself, bravely broke form and tried to mingle. I quickly discovered that my speed and pronunciation of Human, while completely apropos for the station guard, was still a little slow and devoid of slang for the actual Human passengers.

I attempted to listen—eavesdrop is, I believe, the Human term—on one such conversation. The two Humans remarked on the long-standing alliance with the Teek and debated the likelihood of finding other species as agreeable. It was during this focused listening that my concentration was interrupted by a strange high-pitched note, very faint and from no discernable direction.

True, I had been somewhat overwhelmed by various stimuli, but I had the strange impression that the high note was saying, "*Free me!*" in a familiar, purple-facer dialect.

My fins extended on instinct. But looking around I saw that no one else reacted to the sound. The other Tsangharee seemed content engaging with, or insulting, one another. Likewise, the Humans are said to have notoriously bad ears, and Teek don't often interact with things that they aren't already prepared and programmed to handle. Belbehan always appeared scared, so they were not helpful.

I wished to speak to the P'rukktah, who were fitted with three sets of ears. However, at first survey, I saw only one cluster of them on the viewing deck, and I was not one to get in the middle of four giant mammals, even if three of them were the smaller males. Whether or not *I* wished to think of P'rukktah as foes might not matter to people who had been involved in border skirmishes or Segranee attacks, especially if these same fur-faces used tiny, beady eyes that perceived far less color than a Tsangharee could.

As *tessenda* would have it, I turned away from one group of P'rukktah and nearly ran into another. This same tall, lone female whom I'd grinned at in queue, and who now glowered at me. She had prominent cheeks, but a far less pronounced underbite than most of her kind. Though they did not not typically consider fur coloration a notable facet, I certainly made note of the bronze and gold colors of her mane, starting at her brows and arching back over her head.

She was armed with a rod encased in solidified foam, which was not a typical P'rukktah tool to my knowledge but appeared intimidating in her strong hands. Instinct caused me to pull away when she thrust her chin in my direction and started walking past me. Still, I coaxed my vocal cords up out of my chest and began to ask the question on my mind.

"Begging your pardon. Did you just hear—"

She raised a hand, and I stopped, trying to gauge the creature for understanding and general demeanor. She gave no indication that the question I had begun would be answered, but she made a point of demonstrating that her ear was occupied by a translator feed. She tilted her device to me, displaying a rough instruction for passengers to go to their individual pods in preparation for the space fold.

I understood. It was prudent to strap in too early, rather than too late. After all, this liner's stabilizers and artificial gravity could not yet contend with the vector physics of entering and exiting a space fold in a way that was safe for ambulant crew, although many of us had heard the Initiative would be solving that particular puzzle. But I also understood that she did not speak my form Tsangharee, or Human, I would posit. Fortunately, I knew some rudimentary Irruktir and could ask my question quickly.

I imagine the approximation would look like this: "Requesting forgiveness, lady passenger. Did you hear…" And yet again, I hesitated, for I hardly knew how to describe the disturbing sound in my own tongue, let alone a rough approximation. I attempted to pitch my voice high enough to imitate the Segranee's plea. "*Free me.*"

This perplexed the P'rukktah, as is reasonable. Her brow and temples flexed in consideration, or perhaps confusion.

When the call arrived on the speakers, louder this time, she chose not to ignore it. She presented both palms to me, which I catalogued as a formal farewell gesture, and continued toward her pod for the bulk of the journey.

The alert to strap in and close personal pods was repeated in several languages. In Tsangharee-trade, the sentence read in the urgent imperative mode, with a very clear threat to safety if we did not comply.

That the nearest empty pod happened to be adjacent to a P'rukktah's was not a matter of design, although her tusk grinding in my direction gave the impression this one did not appreciate being followed.

I was already well-versed in learning social norms after first getting them wrong. So, the combination of Liesarn's chiding, Human

Gordon's escorting, and this unnamed P'rukktah's coolness was merely part of a learning opportunity, I told myself. This attitude would serve me in my longer-term career, even if I presently found myself distracted by every overheard noise and potential new connection.

As soon as the pod's padding adjusted to Tsanghar specification, I stepped within. Leaning back into my stabilizer cradle, I tucked my tail into the groove beside me and closed the pod's door. I stole one last glance at the P'rukktah, but she had already closed her eyes and curled her ears.

I remember thinking that, given her lack of curiosity and reliance on a translator, she would not make it very far in the Initiative. I would be pleased to be proven wrong.

* * * * *

Chapter Five:
Lidstrom

Phobos Orbiting Station

We were issued matching flightsuits immediately after disembarking. They were stretchy, full-body, forest-green undersuits whose comfort and movability went far beyond any Terra-tech synthetic fibers I'd ever experienced. Next, we got our tags, IDs, room assignments—and many other things I didn't track—in digital form. These were installed into standard-issue wrist devices, like your usual personal device but up to I.I. code. Everything but the undersuit and the wrist device could be subject to change.

Cadet Yiorgos Stratis was excited when he found out we would be, at least temporarily, assigned to the same cadet quarters block on the planet at the Olympus Mons Academy, along with a half dozen other Greenies from the E-group. Everyone from *E* was native English-speaking and originally from the northern States or Canada, which I guess made things easier.

While we ran through our device checks and chewed on the first solid protein in days, a cadet named Rivers took it upon herself to prompt intros. Some of us knew each other from the pre-screening days on Luna, but a small enough percentage of those folks had made it that we were mostly a collective of select strangers.

I marked Rivers as shorter, louder, and curlier than most. She had taken advantage of the Initiative's loose hair regs to wear jagged undercut patterns on the sides of her scalp and was eager to declare herself a computer-tech focus in front of witnesses. She got others calling out where they were from, what their field of focus was, and why the hell they had signed all of their university years away for a life in the stars.

"How about you, Unibrow?" she asked Yiorgos, who was sitting next to me.

More amused than offended, Yiorgos stood, introduced himself with exaggerated Greek pronunciation, and said he was going communications, which surprised me, as I would have pegged him for a tech or research-science focus. "And as for why, I've probably seen every episode of every show with star or space in the title, and I could do better than them, that's why."

A wave of chuckles went through the group. As soon as Yiorgos resumed the bench, Rivers gave me a nod. "And you?"

And me. Though I'd answered the question a thousand times, I discovered that I didn't know what to say now. I'd recited my dream and my reasons to every adult who would listen. Every choice I'd made and every lucky break I'd capitalized on had led me here, so it felt weird to pass it off as a joke or condense it into a single anecdote.

I was still deciding, juggling between a hasty rendition of my first shuttle flight and a cookie cutter TSF-inspiration-comment, when my mouth opened, and the answer fell out of me.

"I'm a pilot," I began, and got no further.

Several teasing *oob*s were thrown back at me. I caught one saying "Damn, check out this 'naut" and a barking "You think you can handle lizard reflexes!" that cut through the rest.

I hadn't thought about being the first one from our group to declare a piloting focus. I was used to most recruits being STEM-focused, but it was another thing to hear so much surprise and what I hoped were good-natured jibes, most of which were about the faster, more experienced alien competition.

"Hey, if he says he can beat 'em, he can beat him," came another voice. A wiry, stern-jawed cadet, with close-cropped hair and mixed Asian features, was nodding in my direction. She hardly had to raise her voice to seem imposing, and she was just serious enough without coming across as dour. "I saw this kid fly a couple times on Luna. Lidstrom, right?"

I nodded.

"Yeah, if anyone can give the scalies a run for their money, it's him."

I breathed a silent "thank you," not so much for the rescue from some laughing challenges, but for keeping me from oversharing. Sadly, I couldn't reciprocate the introduction, for I didn't recognize her by face or reputation yet.

Without being prompted, she told the room, "I'm Helen Shin, security and tactical. Certified in hand-to-hand, de-escalation, neutralization. And I'm here to take on any species they throw at me."

That was my first introduction to Cadet Shin.

There turned out to be a couple other prospective pilots in our section, none of whom earned the ribbing that this first volunteer had. Among the range of focus areas and backgrounds, including some who'd actually lived long term on Luna or Gany, there were some common threads, especially in the tone that came across. Looking back, I would call it a hopeful confidence, that we young Human cadets could contend in this new galaxy-wide community, among aliens who had been doing it far longer.

We received our room assignments and small-issue personal luggage. I also confirmed that Yiorgos and I, as well as many others in earshot, were all in the same category of nerd. We'd all grown up right in the middle of the first-contact, second-contact, and Teek Alliance buzz. We'd all followed every piece of mostly redacted reports on the interstellar conflict known as the W-Wars, and had at one point aspired to join the Transnat Space Force, led by heroes like Admiral Victoria Hass. One cadet had brought a signed holographic Hass: Comet-Tamer trading card, which she eagerly showed us. Then, after the war had ended and the worldwide obsessions with aliens settled into a more comfortable fact of life, people like us stayed obsessed. We were space nerds and had been absorbing every ounce of interstellar fact and fiction we could get our hands on.

Given how little we were allowed to bring with us, it spoke volumes that many of our personal items smacked of some fandom. Most were small: a lapel pin, a hair clip, a pair of non-reg socks, and the occasional collectible. Yiorgos had exhausted the most packing volume with a physical novelty chess-set in both standard and 3-D varieties.

Mine hadn't taken any space at all. While Yiorgos collapsed and put away his boardgame, I rolled up my flightsuit's pant-leg to display my outer calf and the tattoo that was still recent enough for full vivid color. The magenta-haired *Spacegirl Stella*, hero of the most streamed cartoon when I was eight, boldly pointed toward the stars.

"Man, that is some dedication," Yiorgos said.

It was also then that an officer jumped right into the conversation, appearing squarely in front of me, unhindered by the augmented grav of Phobos Station. "You showing off some ink there, Greenies?" I could tell from his voice that he was the trainer who'd woken us, but he was much more intense in person. Dark eyes and taut muscle in the temple, framed by a classic jarhead cut.

"Yes, sir," I said, hoping that I was reading his lieutenant stripes correctly.

"Mm-hmm! Yeah, I got one, too." He rolled up his sleeve, and I was weirdly excited and naive enough to think it might be another depiction of our favorite cartoon cadet. Instead, he showed me the nine-pointed star with an inlaid silhouette of a scorpion and the letters TSF for Transnat Space Force. "TSF, First Division Exo Marines. Oorah." He said it just deadpan enough for the smile at the end to be the most intimidating part. His tag read N Chandan, and I made a mental note never to cross him.

As he walked away, I lowered my voice and asked, "You think he's seen alien combat?"

Murmurs of "definitely" and "affirmative" came back to me. One of the other Greenies remarked, "I bet he's got some stories."

"Yeah," Yiorgos agreed, "too bad all of them are classified."

I would later learn that Yiorgos hadn't meant it as a joke, but it earned a laugh from several cadets in earshot. That was another commonality: when we laughed, we all sounded Human. At the time, I took that kind of thing for granted.

* * * * *

Chapter Six:
Paul Newman

Phobos Orbiting Station

My people do not have long literature. Perhaps it is our shorter lifespans or ongoing mental connections, but our literary tradition never developed in quite the ways of Tsangharee or P'rukktah and is negligibly limited in comparison to the Humans.

Teek communicate so many events in a flash of insight, hindbrain to hind-brain within a hive or through drones to other families. We have names that designate time and place. Our language is so much faster and more precise than anything syllabic—it is also far less poetic or descriptive.

If I were to tell the story of my trip from home planet to Mars-Human via the Phobos Station in Teek, it would be summed up in the word, "Arrived," which would take less than a tenth of a Human second to communicate. If this were with a member of the family, my eye chromae or my hind-brain might betray some exhilaration or exasperation.

In Human, however, I would be tasked with preparing an exposition in the beginning, a conflict and crisis for the middle, and then a favorable resolution, also known as an ending. The beginning began on home planet. The middle started shortly after we arrived at Phobos Station where, to my surprise, I would find conflict in several forms.

My *jiki*, Ella Fitzgerald, would call this a rapid learning experience.

As is typical for the winged molts, she recovered from the travel hibernation faster than I did. She had to lead me by the hands toward processing while my auditory and visual sensory adjusted. I was not sure if my scent receptors would ever adjust to the confusing range of sterile non-smells and sudden—and offensive—presence of uncategorized smells.

I attempted to excuse myself to the Belbeh I bumped into while visually impaired, and I was glad that I did so in Human, without having to actively think about which language I was using. The Belbeh ran away in fear, but that was not surprising.

As I was disembarking with a sizable collection of fellow Teek, both from my home planet and neighboring ones, I was interested in displaying in every possible way that I belonged. From language use to proper posture to not slowing down the immigration queue. Though Ella would maintain that we were preselected for these roles, I felt that I was beginning to understand the Human sense of competition with one's peers.

However, I clearly did not see or hear well enough during disembarkation to catch an error in my registration.

I don't know when precisely it occurred. We gave the original and then Human nickname versions of everything that was asked of us. My *jiki* confirmed that she was Ella Fitzgerald and I maintained that I was Paul Newman. This was a test of my ability to mimic their P and M precisely, a sound which I had learned to mimic with my two vertical tongues. Even while disoriented, I was practiced enough to pass.

We approved, printed, and signed the agreements again, including an acknowledgment guaranteeing regular hind-brain connection with a *jiki* or drone, which I have been told is standard.

However, shortly after exiting the queue, as a visiting citizen of Phobos and Mars-Human, I was able to see enough to detect a potential problem on the printed forms.

My eyes adjusted forward, putting focal distance on the dossier in my hands. I wished to make certain I had read it correctly. Once I was sure, I buzzed involuntarily.

Ella, sensing my distress, asked—in Human, of course—"What is wrong, *jiki?*"

I had not meant to project my distress audibly, but one look at my chromae alerted her. "I might be disqualified and recalled," I told her. Once I had admitted, I am certain I radiated my disappointment. I showed her the incriminating document. "They have me listed as *optera* and not *extramani* designation." Indeed, the printed dossier indicated that I had a pair of wings instead of what were commonly referred to as "extra" arms.

Ella attempted to soothe. "Paul," she said, evenly, "this is merely an error. They will fix it."

I decided to believe her. After all, she sounded assured. Perhaps the Human officials could make an error about the number of wings they needed versus the number of arms. I substituted her hope for my despair, sending gratitude as I assessed next steps.

In the large station, between a series of rectangular platforms known as "gates," I looked to a large display board. It had a cursory map, but it also made note of arriving transports and the schedule for shuttles going to the planet. I did not feel I had ample time before my scheduled shuttle; moreover, the large Terra-Human transports were unloading passengers now, and an interstellar liner with Tsangharee and P'rukktah would be arriving soon.

Deciding that I must resolve this issue quickly, I asked Ella, "With whom should I speak to alter this error?"

* * *

I found some comfort in the lower corridors of the Phobos Station. One lift down into the moon took me out of the high-ceilinged terminal and into tighter, more focused pathways. Many of the walls were made of the rock itself, albeit sealed with an airtight enamel—just in case. There were plenty of handles for those whose hands did not effectively grip in low or variable gravity environments. Either way, it felt like a local asteroid transport or a tunnel from home, and briefly alleviated some of the culture shock. I made a mental note that I should need to recalibrate home to refer to Mars, and then to whatever ship I was assigned, assuming I did not find myself rejected and recalled.

I followed the arrows as presented by my device to the personnel office, which was not far away from the processing center. This was good, as any additional delays could make me delay my rendezvous with the planetary shuttle.

I was fully prepared to knock as practiced, with the back of the knuckles of one hand—not one pair of hands, but just one hand. However, the door was open. Two Human voices were within. Both voices were a little scratchy, as if throats and lungs had been damaged in poorly scrubbed atmospheric environments, but one was quite a bit lower and rounder than the other.

I stepped in through the open door, to see an office setup with bolted desk and magnetic mounts for both technological and simple mechanical devices. One of the Humans, the one with the higher scratchy voice, sat on the desk, and I assessed by the shape of the torso that she was female, which aligned with the lack of facial fur, or any visible head fur for that matter. The top of her jacket was open, showing the more comfortable flightsuit and indicating casual. Casual or not, the markings on her jacket designated a ranking authority, whose structure and notation I had not yet memorized.

"Come on, Claude," she was saying, while shaking her hairless head, indicating a negative.

The man who was apparently Claude was not wearing his jacket, so there was no way to determine rank. But he had a circle of facial fur around his mouth and great enough height for me to guess him as male. Perhaps he was a non-ranked secretary. "Look, I'm not trying to cause a scene," he said, gesturing with one arm, while another held onto a ceiling rung. "I'm just saying, if we're profiling and pigeonholing different groups of people into certain roles, doesn't that sound like racism?"

She shook her head again, this time with closed eyes. "It's not the same at all. Third-planet racism was a series of incorrect assumptions that people of different color skin were born with different capabilities. We're not talking about assumptions; we're talking about facts based on different species."

"Now that's going too—"

"Female P'rukktah are physically stronger than any other species here. Am I wrong? Tell me that I'm wrong. So why not ship security. Tsanghar typically have faster reflexes for pilot work. And obviously—" the man was starting to turn away and the woman lithely shifted on the desk to maintain eye contact, "—*obviously*, we save weapons and tactical for Humans."

"I don't know. It just—I mean, with everything else being so progressive, doesn't this seem a little backwards to you? I don't know." Then, as if unsurprised by my presence, he indicated with open palm. Was he asking me to hand him something? "Jane, what do you think?"

I did not immediately discern that the name Jane was a misaddress. But after a quick analysis, I concluded he mistook me for another of my people and decided to correct him. "I am not Jane."

"Oh, *grepht*," he swore. The woman smirked, unless I misread the expression. To her, he said, "Don't say anything."

She complied, but her silence seemed to irritate him, as if she had tacitly made a point. Perhaps I had been misinformed about the Human's lacking capacity for telepathy.

"Sorry," he said, palm still presented to me, "you are…?"

I rattled off my designation in my formal tongue, which very few Humans could understand, and none could duplicate. Then, I offered translation: "That is, of the queen order you call Bertha, and my Human name is Paul Newman." I said it carefully and watched their faces to see if I'd gotten anything wrong.

"Paul Newman," he acknowledged. "Yes, excellent. Welcome. Your English is—well, it's excellent."

"Thank you," I said. "Much of it was implanted during incubation."

"Right. I'm—um—" He noticed his own lack of jacket, and the fact that he did not have any rank displayed on the dark-gray flightsuit. "Sorry about the complete lack of decorum. I'm Commander

Poissonier, off duty, so you can call me Claude when I'm off duty. This isn't a military establishment—right, Vieve?"

The woman, Vieve, chuckled. "Sure, Claude."

He indicated his head toward the woman and said, "This is Staff Sergeant Genevieve Ramirez." But he said it quickly enough that I did not properly register the acronym or which part of the full name I should use. I resolved not to use any of it until she reintroduced herself.

The commander stood a little straighter and took a few steps toward me. "So, Paul, you're a new cadet?"

"Classified Green Cadet, awaiting planetary shuttle, squad assignment, and I-dot-I-dot training."

Vieve made a barking, sputtering sound that I had trouble placing as aggression or choking. The smiling mouth and eyes displayed happiness, and the sound nested into my mind as a laugh. "Sorry, I just—Gods! I never get tired of you guys."

A little more gently, Commander Claude said, "You don't have to say the dot part. Just I-I. Or we call it the Initiative. So, what brings you to personnel, Green Cadet Paul Newman?"

I presented my dossier. "I was told that this is the place to correct an error. I have a misclassification, and I was told to go to the secretary of enrollments in the personnel office. Am I in the right place?"

Claude glanced toward Vieve. She nodded.

"Yes," said Claude, but with hesitation. "Well, he—the secretary of enrollments is out for lunch, but—here, I can take that and enter it for you. What was the error?"

I gave him the dossier and explained, "They have me listed as optera instead of extramani."

"How's that?" he asked, then quickly self clarified, "Oh, I see, someone wrote down you were a wing-worker and not an arm-worker. Okay, I can confirm that visually." He went around the desk to sit behind it. He drew up the holographic interface and appeared to enter some information. "Here, let me just—" The information entry was paused, and the circle of facial fur appeared to scowl. "*Grepht*—" Widened eyes. "Sorry! Uh—Paul, what's the Teek word for shit?"

I did not wish to sound ignorant, but I preferred to clarify. "Do you mean 'fecal matter?'"

The woman named Vieve chuckled again. "Give it a rest, Claude."

Commander Claude accepted the change of subject without having his question answered. "Okay, I will, under one condition. Can you enter this for me?"

Vieve relocated to the other side of the desk—to say she walked would not accurately describe the low-grav movement. Her motions were very smooth, almost reptilian as she helped to take the man's place on the seat. "Yeah, yeah, move over, you dinosaur."

I considered adding what I had read about pre-Human dinosaurs but waited to see if the comment was relevant. At least I knew it was not literal.

Standing, his awkward height and bearing putting his head dangerously close to the hard ceiling, Claude remarked, "It's amazing. I can understand theory and application of Teek propulsion systems, but I can't keep up with the damn IT updates."

"Yes, sir," I agreed.

Vieve didn't have any issues with my file or entering the information.

"Now, Paul Newman was another famous person, right? This one actually sounds familiar to me."

Dutifully I supplied, "Paul Newman was a 20th-century American actor who appeared in over sixty films and was the owner and founder of a citrus-fruit luxury beverage."

"'Luxury beverage?'" Claude wondered.

From behind the holo screen, Vieve clarified, "Lemonade, sir."

"No kidding! He invented lemonade?"

Although it had sounded like a question, Claude apparently did not require an answer, for he prefaced another before I had a chance to offer correction about the invention of lemonade.

"Hey, Paul, informal question, so don't feel any obligation to answer it. As a cadet, what is your focus area?" I noticed Vieve glance up to him, with an emotion I could not read. "Which fleet path are you interested in?"

I decided to take him as sincere rather than suspect a trick question. Besides, it would be in my best interest to firmly and deliberately demonstrate my intentions toward one of the five paths available. "Communications."

Commander Claude folded his arms and projected satisfaction. "Isn't that interesting. Communications. Why are you drawn to communications?"

I actually felt myself straighten, something Humans call "swelling with pride." My head was up and back, far straighter than the default posture. "I want to talk to everyone, everywhere. I want to learn from every kind of sentient life."

The commander struck his hands together, and I was reminded that endoskeletal creatures have elastic skin for issuing strange sounds. "Yes! Exactly, that is precisely what this is all about—You hear that, Vieve?"

"I'm sitting right here, aren't I?" she asked, but her tone was changed. "Hey, Claude, I—" She made a noise with her throat that sounded like *Hrm!* "Yeah, you're right, they changed something in the interface. And, well...I think I may have deleted some of his information. Sorry, Paul. I'm just going to message the secretary and let him sort it out."

I think I managed to hold my anxious vibration, but my chromae projected my feelings vividly.

"Easy, Cadet," said Claude, also shifting in tone to something I read as much more authoritative. I had always been told that Human hierarchy was learned rather than instinctual, but I was impressed by how effectively the commander donned this new demeanor. "We'll get you processed and down to the planet. You have my guarantee. You might just have to take a later shuttle today."

There was a knocking sound on the door behind me. My antennae detected the Human before I turned about to see. I confirmed that the door had been left open but found it interesting that this individual still knocked. Given the height, I wanted to assume female, but the shape made it more difficult to determine. Fortunately, Humans are not as rigid about gender classification as the P'rukktah.

"Hi," said the Human. "Don't mean to interrupt. I'm G.C. Darren Lidstrom. I was sent here because they got something wrong on my file."

Claude and Vieve shared a look.

Claude took his sleeveless I.I. jacket from the wall hanger and started to put it on. He gave a nod that did not mean yes and verbally added, "Cadet Lidstrom. Paul. The secretary is on his way, but I'm afraid I'm needed back on duty."

The other Green Cadet, or G.C. Darren Lidstrom apparently noticed the rank insignia and snapped to attention in order to salute. I mimicked the gesture, grateful for the presence of a practiced Human to demonstrate what I'd only read about or seen in two-dimensional presentation. Instantly, I found myself wondering if I'd erred by using two hands instead of one.

Regardless of my poor form, the commander reciprocated the gesture as he walked by and out the door.

Vieve endured collective silence for only a few more seconds before standing herself. "I'm following him before I make anything worse. Cadets."

Alone in a room with one Human, a fellow cadet, and I did not know what to say.

For the second time in very close proximity, I was grateful for Darren Lidstrom. The cadet offered me a hand and said, "You said Paul? I'm Darren. Or Cadet Lidstrom. Good to meet you."

"Classified Green Cadet Paul Neman," I replied. I took the hand in one—not two—of my own and squeezed slightly. "Pleased to make your acquaintance."

* * * * *

Interlude:
Kesiel

En Route to Phobos

The ship was wonderfully efficient in design, one of the faster long-range propulsion systems, provided it could go in an aggressively straight line. Pulling from a mismatched mishmash of different organizations' traded secrets, the liner was an effective predecessor of some of the true collaborations to follow, and our heavily mixed presence on the ship seemed to reinforce that. The individual pods were modular enough, filled with a kind of impact gel that could be adjusted in density or pressure to accompany the needs of different species, based, I'm told, on P'rukktah technology.

There are many wonderful surprises that can come from previously untested arrangements of persons and ideas, from a multitude of barely established factors. None of us should have been shocked, but we were utterly unprepared.

Somewhere within a Human light-year of their system, something incredible awoke in the underbelly of the liner and radiated a signal into space.

* * * * *

Chapter Seven:
Arrksh

Mars-Human Orbit - Docking at Phobos Station

I am prepared to dock. We have to remain in our pods wearing proper restraints, in case of turbulence or sudden grav-shift. No undue turbulence occurs. The emergence into real space near enough our destination planet goes smoothly; we suffer no jarring inertial effects, not even enough to disrupt the Human-language acclimation recordings sounding into my ears.

I am *not* prepared for reptiles to begin shrieking. All three sets of ears find it difficult to focus. I can only imagine it is this caterwaul that causes the echoing sound of distortion, filling this section of the vessel. As it occurs shortly after we exit the space fold, I can also blame the adjustment back to real physics.

From places I cannot see, the shrieking compounds with hisses and snarls, and the scrapings of sleek creatures wriggling free of poorly thought-out restraints.

Fortunately, I am prepared to defend myself with non-lethal tactics. I can hear P'rukktah growling in response, demanding to know, in our own tongue, what is the meaning of this Tsangharee madness. I unbelt myself and step toward the luggage compartments, giving my handprint to a scanner to invite it to open, but it remains locked. I only have a few items on my person, including a tiny sword, sealed in expanded polymer.

I glimpse the tail end of a lizard darting between compartments. I see the face of a Human security on the display, giving an order. The translator in my middle ear tells me, "*Stay in your pods! We are experiencing—*" But the last term is untranslatable. As I am already out of my pod, I choose to ignore this comment. I can always blame my translator.

Proceeding through the narrow corridor, I recognize one Tsanghar, a chirpy, chatty one with green fins on her head. But her face has changed, contorted in half-dreaming terror.

As Tsangharee seem able to sleep at any place or time, it is not surprising that she would have been recharging during the voyage, but why she cannot wake now, I cannot tell. The casing of her pod is open, so she is only held in by a semi-elastic crossbelt.

Outer eyelids open, inner eyelids closed—peculiar in open air. The head does not thrash so much as bob, as if trying not to gag. Her nostrils are sealed closed, which would occur if shutting down against a poison or preparing to be submerged, while the lips are parted for breathing shallowly between the pointed teeth.

My gesture is an affront in most circumstances, but as the shrieks have not subsided, I proceed. I press a finger against the closed nostril, hard enough to bruise, and lift.

The seal breaks and the creature takes in more than just a shallow inhale. Her translucent inner eyelids open and she sees me.

I am impressed by her composure, considering how suddenly she was woken. In breathy sentences, she asks me a question, using common enough Tsanghar words that I hardly need the translator. "Did you hear? It said 'Free me.'"

I had not heard such; I do not speak much Tsanghar, but I hear repeated exclamations and wheezes of *hridan!*—perhaps this is a more desperate idiom for "Free me." Either way, I do not argue, do not clarify. The green-finned one is awake and lucid. I will find the others still in distress.

I hear green fin unbelt behind me and follow. I go in the direction where I'd seen the tail disappear, and I find my quarry. A dull orange Tsanghar curled on the floor making a similar bobbing motion with the neck, but more violent and with no evidence of breathing through the mouth.

I go to feel the neck, and the lizard reacts! She rakes at me, claws extended. I do not pull away quickly enough, but the claws hardly make a scratch against my tensed face. They do, however, disrupt my translator. By disrupt, I mean sever the cord.

The green fin one makes a distressed comment I do not fully understand. I am unconcerned with this. I say, "Hold her!"

The green Tsanghar complies, clearly understanding me well enough. I notice that this green helper does not have claws under the top skin of the fingers. Less dangerous, but most likely able to get a stronger grip on her fellow's wrists.

I continue to inspect the throat with my own larger, warmer hands, and the orange Tsanghar tries to jerk away. The coiled tail whips about, hard enough to raise welts but not to cause any real damage. The neck is constricted. The egg sacs in the throat are not inflated with new life, and the glands that swell for posturing are also inactive.

"Swallowed her tongue," I mutter. I remember reading about this unfortunate fork in mutation. The wide tongue base which could block the back of the throat for lizards about to dive or enter a toxic environment is helpful for the various branches of their species, especially for gilled ancestors, but modern evolution of a speaking tongue has increased length enough that said tongue can be fully swallowed. Thus, an extreme fear response results in choking.

I pry open the jaws, which snap shut.

The green-finned one adjusts grip on the arms and uses a leg for leverage. She hums something that I perceive as fascination more than distress.

I hear a door and a Human voice behind me. It barks something unpleasant, probably telling me to let go or stand down. Perhaps it is threatening me with a weapon, but I cannot be deterred.

Fortunately, the green-finned Tsanghar replies in Human, its voice twisting the syllables and intonation, making it much harder to understand. I can only hope it is vouching for me.

My thumb has found the airway, low in the throat, beneath all the tender sacs, muscle groups, and glands.

I take the foamed sword out of my belt and smash the object against the floor, cracking through some of the polymer, enough to draw the blade from its sheath.

The Human yells again, which is partially translated by his machine. I do not pay attention. I do not pause or hesitate.

The point of the sword is sharp, and the airway is apparent. Other than dissection of a corpse, this will be my first time directly operating on a Tsanghar. I do confess my excitement.

* * * * *

Chapter Eight:
Lidstrom

Phobos Station

For anyone who is afraid of bugs, the Teek look nothing short of terrifying.

The two molts who could join the Initiative as cadets stand about four feet tall, with ribbed exoskeletons and occasional spiky bits. They have segmented eyes, the inner part of which can slightly extend or retract for focus, and the outer parts of which change color, vibrantly. Their antennae are independently mobile and apparently move around on instinct, acting as more than one of their senses, including the mildly telepathic hive link. And finally, the mandibles, outfitted with two large grabbing pincers and two smaller ones to pull things into the actual mouth which can be found under the snout. That grinding maw is largely not visible to those who are looking straight on. Tack on four to six clawing appendages, possibly wings, and you have an ant-mantis-crossover nightmare for much of the Human race.

Maybe it was growing up in Detroit, with smog thick enough that it was poisonous to cockroaches. Or maybe it was my fascination—obsession—with space exploration in partnership with the Teek Alliance; either way, I didn't mind being alone in a cramped, egg-shaped office carved into Phobos with Paul Newman.

What's sure to be jarring to any bug-o-phobes out there is that the Teek smell incredible. Now, I'm not trying to get weird here, so don't mistake great-smell for sensual or erotic—from everything I learned pre-academy, there's no way to even get freaky with the worker molts of the Teek species—but the smell is something like fresh laundry hanging over an Ontario flower garden in mid-May. It's the kind of scent that makes you happy and sad about missing home. The point is this: try being afraid of someone when they smell that familiar and comforting; it's like playing happy music over a horror film.

I had never shaken a Teek's hand before. I had felt the plaster model of one in school—and I was the jackass trying to convince the other kids it was real—but this was quite different.

As Paul Newman jogged my memory and told me about the Human actor he was named after, I did my best to take mental pictures of every part of the interaction, committing it to memory as if it would be a singular experience. But that was crazy; I didn't need to remember one handshake for posterity. I was at the beginning of a career that would include *thousands* of Teek handshake opportunities.

"Cadet Lidstrom," Paul said, in his voice that sounded like it was bouncing through a plastic tube, "did I ask the wrong question?"

My mouth fell open. Apparently, I had missed that he had asked a question. "Well...could you please repeat it for me?"

"Certainly. What error prompted you to come to the personnel office?"

"Oh! Well..." I turned over the print dossier in my hands and nearly dropped it.

Officially, there was an age verification stamp, but I was worried about any potential unofficial concerns.

"They flagged my birthday."

I could have sworn that Paul made a buzzing sound somewhere in his chest area. His outer eyes tinged a murky yellow then reverted to their neutral charcoal gray. "I am not certain what you mean."

"Right. Yeah, sorry. When they ran my birthday, some part of the system blocked me as too young. I mean, I turned on Luna before the qualifying date. I just need it approved."

"I believe I understand, Cadet Lidstrom."

That was a relief; I wasn't sure if I would know how to explain much further. In truth, I had very little idea of how Teek even measured age, given their whole molting cycle. I had a desire to ask about that and a hundred other things, but I wasn't sure what, if anything, would offend someone like Paul Newman. For all I knew, he could be very proud and cagey and would expect the same from me.

But that bubble was popped when he asked, "Cadet Lidstrom, what is your gender? I am unable to determine for certain based on your scent, tone of voice, and lack of distinct biological markers."

I managed not to laugh. "Male. Man. Yeah, use he to describe me." I wasn't sure of protocol, but I took a guess on appreciation and reciprocations. "Thanks, Paul. And you...do you have a preferred gender?"

Paul Newman's eyes tinted green, which was supposed to be satisfaction if I had my chromae spectrum right. "My molt type, as well as others you will see, do not have biological sex, so there is no emphasis placed on gender. I use Paul Newman as my name, and I can be viewed as male. If you err, I will not be offended."

I made a mental note that Paul Newman was not easy to offend. I hoped this was representative for other Teek, or that if Paul was unique, I would get teamed up with someone like him. "Cool. Thanks, Paul."

"I appreciate learning about you too, Cadet Lidstrom," he said in a tone that I would have considered mocking if it had come from a Human.

A third voice joined the conversation as a thin man with long hair came down the corridor toward us. "Green Cadets—Human, Lidstrom; Teek, ref Newman." He was reading from an unseen screen as he slipped through the door and toward the desk. An ocular implant supplied the information and his haptic glove was already activating and accessing the console. Though he did not once look at us, the secretary of personnel was determined to help in the most efficient way possible. "Let's get you both sorted and assigned to a shuttle. We don't want you stranded here overnight and missing opening ceremonies."

I saw Paul's eyes shifted toward teal and could hear him vibrate. I admit that I was also a bit concerned, but I was glad I didn't project it as strongly as he did.

* * *

I neither invited nor excluded Paul from following me. Maybe I should have been a bit more proactive, but I wasn't really thinking about it.

After only a few tunnels and one conveyor walkway back to where the E-section recruits were waiting, I don't know if I would've had time to plan ahead. Realistically, though, I probably should have considered the possibility of xenophobia, or even just discomfort at the newness of Paul Newman. Even I wasn't oblivious to how the terminal was sectioned out, or the fact that the Humans and the

Teek were in clusters by species and in arrival groups for easy organization. The uniformed members of the I.I. tried to interact with everyone, though, so it wasn't too much of a stretch.

Apart from those who had gotten really sick or had hurt themselves during docking, the young men and women had gotten into comfortable modes of waiting. Decks of cards and ereaders had come out; for some, ear-pods went in. Some didn't notice Paul Newman, but, for others, his presence might be a novelty or nuisance.

I don't know how many of the other cadets had met a Teek. Even in the geographically controlled E group, there was a wide range of possible contact experiences. The Atlantic Coast and British Columbia folks were most likely to have worked in close proximity to Teek and even had a trade interaction with a rat-beebee or two, not to mention the ones from really wealthy families who had spent months on Luna or had even made a trip to Mars.

But then there were the rest of us. Guys like me and, I assumed, Yiorgos, who was now waving me over from a collection of about fifteen milling Greenies. I recognized a few of them from in-person interactions and from seeing their ID pics on my room assignment list, and I saw that they did not yet have that casual or comfortable look where their new surroundings were concerned, especially when they noticed that Paul Newman followed me over.

"Lidstrom!" called Yiorgos, still a little pale from the journey, but much more robust. "You get it all sorted out?"

I indicated "kind of" with a hand, while looking around to gauge expressions.

Cadet Shin stood and gave me an upward nod of greeting, or maybe it was a way of tacitly challenging the presence of Paul. Even her posture came across as badass, but it didn't yet tell me if I was getting on her bad side. Her eyes narrowed, but her thin lips hardly twitched.

Regarding Paul Newman, expressions ran the gamut: fear, nausea, excitement, curiosity, or ready to challenge, like Shin. Every cadet knew the Teek were our official allies and a big part of what made the Initiative possible, but, in that moment, I found myself questioning how much of the stories or theories everyone else had heard, or believed.

There were those who thought the Teek were dragging us Humans out of a comparable dark age and were grateful or intimidated; others had heard the unclassified war stories and were convinced that the ingenuity and military might of Human beings had saved the Teek and put them in our debt. Of course, there were the Human-firsters, who wanted our species to self-improve on our own merit until we could compete with the other aliens. Which led to the folks who made passive-aggressive comparisons to Separate-but-Equal and other racially charged doctrines from Terra's sordid past.

I figured there was space enough for all kinds in the Initiative, even if I was reluctant to declare my stance and alienate people. Upon reflection, however, me standing next to a Teek before day one at the academy made a certain kind of impression.

Eventually someone forced me out of my silence by asking, "Who's the Teek?"

I awkwardly jerked my thumb in his direction, and explained, "Yeah, everybody, this is Paul Newman. We met in the personnel office."

Yiorgos grinned and bobbed. "Like the actor? Very skilled decision."

"Paul, this is Yiorgos. And—um—other Terra-Human cadets."

Paul Newman's eyes were fluctuating in color when he said, "Hello fellow Green Cadets. I am Paul Newman."

Shin advanced a couple of steps. "Yeah, we got that," she said. If she had been wearing a normal belt, she probably would have hooked her thumbs in it. As it was, she had her hands in the thigh pockets of her flightsuit. "Hey, Lidstrom, does Paul need you for anything else?"

I opened my mouth, then shut it. Paul Newman's eyes went a shade closer to blue. He was not buzzing, however.

This felt like one of those multiverse moments, where I could split off two distinctly different realities and probably launch a chaos theory graphic. On one hand, I side with Shin, of my own people, watch as Paul Newman's eyes go purple; he retreats for now, but vies to take vengeance during our time at the academy. On the other, I snub Shin and vouch for Paul, pitting myself against my own people, and thus beginning a revolutionary friendship that will be the only thing to save both our peoples when the cataclysm arrives!

In reality, the whole thing was much lower key and didn't seem to spark the kind of stuff to inspire award-winning series. To my new Teek acquaintance, I said, "Hey, Paul, it was good meeting you. I'll catch up with you later."

Paul hesitated. But after a second's flash of color, he reciprocated. "You as well, Cadet Lidstrom." He about-faced and started away.

"Skilled, Lidstrom," said Yiorgos. "Already making connections with the Teek."

"Careful," advised Shin. "Academy rankers are looking for people who will support a Human presence in space. Don't want to seem too buddy-buddy with the other types too quickly. Makes you look easy to influence."

Shin stood a little taller than me, with the bearing of someone who had spent more time in low-grav, which gave her an air of authority.

"Fair," I acknowledged, "but I figure hanging out with Teek or even the rat-beebees is okay, right?"

Shin responded with her eyebrows rather than her words. She peeled off from me and Yiorgos and joined another cluster of seated and standing cadets, one of whom was remarking on how good Paul Newman had smelled.

"So, what happened with the registration?" Yiorgos asked me, activating a rising stool from where it had been flush with the floor. He sat down and indicated for me to join him. Other cadets followed suit and listened in.

I triple-clicked one of the floor circles with the toe of my boot, then pulled my leg away while the stool swiveled up to an average height, which I opted not to change. "I got bumped back a bit. Someone else filled my seat for your shuttle, and they put me on a later connection." Seeing Yiorgos' expression change, I assured him, "It's okay; they say I'll be on Mars for opening ceremonies."

"That's good. So, what did—"

But I didn't get to find out what he was going to ask because the klaxons on all sides blared for attention. A pre-recorded voice over the comm loudly stated, in English first, "Incoming vessel, *Cruiser*-class. Clear gates thirty-eight through forty-two and prepare to receive."

The message was repeating in Teek when someone—not pre-recorded—got on the line, sounding a little frantic, "Attention!

Green Cadets stay in your sections and with your groups, except cadets at gates thirty-eight and thirty-nine should cross to gates ten and eleven and wait there. Security report! Foam guns active."

Suddenly, people around me were running in all directions. It happened quickly enough that I didn't even realize we were sitting in gate thirty-nine, not far under the big number. But really, who looks up at their own gate number once they're parked? I wasn't the only one a little slow on the uptake, or who stopped and stared. Though many rushed as if there were a real emergency and security personnel were on their way, there was no continued alarm. No signs of actual code red.

Yiorgos stood and swiveled his stool back into the floor. I followed suit, but we started in opposite directions.

"Wait, where are you going?" he called after me, obviously confused, because he was the one following a very reasonable directive to head to the other side of the giant terminal.

"I'll be just one second," I assured him, my feet taking me toward the hatch and the windows.

I got to one of the transparencies and looked out—"pressed my nose" was less dignified but more accurate. I shouldn't have been surprised to see stars, moving at a notably faster rate than they ever would on Terra-Human or even our relatively slow satellite Luna. I had wondered if I'd witness something strange, something huge and bright and unmissable; instead, I saw stars. Until, without much warning, the alien ship filled the view, moving gradually across the window to docking position and blocking every scrap of space behind its mass.

A hand on my shoulder yanked me away and spun me face-to-face with a staff sergeant. "What are you doing here, Greenie?" she demanded. It was the woman who'd read me in when I was docking, Clancy. She looked considerably less amiable now.

I had no effective excuse or explanation, but a fellow Green Cadet was ready to supply one.

Shin had slipped right beside me. She made eye contact with the staff sergeant and rattled off the same conclusion I'd come to.

"Sarge, we observed no bulkhead alerts or pressure alarms. Security aren't wearing masks—" which ruled out a lot of potential hazards, "—we wanted to offer assistance." I noticed Shin was wearing tactical gloves, the kind that weren't actually considered dangerous on their own and therefore weren't likely to be confiscated but were effective guards and nasty knuckles for anyone with some scrapping skills.

Before I could agree with the logical explanation, Staff Sergeant Clancy responded with an authoritative, "Absolutely not! Look, Punchy, you and Hotshot are in no way trained or prepared for xeno interaction. I'm not prepared to risk your lives or anyone else's because you misinterpreted a situation. Now clear the gate!"

I was backpedalling when the incoming ship scratched its way against the docking arms—still of no actual risk to the station, but not a pleasant sound or flattering to the pilot's capabilities. Shin obeyed the order as well, but only to the edge of the platform.

We both had a pretty good vantage of the doors as they were given the all-clear to open the airlocks, even with all the security personnel blocking the way.

The first person out was Human, waving for everyone to clear a path, while shouting the same. He was the type of man who would exhibit a quiet authority but could augment it by being extra loud.

The second person was not a person but a programmed bot, wheeling something in—but as it got closer, I could see that it carried a some*one*. A lizard-type, the ones called Tsanghar, was curled to one side on a stretcher, which was swiftly escorted from the hatch through the cleared path.

Distracted by the Tsanghar in the fetal position, I might have missed the most important entrance of all. Luckily, Shin was there to nudge me with her elbow.

The third person was an eight-foot-tall werewolf creature, carrying yet another lizard. This lizard was bleeding from the neck, and the hairy beast held a narrow dagger in one hand.

"A P'rukktah!" observed Shin, quietly and with great focus. "Now, *that* would be hard to misinterpret."

This P'rukktah, wearing shoulder plates but an otherwise indistinct pair of pants and vest, did not have that look of pride I'd been told about these species or their family units. I had never been in a room with one before, so I really had no basis, but I did not glean any murderous intent. Rather, as the commotion grew, this P'rukktah demonstrated a great deal of poise.

* * * * *

Chapter Nine:
Kesiel

All Together, But Hardly Met...

Without overshooting my own importance, I can safely say that had I not been in that section of that transport, the minor scuffle which preceded our docking at the Phobos Station would have erupted into an interstellar conflict.

Whether or not you concur does nothing to change the facts, but I will leave you to your interpretation.

The ruckus on the ship and my efforts to placate the on-board security paled in comparison to the response of the Phobos personnel. The somewhat rigid Human named Gordon had seen that some of us would be allowed unblocked entrance, but unblocked does not equate to unfettered. The critical condition Tsangharee were being wheeled out, but my new P'rukktah friend attempted to jump the queue and was met at gunpoint by station security.

I slipped in front of her—much more agile on two, or four, limbs than she—and raised my head to its full extension. "Please!" I entreated, for I have been told that Humans of all stripes love this word. "Please, we must go to your healers."

As I spoke this in perfect Human, they had no choice but to be stunned by my skill and stand down, as had the guards within. Therefore, following Officer Gordon and the one bot with the stretchered Tsanghar, I led the great hairy beast carrying my travel companion Liesarn, whose recently tracheotomied throat was being held open with a crude bit of tubing. The careful observer would note that one of her thermocoils was missing, having been stripped by yours truly, and cut to allow for easy breathing without obstructing blood.

I only wish I could have had more time to take in and properly welcome myself to this place called Phobos, which was much cleaner than Stellar VII and acted as a precursor to the academy on Mars-Human.

I described the encounter four different times in as many Human minutes, detailing the heroic, fast-thinking action of the honorable P'rukktah who had saved the life of my nextmoon kin, Liesarn, and had most assuredly *not* engaged in combat or broken any rules of decorum. I detailed the cacophony of fur and scales in Human and in the most universal form of Tsanghar I could manage. The story seemed to bring enough satisfaction to the Human intake officers and to the Teek on the scene. The other Tsangharee who did not need urgent medical care were being held on the ship to ascertain their condition and likelihood of violence. The other P'rukktah were being escorted into the conveniently emptied platform thirty-nine, surrounded, at a safe distance, by curious Humans who had never seen something so ugly before.

The docking station infirmary was more than large enough for a few incoming patients, but they did not seem prepared to treat and deal with so many lizards at once. I noted with some kinly sympathy that at least two of our number had fully suffocated in the time it had taken to dock and reach the infirmary. The others, however, had been fitted with some manner of breathing tubes or did not suffer the same tongue-swallowing conundrum as Liesarn had.

The Human officer of the infirmary directed my P'rukktah friend to a less urgent side of the room, where she laid Liesarn, dusty orange face, blackened lips, and a charming new scar on the base of the neck. She lay with some rigidity, still clearly in a kind of shock, but from everything I could ascertain about anatomy, I presumed she would physically recover.

This P'rukktah, I had concluded, knew far more about my inner workings than I did. However, I could easily take apart and rebuild, and improve, the sorry excuses for P'rukktah spaceships, so there we were at an impasse of competitive skills.

There was only a moment of downtime while the rest of the Tsanghar were being situated, but something crucial had to be expressed.

I am not a wizard of dialects, but I can attempt some rudimentary P'rukktah. I tapped my new friend on her furry upper arm and growled out in her language, "*I am Kesiel.*"

She gave me a nod and tried—bless her—in incredibly broken universal Tsanghar, "*My name is Arrksh.*"

"Arrksh," I repeated. "*Gratitude.*"

"*Gratitude,*" she reciprocated.

That was all we had time for. A uniformed Human arrived to call me away. Evidently, I needed to impart my account of events one more time.

* * *

The escort led me deeper into the station and I perceived, deeper into the moon, this nearer satellite called Phobos. My new Human was not Gordon, and I was informed neither name nor rank. I did sense an air of importance and nervousness, especially when the door was opened toward my destination.

This room was nearly circular, at about four Human-meters in height and twice as wide. There were ten screens along one wall, and, including the one I had just used, three doors, which remained closed.

All the bolted-down chairs and desks stood empty, and the lights were low. My escort had not entered with me, and all five of the Humans in the room stood. The tallest had peculiar reddish hair, which I suspected to be unnaturally colored, as well as a circle of dark fur around the lips; he was speaking directly to a screen, two-dimensional and severely skewed from my vantage point.

The enlarged face on the screen said to the reddish-haired man in bizarrely accented Human, "How severely would you categorize this incident, Commander."

"Admiral, I don't know if I would call it an incident. Right now, our infirmary staff are reviving and stabilizing every lizard who passed out. There wasn't even a fight or ship malfunction that caused this."

I shifted to gain a better view of the speaker on the screen. Even at an angle, her face appeared wrinkled with dehydration and graying with sun deprivation, but still exuded strength. I recognized this person as a fleet commander of the Humans, whose presence was advertised in the protection of the Human-Teek Alliance.

I was not sure if I should remain out of her camera view, but either way, one of the other Humans in the room saw me, a beige-skinned woman with no notable fur anywhere on her head. She gestured to me with her primary finger, an indication I did not recall from my reading.

Without knowing what this one-finger motion meant, I mirrored the gesture and waited.

"Any theories?" the on-screen admiral asked.

"Their security thinks it has something to do with the Teek drone units resonating a hivemind signal, which interfered with the lizard dreamsharing. I don't know how often that many of both are on one ship, so—"

"Very well," she said, abruptly halting him. Her shoulders lowered, as if the anxiety of crisis had been averted. "Thank you, Commander. I'll contact the liner's captain. Radio my office on secure line if there are any unexpected developments."

"Of course, Admiral." He brought his right hand to his brow, a gesture akin to a Belbeh salute. She only nodded in response before disconnecting the video feed. He did not drop the saluting hand, but instead rubbed at his forehead and the bridge of his nose, which I could only imagine were fatigued from squinting or affecting expressions of authority. "All right, let's pull up the security feeds again. I want to make sure—"

"Excuse me, sir," the bald woman said, interrupting in a manner that would have elicited hisses among my people, "I think the witness is here."

"Oh, yes, excellent." He asked one of his fellow Humans, "Hey, Moore, you speak standard Tsanghar; can you translate?"

Extending my neck forward to indicate my intention to interject, I said, "That will not be necessary, Commander. I am quite studied in speaking formal Human."

He blinked a couple of times and nodded. "How about that? You came prepared. I am Commander Poissonier—" though I would later learn the spelling, it sounded like *Pwah-sown-yeh,* "—this is Phobos Station Director, or PSD, Lang. That's L-T Moore." Lang and Moore each nodded when their names were mentioned. He did not introduce the other two, who each wore "staff sergeant" designations, one of whom was the beige-skinned, furless woman. "On behalf of the Human-Teek Alliance and the Interstellar Initiative, I'd like to welcome you to our home system and to Phobos Station, and to apologize for the complications on arrival."

The furless staff sergeant made a pointed puffing noise when the commander said "complications." He chose not to engage with this and continued addressing me.

"What is your name?"

"I am Kesiel, a Yavamee selection for the Initiative." If I lacked in any formality, I more than made up for it in flourish, magnanimously spreading my fingers and arcing my tail.

"Good. Kesiel," he said, with only a slight error of intonation, which I was magnanimous enough to forgive, "I understand you vouched for the P'rukktah."

From his tone, I took this to be a kind of question, though much less clear than what I would have said. Then again, I cannot fault them too much: ambiguity is an art all its own. "This is correct, Commander Poissonier." I cannot confirm whether I correctly said his name, but I did my best to match inflection but not to use my more dexterous tongue beyond what a Human could manage.

"Good. Why?"

The question was not anticipated and so I hesitated in response. I canted my head at the neck in order to better read him and gleaned nothing disingenuous. Still, I had to clarify, even if that meant questioning a superior officer's meaning and admitting I did not fully comprehend. "*Why* did I accurately relate the nature of the events as they occurred rather than incorrectly condemning the being who saved my nextmoon kin?"

The commander smiled—if you could call it a smile. Once again, the expression was far too muted. Better to maintain one's unreadable *tianego* face than to convey so little. The other eyes were upon me as well, and I was only glad that the admiral did not appear to be on the screen.

"I should think that you would be most pleased!" I said, my own exuberance showing through a smile far less reserved. "Did I act incorrectly or not within protocol?"

"No, you did fine," he said, dropping some of the formality along with the tension in his stance. "Personally, I'm grateful you stepped in and spoke up. And I apologize if this feels like an intense first impression. We're merely trying to ascertain what happened and why, but this is not an interrogation, and you're not being charged with anything."

I canted my head further, for, though I understood his words, I was quite intrigued at this tactic.

"Did I lose you there? Sorry, I can get a translator if you need."

"That is hardly a necessary accommodation, Commander, but I appreciate the gesture."

The furless woman with the staff sergeant patch made a huffed exhale sound, which I took to be intentionally audible. She repositioned herself in relation to me, by a few small steps, but enough to easily demonstrate she was "stepping in." "All right, let's speed this up a bit. Cadet, please respond in the affirmative or the negative."

I could tell I was going to like this staff sergeant's approach less than the commander's, who still allowed for some of the verbal tête-à-tête. However, as I was a foreigner hoping to work among foreigners, I affected my attention posture and prepared to respond.

"You say the P'rukktah did not attack or provoke the Tsanghar."

"Correct."

"You witnessed the—um—" she looked over her shoulder and the one called Moore gestured to his neck, "—the tracheotomy?"

"And assisted," I added. "I held the patient in place."

"Right. And you knew the patient previously?"

"Correct. Her name is Liesarn. She is from a low orbit moon of the same planet, but a different faction and untraceable motherline connection."

Though my final remark caused confusion, the sergeant managed to press on. "Did you have a personal or close relationship with her?"

"I did not. We did not meet until we began our journey to the Sol-Human System."

"And what about the P'rukktah? Did you know—um—"

As the staff sergeant faltered, I decided to intervene with my best assumption of the stumbling block. "Her. She is a P'rukktah female who introduced herself as Arrksh. I briefly attempted a conversation prior to the incident, but we do not speak one anothers' languages very well."

The commander felt a need to interject, with, "Wait, so you had no idea that she's royalty?"

"*Royalty!*" I hummed. "Most fascinating. Is this true?"

Moore shook his head, and tried to convince me, "Not royalty."

"She's from a prominent house," the commander clarified.

"From the sound of it, she was an heir to that household and—"

"Maybe we shouldn't give the details," suggested the shorn sergeant in a hushed tone which would still be difficult to conceal from one so nearby.

"This is an astounding revelation!" I told them. "Please, do continue."

They paused, and the sergeant asked, "Is he being sarcastic?"

"She," corrected the other staff sergeant, the darker one, with a much more sonorous timbre.

"Cadet Kesiel," the commander said, resuming his hold on the room, "what reason did you have to trust a P'rukktah stranger to treat a choking Tsanghar?"

"She appeared medically skilled," I recalled. "Did she not succeed in opening an airway?"

"Yes, she did, with your help."

The silence was practically a song of its own now. Despite their uniforms and badges, the people in this room were clearly very uncomfortable with having interspecies conversations. This script, it appeared, would neither move forward nor conclude without my initiative. "Commander," I began, "might I make an observation?"

"Please do."

"It seems as though you all have a tentatively rehearsed dance around your real concern. Are you attempting to gain information about the conflict between the Tsangharee and the P'rukktah peoples without actually asking? This is the reason for the inquiries: a Tsanghar assists a P'rukktah, even though these people are supposed to be enemies. However, you do not understand our people or our conflicts over the generations. Shall I illuminate?"

Again, this time more sincerely, the Human commander said, "Please do."

"The P'rukktah are not my enemy, nor are they the enemy of the Tsangharee people," I said, explaining as I would to a child whose tongue had not fully developed. "The Segranee faction was at war with one planet and seven recognized households of the P'rukktah. That conflict has ended and the Segranee disbanded. As I am not Segranee and do not know every P'rukktah's house affiliation or planet of origin, there is no reason why a P'rukktah cannot be my friend. After all, there is a peace now."

The commander nodded, somewhat assuaged. "So you would say there's not a likelihood of retaliation or another conflict between the P'rukktah and Tsangharee here?"

"Oh no, Commander. Our people are rivals, and many of us excel at retaliation! The Tsangharee had traditionally hunted and eaten Belbehan, who brought the P'rukktah into space and are their friends, so no peace is guaranteed to last. There is a saying that war is never more than three mistakes away. I should hate for a misinterpretation of today's events to be the first of three, especially in the presence of our new and formidable Human friends."

The symphony of silence returned. Only the furless sergeant smirked. She found amusement in the circular conflicts—as did I.

The commander chewed on his lip and nodded. "Okay. Cadet, I should have asked this earlier. How are you feeling?"

I did not have the requisite time to process and consider my response, nor was I able to gauge everyone's expressions. Even this question was a tactical move. "I am quite well, thank you, Commander."

"I mean…regarding the space hysteria. Most of the Tsangharee in the passenger liner had negative responses when coming out of the fold. Some described hearing a—" He checked his notes. "A 'screaming song' or 'a grieving song.'"

"Yeeessss," I cooed, agreeing my interest, but this caused a minor recoil from all the Humans but one, the still silent and stoic staff sergeant of the darker complexion. So, I turned to her. "Is it not a fascinating phenomenon? Very peculiar."

"A couple of them expressed fear about…" He paused in order to prepare to produce the sounds properly. "*Hree-Dahn*—which we're having trouble translating. Is it some type of spatial anomaly?"

"*Hridan*," I said, gently nudging his pronunciation, "is a superstitious term about misfortune or the convergence of negative factors in space. We use it when known numerical patterns do not fit with outcomes. It is personified as a space ghost that interferes or disrupts, like your gremlin or boogie-man," I supplied, attempting to be as clear and helpful as possible.

This annoyed the furless staff sergeant, who apparently did not wish to maintain her prior amusement. She pressed her lips together for a moment then said, "We theorized it was a combination of the shared dreaming of the Tsangharee and the number of different Teek hiveminds represented. Particularly their communing drones— those large living computer bugs." She attempted to mime the height and shape of a Teek drone, quadrupedal, slow, and elegant, but I was already quite familiar and nodded before she could embarrass herself. "Do you have another theory?"

"Not presently," I admitted. "I fear the mind is too complex a machine for these fingers. But I am pleased that the P'rukktah named Arrksh knew enough to wake me and to save Liesarn. Pity not all of them could be saved."

A minor hubbub issued from at least three voices at once.

One whose name I had already forgotten said, "No, we revived everyone. Our medical technology is very advanced."

I hummed my congratulations. "Then I'm sure everyone will soon look back on this incident with fond amusement. Seeing as no one died and no parties have reason to swear revenge."

Once again, silence had reign for a time. Even though I am not an expert in Human behavior, I do believe my commentary made them uncomfortable. I found this most intriguing and not at all what I expected from a race I had been taught to regard with cautious respect.

There were some furtive bits of eye contact, until the commander resumed the floor. "All right, then. I think that's everything. Cadet Kesiel, thank you for coming down and speaking with us."

"A pleasure indeed!" I announced.

It was not a very large room, but there were enough doors for me to start toward the wrong one. They did not know me nearly well enough to say with certainty that I intentionally stalled. And the commander, to his steadfast credit, was so determined to not look flummoxed that he pretended not to care that I would overhear.

They projected some video feeds on the screens, a balance of visible light that did not have nearly enough color but was sharply focused. As I was being walked toward the correct door, I had occasion to pick out some interesting Human characters whom I had not met.

The commander pointed at a small section, and asked, "Who are these two?"

The darker staff sergeant explained, "He is a hotshot who had trouble following orders, and she was the one ready with tactical gloves."

But that was as much as I caught before the door was gently pulled closed behind me. Perhaps these people were of no consequence. However, experience has taught me to believe in the poetry of convergence, which can make great sense of the universe and its sentient players if one is willing to pay attention.

And, no, I do not believe there is any translation for this poetry in Human.

* * * * *

Chapter Ten:
Paul Newman

Before she boarded her shuttle from Phobos to Mars, Ella Fitzgerald touched her antenna to one of mine and advised me to "See this as an opportunity." The color formation around her eyes indicated a form of sympathetic excitement and a bit of muted envy. She knew that my being "bumped" would allow me to interact with more people, whereas she was only riding down with other Teek and the few Humans who operated the craft and gave instructions. There was a logic to her advice, and a part of me *was* still excited. Yet, given the recent displays of larger groups of P'rukktah and Tsangharee, I was nervous. Even more so that I did not have anyone from home planet or hive to commune with.

I also had to acknowledge that the planetside shuttles were all full—over-full—and tightly scheduled to get everyone down to the academy in time for opening ceremonies in less than one of their solar days. This was simply a fact, and I could not change it.

I watched Ella exit through the circular airlock, and I tried to focus on a positive frame of mind, but I admit to a great wave of uncertainty that almost eclipsed my excitement. After all, though I was surrounded by thousands of sentient beings, this was the first time I had been completely alone and isolated from the hive.

These feelings were hard to explain to the station personnel who saw me standing still, just beyond the edge of the walkway, looking at a now-closed airlock door. After all, they had never been part of a hive and, unless I was misinformed, would not have experienced any mind connection enough to know the absence of it.

One of them asked me if I would like to sit down, while another put out a comm call for someone named Jane, specifically Jane One. I genially declined the offer to sit—sitting is not a natural posture for Teek workers, especially in Human chairs. I am not sure if this agitated them, but they clearly wished for me to go somewhere without telling me where. I did notice that there were very few non-uniformed Teek in sight, that the new cadets had most likely all made their way toward the shuttles. Everyone else appeared to have a sense of belonging and purpose, but as I did not and the Human personnel had not given me a task, I remained and observed.

I was in a reasonably central location of this impressive terminal, and I had time to ascertain and assess. To the credit of my imprint, I have always found Human behaviors fascinating, though I had hardly had time to see them in their natural environment.

Of the two to three hundred Humans I could see walking, working, or waiting, over half were like me: prospective cadets. About a third were in some manner of uniform to designate their role on the Phobos Station or on the passenger liners. The final fraction, perhaps fifteen percent, wore the I.I.-style sleeveless jacket over their flightsuits. These would be instructors, officers, and the odd director, forming a hierarchy much more complicated and subject to interpretation than a hive.

One of these suited types was leading a large P'rukktah from a lower staircase. Though I am not particularly adept at distinguishing

P'rukktah, I recognized her outfit. She was the first to exit the most recent transport carrying the limp body of their rival species. Among other destinations, the sign near the stairs indicated an infirmary below. I wondered if she, like me, felt alone among this collection of Humans.

I was actually somewhat surprised when I was addressed by a voice that was not in fact Human, but the warbling timbre that vibrates through an exoskeleton. "Hello. Paul Newman?" said, or perhaps asked, one of my people. "I am called Jane Austen." Like the other Humans of the I.I., this Teek wore the standard sleeveless jacket over a flightsuit, open in the back for wings which stretched from the shoulders nearly to the floor. With one hand on the upper thorax, Jane said, "I use the Human female pronouns."

She was not presently wearing anything I recognized as an officer insignia, and she did not introduce herself by rank, but I read positional authority from her, both in terms of her demeanor and what I sensed in my hind-brain. She primarily sent me assurance. "Hello, Jane Austen," I replied, searching my memory for that name and finding only the category author.

"I was informed you had to miss your shuttle. The minor error has been corrected and there should not be further delay." She indicated a direction to walk, and I began to follow her. One of the Humans who had been watching me stared open-mouthed, perhaps surprised that I was willing to go once a direction was presented. The other had resumed duties and did not seem to notice my departure.

Jane Austen stepped with more assurance in the augmented gravity than I did, or any of the newly arriving Teek I had observed. I noticed her antennae were slightly longer than mine and flared at the end, which indicated a drier home environment with less wind than mine. Or rather, her home was here, as some combination of this moon and the planet and the I.I.

She waited until we were a little farther away—possibly out of Human hearing range—before saying, "You are not the first to be mislabeled at this station. These kinds of errors of registration happen. That may not sound positive, but I want you to know that you are not being considered any differently by the Initiative."

I had another wonder, which I did not try to conceal.

She interpreted from my mood and answered: "Do not worry, you will be on the planet and able to meditate with your *jiki* before you are in danger of dissociation."

"That is appreciated." I also appreciated that the information was coming from another Teek, one who knew what it was like to be disconnected from the hive. This was something I had tried to explain to Humans before—and one very confused Belbehan trader; even my tutors did not understand.

"Do you need something to eat?" she asked, and I noticed we were approaching a common eating area, something called a "mess hall" or "food court," if I remembered my vernacular.

I felt no hunger urge. "No. Thank you."

"Very well, but bear in mind, you are not receiving the hive's collective call for nourishment, so you may not notice your own hunger until you are literally starving." What she said made sense to me, and she reinforced it by adding, "Many Teek who have traveled beyond their hive and beyond the mental reach of drones fall victim to this phenomenon. I anticipate many of the new Teek recruits will begin to feel faint within three days. Either way, you are joining me for my lunch." She proceeded toward a queue and swiped her wrist across a reader; I saw on the screen that she was approved for a meal from the window ahead, and that the time was marked. There were only Humans in this line, and there did not seem to be a long delay.

"You think I should eat?" I wondered.

"I would. Consider it an opportunity to taste." Jane turned her attention from me to the menu.

I ran a quick calculation about my nourishment needs, realized that I did not know how to translate for Human calories, and mirrored Jane's selection. The screen asked me to present a scannable device or my Cadet ID, but Jane scanned for me before I could make a selection.

She collected both of our sealed "Meal Bags" that arrived along a conveyor and went toward a table, offering and receiving salutations from people she passed.

"Jane Austen, may I ask a question?"

"Yes, Paul Newman." She straddled the oval-shaped stool, gripping some footpads with practiced motions.

"Why did they not recommend all incoming Jyikj'tch'tyeek prepare to consume higher amounts of nutrients?"

"Two things: It is just Teek here; Humans can hardly say our full name, and they do not like it." Her hind-brain gave me something akin to a general admonition or warning. "To answer your question: Despite our alliance and cooperation on this project, many Humans did not want to open the Initiative to incoming cadets of multiple species."

I did not mask my confusion. "But you are part of the Initiative."

"*I* am established. I crewed during the offensive at Syedi-Teek."

My chromae must have flashed cold with fear, not from any firsthand memory, but from collective association of the enemy, where they were defeated but at great cost. Jane did not react.

"I understand the Humans, and they understand me. For example," she went on, unwrapping a spheroid slightly larger than her palm, "I know better than to wear lieutenant stripes among the newest Humans, and I know how to eat a hamburger without shredding it."

Without any ceremony, she picked up the item, turned it sideways and ripped off a section with her outer mandibles.

I attempted to process the bulk of the information, the most impressive of which was her noted, and implied, service record, but the most pressing of which was how to properly handle the hamburger. I had some book knowledge of hamburger as a reconstituted meat sandwich within a reconstituted grain bun, and I believed I had heard one of my tutors mention one. Of course, I discovered it was not only difficult to eat, but also pick up without the ends of my fingers going into the bun. My grip points naturally started scraping and pulling apart the bun, even as I tried to motivate the whole item to my jaws. The interior was not effectively adhered to itself, and I dropped a fermented vegetable which I recognized as a pickle. My attempt to bite into the assembly caused the ketchup to drip out one side. This would indeed take practice.

I saw the Humans at other tables interacting with their food quite easily. There were no other examples of my people engaged in ingestion whose example I could watch. The few Belbehan were gnawing at compact nutrient clusters of their own making.

I set down the hamburger for the moment and asked, "What is your role, Jane Austen?"

"I work on the new deep exploration ships. The *Command*-class vessels, where you will be vying for assignment."

I considered her words: vying for assignment. I found myself intrigued by the nature of Human existence and the choices they would have to make in order to join this program; a program of their devising in their home system for which they would have to compete with one another. Previously, I had thought of the need to prove myself, but my *jiki* Ella had been quite right that much more of my life on the home planet had been predetermined. I could grow and learn, but I had always been right for the task or not. "I don't think I have ever experienced this kind of competition before," I admitted with equal parts anxiety and exhilaration.

Jane smiled—or rather her chromae warmed to orange, and her antennae arced in approval, which I read as a smile. "Congratulations, Paul Newman," she said, "you've just taken the first step toward understanding. It is a long road." Unceremoniously, she devoured what remained of her hamburger and compressed the wrapping into a tiny, flattened square of waste.

Standing, Lieutenant Jane Austen said, "I will leave you to work out your meal without my eyes on you. Once you are done, find somewhere to go and someone to talk to. Barring that, find something to read. Remember, the impressions you make in the next few days could decide your trajectory in the Initiative."

I do not know if that last was meant to sound intimidating or encouraging. Regardless, before walking away she wished me "Good luck."

I had questions I wanted to ask, about her process of gaining rank, or her relationships with Humans of the Initiative, or how long she had been removed from the hive, but I had been given a task. It was, in a manner of speaking, my first order from the Initiative.

I did indeed struggle with the hamburger. Once I was done, I had learned a few new things, and I still had a mission to carry out before catching my delayed shuttle.

* * * * *

Chapter Eleven:
Lidstrom

I was initially pretty ticked off about being bumped all the way to the final cadet shuttle. Not even an official cadet shuttle, but an overflow vessel for a mix of staff, rat-beebee commuters, and P'rukktah whose papers weren't completely in order—or translatable. Apparently, everything was so packed and pre-assigned to get down to the planet that, once I was popped out of my seat with my E-folks, there literally weren't any openings in between.

I stuck close to Shin and Yiorgos until they were picked up, but I definitely felt like I was missing out on important getting-to-know-you moments that might be needed to make the right connections with the right people. So, after waving goodbye, I had to figure out what to do with myself sans other Humans.

This might not have been the right choice for networking, but I opted to kill the couple of vacant hours in a flight simulator. After all, if I needed to impress in any area, it was as a pilot. I also took it as a given that there would be either a fully immersive simulator, or at least a jack that would allow me to run a personal program in a station like Phobos.

I had to investigate a couple of signs and ask a few questions as I worked my way to my target, a trilingual label on the open door. I found a no-nonsense training room, probably the kind without any games or laser battles, but with four full VR boxes, each fitted with standard hydraulics. Not to play up the inner planet stereotype, but I was more excited than scared by asteroid dodging and figured it was the fastest way to get some more training hours under my belt.

I was checking the panels to see if I could log in when one of the boxes opened and out stepped a man in a work suit sporting a Phobos insignia instead of an I.I. patch.

"Good evening!" he said. "I just cleared this one if you want in."

I don't know if I expected to be told to buzz off, but I hadn't thought I would get a genial welcome either. "Thanks."

I went to the box and looked inside to examine the chair and modular controls. They looked like they were configured for shuttle training, which made total sense on Phobos.

As I stepped in, the workman told me, "Yeah, I just installed a new *Command*-class trainer. Got some bugs, but we're working on those."

"Excellent!" And I meant it. "How do I set that up?"

Of course, that was when he realized the fine print and said, "Oh right! You're one of the new cadets. You probably aren't registered yet, so…"

He reached across me to one of the screens and tapped the Settings button to input some information. His suit smelled of an odd mix of oils and off-gassing polymers, and he clearly didn't have any hangups about sharing personal space.

With a thumbprint authorization, he finished whatever it was he was doing and withdrew. "There. I just activated a generic cadet account. It will only get you guest access to the demos, but it's a start. Give it a try."

I logged on, deciding to hold judgment on the demos until I saw how extensive they were. It was pretty limited, with some landing and docking practices and the totally standard slingshot maneuver. Also, as expected, a module named "Rock Hopper Race," an asteroid dodger program, loosely modeled off our own belt, starting at Ceres, employing extreme speed. I'd played versions of the demo before, but never with such limited steering and the absence of shields. Other than being lower res, it might have been the most realistic approach to the program I'd ever encountered, and the hydraulic systems helped me feel out the gravity vectors as I went.

It was a trial-and-error system, which, to tell the truth, was a lot more comfortable for me than interacting with a wide range of aliens who I didn't get at all, and, worse, Human officers who I was *supposed* to get. Dodging fake asteroids, with the opportunity to reset, was much lower risk than dodging cultural blunders and the occasional non-Human fist. There was a time to get out of the comfort zone and there was a time to soothe and self-assure. This was the latter, and I was better off spending it in this flimsy shell meant to resemble a cockpit.

I did reset a couple of times early on, but by my third round, I had found a kind of zen spot where I no longer needed to worry or think too hard about the craft to get it to go where I wanted. I started making faster and faster times through the course. It occurred to me that if I could reset periodically in my real life, I would be just fine.

The film trailer version of this resettable story was playing in my mind when an alert buzzed on my wrist. My planetside shuttle wasn't boarding yet—hadn't even docked—but they had finally opened a platform for us to gather.

With a loud sigh, I ended the simulation. There was a time for comfort, and that was now over. Before I exited, I looked at my final times and scores. They were logged as guest, and there was no one else to compare to, but I thought they looked pretty good. My highest was easy to remember, it had an 84 in the middle of it, like my seat number, and maybe a lucky number for me at the academy. Everyone could use a lucky number.

I opened the door of the simulator's case, which stuck a little on a worn hinge. Stepping one foot out and feeling the compound gravity, I was struck by how alone I felt in this space. If a simulated cockpit was comforting, the process of exiting it provided an even sharper contrast.

I started toward the hallway I'd come through, and I noticed a break in the wall paneling. There were actually several of these in the corridors under the station that showed rock, but in every other section I'd seen so far, the rock was coated with a kind of shiny enamel, a transparent polymer that was good for sealing.

Now, before you ask, yes, I have seen space horror films and played some scary VR, not all of which I'd had the guts to finish. On one hand, you should know better than to touch anything on an alien world without big rubber suits, especially while alone. On the other hand, I was too excited to think about it. I reached out with two fingers, then three, and eventually my whole palm, which barely fit into the gap between panels. I felt the rough, lightweight rock of Mars' nearer satellite.

I had expected it to be colder, as if it would reflect the dead of space rather than an ambient, insulated, and heated station. I think I projected the magnetism I felt, but then again it was totally possible for static electricity to have built up on the rough surface in a manner less common than on the single sheet metalwork of other orbiters.

It may sound cheesy, but I was suddenly quite glad that I was alone to experience this, an actual connection with this moon, sans barriers. In a controlled and safe environment, of course, but I would take what I could get.

"Hello, Phobos," I said, with a smile and an appropriate dash of awe.

I did not jump when I heard it reply, but every hair on my body stood straight up. There was a sound, like the whale calls they play at the aquarium, too full to be like the thrumming of a Teek or the singing of a Tsanghar.

It seemed to come from the rock and yet also from down the corridor.

As I followed the sound, I found a regular hinged door instead of a sliding hatch, which was latched but not locked. I opened it. Like in the case of my first joyride, it was better to ask forgiveness than permission, right?

I was soon disappointed. The space was too big and sectioned to be called a room. It was more like a loading and processing center, like the luggage conveyors of an airport, but for massive interstellar cargo. The sound became more metallic as I entered and turned out to be the less interesting noise of machine treads and servos straining under a heavy load.

It also wasn't hard to tell that I did not belong. The people managing the big, incoming tank were attached to grounding lines and wearing full-body hazmat suits. Everything was far enough away that I wasn't in danger; after all, there were several people wearing goggles but no other protective equipment. I couldn't tell what they were shipping and processing or how potentially volatile certain materials might be. Still, the sight of an all-Human factory or assembly line setup reminded me of Detroit.

"Hey!" one of the men shouted. He was one of the tallest, a combination of genetics and space dwelling. His skin was dark enough that the subtle gray in his full circle of facial hair stood out as light in tone. Most importantly, this authoritative foreman-type wore an I.I. uniform which clearly displayed lieutenant stripes that I noticed as he got closer. His bald head was shiny with the sweat of exertion, even though it was pleasantly cool down here. "You miss your shuttle, kid?"

I snapped a quick salute and said, "No, sir. Mine was delayed. I've been waiting below the terminal. Actually, I just got the alert to head back up."

He chuckled and dropped all measure of formality. "All right, then. You check the doors next time, and don't go assuming you count as station personnel until you're wearing a rank. For now, your job is to focus on being a cadet. Get me, kid?"

"Yes, sir," I replied. "Thank you, sir."

He dismissed me with a nod.

As soon as I was out of the loading area with the door shut behind me, I took a moment to read it. Station Personnel Only. I told myself there were worse ways to have egg on my face.

* * *

I hustled up the stairs, getting my blood pumping in the weird gravity of the station; move your muscles, quiet your nerves, I think is how the saying goes.

The main concourse had a vastness I hadn't appreciated before. It was not all stark white, and there were plants to give it some atmosphere, but I felt like I was entering a bright, clean dome. When I wasn't worried about tripping over people, I was able to look up at the ceiling and marvel at the architecture that I'm pretty sure was mostly Human.

I don't know how many shuttles had actually taken passengers down. Still, considering there had been several waves departing from six shuttle platforms—I estimated some fifty trips—each carrying a few dozen passengers, would put us in the two-thousand cadet range. Now, only a few remained and many of the station workers were off duty, giving this grand hall an eerie emptiness.

I looked at my wrist display then up to the platform sign. I saw one of the final groups gathering for transport to the planet, and I sighed again. It was a mixed bag, the leftovers, the last resort...and not a Human among them. In fact, I wasn't even sure they were all incoming cadets. Some of the rat-beebees and P'rukktah wore generic flightsuits like me, standard issue from one of the waystations or unadorned I.I. suits. The lizards, on the other hand, were completely mismatched. They wore bands of color on their arms and legs, and some of them had stripes across their necks which could have been natural or painted. Every one of them was wearing compression gear with coils, about the shape of a woman's one-piece bathing suit, but weirdly intimidating. Of course, there were a couple of Teek, but most looked like they had jobs to do or were established I.I. servicemen.

One appeared younger, more like a cadet, a four-armed variety instead of the winged ones. He was speaking with a lone P'rukktah wearing an orange-ish vest that reminded me of road workers and night dockmen. Though the Teek had his back to me, I thought the voice sounded familiar, but I wasn't feeling that confident, so I was glad he noticed me first.

His antennae pointed, and his head turned, further than I was ready to see, and Paul Newman clearly addressed me, "Cadet Lidstrom!" He waved me over, and, having nowhere else to go, I accepted the invitation. "I see we are on the final shuttle together."

"Yeah, that's—" I nervously checked to see who might be watching me, "—that's nice, Paul." To the P'rukktah, I said, "Hi, I'm Darren Lidstrom."

He curled his lip and grunted something that sounded like a pirate sneezing.

So, I asked Paul. "Who is he?"

"She," corrected the Teek. "Females are the taller of their species."

I don't know if I looked like I was trying to camouflage with the wall just then, but I'm pretty sure all the blood drained from my face. "Sorry," I blurted, but quickly realized I was addressing Paul. So I turned to the—giant, muscular—P'rukktah. "Sorry."

"This is Arrksh," Paul explained. "Her translator was broken. She'll be fitted with a new one after we land, so this gives me a chance to practice some of my phrases of P'rukktah. I do not know much beyond greetings and names."

"Right," I said. The giant, hairy alien looked like she was scowling down at me, but maybe that was just her underbite and tusks. "Hi, Arrksh. Nice to meet you."

Though she was a good two heads taller than me, and probably double the height of Paul Newman, I reached up for a handshake. She looked at my hand and either did not understand or did not want to touch it. Maybe she understood my mixup, and I had offended her.

Luckily, Paul was ready to assure me. "It is all right, Cadet Lidstrom. I mistook your sex when I first met you, based on the relatively high pitch of your voice and your lack of significant masculine traits."

"Um…thank you," I said.

At least Paul Newman was honest.

I demonstrated my vocal range when I was startled by a lizard with very sharp teeth. I think she said Hello, and maybe Paul thought I was trying to reply in Tsanghar, which is kind of screechy when it's not hummy.

I did not hear or smell the green Tsanghar as she approached. At least in this case, I knew that all Tsangharee were female by some standard of biology, but I had no idea they could be so stealthy. The long-necked lizard was within licking distance when she spoke into my ear, and even after my reaction she maintained very close proximity with no regard for personal space.

"Hello!" she said again, with more emphasis than I thought was reasonable. Her long neck flexed and flared out, which could be taken as an intimidating gesture as easily as an excited one—or just a neutral swallow. I was suddenly confronted by how little I knew about the Tsangharee.

She appeared to be observing me as much as I was looking at her, and I realized it made me uncomfortable. Turnabout was fair play.

I glanced to Paul and was about to ask if he knew the lizard in question, but decided to take the initiative. I shuffled backward like a step and a half. "Hi. Did you need something?"

"*Mmmmm!*" she replied—or maybe it wasn't a reply. "I need to follow a curiosity as much as I need it satisfied. Tell me: are you all new cadets?"

Neither Paul Newman nor the newly-met Arrksh responded immediately, and—because I was in front—I spoke for the group. "Yes. Yes, we are. I'm Darren Lidstrom. This is Paul Newman and that's Arrksh."

Arrksh growled something.

"Yes, Arrksh and I are acquainted. *I* am Kesiel."

She stretched her neck forward again, moving her face within a couple of inches of my own, still with an expression that resembled a smile, albeit with too many teeth. I felt I should say something, so I blurted out, "Your English is really good."

"*English?*" she said. "You mean this dialect of Human? Mmm*mmm!* Yes, so is yours."

I didn't know whether to thank her or to amend that English was a full language and not just a dialect of Human. Then I wondered if the Tsangharee actually called their own language Tsanghar, or if that's just what we Humans said to make it easier to reference.

"*Tessenda!*" Kesiel said. Arrksh jutted her chin out in reply and made a chuffing noise, as if in agreement.

"Tessenda?" I asked.

"There is no direct translation that I know of," Kesiel explained, "but the nearest approximation I know is 'the poetry of convergence.'" She looked satisfied at teaching me that phrase, though I wasn't sure if I'd learned anything.

Suddenly, Kesiel did an about-face and proceeded toward the hatch. I hadn't noticed that the personnel were readying the ship for boarding, but all the Tsangharee had. The rat-beebees scurried out of the lizards' path, practically running between the legs of the stoic P'rukktah.

Soon, everyone was lining up and shuffling toward the hatch, before the announcement even went up. A Human called us forward in English, while a Teek ran the message through a translator into Tsanghar and then P'rukktah.

We were told to activate our wrist displays with our student info so it could easily be scanned. I hung toward the back. I didn't really care where I sat in the shuttle, but I felt out of place among the other aliens. When I did see Humans join the ranks—then cut the line—I wanted to hurry ahead and join them, but these were not cadets. The Human and Teek work crews weren't asked to line up like the incoming students, despite some dirty looks from the P'rukktah and some hums from the lizards.

"We do not sort with our own people, either, by species or rank," observed Paul Newman, still standing beside me.

I didn't know what to say, but I nodded in agreement.

We would be the last three to board: myself, Paul, and the large, hairy creature behind me. I didn't know much about P'rukktah social dynamics, but it did seem weird that this one did at least passively cluster with the others.

The setup at the front of the line was similar to that of a traditional airport, with the little podium and the quick scanner. I would have expected a full bot to do this kind of work, but maybe it made sense for a person to be the last line of defense before the Olympus Mons Academy.

The person handling passenger intake was at least two parts machine anyway, with a basic implant dock on her left temple and a much more invasive bionic graft along her left hand and wrist. Her left hand typed furiously, as it was programmed to do. I'd only seen a couple of these in person, and they gave me the willies, partially because I wondered if I'd be required to get one in order to be a competitive pilot.

"Lidstrom, Darren," she read, then chuckled like she she had heard a private joke. "So, *you're* Darren Lidstrom."

I felt my throat go dry in embarrassment, having only negative notions of what I'd done to earn any reputation, let alone that kind of reaction. Maybe something really had gotten screwed up with my registration.

However, when she preempted the next passenger with a casual, "You must be Paul Newman," I felt a little relieved.

Perhaps it was the fact that the two of us had been bumped later or been in the office of minor screw-ups together. Either way, there was safety in numbers.

I proceeded into the short tube connecting to the shuttle and shuffled my way into causeways that separated the fore and aft compartments. The work crews were rapidly reorganizing behind the rear bulkheads and were visibly relocating cargo that would have otherwise been stored below—that is, if my memory of blueprints and schematics translated to the real thing. Rat-beebees, the commonplace rodent spacers, scrambled over each other to get out of the way of even the likes of timid me and Paul who was at my heels. The I.I. personnel, so marked by the sleeveless jackets and various insignias, were far more confident. One of them, a well-built man, practically shouldered past me after emerging quite quickly from the ladder chute. I recognized Lieutenant Chandan too late to effectively snap a salute but comforted myself with the mental reminder that I hadn't been sworn in yet, and he looked too busy to care about rank in any case.

I entered the forward compartment and saw the other cadets were already belting in. I scanned for seats and wondered if all that was left was the jumpseat in the front corner.

A green head and hand reached above the crowd and the lizard Kesiel waved me over.

"Come sit!" Kesiel called, and informed me, "I procured a row."

Not just a row, but the *front* row of the passenger section. There wasn't a practical need to be in front for entering and exiting, but there might have been some sort of status in Kesiel's twice-lidded eyes.

"Darren, you sit here—" she indicated, "—Paul Newman, here, and finally my friend Arrksh."

She had lined us up in order of height, from Paul to Arrksh. I hardly knew why she had saved seats for us, or how, for that matter, considering the hisses she was getting from other lizards in the back rows.

But I thanked her and didn't question it further. Parked between Paul and a lizard, I was certainly getting my interplanetary culture badge.

I heard the telltale sound of the outer door, then inner door, closing, and the redundant seals being inflated into place.

One more familiar face joined us and went straight for the jumpseat. Clancy was fitted with a modular headset—earpiece, eyepiece, microphone. She also appeared in good spirits as she closed a pack in the wall compartment.

"Hey there, Hotshot," she said, giving me a quick nod. Then, walking front and center, she addressed the group. "All right, we got seats, straps. It'll start beeping at you if you're not securely fastened in three seconds." A few clicks sounded in response, but no beeps.

Clancy pointed above her head at a wall-mounted camera eye. "Photo for I.I. posterity." I never saw a flash or heard a shutter sound effect, but it must have taken. Then, hand to her headset, "And one for personal record."

And that was that. She sat in the jumpseat and cleared our compartment via her headset.

* * * * *

Chapter Twelve:
Lidstrom

Phobos to Olympus Mons Academy

The ride was smooth, far more than anything I'd experienced from good ol' Luna and especially from the planet I was learning to call Terra-Human. Paul Newman explained to me why we would have the longest shuttle flight because of how far Phobos had traveled in the last few hours, and Kesiel was humming, pretty much constantly.

After a while, Clancy put a hand to her ear, and her eyes darted down.

"Clancy here," she said over the comm, without a particularly hushed voice, interrupting Paul and definitely getting my attention.

She grinned. "Copy, I will."

She addressed the whole group. "Cadets! Eyes front. You're about to see something spectacular." She used her device and made quick work of changing the display. What had been an opaque wall became a large screen split across three tall panels, then she gave a voice comand, "Forward view, full."

I couldn't help but gasp.

Picture this: red planet, crescent lit under a setting sun, against the excellent backdrop of stars, and right ahead of us was the biggest ship I had ever seen, which only grew larger as we continued toward, and eventually past, it. It was unlike anything I had ever seen on Luna or in any of the infographics; not quite Human or Teek, but something new.

I wanted to stand up, not because I was having trouble seeing, but in a dramatic response. I would have done a slow clap if I thought anyone else would join me—maybe I should have joined the humming lizard before she went supersonic.

"Wow," I breathed, "is that—"

Clancy nodded. "That is one of our new *Command*-class ships; the kind you might eventually crew for. It's the most deliberate collaboration of our species' technology to date, and we've got three of them preparing for people to fill them." She looked up from me to the other raised rows, at the lizard, P'rukktah, Teek, and rat-beebees and added, "All kinds of people."

From beside me, Kesiel said, "Such an elegant craft; it deserves a justly elegant name."

"They haven't named it yet," Clancy said. "Rights are going to first captains, who haven't been selected yet." This was not announced, merely explained. Anyone could hear it, but I felt like she was talking to the front row, or maybe just me. "We're all at the beginning of something new."

I didn't want to be impolite to Clancy, but I couldn't take my eyes off of the ship. The yet-unnamed I.I. *Command*-class vessel, capable of who knew what.

I didn't realize I was speaking out loud when I said, "I'm going to fly that ship some day."

I should have known Paul Newman was listening, and, more importantly, interpreting via his Teek brain. "Congratulations, Cadet Lidstrom. How soon will this accomplishment occur?"

Even without active camouflage in my DNA, I turned red. The lizard hummed, and Clancy actually laughed, proving that the staff sergeant really was a flesh and blood Human and not an android. At the very least, she didn't mock me by calling me a 'naut.

* * * * *

Chapter Thirteen:
Arrksh

Mars-Human, Olympus Mons Base, 0000 Hrs Day 1

It is past the Martian midnight by the time we land in the Olympus Mons Base. While we disembark with our personal luggage and standard issue gear, I use my wrist device to translate the signs and placards as I go, understanding that most of the station interior signs are warnings about low pressure and lower oxygen count, should any of us attempt to brave the surface. The exterior doors and windows are very thick and very locked.

The interior of the base is oddly comforting, even in the low gravity. Weightbelts and heavy shoes are available to those who need them, but I have experienced both higher and lower gravities than, I would assume, any other P'rukktah on board. The motion is something between a lope and a crawl, and one can distinguish the amount of time spent on the surface from how effectively one walks. Kesiel and all of the other Tsangharee drop to quadrapedal posture, a low pressure crawl rather than a walk. The Jyikj'tch'tyeek, Paul Newman, adjusts easily to this gravity as it would be closer to home. The Human Darren Lidstrom bounces and chortles at himself every time his step is off.

There is only a brief orientation speech in Human which I hardly attempt to translate before we are directed to our quarters. For ease, they seem to be grouping us by species, dismissing Darren and Paul first and then sorting the rest of us. I do not voice complaints over this, but I am still aware that my people avoid eye contact with me. I wonder how many souls I will have to bunk with, and whether there is any danger to myself or others.

However, when the P'rukktah are being directed, I am instead intercepted by one whose tone is formal with a hint of worry, using my name and giving some rationale for why I am to follow them. This Human is in a Transnat uniform, not I.I., and he carries a sidearm, which I have noticed is a rarity among the staff on this base.

Kesiel acts as intercessor between me and the Transnat security staff. She breaks ranks to tell me, with near grammatical clarity but poor pronunciation, "*Arrksh, they needing you go get new translator.*"

I thank Kesiel, first in my tongue then hers. I am aware of the snarls from some of my people over my interactions with the helpful lizard. I follow the Human in a different direction. Our destination is apparently some distance away as we get into a small car, thus saving several Human minutes. I admit that I do not have a mind for maps when there is no sun overhead, but I attempt to sort the layout of the academy. Once again, I find it comforting. The lighting, greenery, and aromas are all conducive to productive learning, for multiple species, if I am not mistaken, as I surmise there are a lot of Teek calming pheromones in the atmosphere. It is also so distinctly nonmilitary that I begin to wonder if what I have been taught about Humans is untrue, though it is possible they are merely flexing their diplomatic or hospitality muscles.

By the time we disembark the open-topped vehicle, I consider myself acclimated enough to the space, even if I need to be very mindful of the gravity. With or without a translator, it is not difficult to follow directions or to recognize that the guards in this section are armed more cautiously than most other staff on the base who do not even carry visible sidearms. These wield suppression weapons; I make out the designs of a foam gun, meant to immobilize. One of the guards has high blood pressure and increased respiration at the sight of me but maintains an unwavering expression; my auditory and olfactory senses are clearly far beyond that of Humans.

I am waved through a doorway into, not a technological hub or medical station for fitting implants, but a conference room with three high-postured Humans, two Teek, including a drone, and one P'rukktah, whom I easily recognize.

Though I feel both relief and annoyance at the Elder's presence, I demonstrate respect, displaying far less emotion than the guard at the door. I crouch into a near-kneel, a gesture which I believe Humans inaccurately call a "lunge."

"Esteemed Elder," I acknowledge in our common language, paying proper respect to a former regent, now an advisor. I have not seen her in many years, and I can see that her eyes are growing dimmer and sunken—yes, a sign of wisdom, but also, I imagine, weariness.

"Rise, daughter of Irrukkt," she says, almost as soon as I have bowed my head.

When I push up to my full height, it is with too much force for this place, and therefore more speed than I wish to show. I notice some of the others flinch; the Teek drone, almost as large as me, does not move in reaction, but emits a low-pitched buzz in sympathy with the connected sentient mind.

The sentient Teek, winged, speaks with a deeper voice than most I have met, saying phrases in Human that I do not fully understand and with very little emotional inflection or affectation. I do, however, notice the device in her articulating fingers.

My Elder steps in, taking the new translator and conveying it to me. It is similar to the previous, with a band to go around the neck and an attached microphone to pick up the ambient sound. The earpiece looks much better, more effectively suited for a P'rukktah ear canal and less likely to interfere with the pitches above or below the Human range of hearing.

While I am fitting and situating the device, my Elder says, "Welcome, Arrksh. I am pleased you are safe."

"Gratitude," I reply.

She takes hold of my chin, pivots my head to either side, presumably in inspection, and whispers, "Courage, daughter. Do not be moved."

As soon as she has said so, she steps away from me, leaving me to accept her words without reaction. With an open hand, she seems to indicate that I am available to speak with the others. She begins to say so in the Human language. I calibrate my personal device, enabling it to sync with the new translator in time to hear my Elder finish her sentiment.

"—and respond in kind. Arrksh will also soon be learning the Human English as well, so her reliance on a personal translator will not be permanent."

This translator is quite adept, much faster and clearer than the previous. At least, that is the case for receiving, I am not certain if it will as easily turn my voice into the Human English yet.

One of the Human women, older, possessing more wrinkles and gray hair, approaches. She looks familiar, even though previous images made her seem taller and younger, though still gray-haired. "Arrksh, it is an honor to welcome you to the Olympus Mons Base and I.I. Academy. I am Admiral Victoria Hass, former head of the Transnat Outreach Fleet and assistant director of the Initiative." She puts out one gloved hand for me to shake.

I am familiar with this maneuver; I understand the mechanics of a Human handshake. Some of the less spaceworthy bipeds have similar gestures. My people consider trust and friendship to be much physically closer and a mutually beneficial relationship with strangers to be something best handled across a room or separated by screens. This is a strange hybrid, but I have already adjusted for it.

However, when I shake the hand of this esteemed hero, I do not expect the fingers themselves to be mechanical. Not an overlay, not exoplating for protection, but a replacement for severed bone and tissue. Despite what I have heard about Admiral Hass, I did not know she lost the majority of her right hand.

She keeps her eyes on me when she releases my hand and says some words that do not effectively translate. I soon realize that she is introducing the other parties in the room, using proper nouns. I activate a setting on my translator to try to pick up these terms phonetically. One of the Humans is another director of the I.I.; the Teek is a visitor, like the P'rukktah.

"And you are already familiar with the envoy, Elder Saerpstra." She indicates my Elder but does not say anything more about the relationship. I cannot tell if it is because she does not know or because she does not wish to reveal me before the others.

"Honored," I say and hear my voice distorted and bastardized into a robotic reproduction.

"Arrksh, we are pleased you arrived safely." The admiral pauses, not in hesitation, but a deliberate silence before proceeding. "You may be wondering why we called you here."

This time, I elect for silence.

"Something about your background and position has been brought to our attention, which was not made clear when you were first recommended to the Initiative," she continues. "As your file was reviewed and referred by Irrukkt ambassadors, this was not your fault. However, the I.I. is not accepting persons of royalty in our first cohort of new cadets."

I wish to look to Elder Saerpstra, but I maintain my stare. I am also aware that I have not personally been dismissed, even though I am also not being addressed as cadet.

"Do you understand?" she asks.

I respond in my tongue and hear the robotic Human voice say *"Comprehend"* in its place. I inhale through my nostrils and let the vibrations of electric current in the walls and overhead lights steady me, before I say, "I am not royalty."

One of the other Humans begins to object. He is a slender man with a hooked nose, apparently losing his hair rather than shaving it off. He stops short when I continued speaking.

Without worrying about the accuracy of the translation, I explain, "My house was dismantled at the beginning of the last Tsangharee conflict. That way, the Elders could serve the cause of peace without dishonoring a house, and the descendents could return after the war without being bound as enemies of the Segranee, or any Tsangharee. I am not royalty, I have no military service in my background, and I have no blood debts to settle. I believe that was requisite for cadets."

Elder Saerpstra juts her chin forward in agreement, her lower tusks catching the light. In Human, she says, "Arrksh proclaims she is not a princess, nor should she be treated as one."

There are sudden responses from two voices other than the admiral's and my translator has trouble adjusting to both so quickly, but I can perceive the agitation and worry. I turn toward the Teek, who has not said much but is now addressing me.

The winged Teek asks, possibly repeating, "Your position here is not based on any station from your home planet Irrukkt or any other territory controlled by the P'rukktah?"

"Correct," I say.

With a twitch of antennae, the Teek continues, "You will be given no special treatment or considerations. You are going to be judged on your own merit, without aid from Elders."

"Correct."

The Teek and the complaining Human defer to the admiral. She stares at me, unblinking; I reciprocate. Eventually, she says, "Very well. You are admitted to the Initiative as a Green Cadet, as Arrksh, without any other titles or station."

Her demeanor changes, she is no longer playing diplomacy with a princess and a visiting Elder from a spacefaring species. Admiral Hass is now the woman in command of this base, perhaps all of the new project known as the I.I., despite sharing the responsibility with two other on-base directors. She gives me a curt nod that is neither complimentary nor particularly friendly. "Cadet. The next time I speak directly to you, it will be because your actions warrant a response. Either an accomplishment worthy of recognition or a misstep worthy of reprimand. Make sure it's the former. Dismissed."

The admiral does not initiate a salute nor ask for one in return. I turn and leave, feeling more thoroughly stripped of title than I have been in the past. It is exhilarating.

A part of me longs for a chance to say one more brief farewell to the Elder Saerpstra. I do not imagine she is going to be present at the academy in the long term, and I cannot guess when I will see her again. Still, as I exit through the doors and between the guards, I can hear her sendoff. Like me, she knows how to speak in pitches below the Human hearing range; unlike me, she is aware of precisely what might be recorded and reviewed and therefore what is safe to say.

Again, she tells me, "Courage."

* * *

By the time I arrive at my designated quarters, I expect everyone to be unpacked and asleep. I manage a brief glimpse of the room with the lights off, but I can also hear from the others' breathing that they are awake and aware of my entry. It is a small shared space with ceilings that are barely tall enough and a floor that is loamy enough to be comfortable under bare feet. Three other female P'rukktah, a reasonable group for rooming, are distributed among the bunks.

The flat beds are acceptable if not ideal. The Belbehan blade sits well on the shelf in my bunk space, just beside my new translator. I am glad to earn my rest and prepare for the coming day.

The soft snarls from the others are not given words, and so can be ignored. They may all know who I am—who I was—and the history of my house, and it does not matter to me if they wish to disdain me or bow before me. As far as I am concerned, I have hurdled over the unpredictable, uncontrollable parts of the journey. The hard work may begin tomorrow, but at least that is in my control.

I close my eyes and slow my breathing. I resume my language lessons, audio input of Human speech through an earpiece, to prepare me for their complex intonation, in an effort to not look like a *lahksa* through mistranslations.

When my subconscious begins to provide the images of dreams, I cannot help but wonder if the Humans are also dreaming, and whether someone like this Darren Lidstrom has any idea of the kinds of people he will be working with. I wonder if he is capable of being as deadly or dangerous as his race's reputation suggests.

* * * * *

Chapter Fourteen:
Lidstrom

0100 Day 1

I was glad it wasn't a strictly military approach at the academy and that there was no official, unavoidable call for "lights out." That meant that I hadn't totally missed the most crucial part of the early days: schmoozing.

By the time I arrived at the cadet quarters and scanned my way into the E-block, I expected most people to be in their own bunks and asleep. Instead, I found Yiorgos and a handful of others, some of whom I recognized, still awake. There was the beanpole-tall Cadet Benjamin, also from the Midwest; Gerhardt, who'd gotten sick in zero grav when we'd landed; and the curly-haired cadet with no shortage of wry remarks, Rivers.

"Glad to see you survived the encounter," Rivers told me by way of a salutation.

Shin joined us and expressed something similar with a rough touch to my upper arm. Cadet Shin did not sit down, but stood at the edge of the group, arms folded across her chest.

Yiorgos just wanted to talk about how state-of-the-science this facility was, how it utilized the best of any amenities Mars could offer. Greater in size, scope, and power than any other surface base, with simulation and training rooms that any of us could kill for.

"And," he said with a raised finger, "it's one of only two installations with both an onsite Uua *and* an Avowol."

"No kidding," Gerhardt said, "can we see it?"

"Yeah, they're putting it in a public plot right in the middle of the North Nexus," Yiorgos said. "You'll walk by it like ten times a day."

"No, I mean the Avowol. I don't even know what they look like."

"Right," he said and started to explain that the the Avowol tank was off limits for the time being. My head started swimming and my ears were ringing. I leaned forward onto one fist and started massaging my brows with my knuckles.

"Hey, you okay?" Shin touched my shoulder and looked a little concerned.

Everyone else paused to stare at me.

"I think I'm just tired," I said. "A lot of adjustment." I go to my feet. Evidently, I would be missing the schmooze tonight. "I'm gonna turn in."

"Maybe you got whammied by a lizard song," joked Rivers. "They *Hree-Dahn* at you?"

"Yeah, maybe," I replied with a grin. "We'll find out tomorrow if I slaughter everyone else in the room. Goodnight."

Gerhardt scolded me, and Yiorgos laughed as I walked away; both reactions reasonable from roommates.

I heard Cadet Benjamin asking what a *Hree-Dahn* was.

"Some kind of lizard curse," Rivers replied. "They sometimes yell it at other lizard breeds if they don't like the shape of their fins or something."

"Racist aliens," Shin said. "Charming."

That was the last I caught before I was out of earshot.

I entered my quarters: four bunks and very little private space, and my home for the foreseeable future. Maybe I was just overwhelmed by the transition. A few months on Luna and any number of orbital stations was nothing compared to the distance to Mars or the vastness of space. But I would be damned—by any Human or alien deity—if I would let a little thing like homesickness slow me down here. No, it was time for a good night's rest, and then off to the races like I was born to run on Mars.

* * * * *

Chapter Fifteen:
Kesiel

The Olympus Mons Academy was one of about a dozen megabases on the Mars surface, but I am told it was the most impressive and the most deserving of its place on the planet's highest mountain.

Like much of the Initiative, it was designed by a Human and Teek team, but with occasional input from consultants and contractors of several more species, spanning dozens of worlds and countless affiliations and ideologies. There is a Human term for this kind of mix, called a "melting pot," which posits that when these elements come together, they become so intermixed that any individual identity is indistinguishable.

Another school of thought, namely mine, would disagree. It is instead a rich pallet used to create a vast mural and, in each brushstroke, the signature of the people who created it or the audience it was created for. Every room design, every choice in lighting, each respirating plant has been planned. Perhaps in a few years or after a few crops of candidate cadets, these unique features would diminish, grow muted and muddled, but as the first set of cadets to trot out and test the space, we had the opportunity to see everything as the designers intended.

Even the schedule was an interesting attempt to juggle the various needs of the species. Fortunately, most of us had similar day and night cycles, even if we counted the intervals differently. I had familiarized myself with Human hours and minutes enough that these did not disrupt my ability to schedule. I also appreciated that the Humans were so entrenched in their own measures of time that, rather than creating a new time-keeping system for this new Martian planet, they simply tacked on a portion of one of their hours to the usual twenty-four, creating an M-Day with a gap period in the middle of the night.

Naturally, I was too fascinated to explore these tenets of a multispecies habitat to want to stay asleep. I withdrew myself from the coil of fellow lizards, trying not to wake any of them. There was more than enough space to do so, considering that three of our roommates had been held for observation and further treatment. Then, after a quick blast of the heat lamp and two caffeine patches on my underarms, I dressed in the Green Cadet uniform and excused myself to explore the facilities. I adored that the Green Cadet version of the universal suit was literally a dark shade of green, even though I had been told that I perceive this shade quite differently than do the other species. I also appreciated the underlay of thermoils around my ribcage and the slight pressure at each of my socket joints, reminding me that I would be expected to stay upright and bipedal rather than the ambi-stance that we are more likely to take in unfamiliar gravity. These notes showed the hybrid design had multiple authors.

The Tsangharee quarters were fully designed for cluster sleeping, a practice which was apparently distasteful for Humans, uncomfortable for P'rukktah, and physically dangerous for Teek, for reasons I was not yet studied enough to comprehend. I had pictured similar sleeping arrangements for the Belbehan, but I will admit that the mental image made me salivate and reminded me why the rat folk were stationed far away from us. Logically, the Teek were closest to us in the north wing, with the furred species in the south and the Humans between.

When I exited, I found several said Teek in the common space, which I had not adequately surveyed the night before. In addition to the main walkway and some social area, the commons broke off into pods that appeared to be workspaces. Each was equipped with an array of holographic interfaces for all sorts of simulations. There were also the easier and much more traditional tables with modular stools. I also found a number of boxes on small stilts, big enough to fit a seated P'rukktah. Closer inspection revealed that these were flight simulators for pilots and that the stilts were hydraulic pumps. This became even more apparent when I saw the box open, and a Teek step out of it.

Acknowledging that the Teek needed far less sleep and that I came in late, I was still impressed by how rapidly studious they were. Though many were occupied, they paused to interact politely with me. Still, neither winged nor four-armed were interested in morning banter, so I made no headway in asking about their living and sleeping arrangements.

Some Humans were emerging, as was the occasional Belbehan, and these were occasionally more interesting and forthcoming. A few seemed to assume I was a formal inspector or officer, visiting to check on them; either way, they indulged my curiosity, relayed to me the rudimentary layout of each of their quarters. The P'rukktah would sleep comparably quite longer.

The signs for "Breakfast" could be used as much more complicated interactive displays. They showed recommended meals and mealtimes for different species, including general energy conversion equations. As I knew what I was and when I might need to eat, I checked out the P'rukktah recommended consumption suggestions, including steps to convert to the Human meal schedule, which would make scheduling shifts easier.

I was about to look up recommended living arrangements for the Avowol—who, as far as I knew, did not sleep—when an alert populated the screen. It was not a personal message, rather a reminder for whoever was using this terminal about the updated orientation sessions for the next two days as well as the opening ceremony for new cadets.

Even the titles of these were simply delicious! Between items like "I.I. Rank Structure" and "Condensed History of Alliances," there were delightful nuggets like "Cross-Cultural Offenses" and "Interspecies Anatomy," which I could only imagine would be a series of warnings about the attempts for the mammalian types to engage in sexual intercourse. I made quick mental tally of the sessions I should like to attend, accepting that some did overlap, and others did not allow for a "normal" meal schedule.

One such orientation had recently begun, early enough that it did not provide any conflict or overlap. The original title was printed in unreadable hatches, but it included a translation: "Human Customs for Teek."

Speeding along the corridors to the course's location, I did make a point of waving at everyone I passed. I do not believe, given their expressions, that I made any fast friends, but I gained greater and greater understanding of behaviors and habits with each confused look or scowl.

One sight nearly caused me to pause: an Uua Prime native was being installed in one of the central hubs, a point of convergence with connecting corridors for the cadet rooms, as well as those to classrooms, workshop spaces, the hangars, and many others that I had not yet explored. This section of the base, officially called the North Nexus, was the largest domed area, and was decorated in ranges of flora, mostly vines and flowers indigeneous to many planets, forming a visual poetry of nature beneath the unnatural but still artistic ring of national or planetary flags. I noticed the Yavamee flags, among others, creating a kind of suspended crown for the great tree.

The tree, a long-lived sentient from Uua, was to be planted in a circle of soil, under a dome of partial transparencies, so as to receive sunlight during the day. There was a satisfying symbolic parallel in this tree's position, at the center, or at least a relative center, of the cadet part of the base, with the roots sprawling out like corridors in all directions. A couple of Humans were working to massage the giant out of its dormant state. Most of the leaves were still curled inward, its bulbous branches as retracted as they would go. I had never been so close to one, and I do admit I had always wondered about the possibility of climbing such a large being. I also knew that it was, most likely, not going anywhere anytime soon, and I had a class to take.

I slowed my step and my heart rate in order to present as casual an entrance. I apologized for being late and took a seat near a Teek I recognized as one Paul Newman.

The Human instructor opened her mouth, then shut it again. I regarded her with an unwavering smile, and she finally spoke, "I think you might be in the wrong place. This course is for Teek to understand Human customs."

"Yes!" I agreed. The only other cadets were, in fact, Teek. A majority were four-handers, with about half as many wingers, and the odd drone in the corners.

Paul Newman did not appear vexed by my presence, nor did the winged one beside him—I assumed his hive-kin companion.

The instructor eventually proceeded, and I absorbed knowledge.

* * *

Never was I kicked out, but seldom was I welcomed during my morning ventures. I acknowledge that I purposefully selected orientation courses seemingly intended for other species, but I maintain that that was the best way to learn all of the dynamics of the academy. It also afforded me that opportunity to see some of the faces I'd met before and to track their interests.

The liveliest discussions occurred where both Humans and Tsangharee were present in abundance, meaning that things like rank structure, titles, and gender expression appeared to be much more engaging than they really were. The "Interspecies Anatomy" lecture turned out to be quite dull by comparison, possibly because it was taught by a Teek. Though Arrksh was present and taking notes, I did not stay for more than a couple of slides. I did anticipate needing to learn about the seven most common molt expressions of an adult Teek, and I already knew about my species' mode of asexual reproduction.

Between courses, I followed the noise to one of the more exciting amenities.

One of the gymnasiums had been set up with variable gravity pads, large enough to comfortably host several people at any given time. Each floor's gravity was set to that of a visiting species' home environment and the tension of the mat was meant to demonstrate roughly how hard the ground might be.

Of course, they could only approximate one Tsangharee moon at a time, but that space was not nearly as interesting as the P'rukktah environment. The sign said that the pad had been programmed to simulate Irrukkt, a higher gravity planet with surprisingly spongy and loamy topsoil. I had never set foot on Irrukkt—point of fact, I had never left the Tsangharee home system before this venture—but I had always had a kind of fascination with the planet which had developed more forms of large, complex fauna than any others I knew of. Perhaps one day, with this Initiative, I would visit an even more impressive array of life than the P'rukktah homeworld.

The only other party exploring this pad was a Human, though I doubted she was using the simulated gravity to imagine the planet of inspiration. Her manner was much more direct and purposeful. She had very short but very straight black hair, which formed an almost spined look over the top of her head, and she wore tactical gloves, even though there were no combatants or targets on the pad. This specimen appeared to be performing a kind of solo dance, a performance by oneself for oneself without any outside interference.

She would push with her feet against the spongy surface, trying to push off enough to effectively jump, learning the resistance and elasticity more with each attempt. Then, once she was assured, she effected a rolling leap, coiling her legs up to minimize distance from her center of mass. When she landed a little off balance and used her arms to steady herself, I recognized her as a Green Cadet from the Phobos Station's camera feed, wearing the same tactical gloves. I would later be told that she was called Shin, like the lower part of the Human leg.

"Mm*mmm!*" I voiced, impressed by the aerial maneuver. It called attention in a manner Shin did not appreciate, but she stepped back and gestured to the space in front of her, tacitly welcoming me to join her.

"Care to give it a try?" Shin panted. "It's about one-point-two gravs. That's double what you're used to, right?"

I categorized her tone as challenging, and I agreed. I did not see any reason to verbally point out that my moon was a little heavier than the typical for a Tsanghar, but I still wished to try the floor. Relative gravity is a strange concept, peculiar but survivable, and purely calculable with the right frame of reference. I was learning the Human frame of reference, like their distance in meters, their liquid volume and pressure measures for fuel, their energy counts for propulsion. However, despite my ample preparation, I did not brace for the change from the light M-grav all the way up to simulated Irrukkt-grav.

The vector forces began to change about a meter from the edge. That I got pulled down and immediately collapsed was actually not too much of a surprise to me. Shin clearly took this as validation and chuckled.

"Mm, yes," I grunted, more tersely than I would have liked, with my belly and neck pressed to the floor. The once comfortable tension suit and thermocoils were now much like a prison. I found my hands, my feet, my tail. None of them were under me or in a position for mechanical advantage yet, so I began to drag each limb in.

"Hey, do you need help?" another voice called out, somewhere beyond the edge of the pad. Shin watched me struggle.

"Not yet," I said. I felt my skin tightening, compressing my muscles around my bones, which were far less brittle than those of Humans. My spine tingled as each vertebra was pushed closer together. Eventually, Shin took two steps toward me, closing the distance. Though I sensed reluctance in her tone, I properly understood the words: "Here, give me your hand."

"No, thank you," I said. Then, with a grunt and more than a little exertion, I pressed myself to a four-legged stance. I let my tail drop as more of an anchor than a counterbalance. I kept a strong, squatting foundation with my legs, and stood upright.

"There!" I smiled at Shin, eager to show teeth, but aware that I was standing much shorter than I would in a lower-grav environment. Once I proved I could stand, however, I had little else I needed to demonstrate. So, my very flexible pride intact, I trudged off the mat, leaving behind the loamy soil and punishing gravity of Irrukkt.

I had hardly returned to the much more sensible M-grav (not adjusted, just returned), when I was interrupted by a hiss, a telltale show of presence, which I chose to ignore.

"Moonkin!" insisted the lizard in our tongue, before hustling in front of me. She was taller than I and would remain so once I righted my posture. Her patchy gray scale patterns did not appear to me like that of my home moon, but I did not correct her.

"Yes, cousin?" I said, widening my eyes to receive her clearly important wisdom.

Patchy-face flicked her tongue out, lashing along her teeth. "Be mindful, Green fin! You already stirred yesterday with the P'rukktah and our cousin, Liesarn."

That she knew Liesarn by name meant one of two things: either she was close enough to refer to me as moonkin or at least a neighbor, or my people had put a lot of attention on Liesarn's minor operation.

"Mm*mmm*! But she is well."

"She still cannot speak!" Patchy-face clearly found this a great and terrible affront, a view I hardly shared. After all the times she had put thumb to my back, I would gleefully deny even my actual moonkin the chance to put her voice to my ear.

Even Patchy-face realized this was not a debatable point, so she returned to her apparently urgent message. Without moving her head, she darted her gaze to an I.I. uniform by the door, then toward Shin. "They'll be watching everything we do. Using the information to form training squads. They might pay attention to who you consort with."

"Mm*mmm!*" I agreed. "I'm counting on it."

She stared silently, her lips working to form a response. Poor Patchy-face could not understand my motives and means, but I could scarcely see any value to her brand of species solidarity in a place like this.

I decided to impart some wisdom of my own. Gently, I told her, "Sometimes *tessenda* needs some assistance."

With that, I smoothly disengaged from the member of my species.

* * * * *

Chapter Sixteen:
Lidstrom

The prospective pilot crop came in all shapes and sizes. There may have been more Humans than any other single group, but the Tsangharee and rat-beebees combined made up more than half, which probably accounted for most of the lizard and rat cadets in the whole facility. In addition, there were a couple of each kind of worker Teek, as well as one of each male and female P'rukktah. The male P'rukktahs reminded me of the classic werewolf look, though slightly larger than a Human and arching slightly forward as if ready to strike but with a bigger head and a near mane drifting into the raised shoulders. The female pilot was even more massive than Arrksh, standing with the presence of a mythological god—or rather goddess—and I wondered if she'd fit in any of the pilot chairs or simulators.

Luckily, the I.I. was super prepared. They had set up modular seats for all five species, as well as others who I had to guess had missed the cut—or not accepted the invitation to the Initiative. Of course, we wouldn't get to test the range of the simulators yet; most of the fun and challenging things were locked while we were tested on the basics.

So, today was shuttles and ground vehicles. The bald woman I'd met at the same time as Commander Claude, Staff Sergeant Genevieve Ramirez, ran us through the basics in lecture and demo form before we got to actually use the machines. I didn't resent or object. To tell you the truth, I was relieved this part of the training was already familiar to me, where the rodents were either scrambling to relearn or unlearn basic piloting protocol. It probably didn't help that the Tsangharee would periodically hiss or hum at them; Ramirez didn't stop them from doing it either.

Like a good cadet, I waited in line then focused during the trial runs. I won't say I was a natural or that I seriously beat out the competition—we couldn't see any scores to compare them. Still, I felt confident that I was making a good first impression with Ramirez and whoever else was monitoring the systems, and I really enjoyed driving the Red Terrain Vehicles on simulated Martian grav and terrain.

I only broke formality once, blurting out a question that I couldn't have been the only one thinking. "Hey, can you flip these things?"

Ramirez and all the other staff paused, forcing me to check myself. Not only had I skipped addressing her as staff sergeant, I might have revealed something they could interpret as reckless.

After a moment of suspense, Ramirez said, "No, Cadet. These were purposely designed to be unflippable on the red planet. Unless you deliberately drive it off a cliff, it wants to keep all six wheels on the rusty ground."

Nodding frantically, I said, "Thank you, Staff Sergeant."

I hoped I hadn't drawn any lasting bad attention.

* * *

I was glad to have the refresher on the rank structure in the I.I. during the "Nuts and Bolts" lesson that afternoon, and I did a good job of not laughing at anyone's attempt to salute like a Human. Throughout the mini presentations, many of the instructors continued to insist that the I.I. was *not* a military program, but that rank and respect were important for the safety of a crew.

I understood the idea, and I think I get why they were so intent on letting species outside of the Human-Teek Alliance know we were not building an army. Still, it rang a little hollow, seeing as the assistant director of the whole program had been an admiral of the Transnat Fleet, and everyone had ranks based on old Terran navy or marine designations.

Commander Claude Poissonier was definitely one of the best at bridging the non-military gap gracefully. It probably helped that he dyed his hair pink, which made the sensible crew cut still look more like a personal choice than a regulation one. I didn't know whether or not he had served in the W-Wars, that semi-secretive conflict that had forged the Human-Teek Alliance, but the fact that he was a commander afforded him the clout of a seasoned officer.

Still, Claude rarely used the podium when he was on stage and frequently interacted with people directly as he demonstrated and adjusted their salutes. At the end of his lesson but before calling up the next speaker, he added a note that I don't think was on his slides.

"We are establishing universal gestures and expectations, because, in the Initiative, you might end up interacting with anyone for any reason. We don't have universal translators, but we still have to be able to work together."

This segued nicely into the next speaker's breakdown of squad assignments and how we would be paired, grouped, and redistributed into different teams throughout our time at the academy. I couldn't help but look around the lecture hall and notice that, once again, we were all grouped by species. I did manage to pick out Kesiel, who seemed to be showing up everywhere, standing out among non-Tsangharee. Arrksh was near the door at the edge of the room. If I recognized him properly, Paul Newman was front and center with a small cluster of other Teek. I was among Humans, Yioros and other E-group folks, and I wondered if I should be taking a page from Kesiel's book.

The next speaker was missing. Lieutenant Nicholas Chandan, engineer of adaptive forcefields, was on the program to speak about emergency procedures. There was a moment of confusion before his replacement entered, creating a wake as she made her way directly to the stage and assumed the microphone with a gloved right hand.

"Lieutenant Chandan is unavailable," she said decisively. "I will be covering the topic in his place." She did not feel a need to introduce herself. Her face was known, even if the gray hair had changed. If there was any doubt, one could simply check the rank stripes on her jacket, which we'd recently reviewed.

Admiral Hass, officially assistant director of the I.I., took a much more formal approach. She marched when at attention and strode when at ease, reflecting none of the awkwardness that many others did in the low gravity, to the point where I wondered if she was wearing a grav-inducer under her flightsuit and coat. I don't know if I had actually imagined her to be friendlier, after all, she was hailed as a war hero for saving the Teek, but I think I had been hoping for an aura that invited more celebrity worship rather than the stoicism of order. The lizard Kesiel would probably say it better.

She used slides to address important commands, including alerts for emergencies. She stressed the importance of following commands quickly and without question when it came to the safety of the ship and crew. Then, near the end of her presentation, she looked down at her hands, possibly checking a note, and regarded us with narrowed eyes and what I was certain was a small smile. "Since many of you are already asking the officers, I'll confirm the rumor: three *Command*-class vessels are in orbit and you will be touring them in the near future."

I felt my chest lift in excitement, thrilled at being one of the first to know about—and see—these new marvels of cooperative invention. Of course, I had no idea about what she would say next.

Hass did not take any questions or entertain reactions, of which few were voiced. After a brief pause, she continued, "And, yes, one of the ships is projected for early departure. We are looking for a handful of cadets to do much of their training aboard the vessel. We do not have set dates or numbers at this time."

My jaw dropped. I wasn't the only one.

Hass exited the stage, inviting Jane Austen to take her place to talk about the types of mechanical failures and hazards that might be encountered both on Olympus Mons as well as in the black of space.

* * *

Usually, I hate things like opening ceremonies. I skipped my own graduation because I didn't want to stand in line to get handed a data chip with a diploma. This was different.

The central dome of Olympus Mons Academy was impressive in its construction, with an unsupported ceiling that looked far larger than anything that could stand up to Terran G. Flags and symbols of not only our nations, but factions and families, and home planets of several species lined the walls. Shuttles and low atmo hoppers streaked overhead, visible through the excellent transparencies.

The music, played by a lizard using both digital mixers and some kind of alien chimes, was eerie and otherworldly.

Officers and representatives wore capes and sashes over their I.I. jackets, along with dozens of badges and accolades. I recognized most of the species on stage, even though I had no idea how to categorize their rank or station.

Sitting among my fellow Human cadets from E-cluster in the audience, I watched with rapt attention and listened intently to every speaker.

The directors gave their formal welcomes, the ambassadors gave their blessings or indications of good faith, the speakers recognized the people who made the effort possible. Except, when they introduced people, they gave not only title and name, but species, planet of origin, faction, if any, and sometimes their city.

Next, the presenters recognized the I.I. instructors, their ranks and positions fully pronounced. A couple of commanders, a mix of lieutenants, and a huge presence of staff sergeants. Nine out of ten of them were Human and the rest were Teek. I noticed only one empty chair, and confirmed that the empty name that went with it was Nicholas Chandan, but everyone else was there and ready to stand proudly when called on.

Finally, before distributing uniforms, they named all the Teek queens who had sent representatives as cadets, then all the Tsangha-ree factions, the P'rukktah houses, rat-beebee—sorry, Belbehan—

homeships, and finally Terran nations. I understood little of what was said, but I reveled in all of it.

Beside me, Yiorgos was making notes of the names he recognized and periodically cursing his translator for being unable to handle proper nouns. Around us, various Humans and other species whooped and cheered for groups or individuals. I saw Shin raise a fist in support of the admiral.

I said nothing. When I received my uniform, I am not ashamed to say that I teared up, and even that I did silently.

* * *

Day 2

"It's all about the *pre*selection now," Yiorgos said at breakfast. "Doing anything you can to stand out and get placed on that first assignment. I hear they're going to be looking for three or four squads to lock in early before filling in the other gaps."

"Three or four Human squads," Shin amended, taking her seat at the end of the row. She managed to be both smooth in her movements but rigid wherever she landed.

"That sounds like a lot of smog," I said. "Where'd you pick that up?"

"It's around," Shin replied flatly, and despite my earlier denial, I knew she was probably right. The Interstellar Initiative was primarily a Human venture, even if it enlisted the cooperation of other species. Shin hammered the point a little deeper by adding, "You need to show that you're the best. And the best way to do that is without any translation barriers or culture barriers on your squad."

I looked down at my plate. The contents were uninteresting, so there wasn't much cause to stare at it. The truth was, I felt a little ashamed. Even though I had nothing against Paul Newman or any of the others, I didn't want to put a potential friendship over getting on that first ship.

"Sure," I said eventually.

"All right. You're going pilot," she said to me, "and you've got comm tech—" to Yiorgos, "—I'm on the military track, security specific, and I've got a couple of recs for engineering and research." That was all five roles. Shin certainly did have it planned. "I figure we all list each other as preferences, get placed in an elite squad, blow the competition out of the water."

"Check," Yiorgos agreed.

"Sure," I said again.

"Okay." Shin stood and walked away with her usual assured posture, along with a slight Martian bounce.

"You know she's making the same speech to like three other groups," Yiorgos said.

"Really?" I wondered, then shook the wonder. Shin did have it all planned. "So, you're not gonna list her on the form?"

"No, I'm gonna list her. Have you seen the way she moves on the mats?" He took the moment to finish chewing and swallow the bite. "But I don't know how our preferences even factor in. I mean, they won't even confirm that the teams are five, even though it makes sense to hit one of each field. So, if we don't know, we might as well say, you know, that we want to work with the best."

"Right." I nodded. It was all a mess of politics; bureaucracy was the only universal constant among sentient peoples. But you would think if we were really smart we would figure out how to do away with it altogether.

I knew that I had to fill out my squad preferences sooner than later and lock in my track, but I left the mess that morning with a strong willingness to procrastinate. The only sessions that day were still the optional orientation types and some of the "head start" or sample ones. I hadn't seen anything for pilots, although there were a couple for reading telemetry and 3D astrogation models that a responsible aspiring pilot would probably want to pick up.

Instead, I played at procrastination. I headed back toward the cadet quarters, pausing only a moment to regard the moving tree that appeared to be teaching low-grav yoga.

I picked out one of the boxes, the basic-on-the-outside cases for the flight simulators, which I hadn't had a chance to log back into since landing, and now I had a cadet login I could use.

Unfortunately, I found the first simulator was not only occupied, but there was a queue, cadet name lists with different people plugged into various times. Of course, I was in the Human section, and I figured maybe there would be more availability among the other species. The furry section of the quarters had queues of rats, from what I could tell of the names. The cold-blooded group topped us all. The lizards and bugs had not just listed electronic queues, but mobs of hopefuls were lined up; some were watching live shares of the simulator on display monitors. I recognized the screen display and the asteroid run.

"Cadet Lidstrom!" said a familiar voice.

"Hey, Paul," I said, with a genuine smile. "Man, what's got everyone so worked up here?"

"The pilot simulators have been made available," Paul explained.

"No, I know that. But—" I gestured around. "Why are there so many people lining up for a simulator?"

Paul's eye chromae flashed a warm orange, which I think was supposed to be excitement—either that or warning. "Cadet Lidstrom, you do not understand. Many of us have not experienced a VR interface like this. It is very satisfactory!"

I didn't tell him that he should have picked a stronger word than satisfactory. Instead, I observed a small huddle of lizards, violet and grayish-yellow, huddled around one of the screens and making high-pitched laughing noises. "Well, they seem happy."

Paul Newman's chromae adjusted to a neutral. "They are using profanity and threatening the machine, accusing it of not responding properly to commands. I do not think they are happy, Cadet Lidstrom."

I was duly impressed. "Paul, you speak Tsanghar?"

"I understand a couple of prominent dialects of Tsanghar with sufficient clarity. I was imprinted with strong language faculties."

"Right." I still found myself watching the lizards, trying to retrain my brain that their "smiles" were not always an indication of happiness.

"Now, they are saying the machine controls are predisposed for Humans over other species," Paul continued to translate. "I do not know if that is true."

"It may be," added another, a Teek whom I'd seen with Paul before, a winged one with a slightly higher and rounder voice. "After all, Humans are known for military might, long-form fiction, and virtual reality."

I guess it was nice to have that spelled out. I put out a hand to the winger and said, "Hi, I'm Darren Lidstrom."

I felt the exoskeletal fingers give a gentle squeeze around my palm and my wrist. She, like Paul, smelled like all the comforts of a warm, freshly laundered bed. "Paul Newman has mentioned you. He and I are *jiki'yt*, or hive-kin. I am Ella Fitzgerald."

Ella was neither inviting nor excluding. If it weren't for her chromae, I wouldn't have been able to read her at all. But she, I assumed, must have read something about me, for she supplied an answer to something I was thinking. "I am not in the sign-up queue. The simulators do not have proper space for wings. This is an opportunity for observation and data collection."

I realized I would have no way of knowing just how many of the people there, especially Teek, were cataloguing others' actions for whatever range of reasons.

"I am, Cadet Lidstrom, and my spot will come soon." That meant one less spectator. I was about to ask him how long ago he'd signed up, when he surprised me. "Would you like my spot, Cadet Lidstrom? I know you are much more interested in piloting than I."

"Oh, no!" I reacted, once again tracking the color changes around Paul's eyes, I tried to explain as nicely as possible. "I mean, thank you, Paul, but, no, you put in your name and waited. But I really appreciate it. Thanks." I added a thumbs up because I couldn't think of any other gesture to punctuate the refusal without seeming ungrateful.

Taking one step back, prefacing my exit, I told Paul Newman and his *jiki* Ella, "I'm actually gonna go take care of some questionnaires. I'll jump back out here another time. I'll see you soon."

My ears burned, and my cheeks felt hot. I was almost as uncomfortable with Paul's offer as I was grateful to have it, so much that I was too distracted to think of the low Martian gravity.

Loping into my quarters, I found I was glad my roommates were all at least briefly occupied elsewhere. I opened my personal device and pulled up the placement questionnaire. When prompted with the five fields for focused cadet training, I did not hesitate: aerospace, communications, military, research, technology. Naturally, I picked the first: aerospace with an emphasis on pilot training.

Next, I found the squad preference screen. And almost every "Who do you want to work with" question was about species or some variation on that theme. I know what Shin wanted me to do, and it might have been the smart choice, but I couldn't stop thinking about Paul Newman, who had offered me his place in line, smart choice or not.

"No preferences," I said to no one in particular, given that the room was empty. However, if I was being recorded, I'd like to think that I was making a statement to the powers-that-be.

I left every response neutral or N/A, and when it came time to list names, I left it altogether blank.

* * * * *

Chapter Seventeen:
Paul Newman

I appreciate the unknown.

Particularly, I enjoy the opportunity to question an occurrence that cannot be answered with a quickly typed query, a mental imprint, or a drone's stored knowledge. While there are still scientific principles to be explored and discovered among the Teek, we have few matters to ponder within our hives.

At the Olympus Mons Academy, so little was known for certain. Some of my fellow Teek found this frustrating to the point of anxiety, and many—Ella included—decided to ignore the complexities that did not directly apply to them. This left a few of us to wonder about everything and discuss it whenever possible.

One of the mysteries the Teek wanted to debate was that of the anonymous score in the flight simulator. From the earliest anyone could log into the program, the "Rock Hopper" module had had a posted high score of 11,840, with no name attached and which no one was able to beat.

As it was a Human-built simulation, fit for Human binocular, single-focus vision, it did not surprise me that the contraption might have been better set up for Humans or similar mammalian sentients. This upset the Tsangharee, who typically prided themselves on having faster reaction speeds than the Humans.

After trying my hands at the controls, enough to gauge how far I would have to go to reach the high score, I advanced a theory: The score was not made by a cadet. Rather, the score was input to give the cadets a goal to strive toward.

"Perhaps it was also planted to create competition," someone added.

"Or it is a way of testing how we will react to an unachievable goal," ventured another. This received clicks of agreement from more than a few Teek and hums of annoyance from the listening Tsangharee.

I did wonder if my new friend, Cadet Lidstrom, aspiring pilot, would appreciate the challenge.

* * *

Challenge was widespread as the orientation courses transitioned into Interstellar Boot Camp. I was informed that the use of "Boot" was a metonymous address to new recruits rather than the term for a technological upload or a literal piece of footwear. The green Tsanghar named Kesiel assisted in this education, telling me that "boot rhymes with recruit." I did not understand this commentary, but perhaps I would learn more later.

Apparently, on Terra-Human the purpose of a boot camp is often to use extreme exercises in order to break someone down and rebuild them. While this process was not as physically taxing on our muscular and respiratory systems, I would quickly agree with the sentiment.

I was assigned a class schedule to fulfill Green Cadet requirements and begin my communications training, but I did not ignore the words "subject to change." After only three minutes of my first class, an alarm sounded, and we were interrupted by an evacuation order, which was more chaotic than it ought to have been.

When the evacuation order was lifted, we returned to the class, and a staff sergeant informed us that we had just participated in a drill. He then reminded us that the I.I. was not a military endeavor, but that cadets could be "scrubbed" for failing to follow emergency procedures properly.

We knew the program was fully elective, but fortunately no one wanted to leave. This was one of the great benefits of the prior selection and self-selection processes. I did not know who among us were motivated by personal goals, a sense of pride, or a duty to represent their people. Also fortunately, I was highly motivated by all three.

We ran emergency drills at random intervals, simulating everything from depressurization to xeno-pathogen exposure. Sleep cycles had to be adjusted, mealtimes rearranged, but I did make a point of eating more than I thought I needed and trying to convince other Teek to do the same. Fortunately, there were not many changed class schedules in the first few days, but we began to suspect that a rearranged schedule was the first sign that a cadet was not doing well in their chosen field.

As a comm tech, I had the luxury of playing with signals, codes, and mistranslations. After all, I had been imprinted with a strong interest in language puzzles and an innate desire to make all concepts presentable and understandable in Human. Some of the tasks were relatively easy demonstrations of acumen, and others were very complicated, but these were usually pre-assessments with no advertised negative consequences. The interruption of unscheduled drills meant that some of the coursework or assessment had to be made up at a later time.

Of the people I could observe in my general classes as well as the communication cohort, I continued to notice some trends and overlap among species. For one, the Belbehan struggled most consistently. According to my *jiki*, who was more well-versed in interspecies medicine, the smallest cadets aged and changed so rapidly that many could be less capable than they would have been when initially invited to join the I.I. The P'rukktah and Tsangharee snarled at each other when at a distance and when working individually with one another but did not antagonize each other when sharing a classroom or workshop space. The Humans were not only ubiquitous but highly versatile, to the point that it was nearly impossible to predict areas of strength or weakness based on species alone. Many of the Teek were competent, but they did not stand out as the best or worst. Some of them began showing signs that they were not eating enough.

By the end of the second full day, I found myself doubting my internal chronometer and debating the benefits of communing with a drone that wasn't from my home hive. Ella Fitzgerald also needed a longer time to commune and reset that night, but even that was interrupted by another drill.

* * * * *

Chapter Eighteen:
Lidstrom

Yiorgos liked to call the Initiative a matrix of double blinds and carefully worded contradictions. It was for this reason, Rivers labeled him a "math head," which, I know, is considered an outdated term for certain neurodivergents Terran-side, but, on Mars, nobody raised issue. Yiorgos quickly pointed out that this was another example of a contradiction, that we could use offensive language around Humans but had to watch our step, tone, and verb tense around the xenos.

I casually agreed with him, because clearly Yiorgos had put a lot more thought into it than I had.

For starters, the Initiative was aggressive about keeping their reputation non-military, even though the majority of the instructors had had some form of military training.

This was actually part of the official systems' accords that allowed for the Initiative in the first place. We recruits were given the bullet points. Hosted on the P'rukktah homeworld, this meeting had involved several P'rukktah houselords, Tsangharee faction representatives, Belbehan ship leaders, Human ambassadors, and Teek hive-mothers, all presided over by a slow-speaking Uua who etched the salient points into its bark for posterity. There, they agreed that none of the recruits for this new venture could have served in any military capacity or be in positions of established political power among their own species.

Apparently, they'd run into difficulty finding the exact mix and setting it as a universal standard. We didn't exactly get a printout of the specific criteria, but some of the vetoes created the exceptionally narrow selection terms.

They needed us young enough to be pliable, interested, and adventurous, *but* we had to be skilled enough to look good for Terra—or whatever species we represented.

They needed people who were open-minded, accepting, and curious, *but* they also needed cadets who were disciplined and committed so they would willingly sign their lives away for technological hybrids and group arrangements that were untested.

This is where I think they must have encountered the biggest roadblocks and paradoxes. The Initiative, and everyone recruited into it, had a vested interest in making themselves look good—and the definition of "themselves" was not necessarily universal. Some races were individualistic to a fault, others wanted those in their own species to win, others had categories only they knew about, like a particular lizard moon or P'rukktah house—which I don't pretend to understand.

So, it's not like we were the only ones with some recruits rooted in a "Human First" kind of philosophy. At the time, I didn't really have anything against the movement. After all, I was Human, and, to be honest, I saw nothing wrong with any planet putting their peoples' problems before those of the rest of the galaxy. The difference, I would be reminded, was that many other planets were already home to multiple sentient species, so their approach was not likely to be the same as the Human one.

I silently avoided these debates. I cared more about being a pilot, getting into space, and exploring than any of the grand-scale politics. With what I wanted out of life, the idea of stubborn loyalty to one species just didn't strike me as practical. That isn't to say I think I'm a better person or more open-minded, just that my form of selfishness aligned with what I needed and what the Initiative was looking for.

Though Yiorgos, Rivers, and Benjamin were making a game of guessing who was a Human firster, I mostly ignored them. For example, I never bothered to raise the theory that Shin was anti-xeno, and I sure as hell wouldn't say it to any of the ex-TSF folks.

Lieutenant Nick Chandan stood out to me as the scariest. Although I'd seen him carry on polite and even friendly conversation, I fully believed he was capable of killing any number of sentients with his bare hands, even if he'd been hired as an engineering instructor. I reached this conclusion after exactly one of his daily low-G calisthenics courses. I was happy to learn he wasn't the instructor the next morning. Instead, we had someone named Gordon, whom I'd met before in the underbelly of Phobos, but who, thankfully, didn't seem to recall me as the trespassing "kid." This lieutenant was deep-voiced and soothing compared to Chandan, at least until we got started, at which point he seemed to take personal insult from anyone who did not sweat enough.

That seemed consistent: The lieutenants were badasses who wanted to present their position in the hierarchy, the staff sergeants were all business and rarely demonstrated their combat training, and the non-ranked instructors were few, peculiar, and often called "specialist."

I think some of the commanders managed the best of all worlds and were in many ways examples of the tight niche they wanted us recruits to be. They were well-educated, very experienced, and at least presented as extremely open-minded. Perhaps this came with maturity more than anything else. Would I say I had favorites? Sure. I mean, if teachers can have favorite students, why not the other way around. Even though he wasn't one of our flight instructors, my favorite was consistently "the French guy"—Commander Claude Poissonier. He was both formal enough to command the authority his rank deserved but practical enough to know that most xenos, and some Humans, couldn't reliably say his last name, so he went by Commander Claude.

Regardless of their demeanor, no one messed around. They were all on a firm, fast recruiting track with fires lit under their collective asses in a way I never would have pictured. I wasn't the only one who assumed the Initiative would involve a lot of long, boring lectures and reading before we managed to actually do anything. But not with this group. We weren't novices; we'd all had preliminary training, and it was only a question of how quickly they could get us ready for more and more hands-on scenarios.

* * * * *

Chapter Nineteen:
Paul Newman

Day 3

On the third day, we were given a communications puzzle, which I suspected did not have enough information to solve.

The scenario provided a scrambled signal during a high-stakes negotiation, which communications cadets were to interpret and present to a captain with a recommended course of action. Commander Claude Poissonier was administering this particular activity and said that he would leave a negative review to anyone who called him something other than "Captain" for the duration of the assessment.

I wondered if it was designed to test perseverance, like the score in the pilot simulator. I also noticed that many others were taking a very long time working through every available algorithm. Though most of the room was Human, there were a few Belbehan and Teek among every cluster of hopeful communicators. The Belbehan struggled with the attention span required by the activity and with the idea of working solo. I noticed that many of the Teek, with sunken eyes and drooping antennae, appeared exhausted, even before they finished converting the signal to effective audio.

I managed the technical side of the activity quickly, but I could not ignore the others' struggles with the interpretation. Instead of running all of the pattern detection I might normally do or testing for various ways to reinterpret the garbled mess of the faux transmission, I reread the scenario description. Then I went with what Humans would call my "gut instinct."

I was the first to leave my workstation. I knocked on and entered the proctor's door.

Claude Poissonier's office had large transparencies on three sides and multiple screens which were not turned toward me, so I assumed he was able to take in much information through observation. He looked up as I entered and put one elbow on his desk.

"Did you have a question about the exercise, Mister Newman?"

"No, Captain," I said, keeping my head upright in the uncomfortable position of attention. "I am here to deliver my recommendation."

"That was—" I believe he was about to compliment me by telling me how quickly I had achieved a conclusion. However, the Human maintained his role and asked, with all seriousness, "Did you interpret the transmission?"

"No, Captain, not fully. The signal was damaged, but what little I received of the tone sounded urgent."

He nodded a couple of times. "Go on."

"Well, Captain, if it is urgent, we should act quickly, rather than spend more time trying to unscramble a signal which might have been irreparably damaged." I attempted to discern whether or not he agreed with my general commentary, but he gave no reaction, so I proceeded, referencing the scenario transcript. "I recommend we return to low orbit, try to contact our ground crew with less interference, and send a shuttle. This way, if we need to intervene, we will have another craft nearby, which will be especially helpful if we need to rescue anyone."

He did not speak for a few seconds, but I held the position of attention.

"Thank you, Cadet," he said. "You are dismissed."

* * *

I did not know if I should feel proud or ashamed of being the first to walk out of the assessment. My feet felt the heaviest they had since my arrival on Mars-Human, which I did not assume was merely a sign of acclimation.

The halls between classrooms were certainly the emptiest I'd seen them, given that everyone else was currently occupied by instruction and training. I considered finding a drone to meditate with, but I had never connected with a drone outside my home hive and I did not want to introduce such factors in my current state of insecurity.

My thorax was audibly vibrating by the time I reached the North Nexus of the academy. Classrooms lay behind me, cadet quarters to the right, hangar and garage straight ahead, and labs and offices to the left. The center of the Nexus was a circular garden in which the Uua Prime had been planted. I paused to regard the tree that stood over five times my height and would easily dwarf the largest Teek queen.

It was still unclear how the natives of Uua Prime perceived people, especially when those people were not standing on their soil or easily reachable by root. They could not see and limited psychic interactions revealed they did not quite hear. From fifteen meters away standing on inorganic floor I most likely would not have registered as a being to its senses. However, I felt like the tree regarded me as well.

It adjusted its posture, making a creaking, stretching sound, and some of the bark around the trunk flared in my direction to increase perception. Two Belbehan, who had fallen asleep in the upper branches, were spooked by the movement and they scurried down and away, leaving just the two of us, a Teek and a tree.

I approached as if entranced—No, I approached as if summoned by a queen, completely aware and willing rather than compelled. As soon as I stepped over the shallow barrier and onto the coarse, rocky ground, I found myself wishing I was not wearing boots.

The Uua indulged me, and I paused to take off said footwear in order to stand bare on the earth. As soon as my exoskeleton made contact, one of the roots arced up through the dirt. It was thinner than my wrist and less prehensile than a Tsanghar's tail, but it was still able to nudge its way toward my ankle and lie against the connective tissue between bone plates, where it is easier to conduct electromagnetic signals.

I heard the Uua's voice, low and absolutely certain. It was clear in both my hind-brain and fore-brain. It told me, "See."

It shifted one of its branches and pointed, seeming to indicate a way down the north passage, toward the hangars. This was not a command, despite the imperative language structure. I interpreted it as a hope that I would listen and attempt.

Pivoting, I left the tree and circular garden behind me.

My bare feet carried me quickly forward. I let my head lean forward, letting go of the posture most common for bipeds. My antennae reached out and scanned.

I kept walking until I heard something that broke my concentration. Before I reached the hangar, a voice drew me toward one of the garages. I was not immediately certain if it was a Human voice; in hindsight, I believe my interaction with the tree was responsible for recalibrating my brain's ability to interpret audio signals.

When I could understand the voice, I initially caught only concepts, namely "shuttle schedules" and "Wayne," which I took to be a proper noun. I did not truly register that I was being addressed until I was already in the garage and proceeding toward a two-meter-long black bag that had been set on a wheeling tray.

I was extending my right arms toward the black bag, too high for someone of my stature to see within, even though it appeared unzipped. Then something—someone—grabbed my shoulder. I reacted suddenly, my gripping fingers snagging the bag and pulling the whole tray rapidly enough that it jostled the bag it supported and body within it.

I do not recall being surprised to see the bag held a body which, once jostled, nearly rolled off the tray. Part of it extended toward me, pointing much like the Uua had, albeit without any intention.

The hand that reached out of the bag had certainly been Human and though now completely lifeless, inert. It had slipped out and was hanging limply from an unseen shoulder socket. The flesh was pale, indicating the corpse's temperature and lack of flowing blood. The fingers were startlingly striated, marred with white and blue that almost matched the paleness of death, but did not fit the usual spectra of Human flesh tones. Perhaps this was how necrotic Humans looked.

There was a mark on the forearm, something I might have thought a natural dermal marking if it had not had such a geometric pattern. No, unless I was mistaken, this was what Humans called a tattoo, not unlike the brands Tsangaree wore or the permadye of the P'rukktah. The mark was several centimeters, possibly a decimeter wide, a nine-sided figure with an inlaid star and the silhouette of something more organic that could have been plant or animal, along with the letters TSF.

"Hey!" a voice said, while her hand motivated my shoulder to turn. I saw another Human—living—in an orange exosuit covering any name badge or rank, but with the helmet off. Not happy. "Man, you got ears in that head of yours? What are you doing in here, Greenie?"

I studied her face. Smooth, peach-toned, rounded cheeks, and hair the color of a sulfur flame in looping curls. Blue eyes that would have suggested fear, were she Teek, but this was the cool blue of anger.

Apparently, I did not respond quickly enough, for she grew angrier.

"Greenie, I asked you a question, and if you want to keep wearing that patch, you'll give me an answer."

"Whoa, hey," the other Human said. This one looked and sounded more male, with a fuller tone and much greater height. His skin was quite a bit darker, and he wore a full circle of facial hair around his mouth. He put on a smile, which I interpreted as an attempt to stave off awkwardness. "Ease up, Burke. Don't interrogate the Teek." With a much softer tone than she, he asked me, "Do you speak English?"

"Yes," I said, glad I knew what the Terra-Humans called their dialect of Human.

"Okay, what are you doing down here?"

I considered remarking that I had not decreased elevation, but I erred on the assumption that this was an idiom or colloquialism. "I concluded an assessment early. The Uua pointed me in this direction."

"The Tree, huh?" He gave a quick non-verbal gesture to the blonde female, apparently "Burke," and she walked around me in order to put the arm back inside the bag. "Sorry you had to see that. Sometimes people get uncomfortable with dead bodies."

I was not uncomfortable with corpses. I understood how they were replanted to fertilize the incubators on my planet, but both of these Humans appeared less comfortable than I. So, I asked, "What is this body for?"

"Cadaver lab," he answered, very quickly. "Research and medical cadets are working with donated dead for mock autopsies and investigations. Yeah, simulations are one thing, but the real deal is preferable for some applications. You in research?"

"No. Communications," I corrected him. My compound eyes kept adjusting focus, to better look at both this Human and the bag containing the corpse.

"Very skilled," he remarked, in a way that sounded more routine than sincere. "Well, I am going to ask you to leave. Cadet presence during prep can compromise the integrity of the assessments, so..."

I understood this rationale. I straightened, made a salute, then began my exit. I was wondering whether Ella Fitzgerald would have an opportunity to work with this particular specimen in the near future, when I heard the female Human ask, "Why isn't it wearing shoes?"

My thorax buzzed with embarrassment for much of my walk back. By the time I returned to the Nexus to collect my boots the

Uua was already asleep again, and there was no one else to remark on the oddity I had experienced.

* * * * *

Chapter Twenty:
Arrksh

The corpse is cold, the flesh irregular. However, without being able to remove this encumbering suit, I cannot tell *how* cold or *how* irregular. Naturally, we have instruments to read these kinds of things, which project temperature and pressure in more than enough units. Still, there is a stark difference between taking readings and feeling for oneself.

I wish to ask the instructor if I may remove my gloves. There is no indication of risk or hazard, and I would be much more effective if allowed to interact directly. Still, I refrain. I keep my voice low and my head down. That is wisest during my first days at the academy.

Today, I work alongside a Belbeh, who appears very grateful to have me as their partner. Though my diminutive colleague is very quick and precise at anything that might require muscle memory, she struggles with committing the facts to memory and continues to confuse vital statistics of any species that isn't Belbehan.

This has left me many opportunities to delegate, and to test my ears and reaction times, so that I may prevent her from doing anything too detrimental to our process. Fortunately, the particular test body we are examining is only semi-organic, so there is far less risk of destroying valuable resources if we—she—should err. Parts of it are purely a mannequin, with lab-grown flesh covering the relevant parts for each day's study and dissection. This one has beautiful scale work, which we have been painstakingly spreading.

"Next we are going to cut through the neck muscles and the lower buccal membrane," the instructor says in Human. I hear a translation in my earpiece and hope that the locational nuances are correctly reported.

I begin with a scalpel on one side of the facsimiled Tsanghar neck while my Belbeh classmate attempts the other.

The instructor continues, "This is an exercise of precision and patience." She keeps her hands behind her back, which accentuates her formal posture even though she is quite short by Human standards. "If you cut in the wrong place, you will run into the elastic sinews which can impede your movement. If you go too deeply, you might run into and puncture the ovarian sac just above the ribcage."

Because my translation arrives later, I hear some of the laughter—both amused and derisive—before the mention of the lizards' egg-forming organs.

The Belbeh makes a derogatory comment about having "one's balls in one's throat" in broken P'rukktah. A Tsanghar at the next workstation screeches toward us, as if in response, causing the Belbeh to startle and cut too far into our specimen, demonstrating precisely what the instructor has just warned against, spilling the sac. The fluids are also lab grown, but a good imitation of the real thing. This makes the same Tsanghar laugh. I wonder if this humor is macabre, given the likeness we are dissecting.

While the Belbeh swears and an instructor's aide approaches, I continue my smooth incisions. I may be encumbered by gloves, but I am not hindered enough to disrupt my motion. I split and separate the muscle tissue, then apply the surgical clamps. I can see the luminescent sac within, unharmed.

I hear knocking on a nearby workstation, and I look up to see one of the only other P'rukktah in the room; a male, jutting his jaw at me in recognition and approval.

* * *

"Y ou are no stranger to the blade," the male says to me after the lab has concluded. He growls an implication I choose to ignore.

"Appreciation," I reply, rather quickly, letting my learned Belbehan lilt flow. "You appear adept as well." The other students, made up of a much more even mix of all species, pass us by. I imagine very few speak P'rukktah well enough to understand us, but I do not deny the possibility of active translators.

"Yes," the male says, "though I imagine you have much more experience slicing into lizard necks than I."

I do not recoil. I know better than to show an emotional response. In fact, his remark does not demand a response from me.

But he presses, "To spend a quarterlife in the reaches of space where no lawmakers can record your triumphs or your savagery." Again, he juts his chin, expands ribcage and shoulders, an aggressive gesture but not wholly hostile.

I hear myself growl in response before I can temper my own neck. My lowermost ears pick up the low thrumming of his hearts and I register the scent of the pheromones and adrenaline. "Stop dancing; say what you mean."

He closes the distance between us, lifting his head to match my height so that we are practically chin to chin. I have endured the cold looks and casual growls of the females, but I have not had occasion to receive overtures from a male since my arrival. Though he is short, even for a male, and most likely incapable of matching my strength and prowess, I feel my blood racing in anticipation of a collision, but he withdraws a few fingerlengths. His brow muscles relax, and his ears press back in a form of smile.

We are not alone in the corridor. All kinds of eyes are upon us, from double-lidded lizard slits to compound and chromaed, to the comparably dim eyes of more of our kind.

Very quietly, he tells me, "Solidarity. I am for you, *Kirshka*." I do wonder if the word would translate to keen listeners or if it would sound like anything more than "ma'am" in Human. Fortunately, it is too general a term of respect to mean "princess."

He lowers his posture, sinking down to his more natural standing height, and turns away.

"Name?" I ask.

He chuffs, seemingly amused but tells me. "Aijla."

Aijla. No house name, not even a mention of a home territory. I cannot blame him, but I do watch him join up with two other males and proceed away.

I exhale through my nose and work to settle my blood pressure. My body is still primed for a form of collision, but I do not show this to the onlookers, who are dispersing, believing any confrontation is concluded.

One person does linger, a Teek with long wings and a surprisingly long cranial ridge I have seen before; I believe her name is Ella, but I have never formally met her outside the medical training. I consider growling or barking at her in accusation, but her chromae are so neutral it would seem untoward. I do not expect her to speak.

"Impressive work," she says in a manner that is completely devoid of innuendo and which reminds me further of where I am and with whom I share company. This is not a place for aggression.

I nod in acceptance and the Teek turns away, leaving me in peace to slow my demanding organs.

I am in the process of quieting my pulse when I hear a voice of concern, Human frequencies. The instructor is "checking in" on me. This is apparent even without my translator enabled.

"I am fine," I assure her in my language, letting the computerized version relate the words. Then, recalling Human decorum, I try one of their phrases in the best pronunciation I can manage. "*Thank you for asking.*" I prefer just saying "gratitude."

The instructor is placated. She relaxes more. "Very good! I'm glad to see the translator is working well for you." She looks down to her own wrist device and thumbs something available to her visual interface. I surmise it is a message for notification for she tells me, "If you have a moment, you are requested in one of the med-labs. I'll share the directions." With another couple flicks in the space above her wrist, she sends information from her device to mine.

I recognize the lizard's name.

* * *

"Liesarn," I say.

"Aarksh!" she wheezes in response.

The bandages around her very mobile neck look far more comprehensive than what should be required for the size of the incision I made. I wonder if this Tsanghar has access to the right nutrients she needed to heal. I wonder why the Human medicine is so much less efficient than P'rukktah biochemical techniques. I also do not voice my concern or my confusion, knowing that this too would indicate my level of familiarity with Tsanghar physiology.

Liesarn is paler than the last time I saw her, but that could merely be an automatic camouflage with the whiter walls of the medlab. She stands normally, however, without any sign of strain to maintain balance; even her tail is upright.

"I wanted to thank you, now that I have a voice again." She grins at me. I notice that her voice still rises and falls in the usual fashion of Tsangharee, but without as much control of pitch. "According to the doctors, you did an excellent job. I shall be rejoining my fellows soon and formally enrolling in the academy."

"Congratulations," I say. I have folded my arms across my chest, displaying my skepticism. "I would think Tsanghar flesh could repair by now. Was there a complication in healing?"

She pulses forward, their kind of nod. When she next speaks, it is with both eeriness and intrigue. "Yes, Arrksh. After you delivered me, I woke screaming. I thoroughly damaged my healing tissue." Though her volume is hindered, her tone still sounds fascinated. "Apparently, something terrified me, and also impacted the dream minds of my moonkin."

Liesarn does not take any precautions to not be heard. Someone on the I.I. staff—an aide, I assume—is working nearby and has paused to listen.

I follow Liesarn's lack of modesty or secrecy. I suppose I have no reason to suspect that anything spoken here could be damaging, to myself, the lizard, or the I.I. "What was it?"

Liesarn wags her head back and forth, the length of her neck making the arc impressively long. "I cannot remember. None of us can. Not even with the assistance of the Avowol." She absently flicks her tail in the direction of the sealed water door, where the Avowol dwell.

I am torn between asking the medical aide, who has now completely ceased her tasks, about it and asking about the experience with the Avowol, a strange cross between cnidarian and cephalopod, with multiple, movable brains and semipermeable psychic skin. Instead, I ignore both and push forward. "What do you think it was?"

"The common theory among the *experts*," she begins, hissing even more at the word, a challenge of their title, "is that there were too many psychic signals in the vessel when it passed through a spacefold. Between Tsangharee of so many moons trying to dream together and the presence of the Teek, each longing to unconsciously connect with their own hives."

I give the theory its due muse. While these factors may be plausible, it is also assumed that Tsangharee only dreamshare when breathing the same air, which could not happen in the individual safe pods. And Teek—I know little about Teek brain chemistry other than what is common knowledge, but I have been told on many occasions that the workers can only create very weak, person-to-person psychic connections.

"But you do not agree," I say.

"What other explanation is there?" Liesarn asks, drawing back her cheeks and lips in order to reveal the interlocking pointed teeth.

I recognize this kind of question from Tsangharee, and I shudder to witness it. It is both rhetorical and direct, creating thoughtful silence while demanding an answer that is not known. These kinds of philosophical puzzles have managed to force rash action and to halt progress of the lizard kind for generations.

We let the silence remain. Liesarn continues smiling, hardly blinking. She does swallow, rather painfully, but she keeps her eyes open.

Eventually, I wish her, "Positive days and a speedy recovery."

"Yes, indeed. Thank you again, swift surgeon."

I know that the remark is not sarcastic, but the tone is still off-putting.

I take one last look at the Avowol tank. There is a small window, where I catch a glimpse of a moving body—the Avowol's umbrella frame compressing around the water and propelling itself by.

* * * * *

Chapter Twenty-One:
Kesiel

The tree in the atrium flexes its leaves
And teaches the people who cluster to breathe
In wisdom that stretches their baser beliefs
—Kesiel, Human Language Poetry in Tsanghar Meter

The tree people of Uua Prime have trouble fitting into the attention spans of other minds. While they can communicate, though very slowly, they also have a habit of slipping out of consciousness whenever it suits them. They have no concept of the passage of time and can rarely be held to any form of schedule, even with frequent reminders. This is why no one has ever bothered to call them allies, even if we know better than to make them enemies.

I have been told that there are only two Uuas on Mars, a handful on Terra-Human, and one particularly chatty one in an "International Space Station" orbiting the Human home planet who has been known to express more than three thoughts a day.

The one in the Olympus Mons Academy might as well have been representative of all Uuas as far as most of us were concerned. After all, few people had been among enough Uuas to develop a scientific sample set. Though there were more of them than any other group, I quickly assessed that the Human cadets were more fascinated with the tree and flocked around its grounds in greater numbers than any-one else. Of course, the Uua slept at random intervals, so this left quite a bit of downtime.

I could only theorize as to the cycles of the Uua, or how and why it decided to respond to certain stimuli. Doubtless, Arrksh would have an easier time telling head or tail of this great alien oddity. I imagined she had more of an idea of how to dissect this specimen and would learn more in the medicine training. That said, everyone knew better than to approach an Uua with a weapon.

While I did not "wait around" in order to interact with the tree species, I did extend the courtesy of a pause and a salutation when-ever I passed the majestic form. I found its tableaus altogether en-riching to witness, be they a lone sleeping tree or a congress of mammalian types stretching their limbs in grateful imitation. Uuas are considered wise and, though slow, can demonstrate the wisdom in the art of body flow. So, while our Uua stretched and waved, Hu-mans did something they call tai chi, which comes from a very dif-ferent dialect of Human than the English one. These movement forms, with one palm up and the other down, are actually quite simi-lar to those of my people. Bear in mind, we use a tail for counterbal-ance, thus completing the flow that could not be achieved with an even number of limbs.

It is also telling that we all have trees on our worlds. That the trees of the Teek home system are massive sprawling structures whose bark consists of hard deposits of vegetable bone does not stop them from being trees. Even the underwater Avowol have trees that grow downward from what are essentially kelp islands.

Furthermore, all of us interact with our trees. Structure, worship, inspiration; a source of food, fuel, building materials. It is possible that some grand seed-sowing across the galaxy ensured the presence of trees on all planets that support intelligent life, but it is just as likely that some root factor is required for both, a complex causative relationship billions of years in the making.

The trees of Uua Prime, as well as the other interstellar plants expertly arranged throughout the corridors of this base, reminded us that we were all relatable on some level, even if my sister Tsangharee did not wish to acknowledge it. In those early days, I continually heard them hissing and gossiping, sometimes above the hearing range of all but the P'rukktah, about Tsanghar superiority and how the Humans were unfairly rigging courses to deny us that.

It was a peculiar balance, much like that which the Uua taught through its example or the well-used tail of a Tsanghar. The Humans were potential allies and yet they were rivals of the weapons game. Many species wished to capitalize on their sudden presence, but we also feared them.

I had long been part of the we who found them more subjects of curiosity than an assumed help or harm to the shared galaxy. And as for their weapon technology, I had the Uua-like wisdom to see that as a mere footnote to the Humans' true technological importance: they were succeeding in bringing together more species' scientific advancements in a shorter time than we had ever seen before.

The technology field, I was told, was even more segregated than the others. For one, those of us with an engineering focus shared very few classes, if any, with those studying information systems. And, among the engineers, I was the only lizard. Eager and much taller than anyone else, I was picked out by every ranking officer and, possibly more important, non-ranking expert for questions and demonstrations.

One particular specialist was a Teek wearing lieutenant stripes who went by Jane Austen. She selected me immediately and inquired as to whether I was playing a prank by pretending to be an engineer. Apparently, she had been warned about me.

I informed her that I was entirely sincere in my interest in the field and completely committed to learning. I did have the luxury of playing at obliviousness, pretending that I did not recognize her dismissiveness and disrespect. Unlike the Teek, with the rings around their compound eyes, I do not spontaneously change color when I experience change of emotion.

* * * * *

Chapter Twenty-Two: Kesiel

B y the time I arrived back in my section of living quarters, the bidding and betting over the cadet pilot simulation program had increased dramatically.

Many amused, frustrated, and intrigued *Mmm*s rang out in chorus
from collected Tsangharee. Their gestures and energy were so unlike
that of the grounding tree, that it was difficult not to immerse in and
adopt their emotional energy, and all surrounding a crate on stilts!
Yes, I know that in the hands of the brilliant Human VR engineers,
this crate looked and felt like a real pilot's seat.

One of the red-backs with a long snout shoved right up against
me, blocking my path as I tried to proceed toward my room. Instinct
wanted me to ready for combat, and instinct nearly won. I raised my
tail behind my head and opened my mouth, showing teeth in response to the challenge.

"Sister," oozed the red-back, a forced friendly greeting under a
threatening tone. "I have wagered, and I wagered on you because
you are strange. Can you corroborate my theory?"

I put down my defenses but raised my head, trying to see over
who I could. Though I caught a few eyes, I did not gain any sense of
what was being asked of me or why.

"I shall endeavor, sister," I returned. Pleasantly, I might add. "Please say more."

"The high score made by the guest student! You have a different schedule than we, and you rise early in the morning. Was it you?"

I admit that I savored the moment longer than I probably ought to have. I closed my eyes—both pairs of lids—and slowly exhaled through my nose. I brought my declawed digits to drum on my chin, before finally breaking the news. "No. I have yet to sit in the chair."

There were some groans and snarls from onlookers, who had also wondered if, or assumed that, I had made the higher score. Bets were paid out, which mostly consisted of home incense, muscle soothers, and imitation live food. The red-back protested, then lamented loudly.

From not too far away, I saw two Teek staring at the strange proceedings. One was taking notes. I grinned at the Teek and waved, while the red-back continued to embarrass herself, wagging her tongue as well as an upturned head.

"Do not so tax yourself, sister!" I said, surprised by my own sudden excitement. "I think I know who created your mystery score."

She rapidly put her lips by my ear and intoned, "Really? Have you already wagered?"

Prudently, I surveyed the board. Any appropriately managed betting or bidding pool required a well-maintained display board, and this was no exception, even if the characters and numbers were in an acceptable form of Tsanghar shorthand rather than a full, easily readable language. I could see that there were clearly forms of bets on individual scores, as well as scribbled-in names and home clans of those most likely to either beat or already have the high score. So far, every listed name, including mine, had been eliminated.

"I have not wagered," I responded, with a calculated pace. "But what would you stand to win if I could correctly find the one Human cadet who managed the unbeatable score?"

"I would recoup what I lost, surely." The red-back attempted to look hopeful but was shot down by a legitimate concern. "Why wouldn't you simply use this knowledge yourself?"

I showed all of my teeth. "It is not my wager. I put forth no risk, but I would appreciate compensation, should my insight prove correct..."

Red-back initially missed my meaning, but that mattered little. I did not work out every emotion or interaction, but it wasn't long until I was searching for my recently acquired Human friend.

As they were creatures governed by clocks—clocks that were fairly similar on Mars-Human as their Terra-Human—many of the Humans could predictably be found dining or slumbering at predictable hours. As I had no need for a late meal, I did not frequent the mess at this hour, but I believed the Human in question would.

The tapestry of Human activity queued up, self-served, and populated the tables. Some examined tablets, either frantically studying or self-soothing. Some tested wits or bluffs against each other in the form of games of strategy or chance. And off-center, a short, sandy-blond specimen of Human adaptability was using a tined instrument to gather noodles, for his tongue was not long and dexterous enough to retrieve them.

"Lidstrom!" I sang when I arrived, taking a seat on the bench. One of Lidstrom's Human companions, the one with the thick and nearly connected brows coughed in surprise.

The buzzed-haired female named Shin fixed me with an expression that was neither a scowl nor a sneer but flirted with both. She asked, quietly enough that I only just understood it, "Why do they all seem to know you?"

To his credit, Darren Lidstrom ignored the comment. "Hi, Kesiel, did you need something?" He also stammered to get around his mouthful but managed not to issue food particles from his mouth.

"Yes! The flight simulator, have you played it?"

"Um—Played?" His small neck pulsed as he swallowed. "In the pilot program, we're learning the basics and looking at docking procedures for shuttles. They won't even let us on the *Command*-class ones yet."

"I see…" I continued grinning, prompting the Human to dig a little deeper and supply an answer.

His shoulders squirmed a little under the collective gaze of myself and Shin. "Oh, and on Phobos I logged a couple hours just messing around."

Shin asked, "You did? We didn't even have access to the sims when we got to Mons."

"Well, yeah," Lidstrom responded, "but I was stuck there waiting for the next shuttle, and—"

"Please," I interrupted, letting my excitement get the better of me. "Are you familiar with the Rock Hopper module?"

"Yeah, the asteroid dodger. That was one of the only ones available, so that's what I was on."

"*Mmmm*mmm!" I observed, which caused a ripple of unease through the several Humans at the table, all of whom had stopped eating to stare at me. "Do you recall your score?"

"Uh…" Lidstrom chuckled, showing a little embarrassment, possibly of me. "Sorry, Kesiel. I didn't—We don't typically—I mean, I don't have my score memorized."

"Was it 11,840?"

He gave this due pause, considering it, but I could tell from his eyes—read them like a Teek's chromae. "Wait, yeah. How did you know that?"

"A 'guest user' has the high score. I thought it might be you." Having acquired my information and swiftly delivered a message, I stood from the bench. I extracted my legs smoothly, but I couldn't resist running my tail across one-brow's shoulder.

"Jesus!" he exclaimed and upturned his plate.

"Lidstrom," I acknowledged. Then, "Shin. Others." And I about-faced to slip out again. I anticipated a very grateful finder's fee from the red-back.

Behind me, I heard the Human named Shin say, "Damn, son! I think I need to update my squad preferences."

* * * * *

Chapter Twenty-Three:
Lidstrom

2000 Day 3

The steps for inflating a man's ego are pretty straightforward and repeatable, even if they are not always easy to arrange. First, make sure that he is actually pretty good at something. Then, tell him he is good at that thing. Next, find a way for him to get that thing publicly exhibited, possibly on a scoreboard, in an environment where that skill is actually valued and praised. It works for pro football and VR players. My dad used to joke that hockey players were too down-to-Earth for that kind of thing, but I'm pretty sure the theory would hold true if they'd kept a professional league into the twenty-second century.

So, on the third day of my stint in the Mons Academy, when I was told that I held the high score on the "Rock Hopper" simulator, I was feeling pretty pumped. Once I found out that pretty much all the Teek and lizards knew about the guest score and were competing with it...well, I don't know if there is a word in English for that feeling, maybe in German or Tsanghar.

The rest of the dinner and the walk back to our quarters was excellent, definitely the coolest academy experience so far. It started with a series of congratulations, first from my close colleagues and then from acquaintances and even strangers. Only one of the other Human cadets expressed doubt that it was actually me who put up the anonymous score and that was because a very loud group of the

Tsangharee began jeering and heckling when I returned, saying that I could not have actually beaten all of them and was just pretending, which inspired the Human cadets to form up and start cheering me on.

Here's the weird thing: I don't think all the accusations were actually derisive. Some of the lizards were impressed by my gall at claiming something so outlandish. I heard some weird comments about crediting or blessing the throat of she who bore me, which could have been a product of poor translation or broken Tsangharish-English.

I think it was inevitable that the crowd would challenge me to do it again. Among waving hands, tails, heads, and various shapes of fins, more than a few Tsanghar suggested that I couldn't repeat the score.

Kesiel played ringleader and called to the group with a very strange high-pitched squeal, commanding silence from enough of the crowd to speak over them.

"Well!" she announced, with that same pointed grin and her neck at almost full vertical extension. "I contend that Lidstrom *can* repeat his "Rock Hopper" score. Would anyone care to wager?"

I pretty much lost track at that point. Not only was much of the betting not in English, but the rat-beebees and P'rukktah quickly joined in, adding things that were even harder to understand because every growl and squeak sounded angry or scared. It was hard to tell if any of the Humans could work out the betting structure either, and it's not like anyone's form of currency worked for any other species or could really get you much of anything on the base.

I was also wondering why a simulator score was so important to the lizards, but I wasn't given time to figure that out.

"All right, you ready for this, Lidstrom?" Yiorgos asked me, one hand on my shoulder, either to bolster me or to make sure I wouldn't rabbit away.

"Would it matter if I said I wasn't?" It wasn't exactly a joke.

Ahead of me, clearing the path, Shin said, "Hey, you get in there, and you show 'em."

I was pretty sure that Shin wanted me to prove it to her, too.

I tapped my wrist against the outer console. Someone had already cleared the schedule for me, so the simulator would be available. The door drifted open, revealing the seat and the Human-friendly controls. I stepped in and sat.

"This is kind of nuts, isn't it?"

"It's not nuts; it's 'naut, yo!" said Yiorgos, straining the definition of pun.

Shin instead went for the logical argument. "Look at it this way: you do it and you prove to everyone you're the best that ever was. You try and come up short, you show people you got the guts to follow through."

I considered asking what would happen if I failed to get on the scoreboard, but I didn't think Shin wanted to hear it. Instead, I fell back on an old favorite: "Do or do not; there is no *try*."

"Hey!" Yiorgos called out. "Can I get some help setting the feed?"

I became suspicious and asked, "Wait, you're gonna broadcast this?"

"No, just a local duplicate feed. On that screen." He pointed to the biggest one in the common area.

"I can assist in this endeavor, Cadet Stratis." Of course, it was Paul Newman. Paul trotted in, at least a head shorter than the shortest Human there and looking like any of the Tsangharee could swallow him whole. "I am quite excited, Cadet Lidstrom," he told me, not very confidentially. "Although, if you do not manage success, the experience will be embarrassing."

"Thanks, Paul. I'll keep that in mind." I familiarized myself with the controls as quickly as I could. As far as I could tell, the interface was identical in almost every way, except this one was newer, and all controls could be adjusted and recalibrated for other shaped hands. It was nice being the default species.

Yiorgos ducked his head in one more time, a little closer than I would have liked, to jack into my video feed, but it gave me a chance to make a final request.

"Hey, do me a favor, don't record my audio."

"Yeah, sure, why?" It all came out in one breath.

"Because I don't want to worry about how I sound when I'm singing my own theme music. Now get out of here and let me race."

Yiorgos laughed. I don't know if he took me seriously, but he did stop leaning into my pilot space.

The crowd began to quiet. They weren't exactly roaring before, but a few Tsangharee can whip up an impressive amount of volume and range. Apparently Kesiel had finished arranging betting terms and now wanted to give me the final breakdown.

"Ah! Lidstrom, I have 'haggled,' as I believe you would say. Since no other contender has reached the eleven-thousand mark, you only have to hit that. You have three tries."

"Three tries?" I balked. "Haven't these guys been at this for a couple days?"

"Yes! That is why you get three."

I opened my mouth on instinct, but I had no idea how to protest against Kesiel. "Well, okay then. Tall order."

"Hmm? Oh yes! An idiom." Kesiel found this highly amusing and made a noise that was eerily close to a giggle. "I have one of my own: *tessenda*. You will win, Lidstrom."

Despite her encouraging words, Kesiel did not attempt any grace when she closed the door on me.

I was alone in the fake cockpit, which didn't have much sound insulation. I found myself wishing for the black of space around me instead of onlookers and hecklers. It would have been much more peaceful.

I took a deep breath and shook out my wrists and my neck as I pushed the air out. I popped in a piece of gum; a basic creature comfort, helpful for focusing.

For most of my life I'd done pretty well under pressure. More so when internally motivated, and even more when I already believed I could succeed. This was a bit of a new experience, a cut above in challenge and consequence.

I didn't see any point in waiting any longer.

I fired up the simulator, felt the hydraulics pulse and self-check. I formed a bubble with the gum and popped it twice while I worked through the selection screen.

"'Rock Hopper' is a go," I told myself.

The first heat was truly pathetic. I got off wrong at the gate, veered, swiveled, overcorrected, and blew myself up. And yes, there were chortles outside.

While I resettled myself, I heard a knock on the door.

"You okay in there?" Yiorgos asked.

"Yeah, these controls are just more responsive than the Phobos ones. I'm just getting my bearings."

BS or not, I still had two more tries.

I tried the steadying breath again, hummed it out to the tune of an inspirational film score. Of course, I was distracted and shaky, and it didn't come out well. I looked at the corner of the HUD and saw the score marker, currently zero. I would make myself nuts watching that score, so I did what any sane pilot without much conscientious hygiene would do. I took the gum out of my mouth and pressed it over the score, so it covered the high digits. I wouldn't watch my thousands.

New piece of gum, a little more settled, a little more calm.

I tried to remember back to the flight on Phobos, the sequences I had seen and used then, the mindset I'd had. Also, if the controls here were better, then hitting my high score should be even easier.

What occurred to me next is kind of hard to explain. It hadn't felt important at the time, but for some reason the memory of the raw Phobos rock popped into my head. I had touched another planet, or at least a moon, and it had sung to me. A whale song, distant, longing, very settling.

I started up again, only vaguely aware of the noise from the people outside the simulator as I went on my next run. I worked with the controls, not against them. I felt the hydraulics shift and push as I picked up speed. The asteroids practically avoided me, drifting and creating the openings I needed.

I started making tighter, closer, riskier maneuvers. I pushed the ship's boosters whenever I needed and rarely pressed the decelerator.

My speedometer kept ramping up, faster than I remembered going on Phobos, and the three low figures of the score kept shuffling.

All the while, a whale song played in my head. My arms tingled, every hair stood on end, fueled by the thought of touching Phobos.

I pushed faster, harder. The turns got increasingly more difficult; each new obstacle and dodge looked like it would be my last. The rocks got closer together, and I kept trying to dart between them, even the smallest openings, until, inevitably, there was no escape, and I exploded in a flurry of pixels.

It wasn't until then that I noticed the volume of cheers outside of the simulator. Clearly, I didn't need a third try, but this ego wanted something to brag about.

* * *

No matter how many times the instructors said these were our *first* squad assignments—with the clearly explained expectation that they *were* subject to change—everyone placed great importance on who they were grouped with. After all, first impressions were lasting impressions, and those impressions could decide who got pre-placed on the first *Command*-class vessel.

Naturally, as a pre-vetted ace pilot, I assumed I was a shoo-in—even if I had no idea what that term actually meant. After all, I was the new hot commodity, even to the lizards, who I'm pretty sure wanted to slit my throat, but they still knew who I was, and they requested me for their squads.

Yiorgos let me have my moment in the sun and did not once tell me to be careful or take it easy—maybe he knew that that would just make me dig in my heels more and make crazier, more outlandish claims.

With no alcohol available for cadets and the only real high being from hypoxia, I didn't say anything too stupid. I do distinctly remember telling Yiorgos, and whoever else was in earshot, "Whoever's on my squad tomorrow, we're going all the way."

"Well, let's hope they put me with you," he said.

* * * * *

Chapter Twenty-Four:
Lidstrom

0500 Day 4

Morning involved high tension and calisthenics. Literally.

Almost everyone was so buzzed about squad assignments that the powers-that-be actually tried to tire us into submission. However, for a sizable complement, it just pumped us even more. It was cool to see how Humans, P'rukktah, and Tsangharee hopefuls—all young, non-military-types with dreams—were stoked for the same opportunity. The Teek vibrated, jittered, and flashed various colors from their eye chromae. I think the collective exuberance just scared the rat-beebees.

The assignments were not going to be posted, as had been originally planned, instead, we were told over breakfast we would each be pointed toward a wing of the base and then a specific room number via our wrist devices, individual prep rooms or ready rooms, where we would find our squads, check in and be given our first assignment. The whole thing was like a spy VR, with disconnected directions from various cells, the kind that would be hard to trace.

Admiral Hass even came to the mess to deliver this particular bit of news, keeping her usual professional, at-attention demeanor. She was flanked by the other directors, who were just as serious as she, even Commander Claude, who was typically a much more down-to-Earth—or Mars—kind of leader.

"Know this, Cadets," she said, without needing to raise her voice to be understood perfectly by everyone, "any complaints or reassignment requests will not be accepted and will reflect very poorly on you. You are also not to speak with anyone about your specific squad assignment until every squad has completed the first scenario."

There were some groans over this particular twist. I think we wanted to see public lists of names so we could gloat and lord it over each other. A few of us caught the note of a "first scenario." I, for one, hoped it would happen right after breakfast.

I soon got my wish. Alerts started popping up on wrists all around the mess, but only to about a quarter of us. I was in that first wave and, yes, I managed to look more smug than I had in my recruit photo.

I stood, nodded to Yiorgos, Shin, and some of the others from E-group. "Duty calls."

I was more than excited walking down the corridor. I'd been to non-gravved parts of the moon, but I don't think I'd ever felt so light. If there hadn't been a ceiling above my head, I think I would have skipped straight off into space.

And why wouldn't I? I had made one of the best impressions ever, and not just to a boss or a teacher or a would-be captain, but, more importantly now, on hundreds of peers who were both my competition and my best line of defense.

The directions on my wrist took me toward the hangars, and I picked up my pace under those excellent windows. I saw shuttles and freight-craft coming in overhead, noiselessly in the nothing of space and further out along the horizon, somewhat jagged from the Mons ridges.

The few cadets who had left the mess about the same time as me veered or darted off in different directions, so that by the time I reached my door, I was alone. I took one final look around, and let myself in.

The ready room was small. Two benches, lockers, a tall exosuit closet, and a standing console with my first squadmate standing beside it. Of course, she was first, standing there grinning, all two feet of neck and four feet of tail ready for anything. And you know what? I wasn't any less excited.

"Mmm!" she hummed, arching her neck forward, every one of her green fins standing on end. "Lidstrom, we have been assigned to the same squad."

I nodded. "Kesiel."

"Ah, Cadet Lidstrom. Cadet Kesiel," said a familiar voice, as a third person entered our ready room.

I whirled around, and in my haste ended up looking right over the arthropod's brick-red head. I adjusted down from his antennae to Paul Newman's eyes, which were a warm orange, more than I'd ever seen them before. He craned forward, and his mandibles flared open; I heard his thorax thrumming.

Unlike me, Paul headed straight toward the console, swiped his wrist to input his cadet information, and his name appeared on the screen, both in its original Teek, which looked like a bunch of stick marks, and his chosen Human one: Paul Newman, Communications Specialist, right under Kesiel Y-T, Engineer.

I added myself to the squad and saw my name come up as "Darren Lidstrom, pilot," just as our fourth arrived.

Shin got about two steps into the small room. She had been learning Mars grav quickly, and could even march in most circumstances, but when she saw Kesiel and Paul, she dropped every bit of formality and enthusiasm.

"You've got to be kidding me," she said. I knew how she felt about it, but I didn't expect her to say, "We got two aliens?"

What happened next was Flix-level cinematic. Despite his name, I don't think Paul Newman appreciated it, but I hoped Kesiel did, with her sense of drama and weird aesthetics.

Before the door even had a chance to close, the largest member of our group slipped in behind Shin. With a quiet growl, Arrksh repeated only, "Aliens…" in a voice that did not read as either a question or a statement.

Shin reacted quickly, not exactly a jump-scare, but definitely discomfort around such a large being, and took two awkward steps back from the P'rukktah.

Arrksh appeared to glide whenever she took a step. I don't know if her legs were specially designed for absorbing shocks, but she made walking on Mars look like an elegant crawl. She only needed three steps to close the distance to the console, where she entered "Arrksh, Science: Medical."

The furry female growled, "Hello, squad," in her natural voice, before switching on her translator, which supplied a flat mechanical "I will leave this machine in Human" over her next sentence.

I looked at Shin who was moving her jaw from side to side, as if chewing on something hard to break through or swallow.

"Shin, it's to you," I told her.

She needed a moment to compose herself, then she clicked her tongue and said, "Yes, it is." I'm not sure if it was for my benefit or her own when she muttered, "Welcome to the interspecies experiment." Either way, the final name, "Helen Shin, Security," was added to our squad.

Though I couldn't read Arrksh, and I couldn't *not* read Paul, courtesy of his vibrant eyes, I had the impression Shin was the only one who was really disappointed. Tell you the truth, I was probably as happy as I could have been. I was also willing to bet that Kesiel had predicted it perfectly; knowing what little I knew about Kesiel, she probably *would* have made some bets on her squad assignment.

* * * * *

Chapter Twenty-Five:
This Fine Crew

0700 Day 4

Paul Newman

"Klaxon" is one of my favorite Human words. I am told it does not come from English-Human, but originally from some combination of other Terran tribes, one of which is called Greasy-Human. It means some combination of a machine produced sound and a shriek. It is also very close to a Teek word for the same, which is probably the best evidence that it was named for how it sounds, even light years apart with very differently evolving languages. At the Olympus Mons Academy for the Interstellar Initiative, klaxons had to be programmed for optimal reception for all our ranges of hearing.

Just seconds after the last member of our first trial squad confirmed her identity, the station's klaxons sounded, calling us to attention and making communication very difficult. We knew certain signals and sounds from running the emergency drills. Each of us knew that this was a kind of drill. I assumed it was a first test, a way of seeing what each squad was capable of.

Our wrist devices vibrated and the screen showed our squad's number and color designation in addition to a new destination. We followed the directions at a fast trot, out of our ready room and into the corridor. Two other squads of five cadets had already been cleared. One group of all Humans was running at full Martian sprint.

Shin yelled, "Pick up the pace!" so we did, as if we were racing. It hardly occurred to me at the time that we *were* racing, toward the hangers and the sectionally sealed garages.

I was the last to arrive in our next room, where another console was set up. This room had more cameras and a Red Terrain Vehicle, a six-wheeled tank, pointing toward a locked and air-sealed door. In other words, pointed outside to the Martian surface.

Lidstrom waved me over, saying, "Paul, come on! It needs all five of us." He wore a smile when he said this, welcoming rather than ordering. I scanned my wrist, completing our squad and the video monitor began playing.

The face of Commander Claude Poissonier appeared, with shorter hair than he'd had this morning, indicating a pre-recording. I heard the hiss of the RTVs rear door opening as well, clearly prepped for our arrival and successful sign in.

The commander addressed us. "Squad, your clock has already begun on your first scenario. I will provide directions on this console, and there will be prompts inside the vehicle."

That was apparently enough for some of my squad, for they split off and started toward the RTV. Shin was the first away. Kesiel hummed and followed. Lidstrom was unsure of which was more important. Arrksh remained, squatting low on her haunches so she was only centimeters taller than me, her arms folded across her chest.

"This scenario and task is being given to squads in waves," the commander continued. "You all have the same directions and the same equipment. This task was set up so you cannot do it alone. It will take all of your training and skillsets working together. So let us begin."

"Hey!" Shin called from the RTV while the commander started laying out the directions. "They have stations in here. One of them's life support!"

This overlapped with, "Your Arteevee has been set up with some simulated functions disabled and it is your job to set them up in order to make a surface drive to a destination in order to complete a time-sensitive task. Even though you will be restoring this Arteevee for functional use, the danger is simulated, so things like life support are fully functioning, even though you have to configure the simulation to proper parameters."

Arrksh made a chuffing sound. Apparently, that amused her.

Shin, however, had not heard this last and called out again, "We need the science officer to start on the life support!"

Lidstrom, who had been hovering between the console and the tasks tried a different tactic. "Hey, Paul, are you good to listen and relay the directions?"

"Yes, Cadet Lidstrom," I told him.

After a quick nod and a "Thanks," Lidstrom got Arrksh's attention and started her toward the RTV.

Fortunately, I had every ability of hearing and understanding two conversations at once, even if I could only act on one at a time, so I did not miss any of the commander's information.

The overall task made a great deal of sense for a newly formed, cooperating squad, and it began with distributed maintenance tasks. The pilot was meant to reconfigure the operating controls for optimal use over the terrain. The engineer was to find and fix some hindrance on the accelerators. The science officer—in our case, medic—was to set up proper life-support parameters, including atmospheric pressure, albeit simulated. The communications specialist—in our case, me—was to arrange our scanning and signaling systems. Finally, our military track specialist, Security Cadet Shin, was to properly configure our simulated weapons and shields.

I continued listening to the directions, but I began rigging a configuration of my own.

Lidstrom had given me an idea.

* * *

Arrksh

While the arthropod continues to hear the directions, I make my way to the ground vehicle, known to them as an Arteevee.

It is surprisingly large within—not spacious or comfortable, but more than large enough. It is segmented, much like the arthropod, into a fore, mid, and aft section, each with bulkhead-style doors that could shut rapidly in the event of breach. Having lived on the far riskier Belbehan vessels, I naturally look to the emergency panels, which supply masks, oxygen, and emergency sealants. Of course, any danger we might experience during this mission is simulated, so the safety features are not as important as they might be otherwise. We will be wearing helmets and probably seat restraints, and I notice—with amusement—that the helmets are already properly shaped for the range of species; mine is by far the largest.

The shorter Human, Lidstrom, has already made his way to the far front of the largest compartment and seated himself in the pilot's chair. He works at a virtual interface at impressive speed. The other

Human, Shin, is past the virtual part of her setup and is now physically adjusting and orienting the weapons and shields from within the craft. The lizard has slipped out of sight, but I can only imagine she has found an undercrawl where she can deal with our propulsion systems.

I see a "life support" station, as designated by the Human script I now recognize, as well as the universal symbols we've been taught. The interface begins as virtual, partially holographic, with a camera and reference plate for my movements. I swipe my wrist device by the scanner. It asks to confirm my species and preferred language, and I acknowledge.

From there, the directions are brief; I assume they are more thorough at Paul Newman's console. As the medical staff of the craft, I am to check and adjust the life-support parameters before we depart. As the science cadet, regardless of my specialization, I also have the responsibility of interpreting some scans while on our journey, an aspect with which I'm less familiar.

Just before I click past the virtual interface, I am issued a warning: if, at any point, the simulated environment is not able to sustain the crew, the program will abort, and the Arteevee will return to the base on its own accord. I wonder if the others are receiving similar warnings.

I hear Shin cursing at her instruments. Even if I don't understand the words, Human tone is incredibly easy to interpret for emotion. It's as plain to me as the Teek chromae.

I hear the hiss and slither of scales and tail just before I see Kesiel emerge from below.

"Success!" she declares, in Human, then repeats for my benefit in Tsanghar. I have no way of knowing if she has already completed her task, whereas I am only beginning mine.

Of course, I can only suspect the specifics of each crew member's task based on their area of focus. I suppose I will not know how effective they are at each task until we have completed the scenario.

I am familiar with Lidstrom's overnight reputation and for some reason I want to trust Kesiel's innovation skills.

Paul Newman then enters the Arteevee to give me faith in his abilities.

* * *

Kesiel

The first scenario was an impressive concoction of controlled and variable problems that tested our skills individually and in tandem, as well as our tenacity and reaction time.

The initial instructions did not say "race," and yet that was the common interpretation. That we knew we were competing with others was enough, even if we did not have any way of monitoring at what stage they were.

For my part, I have always adored the strange symmetry of engine systems, especially those with gears. I will not say that there is always a way to increase efficiency, but in this case, they left me so much room to play! Six wheels to operate at independent speeds with various degrees of control for turns, stops, and anything else. How could I not hike up our forward speed, our power, albeit with some minor sacrifices to our control on the rusty surfaces of Mars? Of course, I was given a note that should we "stall" or "burn out," according to the scenario, we would be returned to the base—slowly and in shame.

Naturally, I did not see a point in playing particularly safe. After all, high-risk success would speak much more highly of us than a poor comparative performance due to safety.

I finished in the undercarriage while the others were still working on their stations. Paul had yet to begin.

Paul Newman did impress us, however, by bringing the full scenario instructions into the Arteevee.

"Squadmates," he said in that flat artless voice I was growing to adore, "I have relayed the signal through my wrist device. We can listen here while we work."

I assisted Paul in the quick adjustment of the internal speaker systems, and I soon heard the voice of another Teek—a recorded officer—telling us about the scenario objectives beyond fixing the vehicle. They gave a description of a heading, an object to scan, and an obstacle on our return. Here they finally indicated that we would be evaluated on "our quick completion of the task, as compared to other squads." In other words, a race.

I hummed with delight, convinced that none of the other teams were anywhere near as far along as we. As I was already finished with my part, I could easily be of aid to Paul Newman. He did not seem particularly troubled by the interface as he arranged the proper thresholds for the scanners, but he was very grateful to send me onto the roof of the craft to physically adjust the signal array. With no claws to get in the way and effective gripping fingers, I did not need to go to the ladder to climb it, and I had Paul in my earpiece, giving me quick instruction for fixing the signal mount.

While above, I happened to notice one of our instructors, or perhaps evaluators, observing through a window, which separated us from an office on the second floor, just above where we entered. The observer faced the Arteevee from the rear and could see the airlocked garage door. I believed I recognized this Human woman as "Clancy," and I gave her a wave and a grin from my position.

Paul's voice in the earpiece interrupted my grand moment atop the vessel. "That is ideal, Cadet Kesiel," he said, likely unaware of his delicious soundplay. "Our signal should be much clearer."

I acknowledged, humbly making note of my handiwork. I was about to climb back the way I had come, when, with a glance up at the observation window, I changed course and made my way down the side of the craft. I had a feeling—call it a tingle of the fins—that there was more to observe on the outside.

Sure enough, I discovered a present on our rear wheels, left by our dear instructors. It was a kind of clamp, like an extra compression brake, which would doubtless counter some of our thrust, had been installed. Clearly, not every obstacle was declared outright. I took a moment to remove the hindering device and held it up toward the same observation window. I noticed Clancy had been joined by another party, Commander Claude, who must have been making his way from garage to garage to check progress. They knew of my ingenuity, even if my fellow crew would not.

Once again within, I saw that Shin was still working on our shield apparatus—faux shield for the purposes of the exercise. Naturally, I moved to assist.

"Back off; I got it," she said, so suddenly that I actually bared teeth on instinct.

At least I refrained from any direct confrontation.

I continued toward the front of the vessel and adjusted a seat so the back would allow for a tail, or a Teek abdomen. This proved to be more foreign to me than fixing the engine, but I was thankful for the Human's attempt at modular design.

While strapping myself in I heard young Lidstrom taking the opposite approach of his planetkin Shin.

"Hey, Paul," he said, "some of these controls are set up for four arms rather than two. Can you help me re-map the functions?"

Paul Newman was happy to oblige.

* * *

Lidstrom

I think I was only vaguely aware of any of the surrounding noise, including comments directed at me, as I readied for takeoff. I even had to remind myself that I wasn't looking to clear the ground...unless the moguls of frozen rust acted as jumps.

Shin made some crack about being stuck on an experimental squad, and Kesiel said something in English about the gamemakers being very sly. Paul was a wizard at reconfiguring systems, and Arrksh...Well, despite being the largest of us in height, girth, weight, and ability to crush with her bare hands, she was impressively silent.

I had pulled up the map, portions of which were only viewable with Paul's rejiggering of the scanning systems, and was mapping out and mentally timing some of the maneuvers, when Paul told me he had finished adapting the controls for two-handed use.

I think I startled Paul with the volume and fervor of my response. "Excellent! All right, are we ready to kick this sucker off?" I asked, adrenaline most likely impacting my word choice. I assumed Paul's confusion and didn't even bother to guess about Arrksh or Kesiel's interpretation, so I clarified, "Are we ready to go?"

We had already sealed up the rear hatch, and Paul had pulled up the request to open the garage. It was waiting for five checked systems, five statements of all-clear.

"Communications, ready," Paul said.

"Helm, ready," I added.

"Engines, ready," Kesiel said, practically singing.

"Weapons and shields are go," Shin said. Paul punched it in, but I paused to look back at her, and I realized she was frustrated.

Arrksh made a growling sound, almost as a response to Shin. Then she clicked on her translator, and the robot voice said, "Life support is ready."

Paul input the last check and submitted the request. The confirmation appeared in the form of a green light and a written display. If someone in observation was punching in our approval, they clearly did not delay. Almost immediately, I heard the *whoosh* of air being sucked into the garage's O2 reclaimers, so that as little atmo as possible would be lost when the outer door opened. A klaxon, complete with flashing lights, started above the garage door, indicating imminent exposure to near-vacuum outside. The inner door opened, then the outer, slowly revealing the bright orange expanse of Mars.

"I have programmed the navpoint, Lidstrom," Paul Newman said. "And scanners show no signs of other Arteevees yet."

"Excellent. Keep your helmets on and your hands and arms inside the vehicle."

The outer door finished opening, and I gunned the accelerator.

* * * * *

Chapter Twenty-Six:
Lidstrom

I want to make something clear from square one: we were winning.

More importantly, *I* was winning. Sure, the whole thing was meant to be a "team effort," and I'd never say this to an academy instructor, but the fact of the matter is this: it was a race, and I was in the driver's seat. Like hell I was going to let any other team beat us, experimental squad or not.

At our velocity, the reduced planetary grav was doing little to temper the impact of each ice mogul we launched over. I thought Shin was going to lose her lunch, which—to be honest—I wouldn't have been able to tell from the rest of the group, different species being what they are.

Paul had his two primary arms busy with the scanning equipment, but one of his secondary hands was ready to pull the backup E-brake, should the helmsman fail to do so.

I could hear Kesiel humming in the seat behind me, each time I overcame a terrain obstacle with greater speed rather than erring on the side of caution.

Careening along the frozen hills of Mars on six beautifully balanced wheels, I knew that our craft was safety-rated from here to eternity and back, so there was no real risk. Academy-contrived obstacles mixed with natural formations kept it challenging. The dummy fire sounds from our sensors and our mounted cannon only added to the sense of adventure. The whole event was fulfilling a fantasy, greater than my first jet around good ol' Luna. If the camera evidence had survived, I bet I would have been grinning like an idiot right up until Paul got the bogey signal.

"Cadet Lidstrom," he addressed me, fast but formal through his clicking mandibles, "unidentified signal fifteen degrees right of heading." His large eyes pulsed with yellow luminescence, bright enough for me to see in the corner of my vision.

"Forward display," I told him, and the info was immediately projected on a portion of the front transparency. Sure enough, there was an unknown object signalling, on a frequency that would primarily be used for distress if I remembered my emergency training correctly.

"Is that for us?" asked Shin from the gun mount.

"Nothing in the briefing indicated distress signals," Paul stated. I had to tell myself that this was not an objection to checking it out. In fact, as he spoke, he populated the screen with information that I didn't really understand, but I could see the numbers shifting and changing.

"Apologies, Lidstrom. I am having trouble getting a lock on the signal." Paul had dropped "cadet" from my address as though he now had a challenge hard enough to fluster him.

I maintained breakneck KPH, but my eyes had always been excellent. I squinted into the distance, at the closer horizon and bright red surface of Mars, and I spotted the source. The shape was familiar enough to me. Even from a distance, I was pretty sure I had spied one of our external vehicles, all six wheels turned up to the stars. It was so weirdly fitting to see an overturned Arteevee—somewhere between ironic, predictable, and inserted by the instructors for my benefit. But I had to keep my attention on the off-road, so I asked, "Paul, is that an Arteevee?"

"I am not—" He cut off suddenly, and his chromae shifted greener. "I see it, Lidstrom. Yes, it appears to be a Red Terrain Vehicle."

Kesiel hummed a high note that morphed into, "Intriguing. Do we have time to check?"

Arrksh grunted something in reply, but I didn't catch it, and her translator did not give me any info.

"Wait, what if it's one of the other squads?" Shin asked, but in the tactical position, she had to see that every other squad was way, way behind us.

I shook my head and said, maybe a little too confidently, "I think it's a hidden objective. Paul, was it hard to find?"

Paul Newman clicked to himself, considering, his exoskeletal fingers working furiously for maybe a second before he informed us, "It is obscured by interference."

"Sounds like a bonus to me," Shin said, then she asked me just the right question: "Lidstrom, can you get us close without losing our lead?"

The Arteevee would have answered for me if it could, spraying red dust and ice in its wide wake. I admit, I did not run any mental calculations, but a quick glance at my rear sensors assured me. "Hell yeah! I got this."

So I veered.

Shin laid down some cannon fire in an arc behind us—tiny, non-lethal silicon scattershot—to kick up enough dust that even the closest pursuer would lose our visual heading. We were going in for a quick scan, maybe a grab with one of the external crane arms, hopefully all of it before our dusty wake settled.

I had maybe another half-k to go when Paul's eyes suddenly glowed a shallow blue, and his jaw clicked wildly. He only managed one English word: "Peculiar!"

Before I could ask, I was overcome with a sound, a voice, a shrill screech. I shut my eyes for an instant, then opened them to see where I was driving, but everything was awash in that strange blue light. If I thought it would do any good, I might have tried to plug my ears.

Paul didn't have the luxury of closing his eyes, but his primary hands covered them and his antennae.

Shin had half fallen from her pivoting cannon chair, both palms cupping her ears, which told me the sound wasn't just in my head, even though I surmised it went beyond normal hearing range.

Kesiel bared her teeth in something that resembled a smile but which I recognized as predatory. A rattling hum escaped her throat, in a way that didn't harmonize with the screech.

Only the P'rukktah, halfway into the spaceworthy compression overlay, appeared to weather this unexpected cacophony with grace. In blocky computer-generated words, her translator pulsed out, "What...is...that?"

Facing forward again, I was able to see the signs of wreckage ahead and of distressed ground. I think I was about to ask if I should turn away when the choice was taken from me.

An explosion under our vehicle heaved us upward, nose first. Even with four wheels off the ground and fine red powder blocking my view, I prepared for a course correction to recover our heading or even to stop and assess what had felt like a bomb.

A second blast, larger than the first, pushed us from behind, probably just off my right rear wheel, spraying more particulates and lifting us again.

One screech was replaced with another. Where the first was almost organic, this new one was clearly the sound of tearing metal.

The safety belt caught my collarbone hard as my body tried to torque out of the seat. Keeping my eyes open, I saw one of our tires—maybe two thirds of a tire—whip off into the distance on a strange trajectory, made even stranger by the fact that the horizon was spinning.

The reptile cried out, something I couldn't hope to interpret, and a loud *crunch* accompanied Shin's collision with the inner wall of our vehicle.

I was turned sideways and jarred and still trying, futilely, to coax our Arteevee forward, while five wheels spun helplessly against nothing. I couldn't tell when we stopped moving, but I was pretty sure we were nearly upside down, and there were hissing and blaring sounds everywhere. The front transparency was pressed against dirt. The strange blue light and distant shrill were still in my head.

"Paul!" I shouted, but my voice sounded foreign to me.

Paul's chromae went blue-white and his compound eyes retreated into his skull. He shut his mandibles tight and pulled all his limbs against his torso, looking more like a dead bug than any Teek I'd ever seen.

An echoing squeal merged with the ringing cacophony and turned into Tsanghar speech, which Kesiel eventually translated into English. "We're venting!"

I turned to see her rushing to the torn metal and trying to use the quick foam to seal the breach. It was a jagged slash, the kind made by a horror villain's rusty knife.

I coughed, a natural reaction to feeling like you suddenly don't have enough air or have had the wind knocked out of you but unhelpful on Mars.

"Mask," said a shockingly calm mechanical voice behind me. The P'rukktah appeared to be walking only slightly askew, having managed to hang on through the mad spin. She repeated a growling word that came through as, "Mask."

With shaking hands, I finally let go of the controls and scrambled desperately to put on the emergency gear. I know it's a cliche, but I protected my fingers first. The bulky gloves slipped on over the moderately insulated flightsuit and cinched at the wrists, their heated coils and pressure tech protecting my fingers in the event of the intolerable cold vacuum outside, which was making its way gradually inside. The thick fingers interfered with my application of my helmet's facemask, until I realized that one of the catches had broken off. Probably banged against something while we were spinning.

I wanted to check for a concussion. I wanted to unstrap and help Shin. I wanted the horizon to go back to being in front of me and horizontal. Most of all, I wanted the damn noise in my head to shut up and let me listen to the hiss of escaping air instead.

It looked like Paul had fully shut down into that insect-like hibernation his kind is famous for. Kesiel gasped and wheezed before she collapsed, her unguarded hands blistering, and ballooning under her elastic skin.

The P'rukktah, a little too close for comfort and still intimidatingly large, grunted at me to, "Still." She held my facemask in place and started trying to seal it with that black goo that's supposed to work as a general fixative; I remember training about using it for just this sort of thing, but that feels like a dream. "Trust," said the robotic voice of her translator.

It was a comforting last thing to hear as I started to slip from consciousness.

Though it's hard to know for sure, I think I tried to tell her, "We would have won!"

* * * * *

Chapter Twenty-Seven:
Arrksh

1200 Day 4

I open my nostrils first, then my primary ears. The sound of footsteps and a door have woken me, but I keep my eyes closed. I keep my breathing slow, so my chest does not rise and fall.

Two voices, both Human. The male sounds like Commander Claude and the female is yet unfamiliar to me. Their tones are plainly obvious, even though I do not know all of the technical terms they use. Unfortunately, my translator is not in my ear to clarify, and though I have been growing stronger in interpreting Human through focus, my head hurts. There seem to be sensors on me, sticking pads affixed to my fur, machines that are ticking rhythms; I hear the give and take of both my hearts beating steadily and consider drifting back to sleep.

Still, I listen and focus all my efforts on memorizing what they say.

The woman speaks more clearly and evenly, though not as loudly. Sounds of plastic, the echo of polymer floors accompany her. She is answering a question in Human. "They must have found an early way to prevent extreme loss of pressure and O2," she says, "otherwise we'd be looking at much worse."

235

"They were fully venting by the time we arrived." The commander frets, for even below his steady speech patterns, his heart beats fast, his respiration is shallow; limbic system response for a looming crisis, not uncommon in endoskeletal organisms. I imagine him shaking his head in the Human gesture of disbelief when he says, "I feel like I'll get ostracized from the scientific community if I dare to say miracle, but there is no way they should have survived more than a minute in that state, especially the ones who couldn't get masked."

They are discussing our accident during the scenario. I must be back at the base, most likely in the Mons Academy medical ward, under the care of one or more doctors. I do not hear the bustle of cadets, either training or observing, so I wonder if the damage was serious.

Responding to the commander, the doctor begins to answer my questions as well.

"Most of them made it out with little more than bruises and chills, and they're stable now, so we can count ourselves lucky." She sets something down. A tablet perhaps, or maybe a physical clipboard for those who prefer analog. "Do you have any more information about the crash?"

"A lot more, but not all of it adds up—"

"Claude," she says—I imagine she has made physical contact with him such as a hand on the arm, or whatever Humans do to halt their fellows. "It's me. All right? I'm here as a doctor. Forget the rank and politics. Tell me whatever you think you know for the sake of the patients."

"Right. I've only got a couple of minutes before—Okay, here's what we can extrapolate after their signal went offline. They ran into a buried oxygen tank."

"What?" She echoes my own confusion, which I still don't voice.

"Yeah. Compressed O2, a big one. Used to supply one of the underground labs that's no longer in use. There might be a hundred of them around the old survey bases, in use or left behind. This one was buried and far enough off course that the sweepers didn't catch it."

"If the lab's not in use, why was the tank pressurized?"

"Negligence would be the best guess," he replies. "I checked the record; the lab was definitely marked closed."

I hear the shuffling sound of nervous feet, then the commander resumes.

"I mean, there were a combination of factors. When the squad left the garage we logged that their scenario shields were low, not properly set up before departure, which meant the agitator would rock them whenever they hit anything or took simulated fire. That extra instability with the speed they were traveling *and* an oxygen explosion under the wheels was enough to flip the Arteevee. From there, the torque of the flip and the landing on the rock ridge ripped both inner and outer hull. The craft took a huge beating, but not the crew. Even in M-grav, they were lucky to land like they did."

"All of them?"

"Yeah, it was like they fell in slow motion or something. I mean more than M-grav slow motion. Which is bizarre because the result suggests that the force would have been extreme. The size of the planet doesn't change the force of an explosion or exposure to the elements." He paces.

I consider opening my eyes, but I am intrigued enough to listen further. I wonder if they will address the blue light or the signal our Teek found.

"Right."

"And on your end?" he wonders.

"Right." Her voice takes on a new tone, different enough that I almost miss most of her words. "Official report: They all suffered from exposure, but some more than others depending on how much of a seal they got on their masks. Cold, low pressure. Doesn't seem like we're dealing with any long-term effects of oxygen deprivation. Some contusions, no broken bones."

"So just the one coma."

"Yes, as far as I can tell, but I haven't done much work with Tsangaree or P'rukktah, and even Jane-Two is working out of a textbook on this one, so we're really not certain. For one, I've had to induce sleep for the Tsanghar because the painkillers were not working. She'll probably need to fully shed her outer layer of skin to recover."

"But that's okay for them."

"Yes, according to everything I've read, but I'm not exactly able to consult anyone right now, am I?"

"True."

"Look, Claude, there's something else, and I'm telling you now because it's not in my official report. I've run brain scans on all five of them, and they're all showing evidence of psychic interference."

"Wait, like—"

"Like the Tsangharee who swallowed their tongues on the trip in. No mapped trauma and no evidence of a synaptic assault, but…something."

"Hmm."

"Maybe there's some credence to the Separationists." She says this word differently too, and though I do not recognize it, I hear a form of respectful fear around it. "For all we know, the psychic fields of Teek and Tsangharee really aren't supposed to interact."

The commander makes chopped "mm-mm," sounds. Then, "No. Not yet. We don't share this. Not until we know more. We're not sinking the interspecies part of the Initiative on some bigoted hunch—"

I hear clicking footfalls before he does, but he drops into silence when the door opens. I would have been able to tell him it is a single Teek.

"Commander," she acknowledges. Then, "Doctor."

"Jane," the doctor says, "how are the others?"

"Stable," says Jane the Teek, but a different "Jane" than Jane Austen. "Paul Newman is being set up to commune with an off-hive drone to revive him from hibernation. His *jiki* wishes to be admitted to see him."

The commander responds, "Not yet. Debrief first. Once we get the all-clear."

"Understood. And the P'rukktah?" Jane asks.

With my eyes closed and my breathing unchanged I hope they still read me as asleep. And yet, I do not glean nearly as much from the Teek tones as those of the Humans. She approaches me, possibly to inspect some of the machinery, but she neither attempts to rouse me nor broadcasts my ruse.

Another pair of people enter, now enough that I cannot easily keep track of who is where and what they are saying. Still, the voice is unmistakable: Admiral Victoria Hass, whom I have heard over video and met in person. The servos in her mechanical wrist and hand are quiet enough that they would be silent to Human ears, but they are also familiar to me.

"Tell me the P'rukktah is unharmed," she says quickly, forcefully.

The doctor does not disappoint. "She's fine. Just recovering."

"Good. The last thing I need is a dead princess to start the Initiative." Hass asks another question, "Were any of the others politically significant?"

The commander responds with, "Jesus! Vic, this was one of *my* crews and *my* responsibility, whether they're the son of a royal or a ditch digger."

"I understand your position, Claude. Now try to understand mine. I am balancing a delicate working alliance based on the cooperation of several different species. We could lose it all if the various factions and houses out there even start a rumor of attempted assassination. Now, apart from Arrksh, is there anyone with important political ties?"

The commander makes a *tch* sound with his tongue in something like a scoff. Then he relents and says, "No. Neither Shin nor Lidstrom come from well-known families. I think Kesiel was a relative unknown—very clever, but a declawed engineer from a small motherhood on a small moon. Really, Paul Newman's the only other one with a distinct connection. He was Bertha's first pick—"

"She'd understand," the admiral says confidently. "Bertha and I have enough history between us."

I wonder if I've heard the name Bertha before in reference to the W-War, but I quiet my mind as the admiral approaches my bed.

The next question from the admiral feels as if it is directed at me. "So is there any evidence of sabotage?"

"No. Not yet. There was more debris than I'd expected to find. We can speculate, but—"

"I want you to rule out sabotage."

The commander hesitates a moment. "You mean you want me to find evidence to prove it isn't sabotage."

"No, I want you to rule it out." She is resolute on this point, speaking so assuredly that she is one of the easiest Humans for me to fully comprehend. "Let's let this be an accident. Understood?"

"Understood, Admiral," comes out in various timbres and levels of enthusiasm from the others in the room.

"Good. Send me their statements when they're coherent enough to give them. I'll issue a debriefing before I head back to Phobos."

The commander replies, "Thank you, Admiral." She swiftly departs, leaving the others to either trickle out after her or remain.

The footsteps are neither loud nor many.

I do not know who is still present until Teek Doctor Jane says, "Doctor Koba, you should take a break and find something to eat. I can remain."

"Yes, you're right," she agrees and says on her way out the door, "Thanks, Jane-Two."

The Teek approaches me. "You can open your eyes now, Cadet Arrksh. They are gone."

I do so. The Teek is leaning over me, very close given her small stature, and I assume the height of the hospital bed. My eyes are sore, pressured, and my vision is blurry, but I can still see the Teek's chromae are a soft yellow, for "minor concern" if I am interpreting correctly.

"I hope that was informative," she says in a manner that I think is sincere, "even if you don't speak Human."

"Speak" being the operative word.

I start to sit up. Signaling devices pull at me as I lean forward, and Jane-Two assists in removing the little monitors attached to my neck. I am not sure if she is showing a doctor's or a Teek's sensibilities with her physical interaction. I have to remind myself that Teek workers do not experience any form of sexual urges or interaction, and, as such, they have no sense of modesty where it pertains to nudity or touching another's sensitive areas. I am pleased to know that none of these sensors are currently between my thighs and that I am still wearing my flightsuit, even if the sleeves are rolled up and the shoulder snaps are undone for better access to my neck, back, and chest.

"Very good," Jane-Two says.

I want to ask a question, but she is right that I do not speak enough Human. Without thinking, I ask for my translator in P'rukktah.

"I do not speak Irrukktir," she responds, surprisingly using the proper name for my language. "I have a new translator for you though."

I laugh a little at the irony. My eyes continue to gradually adjust, for even this dim light looks bright to me. I can see well enough when the short arthropod hands me a translation device. Jane-Two is indeed a Teek, in particular an extramani, or four-armed, who looks very similar to Paul Newman, enough that a notably different uniform is helpful in distinguishing them. She wears a kind of lab coat and does not seem to have the usual flightsuit underneath. The rank insignia on her shoulder is for a specialist, a lieutenant-equivalent in authority in her area, which I have to assume is similar to mine.

"I am Jane Goodall," she says, while I set up my translator, "named after the famous Human scientist." This does not mean anything to me. "Many of the other officers call me Jane-Two."

Once I have the translator attached and activated, I ask, "Why do I have a new device?"

This one speaks in more blocky, choppy terms than my previous.

"Your previous one was damaged during the accident." She speaks nonchalantly and her chromae have drifted to an emotionally unaffected neutral. "Possibly when you passed out and landed on it."

I refrain from cursing. Instead, I take stock by looking around the room. I had expected to see squadmates here. Instead, I see three empty beds—hospital-style modular stretchers like this one. I can see a clock, indicating that only a few Human hours have passed since we began our scenario this morning, even though it feels like I have slept considerably longer.

"Am I the last to wake?" I ask.

"No, you are the first."

I start to get to my feet and realize how much my head is opposed to this plan.

Jane-Two also indicates for me to stay seated with her right hands. "Please. You will make a full recovery either way. It will just be more pleasant if you don't strain."

"And my squad?"

"They are resting. We are once again encountering some hazards of Tsanghar physiology and psychology that were not in the primers."

This is understandable, and I consider offering my expertise. Instead, I nod evenly and let her continue.

"A drone has been arranged to help recall Paul Newman out of hibernation."

This piques my interest much more effectively. I have never seen a drone spark another Teek into waking before. I realize my intrigue could sound hollow, however, given two names that have been skipped, I must ask, "And the Humans?"

* * * * *

Chapter Twenty-Eight:
Lidstrom

1230 Day 4

I was swimming in blue light. It was so bright that it seemed to take form, like a construct from the Green Lantern's ring. I could push off it, or I could let it carry me, drifting like some kind of current. The light counteracted the gravity of the bright red-orange planet drifting up to me.

I knew it was a dream—I've had enough physics-defying flying dreams to know the difference, but I wouldn't say I was lucid or in control.

I was also aware of an overturned car on Mars, and I knew better than to drive with the convertible top down on an alien world, especially at such an early stage of Martian terraforming.

The wheels of the car were still spinning, gripping nothing. They were humming, sending a sustained revving sound through the minimal atmosphere. I wondered if the sound was conveyed by the blue light.

I swam close, swishing my way down through the blue. The hum got louder, vibrated, roared, until the sound was so loud that I sat bolt upright in the hospital bed, yanking off a number of suctioned monitors. Just out of arm's reach stood a Teek drone, sustaining the tone in a rough bellow that visibly vibrated its thorax.

My own head pounded as if a migraine and a hangover had re-produced a screaming two-year-old, and I briefly shut my eyes. The Teek drone continued and I heard some mix of tense voices trying to react to it, apparently surprised.

When I reopened my eyes, I saw that a Human in lab coat and gloves had grabbed the drone around its middle and was trying to pull it away. The drone didn't seem to resist exactly, but it clearly had a lot of inertia and no concept of being moved. Drones were typical-ly a little shorter than the average Human, but they walked on four sturdy legs and had front shoulders like a P'rukktah. All four legs were rooted to the floor while one of the manipulator arms was still in contact with a much smaller Teek worker, also in a hospital bed.

Paul Newman lay facedown, perfectly still, even with the ruckus around him.

"Paul!" I yelled, though my throat felt hoarse and raw.

A doctor hurried to my bedside and told me to lie back, I think, but I was kind of distracted by the state of Paul Newman and the giant drone that didn't want to be moved, despite the fact that multi-ple Humans were attempting to pry it free.

Another Paul-Newman-shaped Teek scurried across the room on all six limbs, then righted itself before the drone. It touched the larg-er creature with an antenna and made some rapid clicking noises with the lower mandibles.

The drone's hum turned into a whine, like a children's toy run-ning out of batteries, before the creature collapsed altogether, falling onto one of the three Humans who'd been trying to restrain it.

Amid the chaos, the doctor at my side said, "Lie back."

I did so, but at an angle so I could watch them sort out the fallen drone. The four-armed Teek who'd deactivated the large organic computer faced Paul Newman. Before they could reach him, Paul suddenly twitched awake.

Quickly, but without any sign of panic, Paul pushed his way to his feet and stood on the bed. He turned toward me first. "Cadet Lidstrom, are you all right?"

I can honestly say it hurt to laugh, but I tried to assure him, "Yeah, I'm okay. You?"

Paul assessed his surroundings, including the Teek drone on the floor and the Teek doctor standing by his bed. "I surmise I have just emerged from hibernation." Another quick check and he announced, "Cadets Kesiel and Shin have not."

Despite the doctor's efforts, I sat up again. On the other side of the room, mirroring mine and Paul's, there were two more hospital beds. Kesiel was belly-down, like Paul, but with bandages on her hands. Shin was on her back with a wrap around her head and a monitor beeping steadily.

* * *

I don't think I'd ever been told to "settle down" so many times in my life—not that my parents were big on the phrase in the first place. I remember one time when I was really little hyperventilating during a live speech from a Teek on Terran soil. And, after my joy-riding incident at fifteen, I'm pretty sure I was giddily compliant with the law enforcement.

Not today though.

First, Doctor Koba, the facility's chief physician, tried to coax me verbally. When that didn't work, she attempted to restrain me physically. I may have been dizzy, but I'm not weak. Paul Newman, bless his heartlike-organ, advised me that a "supine position was proper protocol," again in a completely calm and level manner.

I wanted to get to my squad, to check on Kesiel and Shin and figure out where they'd taken Arrksh, and I was definitely raving about the blue light. The part I'm not proud of—I practically demanded a rematch, proclaiming to the medics and instructors, who would surely view the security footage, that we had been winning.

The transitions from there turned into a bit of a blur. I didn't realize I'd been given an IV for a chemical compound meant to revitalize me after exposure to near vacuum. Up until that day, I'd never known that such a compound existed. Apparently it was one of many direct results of our cooperation with the P'rukktah, or maybe it was the Tsangharee. The IV was then used to put me in a less-than-functional state, where my mental commands to my limbs didn't seem to work on time or in the right order. It was kind of like the worst body high I could imagine from the few substances I'd tried—but denied in my application to the I.I.

Once I was safely out of commission and no longer a danger to myself or anyone else, the staff began putting the room back in order. Doctor Koba, who might have been pleasant under other circumstances, scowled at me from under her dark brows and bleached bangs while she reattached the monitors and checked my vitals. At least, I think she did, but I was later told I was not a reliable witness.

I didn't notice when the Teek drone was finally hauled away. At some point, the Teek who had dropped the drone was replaced by one who stood much taller and had wings.

Though I couldn't control my tongue, I tried to ask about the blue light and the whale song on the planet's surface. I think my woozy brain was trying to forge a connection between the hum of

Phobos and the whale song of Mars and the Mons crater ridge; the most beautiful place I'd ever seen, and now the most dangerous.

When I started mumbling my way back to sleep, I did receive one comforting answer. Arrksh showed up by my side, standing and looking surprisingly normal according to my slightly skewed perception. I think she put her hand on my shoulder, which may have been to restrain me. It's hard to say for sure in retrospect.

* * * * *

Chapter Twenty-Nine:
Paul Newman

1300 Day 4

In many cases, I enjoy puzzling at an unknown, and yet the number of unknowns in this situation were perplexing enough to be stressful rather than intriguing. It was not just the quantity, but the nature and the treatment of these mysteries.

I cannot say how much of this was due to my proximity with death and a form of cognitive dissonance about the idea of ceasing to exist so far from home. Neither my queen nor even an active home-hive drone would be able to receive my body and the remnants of consciousness. After all, I was taught not to fear individual death as long as I was performing first duty to my hive and near enough that they might retain my final thoughts, as well as much of my imprintable knowledge. A minimal fear of death, but an ingrained sense of self-preservation with a bolstered yearning to explore: I had been told that this evolutionary balance had been difficult to perfect, and even now sometimes failed with mutations and malformations.

My recent near-death encounter had occurred quite differently than anything I had been prepared for, and I had very little time or peaceful space to muse about this in the medical facilities while handling directives from a Teek Doctor called Jane Goodall. Everyone who questioned me wanted to know why we veered off course, when

251

we noticed the breech, and, finally, how we managed to stay alive in the leaking compartment.

I explained to them that there was an overturned vehicle, which we assumed was part of a test or bonus. I admitted that I lost consciousness shortly after our craft rolled, so I did not know to what degree a breech had occurred. I also observed that the I.I. staff should know better than we because it was they who rescued us.

Some of my responses confused them further, but I did not have the impression I antagonized them. There were several disconnects I observed but could not effectively interpret, so I decided to take stock in the facts.

The five of us had been in an Arteevee that had capsized and split open on the surface of Mars during a scenario. Five of us had been retrieved and stabilized in the Mons facility. Arrksh was already up and walking, and even beginning to assist the physician. Doctor Koba, a Human with yellow hair that registered in a strange, synthetic part of the spectrum, appeared both appreciative and frustrated by her aid.

I had been woken by a drone who had suffered a kind of overload, difficult to describe to species without drones, and was therefore removed. Otherwise, I felt fine and my doctor, Jane Goodall, assured me I was safe. She did not give comment or theory about the fallen drone or cause of the accident.

In the bed next to mine, Lidstrom eventually re-awoke as well. This time he calmly answered the same questions I had been given. Shortly after he was deemed lucid and physically capable, Commander Claude arrived to escort him away.

Kesiel eventually woke shrieking, clearly disturbed by her hands, which had been securely bandaged. She appeared far more damaged than the rest of us.

Finally, Shin, who appeared healthy to my untrained eye, stayed asleep, even during Kesiel's waking reaction. Doctor Jane Goodall explained plainly that Shin was in a coma. I am told this is somewhat like our hibernation, but considerably more frightening. I would not wish to fall asleep without a queen, or at least a drone, to wake me.

Commander Claude returned shortly after Kesiel woke, bringing Lidstrom back with him. Then he and Doctor Koba wheeled out the groggy, wincing Tsanghar, possibly for more tests, but I suspected a private interview more akin to an interrogation.

* * *

Admiral Victoria Hass was an intriguing mix of fierce reputation, commanding tone, and surprisingly imperfect physical stature. For one, she was shorter than the other directors of the facility, her shoulders and hips were somewhat askew, most likely the result of an injury which I could only surmise was sustained in a military action. The mobile prosthetic hand was one which, though I understood, I found unnerving, knowing an inorganic replacement would be impossible for a Teek.

However, I felt a hind-brain draw to her as soon as she entered the room, similar to what I would feel from hive authority. Officially, Humans do not have psychic presence, but I felt a commanding force in former TSF Admiral Hass.

She nodded to a couple of people as she moved to the far end of the room. Some gave her a quick salute; everyone gave respect. As soon as she passed each person, they turned to leave. An aide wearing an earpiece and eyepiece pulled up a quick recording interface and pointed it toward her. With a final signal from her gloved right hand, she dismissed Jane-Two from the room, so that the only people remaining with the admiral and her aide were Doctor Koba and we five cadets.

"Good afternoon, Cadets," she said.

"Good afternoon, Admiral," I repeated, but realized I was the only one. I felt myself grow colder while my chromae also took on cooler shades of embarrassment.

The admiral did not look sternly at me. In fact, she exhibited a small smile on one side of her thin lips. "You are all at ease. This is not a formal debriefing, but a check in. Given the nature of the accident, I wanted a chance to address you in person. And to apologize."

I heard a stirring and turned to see Lidstrom adjusting his posture while chewing his lower lip. He had clearly not expected this, and his body was hardly ready to respond.

"First of all, I am deeply sorry, on behalf of the entire Initiative, that any of you were put in such dangerous circumstances. That scenario was ruled completely safe, and, while it was monitored, no one had accounted for the possibility of running into an oxygen tank and exposing any of you to the surface.

"Second," she went on, looking up, "despite the challenge and danger, the five of you worked together to suit, mask, and protect each other, giving enough time for our rescue vehicles to arrive. I am proud of the skills and courage you demonstrated, Cadets, and you should be proud of yourselves."

I followed her gaze and I saw she was specifically regarding Arrksh. I did not know what the P'rukktah had managed to do while the craft was overturned.

"Third..." She paused long enough to swallow. "The doctors have told me that your squadmate Cadet Shin is stable and there is every hope she will make a full recovery. As for the rest of you, they will monitor your progress, but it is believed that all of you will be fine to return to training after a nominal three days' rest." She pivoted and stepped deliberately toward Kesiel. "Cadet Kesiel of Yavamee, I am told your hands will be as good as new when you next shed your skin, and again I apologize that we do not have painkillers for Tsangharee physiology."

"Mmm..." agreed a strained Kesiel. "I shall be well soon, Admiral. Thank you for the concern."

During the pause, Lidstrom shifted uncomfortably again.

"Finally, to address your future in the Initiative and the academy: after the three days, when we update the cadet squad assignments, you will return and be assigned. And, in case you are wondering, all four of you performed impressively during the portion of the scenario you completed."

Lidstrom exhaled effusively. If I had to guess, I would assume he was relieved.

I had the impression the admiral was not accustomed to this kind of direct address, but she broke form here, for her smile changed from its formal symmetry to something lopsided. Hass looked specifically at Lidstrom when she said, "I'm sure you're eager to get back into your training, and so are we. But for now, you have the remainder of the next three days to rest and recover. Progress will continue to be monitored, but you should be released soon."

Her demeanor changed again, quickly and smoothly enough that it was difficult to register. I would have missed it if her face and voice had not already been shown to many Teek, but I saw her slip back into formality without going fully into the position of attention. "Once again, I apologize for the accident and the danger it put you in, and I wish you all a speedy recovery."

Although her words did not directly state it, I knew enough about Human communication to read this as a "farewell," or a prelude to an exit. Yet, there was so much that remained unanswered.

I felt a thrum in my thorax, and my mandibles twitched. In a moment, Admiral Hass was passing me, and I had hardly begun to work up the courage to stop her.

"Wait!" It was Lidstrom who had blurted out, seemingly without thinking. Then, resuming the rank structure, "Sorry, Director Hass, I just—Can I ask you a question?"

From across the room, Kesiel hummed. Arrksh did not react.

The admiral, however, paused. "Speak freely, Cadet."

"Well, just—" He floundered and glanced at each of his non-Human crew. "What about the signal we followed? There was an overturned Arteevee and th-the blue light. What was all that?"

She paused. When she spoke it was with a slower, more deliberate cadence, like what my speech tutors would use. "Cadet Lidstrom, I was informed that you were asking about another Arteevee and a distress signal out on the surface of Mars. Your squad's feed did go out and we cannot confirm what rogue symbols you tried to interpret, but there was no other Arteevee. As for your blue light—"

"What? No—" he exclaimed. I could tell he did not wish to argue with the admiral, but still he could not contain his protest. What I saw in his eyes was not anger or defiance, but confusion and fear. He shut his mouth after realizing his outburst.

The admiral paused, granting him a courtesy that I believed she'd only extend for unique circumstances. "Go on, son," she said, in a manner that suggested a non-literal use of the familial address. "Speak your mind."

"There was a-a signal, which was weird enough. We thought it was a test, and then we saw a-a flipped Arteevee, so we went to investigate. And then when we got there—" He seemed to realize he sounded increasingly agitated. Lidstrom turned to me, and entreated, "Paul, you saw it, too."

I did not react quickly. I had not expected to be called upon to give testimony. I felt my cheeks cool with embarrassment, for I was aware of a difference in species that perhaps Lidstrom was not. "I cannot recall, Cadet Lidstrom. The space before a rapid hibernation due to danger is not stored very effectively in the Teek mind."

"Wait, so you—you don't remember?"

"Not in a clear enough manner to supply accurate account."

"But—" Once again, he looked from crew to crew. "Kesiel, you saw it."

Kesiel raised her head, extending impressively at the neck. "*Mmm*mmm. Apologies, Lidstrom. While I was intrigued by the scrambled signal, I never managed to make out your phantom Arteevee."

Lidstrom considered, but did not ask Arrksh, who would have had a worse vantage point than anyone. Shin, naturally, would not have been able to respond to inquiry.

"But what about the blue light? There was this—" Here, he did turn to Arrksh, but she remained silent. Lidstrom turned his attention down to his own hands, but they likewise supplied no answer. He did not voice anything further.

The admiral, who was waiting patiently, made an expression I was not familiar with, but which I did not read as hostile. "Cadet, you're not crazy. It is common for people suffering exposure to have disjointed recollections, and I have seen seasoned veterans supply much more outlandish narratives than yours after near-vacuum experiences. Humans often have vivid dreams and temporary dissociations in response to trauma. You may have seen and experienced a flash of blue light, but the only overturned Martian vehicle was yours."

The explanation she gave was reasonable to me, easy to accept. Even Lidstrom did not attempt to dispute it. But there was something about the way she said it which struck me as familiar, in a way I could not place.

She tapped one hand on the foot of Lidstrom's hospital bed. "Rest up. As I said, we're eager to have you return."

With that, the admiral gave an informal nod and exited. The doctor did a quick check and also slipped away, leaving the five of us alone, four alert squadmates and one sleeping Shin.

Shortly after the door closed, Kesiel turned to Arrksh and asked, "Could you render assistance?"

Arrksh shifted, then shuffled forward. Kesiel held up both hands in the bandages to the P'rukktah. I did not actually expect Arrksh to begin unwrapping them. Apparently, neither did Lidstrom.

"What are you doing?" he asked, quietly.

Arrksh said something in her first language, but her translator was not enabled.

Kesiel supplied, "Assisting. In a manner foreign to the Human doctors." She winced and hissed as one hand was revealed, a sticky salve coming away with the wrap. The skin had expanded and then deflated, stretching against its own elasticity during the pressure loss.

I did not know how painful it might be for the Tsanghar, my exoskeleton would have behaved very differently.

She said with some strain, "If you don't mind—" she lifted her chin, "—I'm feeling dry."

Arrksh paused and glanced at each of us. She saw fit to switch on her translator and the blocky voice said, "Medical purposes." Then, using one thumb she massaged the side of Kesiel's throat, which swelled in response.

There were a few other visible movements of the throat, before Kesiel tipped her head toward the revealed hand and essentially salivated on it, using her tongue to distribute the highly viscous liquid. She squeezed her eyes shut, the double lids pressing the eyes deep into the skull, not in pain but disgust. "Their medicine is so vile tasting."

Arrksh repeated the procedure for the second hand, very swiftly, using practiced motions.

I could not see any physiological change to the hand, but Kesiel's movements became less tense, indicating that her saliva was soothing or numbing the ailing flesh.

The final step was also executed too quickly for either myself or Lidstrom to properly catalog it.

Arrksh brought a palm to her mouth and pierced the skin with the tip of a tusk, causing it to bleed a largely clear blood, which she fed to Kesiel.

"What the hell are you doing?" demanded Lidstrom.

They did not stop on Lidstrom's account, but the exchange did not last long. The Tsanghar drew at the P'rukktah's blood for a few seconds more, lapped at the minor puncture with her tongue, then cleaned her own teeth in order to prevent waste.

"My gratitude, sister," said Kesiel.

Arrksh only jutted her chin out in reply. She then pulled one tiny round bandage from the medical supplies and pressed it to her palm. Rewrapping Kesiel's hands took much longer by comparison, long enough for Lidstrom to wonder again:

"Hey, what was that?"

Smiling, Kesiel informed him, "Healing, Lidstrom. This is healing."

"No, but did you just drink her blood?"

Kesiel replied, "The P'rukktah endure, and the Tsanghar adapt."

This did not seem like a thorough explanation to me. I assumed that it meant there were certain properties in the P'rukktah fluids which the Tsanghar could ingest and use. I was curious as to whether my *jiki* was aware of this.

Lidstrom took a different line of questioning. "Why didn't you just do that earlier? Or why didn't the doctors do it?"

Both Arrksh and Kesiel were struck by the question and they regarded each other as if to reach a tacit agreement. Kesiel responded first, "We do not choose to reveal everything to Humans."

Arrksh's translator added, "Dangerous."

"You understand, surely," Kesiel said.

Judging by Lidstrom's expression, I would guess that he did not. My people had of course welcomed the military minds of the Human race in our hour of need, but if we had not become allies, I did wonder if Teek hives would be just as hesitant about passing such information.

* * * * *

Chapter Thirty: Arrksh

I avoid looking Lidstrom directly in the eye until I am released by the doctors. Usually, I would not feel guilt over staying silent. Tacitly accepting, or pretending to accept, another's inaccuracies has been instrumental in my survival while between planets.

However stoic I manage to present on the surface, I am moved by Lidstrom's passion and desperation. I understand his desire to call for aid and to hope his fellows will back him; my experiences with similar circumstances were how I learned to stay silent when it is necessary for one's position, reputation, and—once again—life.

So, I respond in the affirmative to every question about stability, sanity, and safety from the doctors. I respond in the negative to the offer of extended time in the infirmary or an escort back to my quarters. I keep my lips sealed against my tusks when they ask me "if there is anything else" I might need. I give the doctor my thumbprint, which, coupled with a quick scan of the regulation wrist device, might as well be a blood oath to the Human people. Fortunately, I have not overtly lied, so if there *is* a blood oath, my spirit is safe.

I cannot ignore, however, that I *do* remember Lidstrom's blue light, even if not the overturned vehicle. I find myself on edge and expectant as soon as I've donned my boots and reentered the public corridors. All three ranges of my ears are on high alert, scanning every corner, ready to respond to that indescribable pitch, which I am certain was present prior to the explosion which turned us. I too had felt a strange presence, and I know that I had not properly sealed the gaps in the land craft or affixed all of the masks before I lost consciousness. I also know that I am being given some credit for maintaining my squad's lives, and I realize my ministrations should not have been enough.

Something does not add up. I am neither an engineer nor interested in the theoretical, non-applicable sides of science, but I *know* something about that encounter was amiss. Both the explosions—two not one—and our survival strike me as odd. Too odd to be effectively planned, but also not wholly random.

As always, I am incapable of fully escaping politics, so the threat of assassination is more than a peripheral thought.

In the Nexus surrounding the Uua's garden, the informational screens still indicate that waves of squads are running their opening scenario. I imagine this is taking place in controlled, indoor environments using virtual interfaces. I scoff at the idea, aware of my own disdain. Once again, I am amused by how bureaucratic and timid the Humans are in their home system considering their reputation just a few stars away.

Perhaps with more cadets about, I can gauge from their tones and expressions how they felt and infer what they had experienced. However, it seems I am alone, and that everyone else is otherwise assigned to a squad task, a briefing, or a designated waiting room. I pass only one non-ranking Human custodian on the way back to my room. None of the other females who share my space are present when I arrive; no one growls or snarls at me.

I sense enemies are ready to assault me from any angle. I prefer to see them gather, hear their threats, determine when it is best to talk, fight, or run.

For someone who so rarely had a permanent home or bed, I am surprised by how much I long for one today, and how much the cadet bunk offends me. Not its construction, but the fact that it will be alone save for myself. I do not know if I long for the comforting embrace of a parent or the rush of shared space with a lover, but the solitude is a sudden and deafening blow.

This sensation is stronger than a yearn; it is a voracious hunger, a need for contact and reconnection the likes of which I can hardly claim in memory. I know what it was to dine and sleep amongst tiny rats and not think once of my lost mother.

Once again, I shut out all distracting memories to focus on the present matter. I must make use of this solitude while I have it. I can further guarantee such in the lavatory, where I shut and lock the door behind me.

I waste no time. I activate the full mirror and begin filling the bath. Before the steam has clouded any of the reflective surface, I remove my flightsuit and inspect every patch of skin and fur. I know my body better than the doctors, and I will judge if I have changed since my surface encounter.

I see…no physical evidence whatsoever. I can tell my posture has lengthened and some of my muscles have lost a bit of their tone in the lower gravity environments since my arrival to this planet, but my shoulders and neck are still my own. My thighs are still impressive for a space-dwelling P'rukktah, the sinews apparent where the fur is shorter and paler. Each of my hands and feet check out, as do my nose and my ears, all three canals on each side in perfect working order. My eyes, however, are somehow different, indescribably so. It is as if I am seeing a picture-perfect, statuesque copy of myself in full immodest glory; and yet it is not exactly me.

"Psychic interference..." I echo the doctor's words as I recall them. Carefully overheard and retained, now repeated into my translator to confirm. I do this with every peculiar phrase I latch onto, to build a picture, then a suspicion.

The tub is full. It is too hot, painfully hot, but absolutely necessary.

I step in, one foot at a time as I pray to the all-mother, even though I am several systems away from her planet and influence. I pray as I have not done since I was a child.

I take a deep breath and pitch backward, submerging myself in the water, feeling the sting as the water enters my ears, causing the sensitive tissue to swell and then to block them off. I open my mouth and allow the heat to temporarily overwhelm my sense of taste. My smell has already gone from my nose. Finally, with little more than a steadying wince, I open both eyes and let them heat, until I can see nothing. Other than my overtaxed nerves, I have shut off all external sensations.

I am now free to seek memory.

It takes me longer than I like to focus and find with precision the memory I seek. I have to wade through glimpses of my homeworld, of the well-worn terraced path, and the scarred and pitted hands of my father as he teaches me to find awareness and center. I push ahead, through years of running and redirecting, hunger and loneliness, of the rattling engines of the first Belbehan vessel I crewed on, where I would bump my head on the low ceiling. A captain with a split tail—a genetic anomaly that he was too proud of to let me fix—and a rudimentary aft filtration system, which I am more than certain was held together by collective consciousness.

The same was not true for this morning's sojourn across Mars-Human. The craft was built better but crewed by disparate people working at cross purposes and individual aims, even when on a common mission. Five beings, including myself, forward in the craft.

I had been near the back of the main cabin, the first bulkhead door nearby. A Human, Shin, had been closest to me; her heart beating rapidly, her breathing shallow. She had failed to properly deploy the simulated forcefield system. Incompetence, not sabotage.

Three beings ahead occupying as many seats. There were several touch screens, analog controls, and a transparency, a hard glass composite that could adjust on high impact to flex without shattering. Through the transparency, the planet's scarred landscape to our right.

When Lidstrom and Paul Newman found the signal, had I turned ahead? Had I looked? There was a blue light, but not from a fixed point or source. Somehow, I knew that it had some direction, a traceable vector, though I felt it was both outside and inside the craft; barriers didn't matter.

The decision was made to investigate, taking us off course. Possible ill intent, but unlikely.

I began squinting when we were thrown. Perhaps just an oxygen tank—scraped and pitted, finally rupturing below layers of rusted dirt—perhaps not. I saw Shin fall, then Kesiel shifted; my nonconscious system had taken over, forcing my body to react, reaching for grip points on the walls and righting myself as we tumbled...

To a softer landing. I cannot explain, but I would compare it to being caught by a net which had ripped. My lungs remind me of my need to breathe, but I am still in the craft.

It has tipped and torn. Not a large hole, but enough to be deadly.

A rapid change in pressure.

The lizard unbelts, tries to foam seal the gash in the hull. Not sabotage; personal risk and danger to swelling hands.

The tactical Human is limp, possibly dead. Triage dictates moving to the pilot Human.

No, first the P'rukktah must save herself, or at least delay oxygen deprivation and exposure, by affixing her own mask.

The Teek has begun to curl into hibernation. No known reason for sabotage.

The blue light surrounds.

Six beings in the craft. The sound from the sixth overwhelms.

I cannot breathe.

I gasp. I claw at the sides of the bathtub, work my way up from the water. I am dimly aware of knocking.

My hearts pump irregularly; one side of my chest is sore. I check my ears and feel them gradually make their way back to a livable temperature.

The knocking—literal, present—has been dull, but grows louder. The door to these facilities is neither soundproof nor impervious. There is a voice which I cannot interpret yet, but I am aware of it.

I feel my way toward standing. I shake off the vertigo and disorientation. The scent of the steam is sweet, synthetic, and tinged by iron, like the rapidly oxidizing low atmosphere of Mars-Human. It gives me an idea of how to respond to the voice I cannot interpret.

"I am washing off the Human infirmary smell," I say, aware that I sound somewhat breathless after several minutes underwater. I don't need to seek her gratitude over so common sense an action as a courtesy deodorizing. I am sure they do not want their space smelling of Human rivals any more than it has to.

From the other side, I hear a grumble, which I believe is an acknowledgment. My lower ears have adjusted enough to recognize a word that means "congratulations for your safety."

I express gratitude.

My head is awash with ideas, excitement and fear, but now that the cadets have begun to return from scenarios, I must slow my hand and most likely my jaw.

* * * * *

Chapter Thirty-One:
Lidstrom

Paul and I had a couple more hours to recoup in the infirmary after Arrksh left. We were told Kesiel would not be released until later, most likely after a full shedding had occurred.

We were each subjected to our own battery of tests and check ins. I did wonder if I'd get to spend some time in the tank with the Avowol, get a real brain scan from a first-person-plural space jellyfish, but apparently it was too early to introduce non-standard Human brainwaves to the acclimating xeno-psychologist. I tried not to take offense at the remark, coming from the neutral voice of Jane-Two. I noticed they did not opt for such treatment for Paul or Kesiel, either.

The combined efforts of Paul and Kesiel got our wrist devices reconnected with the general network, at least on the receiving end, so we could get updates on what was happening outside of the white walls. Eventually a feed was switched on in our room, but I was happy for the time-occupying effort.

The academy news was uninteresting. Most of the information was focused on the ever-updating schedule, including class redistributions and cancellations. Some of it was pretty standard, but several of the changes smacked of a reaction to the first scenario, even if they didn't formally blame our accident. We found the public statement about the event itself and the debris and were pleased to find the line "no fault of the cadets" included. There was no mention of either the overturned Arteevee or of the fact that Shin was in a coma. No scores had been posted for public or private access, and there was no indication of any squad redistribution either. I wondered who, if anyone, was getting blamed. Paul noticed that some of the instructors' names did not appear on the schedules anymore, including Admiral Hass and Lieutenants Gordon and Chandan—the last of whom specialized in "adaptive forcefields" in a military capacity. How this related to damage control, I could not say.

When I prompted Paul to look up our names—narcissist that I am—he found that for all five of us, squad assignment and schedule listed "No Information Available," even after our three-day break.

I did my best to hide my disappointment, but I didn't try to dig in deeper while in the infirmary.

There were a few minor arguments among various staff before we were given the all-clear, including at least one additional doctor and a very tense consultation outside our room. I know the Human doctor, Koba, wanted to hold Paul longer—something about the drone passing out when drawing him out of hibernation. Jane-Two insisted there was nothing to worry about and eventually won.

Koba told me, "I expect to see you back here first thing tomorrow morning to take another scan." Then she glared at Jane-Two until her colleague repeated similar instructions to Paul.

Eventually, we were dismissed. I waved to the waking, wincing Kesiel and solemnly nodded toward the sleeping Shin.

As we left, Paul Newman touched my arm and said, "I hope we will be assigned together again when we return to duty."

I think I gave him a half-smile. I wasn't prepared for his positive reaction, and I wish I had acknowledged it. The truth was, I would rather have talked to Paul than the dozens of other chirpy interrogators I encountered throughout the evening.

* * * * *

Chapter Thirty-Two:
Paul Newman

The original Ella Fitzgerald had been a Human female known for her voice. She lived in the twentieth century of what is known as accurately recorded Human history. She honed a very singular voice that I am told has not been matched since. The voice itself was an impressive "instrument" to Human audiences, and the musician who employed it developed styles through improvisation that heavily influenced music development in her own century and then again in the mid-twenty-first. For Teek, the original Ella Fitzgerald's voice is haunting; to some it is literally terrifying. It reminds us of an enraged queen, whose signals vibrate through our heads and could elect to end our lives.

My *jiki* chose the name with this quality in mind, to be as powerful as something feared. She told our tutors that because the enemy could invade our sounds and signals she needed to embody something frightening. She also had more control of her speaking pitch than most Teek I had met, and she used this in order to be heard in loud environments, but she claimed this factor was incidental.

As a companion and sometime coach, my Ella Fitzgerald, now Cadet Ella Fitzgerald, is indeed one of the most intimidating beings I

273

have met. When I arrived in our quarters, I had hoped for sympathy and rejuvenating meditation; hoped but did not expect.

"*Jiki!*" she hissed at me as soon as I had entered our room, and then proceeded to rattle off commentary in idiomatic home-planet Teek. There were comments on my safety, my failure to contact, and my ill-advised friendship with a reckless Human pilot.

"Ella, please," I said, "we speak Human." In retrospect, I admit it was not the best response.

The next several clicks and spurts would be difficult to translate for a Human record, but they all amounted to some form of admonition or insult.

"Can you not say, 'I was worried about you?'" I suggested. "Or 'I am relieved you are alive?'"

She flared her lower mandibles, clearly ready to argue again. We had grown up close enough in proximity that I knew her temperament and so was ready to defend myself from a minor physical skirmish. However, Ella knew I would not give her a satisfying fight should she aim to have one. Either that or she deferred since I was appointed the linguistics and communications expert by our queen.

"Very well, Paul. I was worried about you. And I am relieved you are alive." She relaxed a little, lowering her fist and letting her wings relax. "But these are not necessary sentiments to say out loud when we can just use our hind-brain connection or fully commune. And, *jiki*, we would not need to have this conversation if you had not fallen into hibernation on the surface due to reckless piloting."

"Yes, I understand," I told her. "Are you feeling all right?"

Her chromae became warmer, but not yet soothed. "I have heard rumor and report. Perhaps you could corroborate?"

"I am afraid not. The events immediately preceding the accident and hibernation are...not fully clear," I began, but she had a different idea in mind.

"I refer to the period after hibernation, when you woke."

"That is also unclear," I said. I did recall some commentary from the doctors, but even that had been non-specific. "What do you know about that?"

Her chromae went through a triple shift as she tried to sort out how to express it. "You scrambled a drone!"

"What? No," I said but...

"I asked some questions of the medical personnel. They said the drone sent to wake you collapsed. When I questioned a fellow Teek—"

"Are you certain that's not just incompatibility between hives?"

"Paul, listen: you scrambled a drone. Which either means that you are not capable of communing off-hive or something happened before or during your hibernation that the drone could not process."

"But if I am not off-hive compatible I cannot be an Initiative cadet!" I protested. I felt my thorax begin to vibrate.

Ella's demeanor shifted. She had always been able to shift toward a mode of sympathy when she could see I was in need. In an odd way, my distress was the most helpful thing for tempering her anger.

She reached out to me with one hand and placed it on my chest while one of her antennae touched mine. She offered soothing; then, after I'd stopped rattling, she informed me very plainly, "Paul, we have already confirmed that you can commune with off-hive drones before we left. You are *not* incompatible. Rather, what you experienced pre-hibernation or during hibernation..." She trailed off. "Something disrupted the drone. I was not there, but the witness was very sure the drone collapsed. Considering they sleep standing up, I conclude your accident experience scrambled the drone."

The logic was reasonable, even if there were inferences bridging it together.

I hesitated to ask more. I wished to know, but I did not wish to know bad news. This was like an example of the Human phrase "ignorance is bliss." I checked to verify the door was shut and that I was otherwise alone with a sibling from the same hive. "Am I damaged or in danger?"

"I cannot be certain," Ella said with far less empathy than I would have liked. I did not feel it was an appropriate tonal response when speaking in Human.

"Perhaps you would know more if we communed," I suggested, knowing the shared meditation with my *jiki* was often grounding for both of us and very informative for my medically inclined counterpart, but she surprised me.

"Not yet. If your hind-brain is causing drones to collapse, I determine that we should not commune without a witness, just in case you were exposed to some contagious mental abnormality."

I was about to protest, but she cut in again.

"I am aware that we are capable of voicing when we are overwhelmed or distressed, unlike drones. That is why I insist we have at least one more Teek on hand to see or hear any such distress. For now," she went on, changing the subject as easily as a Tsanghar sheds her skin, "I would like to know what other witnesses saw. Can we bring in your pilot?"

"I see," I said. I thrummed, then quieted my bodily response. However, I did not reply immediately. I did not want to expose my new friend Lidstrom to my shortcomings, whether species traits or personal instability, and I wasn't sure which sounded more damaging to me. "Could we wait until tomorrow? I will be seeing the doctor one more time."

She stared at me. Her chromae pulsed through a range of colors. I imagined she was weighing a number of factors: my level of sincerity, Lidstrom's probable availability, known and unknowable medical dangers and whether the doctor would catch them, and the likelihood that we would go thirty or more hours without communing—which was low, but a risk nonetheless.

"Very well," she said, using her favorite Human expression. "I do have to rest as my squad is still on duty tomorrow morning."

I thought that would be the end of it and began to turn away, but Ella suddenly flared her wings and her hind-brain communicated intimidation. "But, with certainty, Paul Newman, we will commune immediately following my early morning squad assignment or we will both report back to the infirmary." And in case I would object, Ella reminded me of her position relative to mine: "I have Her royal voice."

"I follow my queen," I replied, feeling both due respect for the responsibility delegated to my *jiki*, as well as a personal amusement at the namesake of Ella Fitzgerald having her royal voice. My *jiki* may have been more attuned to matters of anatomy and physiology; but I was a student of communication and linguistics, a field that allowed for simultaneous reverence and humor. I wondered if that was a common Human juxtaposition.

* * * * *

Chapter Thirty-Three:
Lidstrom

"Lidstrom! Man, welcome back to the world of the living. How're you feeling?" Yiorgos asked, making room for me on the bench, not that there was much competition for space in the mess.

"Fine," I said, taking the seat. "Definitely had my bell rung, but I'm ready to get back to work as soon as they let me. How about you? How did it go?"

There were only five of us at the table, all Human and all from E transport. Rivers scoffed, "It didn't."

"Yeah," Gerhardt said. "Thanks to your crew, we were grounded."

"Wait, what?" I received generally annoyed looks. "You guys didn't get to run the first scenario?"

"Well, we ran it on VR—"

"Extremely limited VR. My grandma had better interfaces in her neighborhood bar!"

Yiorgos cut in, stealing focus from the gripe fest. "Man, that must have been so cool to drive out on the surface...before the whole accident and everything."

"So, you never had a challenge in the Arteevees?"

"Uh—" This seemed to be a sorer point. Yiorgos glanced at the others, who didn't give any outward reaction. "Well, I did a little. I

279

was part of the first set of squads assigned, so I got to *hear* the full scenario and we started working on the Arteevee. But we weren't anywhere near ready to go out when they announced there had been an accident on the surface and shut down the whole scenario."

I tried to remember if there'd been signals from other Arteevees on our six. I asked, "So who else had a chance to go outside?"

No hands went up at our table.

"Hardly anyone did. Two squads had crossed the gate, but that's about it. You guys cleared your craft and exited before any of the other teams even knew what was going on. Everyone's shooting theories around, everything from something being rigged in your favor or your lizard threatening an instructor if they didn't open the doors for you. Care to illuminate?"

I gave an unconvincing shrug. "Not sure if there's much to tell. Paul got us set up so we could hear the briefing while we worked, and I think Kesiel did something to our engines, but really it was just a good team."

"Wow." Rivers' expression showed some genuine surprise, if not enthusiasm. Trying to tiptoe around any stereotyping, she said, "I mean, I would have thought—Like, how did the P'rukktah work out?"

"Actually, after we tipped, she was the one who sealed up the Arteevee while we waited to be rescued." I spoke quickly with a sudden almost physical urge to defend her, but I tried to finish calmly. "Like I said, a good team."

Yiorgos blinked a few times. The shape of his mouth didn't change but I could see him working through the confusion, maybe wondering about her translator or even something more specist altogether. Eventually, he settled on, "Man, that's crazy. Too bad they're probably not going to keep you together."

"What? Why not?"

"Because of everything, man. They had to shut down the opening scenario after the accident, which impacted like a hundred squads."

"What else are they saying?"

The collective started to respond, but Yiorgos remained the spokesman with, "I mean, it's all rumor and hearsay, but everyone knows you kind of shot out of there, and then apparently you hit some debris. Wasn't it like an oxygen tank?"

"Yeah, an oxygen tank," I repeated, numbly. It was the theory I had been given, too, though my gut didn't want to accept it.

"Well, then they immediately called back the few others who were just starting. They shut it all down while they swept the field and cleaned up anything else they might have missed."

So, they *had* investigated. They must have. They surely would have found the other Arteevee and the source of the explosion. *Unless* someone got to it first and covered it up, or hid it, or destroyed evidence. After all, they would have been too occupied rescuing cadets, wouldn't they? Followed by preventing the rest of them from hitting the surface. Who's to say any authorities would have reached anything in time?

"So how about you?" I heard myself blurt, changing the subject as artlessly as a high-school freshman. "How's your squad?"

Yiorgos shrugged his shoulders separately, as if to say "yes" and "no." "They're okay. I mean, pretty standard interstellar crew: three Humans—one of them's Cadet Benjamin—plus two Teek. About what you'd expect. I was a little disappointed, but I don't think they followed people's preferences anyway. Later I found out that a bunch of people were never actually assigned to a squad and were being put through additional evaluations and preliminary training. After that, I felt like I dodged a whole lot of bullets. I mean—" he started numbering them on his fingers starting with his thumb, "—

I'm first wave, with a mostly Human team, and no rat-beebees. Don't want to tempt fate by asking for too much more."

I arced an eyebrow and pressed him about the preferences. Yiorgos explained what he'd heard about the species lines and statistically valid reasons to be mostly Human, but I only half listened. Part of me was still on the surface, in that Arteevee chasing a blue light, which he hadn't mentioned.

"I mean, out of all of the assigned squads—three waves worth—there were only like seven beebees. The rest weren't chosen. Oh, here's something weird: one of the rats chosen turned out to be pregnant! Then the powers-that-be had to debate safety standards. A few of us have started a pool on how long it will take before the beebees wash out of the Initiative. You in?" he finished, drawing me back to the discussion.

"What?" I couldn't explain why, but the whole premise sounded off to me, even if Yiorgos turned out to be statistically supported. "No. Um—Not now. Isn't it a bit soon?"

"The whole Initiative is a bit soon in the scale of things, Lidstrom," Rivers said.

"And inviting the beebees," Yiorgos said, "even if they're everywhere in our system, seems like poor planning to me. I mean, do you know that the average lifespan for one of them is like twelve to fifteen solar years?"

"Really?" Though I'd probably read something similar in one of the primers, it was hard to believe once they were real flesh and blood sentients. "That can't be right."

"Uh-huh! That's the average, and with really poor data. Some of them die way younger than that. I was talking with one Teek, who says that only some of the beebees actually use intraspace folding technology, so that means there are tons of them who are probably over-calculating their ages because they don't know how to factor in time dilation at high-v in real space."

This was Yiorgos at his finest, fussing with numbers and data comparisons and casually ignoring social graces. I feel a little guilty admitting it, but this kind of interaction was a welcome slice of normality, separationistic and Human-first though it sounded. A part of me wanted to dive into the blue light and the second Arteevee, but another part of me was enjoying just hanging out and chatting with the crew. They might have been annoyed that the scenarios had been shut down, but, weirdly, it was easier to be around this handful of semi-snubbed but familiar Humans than trying to navigate the space with a grab-bag of aliens.

Then Gerhardt totally changed the game on me. When I asked what else was new, she laughed, and then told me from across the table, "Oh yeah, you know that Rock Hopper module that made you the 'naut? Well, while you were out someone beat your score."

"What? Who?"

Gerhardt shook her head. "They didn't log in. You were beaten by a guest."

I didn't think through the idea, but I wondered, "Why didn't you just assume it was me accessing a guest terminal from the infirmary?"

"Did you?" Yiorgos asked.

"No," I admitted, "but I'm totally up for the challenge."

And that was enough to point me away from the accident for the time being. I knew it was shallow, and I shouldn't have gotten so involved by a stupid VR competition. I rationalized: Shin was stable, we'd all made it back in one piece, and maybe some discrepancies weren't all that important.

* * * * *

Chapter Thirty-Four:
Paul Newman

2200 Day 4

My first indication of an inaccurate reality was that the fellow worker standing before me had both four arms and two wings. These molts had been attempted before; I had some imprinted memory of the trials in an extra-winged, extra-limbed evolutionary mold, which, unfortunately, overwhelmed the capacity for independent thought in a worker brain and left the being with this programmed body either entirely queen-controlled or braindead.

Even so, I saw two wings and four arms on a clearly asserting being.

The second indication that something was wrong was that this Teek body happened to be Ella, my *jiki*, who had never before had four arms. I knew this kind of spontaneous growth was impossible, so I said, "That's impossible."

The moment I said it, she ceased to be Ella and became someone else. The nature of the universe appeared to unravel. I was aware of the spectral wavelengths of the planet Mars. I knew it was not supposed to be blue and that no substance on the surface nor the light of the sun or moons could reflect such a hue.

The sensation of Mars gravity was also incorrect.

285

Everything I observed within this rendition of the academy was slightly amiss; a little too far or a little too close, a little too big or a little too small. Some things were drastically wrong or different or simply empty, as if they did not exist until I looked directly at them and focused on them.

This led to a conclusion: Either the universe as I knew it had shifted and changed irrevocably or I had gone insane. It was more likely that I alone had cracked than the world had. Usually, I am not given to such binary modes of thinking, and I wished to gain more data to better assess the situation.

Any strange phenomenon requires shared observation and corroboration. So, I looked for a person who could help me. Not a Teek, but a Human more capable of variation and adaptation. I searched for my Human friend Lidstrom.

I ran down the halls and corridors of the academy, and I found the distances to be inconstant and actively shifting. What had been a short distance away seemed to retreat from me, and what was once far disappeared.

The last place I could speak with Lidstrom directly was in the infirmary. Even though he had been released, that location was the nearest association, so I decided to go there. Or rather, that was where my feet guided me, whether I moved them or not.

The infirmary lay shockingly unguarded, unprotected by people, protocol, or any security measures. When I entered, the number of beds seemed to be far too many, and there didn't seem to be the right kind of walls or the room was, in some cases, lacking a ceiling. Shin was the only person there, Kesiel having been released.

Our wounded squadmate was sitting up, pointing at me, while she scratched out words in a form of idiomatic Tsanghar that sounded to me more like Segranee than anything I would associate as commonly used. And though she used a dialect I should not have understood, the speech reformed in my brain into two words: "Free me."

I woke up.

This might sound unremarkable to some. For Tsangharee, for P'rukktah, for Humans, and even the Belbehan, I believe, all of these occurrences and sensations could be easily explained. For many, similar has already been experienced.

Understand that for me this was quite unique. Teek are not Human: worker molts do not write long fiction, they do not experience sexual desire of any kind.

And they do not dream.

* * * * *

Chapter Thirty-Five:
Arrksh

The floor feels more comfortable against my bare feet now that everyone else is asleep. The hallway lights are dim but not off. The cameras still track movement, but I am not focused on them.

I stand beneath one of the windows in the Nexus, watching the mesmerizing comings and goings of the various landers and shuttles. I cannot guess with confidence which ships are Human, Teek, neither, or both—even the Belebehan vessels, while plentiful, are not often distinct, and P'rukktah have little presence in this system. My eyes are far less keen than those of the Human or Tsanghar people, but I imagine I can see more than the Uua, planted in the soil beneath me.

My feet prefer soil to the floor. In the presence of the Uua I close my eyes and try to picture the ships passing in the night as she must. I wonder if there is any way to feel them at their distance, especially with the thin atmosphere where they cannot be heard overhead. I switch off my translator and am annoyed by the fact that my cadet-issue wrist device cannot be fully powered down. Instead, I remove it and set it at the base of the tree.

I listen so deeply, however, that I seem to manifest a trick of the ear, as if spoken by a tied and near-strangled Tsanghar.

Free me!

Perhaps it is what I remember of the Segranee in the station before Phobos, which now feels a part of the distant past.

I shake off the sensation and turn my attention to the calming Uua. Her limbs extend and arch majestically. The lines of the bark acting as visible sinews, ready to part for a rare moment of fast movement should I ever be lucky enough to see it.

One of these unmoving branches holds my notice. It appears to point down one of the corridors. From my vantage point this indicates the hangars and garages. I would not say that I believe this being is showing me a sign, but I wish to know the source of this Segranee voice…so I follow the path shown to me.

I pass a couple of staff, night crew folk. There is a Teek custodian on his rounds and a collection of four Belbehan who wear neither Transnat nor I.I. uniforms, apparently making a delivery.

Further down the corridor, one of the garage doors opens upward, with metallic groans and screeches. A Human emerges, stomping loud enough to command my notice. Suspicion urges me to remain unseen, so I hide behind a contour of the wall which provides shadow as much as cover.

Peering out around the corner, I watch the Human. She is dressed in a different style of flightsuit than the one we were issued for the I.I.; I suspect she's part of a Transnat crew. Her head-hair is yellow orange, which appears dusted with a darker rust more consistent with the surface of the planet, and her curls have been pressed and dampened. Her stance shows an exhaustion I do not typically associate with the low planetary gravity. However, when she reaches another door across the corridor, she pounds with fervor.

"Gordon, if you're in there—"

The door hisses to one side, and a taller, darker Human's face greets her. His head is shaved on top. It is difficult to distinguish facial hair at this distance. I have to tune my ears to properly hear him for he tries to keep his voice at a low decibel measure. "Jesus, Burke, you trying to wake the station?"

"You left me out there, Gordon! What was I—"

"Keep your voice down. Come on." He maintains a whisper, too low for my translator to pick up, even with settings turned as high as they are able, but his tone is one of frustration and tension. "Is it secure?"

"Yes, Gordon. Christ."

I have heard this name and this voice before, this Gordon. He is a lieutenant, but he typically sounds much warmer and calmer, even when giving orders. Presently, he rasps an uncomfortable, "Where?"

"Where else?" she says, more flippantly than she ought if he does outrank her. "Hangar four."

"Show me," he says.

He steps into the walkway, then closes and locks the door behind him.

They return the way she came. They are not worried about being spotted. Various maintenance, delivery, security, and other staff are not out of place. With no curfews along the public walks, study rooms, or mess hall the odd cadet would not raise too many hairs either.

Still, I keep my distance, even more aware of the cameras. I find myself wondering how Kesiel would handle being caught in pursuit and resolve that she would merely smile and make everyone else more uncomfortable than she. I am beginning to admire Kesiel. Though I cannot climb like her, my unshod hands and feet make no sticking or scuffling sounds Humans can detect; I believe she would admire my stealth this night.

Gordon moves quickly and the woman scurries to keep pace, grumbling wordlessly. I follow them down the corridor, further away from what I know to be safe or secure, but arriving at Hangar 4, where I had first disembarked.

The curly-haired female named Burke speaks as soon as they are inside. "I cannot believe you, Gordon! I nearly died today."

"Hey!"

His voice is loud and sudden enough that I nearly sprint away for fear of being seen. My back is against a wall that hardly feels secure, even though they would not be able to see me unless they exited. My breathing is too noticeable; any P'rukktah would have heard it. But he is not talking about me. He is responding to Burke. I maintain my stealth and cannot see what he is doing. What I hear hints at my immediate safety but stirs strong suspicions.

"Okay, good," he says. "Cameras and microphones are already on loop."

Her harsh laugh echoes off the hangar walls, with some distortion from the primed atmospheric bubbles.

"What do you take me for? I've got it in my hotkeys. But seriously, Gordon, this is too much. Explosive decompression from our own oxygen source! You believe that?"

"Yeah, I know. But you're okay, so—"

"Define 'okay.'"

Instead of answering, he presses a command for the door to close behind them. They are far enough ahead that I am able to slip in after without needing to duck under the door. I see there are many objects behind which I can hide, including shuttles and maintenance rigs. I hear the door seal, which chills my nerves, but I am too intrigued to depart now.

The two Humans have turned their backs to me, clearly with a destination in mind as Burke continues to bark at Gordon.

"I was lucky I was halfway into my exosuit at the time. Got sprayed with a ton of Mars before I could get the helmet on." I catch a gesture where she indicates her hair, which bore evidence of the local dirt and dust. "Then I had to lay low while the cleanup crew came sniffing around. I don't know how many years that thing took off my life when I popped it into its cage and lugged it back here. And in case you hadn't noticed, our barriers aren't perfect and that modified mask Vee made doesn't keep it from screaming at you."

By the time she finishes, I am behind a parked shuttle, blocked from their view should they turn around. The lights are too dim for me, but perhaps Humans can operate effectively in low light.

"Hey, hey, look, it might not have been an easy hike back for you, but guess who was the one flying the rescue chopper?" His voice was raised in both intensity and crispness, but not in volume; his dim outline is pointing at himself. "Yeah, I had to scramble to pull those cadets out, and while I was at it, scramble the scanners before they found you. Okay? Do you know what would have happened if someone had found you out there? You and Wayne? It's bad enough that people are asking about Chandan."

Her tone and demeanor soften slightly. "What are they saying about Chandan?"

"Well, the cover story about being at a classified off-site base would've been good enough, but one of the high brass has a connection there, so—"

"*Grepht*," she says, using a term for which I do not need a translator. She drops her hands from her hips and slows down. "Gordon, what are we supposed to do? The lab has been compromised and we can't keep it here."

Gordon is not paying attention. He has already reached the prep closets where the EVA gear and decontamination shower are housed. He opens a storage space, which glows from within.

"Jesus!" he exclaims, a word that my translator still struggles to interpret—an idea that is both revered and profaned. "You didn't even lock it! Anyone could get in—"

"That's exactly my point. We have to move it out of here now."

"No. They're not ready for a transfer."

"Who cares? Everyone's on high alert after the accident and the Teek officers have started sniffing around."

"No, we wait for the order."

"How? Boss is on radio silence. Look, if all the higher-ups are asking about Chandan it's only a matter of time before—"

"I've got it under control. I'm covering for Chandan. I'm covering for you. I've got Vieve accounted for." I hear a rattle in his voice, a lack of assurance to support the words he is saying. There was beeping as he closed the door. "And now I've got a lock on here that even you can't override."

"Great." Sarcasm.

"You wanted it secure." As soon as he says so, however, there is a jolt, a sudden crackling of electromagnetic discharge. This frightens me even at my distance, and it causes Gordon to leap back, a little too late. He shakes his hand, apparently conflicted about how to nurse the wound. Muted striations of white and blue now cover the fingers. It's like no electrical burn I have ever seen.

"See! See what I've been dealing with?" Burke says, clearly satisfied Gordon is also experiencing pain.

"All right! I'm sorry. Why didn't you magnetize it?"

"I didn't want to get zapped again," she says. She shows him her own hand which has similar marks, though mostly healed.

"All right, fine. You got a coil on hand?"

I cannot see enough of their exchange and try to move around the shuttle. What he's holding does not look like a complicated device, some copper wires and a battery. He quickly makes a ring out it and roughly shoves the setup inside the locker. Reclosing and locking it, he says, "That'll hold it for a while."

"Yeah, until it drains that coil, too. Face it, Gord, we haven't been able to contain it since the counterpart got within a light-year of Mars. The levels keep increasing. It's reaching out! It's already flashing in my head and screwing with my dreams."

"Right, but we don't really know what—"

"Dammit!" I hear banging, but I cannot see the source. "Listen to me! We don't know shit about them, and that's what's so scary. Maybe it really did reach out and drag that Arteevee off course. Maybe it'll crumple the next shuttle like they did the warships at Syedi-Teek. Okay, if we're not going to destroy it, it needs to get to the station."

She sounds scared. I have seen such terror before, in the eyes of reptiles for whom choking on their own tongues seems like a mercy.

He stalls a moment before admitting, "Yeah. You're right. We should get it moved sooner rather than later. Give me a day, two tops, and I'll get everything worked out from here."

Now that there is no further need to see either the people or the secured wall compartment, I begin shifting back behind the shuttle and make a misstep, a slight slip on the textured floor.

The woman has not noticed me. "Thank you," she says, relief evident in her voice. "In the meantime, I'll check in on Chandan and Wayne as often as I get a chance. Can't have anyone wandering in on—"

"Shush!" he says suddenly. "I might've heard—"

I do not see his next gesture. I am now fully behind the shuttle.

There is the sound of machines, metal and acrylic sliding and locking noises. I imagine a weapon being primed.

Burke yells, "Is someone in here?"

I hear her footsteps approaching. I work to silence my breath, slow my hearts. However, if she comes around the vehicle, I am visible.

"Hang on, let me check," Gordon says calmly, a coolness that could be deadly if directed. I have no idea what he is doing, until he says, "I'm reading no other wrist monitors here. Just me and you."

"Yeah, okay…" Burke says. Though her words agree with him, I can tell this is a ruse. She suddenly runs around to my side of the shuttle and sees nothing.

I am already on the roof of the craft, still holding my breath. The climb was easy in the low gravity, and I am wearing no boots or rough clothing to produce loud noises. My wrists are both bare as well.

"Satisfied?" he asks.

"Yeah, just—You never know." Burke's footsteps carry her back toward Gordon.

"You need to get some sleep," he says. "Being around Wayne can mess with your energy. And make you paranoid."

"Which is why we need better shielding."

"Right."

A rising door sounds. They continue to converse idly as they exit. Burke is discussing how to most effectively shower all the "Mars" off when the door closes behind them.

I finally resume breathing, and my hearts work to compensate. I feel my left wrist, grateful for the lack of band or screen around it. My device, and apparently monitor, is with the Uua, where I left it, where it will not reveal me to Gordon's scanners.

* * * * *

Chapter Thirty-Six: Lidstrom

0400 Day 5

I woke up a little before 0400 M-time. I rinsed off in one of the most uncomfortable shower experiences of my life. It was like I was convinced the water was burning me, no matter how much I turned down the temp. After about a minute, I was shivering uncontrollably but worried about blisters.

I hadn't slept well. My dreams were unsettling but hard to remember. Flashes, traces, images, and a lot of blue light. I thought I had seen Shin, trapped in a coma but calling out "Free me!" in a high, scratchy voice that didn't sound Human. I'm not even sure it was in English. And there was a compounding set of flipped vehicles, where every time I looked at one, another would pop into existence. Finally, I found myself smashed by an asteroid.

I pulled on my flightsuit. That at least was a comfort. I'd grown to like the basic universal design. It was both flexible and a welcome compression; it was breathable but was able to become nearly airtight if the ambient atmosphere was lacking or too cold. I'd tested this only the day before.

The next couple of hours found me trying to shake the weird. I went for a run in the gym, as hard as I could manage with point-eight-five grav enabled. I wasn't alone, but I wasn't paying attention to who else was around or what they were saying.

I still had a bug up my butt about the Rock Hopper module, so I tried that next. I logged some nice highs, but never managed to eclipse the anonymous high score or even beat my last record.

By 0600, I was more than ready to go to the infirmary, partially to talk to someone, but also to confirm that I wasn't cracking. I jogged there, loping in the low grav, and tried to psych myself up for the checkup. I passed a couple of early squads who were slotted for trainings and scenarios—all in-facility of course. I gave Yiorgos a wave as I went by.

Passing through the Nexus, I saw Arrksh squatting near the base of the tree doing an exercise similar to tai chi.

I arrived at the infirmary, and Doctor Koba logged my vitals. She was a little less overbearing when I wasn't trying to shove past her to freedom, still, she had harder eyes than I'm used to from doctors and her dyed blonde hair was pulled back tight. I supposed she wasn't the type to turn to for sympathy, but she soon gave me the all-clear on all physical counts.

For the psychological side, she read off a questionnaire. She had disconnected me from the heart rate and BP monitors which made it feel less like an interrogation. I had to ask her to clarify the question about "seeing auras" and I admitted to the somewhat restless sleep. I also confirmed that I had not seen anymore blue lights, which, strange though it may sound, was a little disappointing to me.

Jane-Two was in the examination room for much of the time, prepping for another patient who I assumed would be Paul, but that may have been because she looked so much like him. I noticed the Teek doctor was watching me, looking up periodically, her chromae occasionally shifting to cooler colors before I answered each question.

After Doctor Koba had gone through her list she asked me if I had any questions or concerns. I can safely say I lied. However, my flat "No" did elicit a raised eyebrow.

I don't know if Doctor Koba was a particularly good judge of character or not, but she clearly wanted to know where my eyes were looking when they weren't directly on her, as if this would be a good gauge of what might be going on in my head. Whenever I fidgeted or looked around myself, she tried to shift and follow my gaze.

"Hey, um—" I paused and chewed on my lower lip. I'm not actually good at faking emotions, but I could fall back on a couple of key tics. Acting uncertain and waiting for a prompt could deflect focus away from my true concerns.

"Yes?" the doc eventually asked.

"Is it okay if I stop into Shin's room. See how she's doing?"

Doctor Koba relaxed. This question was in line with what she expected. "Sure. I think the Tsanghar will be eager for the company as well."

I nodded, pressed out a smile. "Thanks."

Kesiel, I was pleased to see, had regained full use of her hands. She was situated on a kind of chair that, once I thought about it, made a lot more sense for Tsanghar physiology. To me it looked backward because she leaned her chest into it rather than laying back against it. There was more than enough space for her neck to move around if needed, but there was also a bit of a scoop for her to rest her chin. Her forearms were propped on an armrest. It reminded me of those forward-leaning massage tables they have set up in the mega malls.

The moment I stepped into the room Kesiel looked up from the device in her hands. I don't know if she was engaged in academics or pleasure; at the rate her fingers moved, it was hard to tell.

"Lidstrom!" she cooed at me. It was a tone I was beginning to understand and even find endearing after spending a few days around the Tsanghar. I appreciated her excitement and her sense of intrigue and intention. "How are you feeling this morning?"

"Good," I said, as one Human might to another, but I had sensed Tsangharee were a little more wordy, so I filled in, "I'm feeling well, Kesiel. How about you?"

"Splendid," she said.

I gestured at her hands. "I notice you're—"

"Yes! Unbandaged." She waggled free fingers at me to see. They looked smooth and glossy, practically reflective. New skin, post-shed, I imagined, with some tension blisters underneath still visible. "Doctor Koba advised I leave the bands on, but how could I possibly?"

I found myself smiling for no particular reason. "That's good, Kesiel."

I was reluctant to steer the conversation toward Shin. From someone as vibrant as Kesiel to someone so…someone who, up until recently, had been vibrant.

"How is…" I couldn't finish, and Kesiel did not do me the favor of interrupting me.

Shin was still. I saw the rise and fall of her breathing, courtesy of the apparatus that was both monitoring and assisting. Her face was pale and bruised. Otherwise, it was hard to tell how she was doing.

Kesiel, however, did not seem worried.

"She is resting," the Tsanghar told me. "She will wake."

Some people are good at being arrogant and making certain sounding claims they cannot possibly support. However, the way Kesiel said it, it was as if she knew some pertinent piece of information that I didn't, but which led to a conclusion I could accept.

"That's good. You keep her company."

"Until I myself am released, Lidstrom," she replied.

I nodded. "Yeah. Until you're released."

I was about to leave, but Kesiel clearly wanted me to stay.

"I will say," she began, or maybe that was a full sentence in Tsanghar. "Yes, I must say that I have been feeling rather trapped here by myself with Shin, who is not a very good conversationalist. At least, not when she is awake."

I looked behind me. I don't know if I felt like I was talking about something out of turn, but I did know that I didn't want Doctor Koba to walk in on our conversation. "What do you mean?"

"Yes. Dream sharing is not common among Humans," Kesiel said, as if it were an observation rather than a deeper implication.

I smiled. "No, I guess not." Again, before I could turn and leave, Kesiel spoke.

It was a scratching Tsanghar word, as if spoken with a different voice or imitating an accent, maybe from a specific clan or moon. It sounded familiar, just a couple syllables, half-sung, half-screeched.

"What?" I asked.

"Hmm?" Kesiel said. I could tell she was teasing me.

"What was that? What did you just say?"

Kesiel grinned, which is to say she drew up her lips to show all of her teeth and pulled her cheeks to the sides, exposing things that were almost like the lizard version of dimples. Then she let her tongue flick out the words as she enunciated, "Free me."

I startled and checked to see if the doctor was watching. I shifted uneasily from one foot to the other. I had recognized the Tsanghar phrase, except in my dream it had sounded like Shin was speaking.

"Free me," Kesiel repeated in a very different tone, "from this very boring infirmary. I do wish that you could."

And with that, Kesiel returned to her almost innocent ways.

* * * * *

Chapter Thirty-Seven:
Paul Newman

0700 Day 5

I awoke relatively late into the morning, just as Ella was leaving for a training.

"Ah, I see you have woken," she observed. "I will be gone for the next three hours, according to the schedule, but I will send a message if times vary more than ten percent of predicted."

"Yes," I managed weakly.

She paused. "It is good that you have had additional sleep. Perhaps you required it after yesterday's encounter. Once you have seen the doctor and have been cleared to commune, we will commune." She swiped for the door, which opened into a Teek common area, and left our pod.

I have been told by other people, particularly Human people, that Ella appeared insensitive or cold. This is not exactly true, as she is a different species than they. What would be more accurate to state is that I am more sensitive, and therefore—I conclude—warm.

My form of emotional sensitivity made me a better pupil for our Human tutors, who commended my ability to not only learn quickly, but fully. My tutor often said that I was her only protegé to understand the depth of Human phrasing and expressions. I found that I did not have an appropriate expression for my current circumstances, Human or otherwise, and wished I could speak Tsanghar.

I attempted to work backward through my dream experience in order to understand it better, marking out times and as much quantitative data as I could manage. I did not recall more than one episode of dreaming and I was as sure as I could be that I had never dreamed prior to that night. Though I had received input from drones or my queen before, I had never personally established a subconscious narrative while otherwise unconscious. Most of all, I was certain that this manifestation of imagination, or dream, was inspired by the strange encounter during our first scenario, which I could not remember.

* * *

I went to the infirmary, but Jane Gooddall was not there. Doctor Koba was tending to another patient, who might have been Kesiel or Shin, or perhaps Lidstrom had arrived before me.

The medic running the intake desk did not have an officer's patch. He was not even wearing an I.I. uniform, which suggested he was Transnat staff.

I asked if Jane Goodall would be returning soon, a question which he did not answer. Instead, he told me, "Paul Newman, right? Doctor Goodall indicated you would have your vitals measured and recorded and then be assessed by the Avowol. It's just been cleared as calibrated for Teek worker minds, so that's pretty nifty."

I did not know what "nifty" meant, but I had the impression that this final sentence was said mostly to himself.

I had very little left in terms of reaction brainspace. I believe that, on another day, I would have either been excited or nervous. I might have voiced a concern or a particular goal. Instead, I could only numbly assess the facts. I did not enjoy being mostly or partially submerged, but I knew I could survive partial submersion for a very long time. Organic mind scans from non-Teek were new to me and interacting with an Avowol had been a curiosity for many of my hivemates who had also been imprinted with a desire to explore.

I was given privacy to step out of my jacket and flightsuit and put on a water gown; this was for the benefit of the Human. Giving no objection, I was escorted up a short lift to the Avowol's tank.

The medic who prepared me expressed envy as he set me up on the tray—I am not sure if this is the correct approximation. It was not exactly a bed, more of a slab, which was then lowered into the water.

"Okay," said the medic. "It will be a quick scan and then the Avowol will send information directly to Doctor Goodall's system. You don't need to worry about me or anyone else peering into your brain." He put on a friendly, almost smiling, expression at the end of this.

I admit, I did not find it comforting, but I acknowledged I had heard him from my supine position.

The medic lowered the tray into the water, which was neither as cool or as salinated as I expected it to be.

"I'm told the process is very soothing and that you will feel refreshed when you are done."

I nodded as I was lowered. Soon, only my hands, toes, and snout were above the surface. I felt the electricity in the current moving beneath me.

"One more thing," the medic said, "apparently Teek workers experience some short-term memory loss when interacting directly with an Avowol."

My eyes went cold and doubtless shifted to an icy shade of blue, while a silken, watery ribbon wrapped around the top of my head, just behind my antennae. One translucent appendage reached out of the water near my feet in order to grip the side of the tray on which I lay.

I didn't remember anything else about the Avowol.

* * * * *

Chapter Thirty-Eight:
Lidstrom

0900 Day 5

"Hey, Yiorgos, are you busy?"

"Not really," he said, not looking up from the chessboard. I knew that other than a couple of half-assed simulations, few of those who had actually gotten to attempt the first scenario were getting much play now. Hence in-person chess on a physical board. "What did you have in mind?"

Rivers, his opponent, said with exactly zero enthusiasm, "Dude."

"I want to check out the wreck."

"What?"

"Yeah, my Arteevee. I mean, *our* Arteevee, like the one I was driving when—" I made an artless motion with my hands to demonstrate flipping. "Look, it's going in to get repairs later today and Cla—um...someone is going to let me check it out before they patch it."

"Seems cool, but what do you need me for?"

Rivers cut in, "To save you from an embarrassing loss of your king. Check, by the way."

"Shit," Yiorgos muttered, before taking his turn.

I moved closer, hoping to disrupt some of his concentration. "Look, they said nothing on the camera survived and that for some reason our scanners got scrambled. But I have a feeling that there's something they missed."

"What makes you think I can find anything if they missed it?"

"Well…" I floundered.

"Maybe it's a big damn conspiracy, and they're purposely not telling you," Rivers said, taking his next move.

I rolled my eyes, but Yiorgos answered as if it was a serious remark. "Well, then they'd also purposely remove everything." I attempted to interject, but it wasn't very forceful, so Yiorgos continued. "And you said they're letting you in there, right?"

"Check."

"Shit. Unless letting you in to check out a bogus Arteevee is part of the conspiracy."

"Ooh, the plot thickens," River added, still totally deadpan.

"Hey!" I said, more forcefully, loud enough that I turned more than a few heads, but finally I got their attention. "Look, Yiorgos, I have one chance to check this thing out before they patch it up, and I can't do it alone. I don't know those information systems, but you do. And maybe…" I crouched to speak directly over his shoulder like an angel or devil; I wasn't sure which. "Maybe the staff didn't find anything because they weren't looking for something weird, something they would normally throw out as ridiculous. But you might be able to find what they missed."

In a soft voice, Yiorgos rebutted, "Why don't you just ask Paul?"

As soon as he said it, it clicked: Yiorgos evaded me because of Paul Newman. Whether it was because Paul had done better in the first scenario or something else, Yiorgos had some very Human pettiness to him. I couldn't quite say why I didn't ask Paul. I think the species divide made me wary in this case, which was exacerbated by

Paul's inability to recall the accident along with all of the conspiracy talk from my fellow E-group cadets. So, I made something up:

"I need someone who can think outside the box, and Paul's all box."

Yiorgos chewed on this near-truth for a moment, then stood. "All right, let's go."

"Hey," Rivers said, "we're still in the middle of a game."

"Yes, and we'll have to call it a draw."

"I would have beaten you in four moves."

"Unfortunately, we'll never know." He turned away and said, "Lidstrom, lead the way."

I don't know if Yiorgos was the kind of person who would join my quest just to keep from losing a game of chess, but I really didn't care.

* * *

"**Y**ou didn't tell me you were bringing a plus one," Clancy said when I arrived at the auxiliary hangar. She was standing in front of the door in a deck crew uniform rather than the I.I. jacket, with her sergeant's stripes on a removable shoulder patch.

"Yeah, we'll just be in and out," I said, maybe a little too eager, and much more ready to ask forgiveness than permission.

She scrunched one side of her face, as if reconsidering her offer to indulge the greenie, but she'd agreed I needed closure. I was secretly hoping to find something that would open up a can of worms, and I was hoping even harder that Clancy wouldn't be able to tell.

"All right. You've got fifteen. Don't do anything stupid." She swiped the door lock and opened it. Before I could step one foot inside, she blocked me. "Hey, you try to take anything out with you, I'll know."

Clancy was not a particularly large person, despite being a couple centimeters taller than me. I was wider in the shoulders than her and even though she had a good decade of training on me, I figured having Earth grav on my side for my entire life would give me a one-up. After being shut into an infirmary and grounded for a few days, I wanted to play up on the defiance, so I countered with, "Why? Are you gonna frisk us?"

"No, *Lahksa*, I'm going to scan you and anything other than your wrists will show up." She flicked her gaze at Yiorgos and did a good impression of a P'rukktah chin thrust. "Got that?"

"Yes, Sarge," Yiorgos answered.

"Good. Now, I'm doing you a favor here, so don't get cocky."

I wanted to add, "Or I'll find myself floating home." Instead, I apologized, in word and body language. "Sorry, Sarge. You're right." I shuffled inside.

Behind me, I heard Yiorgos say, almost cheerily, "Thanks, Sarge."

I shouldn't have been surprised that Clancy followed us into the hangar or to the Arteevee, which was on the sick-car version of a stretcher.

I shuddered a little at the sight of the rear tire, which had been completely shredded by the O2 explosion. I wasn't a Human calculator, but I had a pretty good handle on vector physics and in seconds I was trying to work out how much force it would take to rip away a two-meter-wide all-terrain tire. Apparently enough to flip the vehicle.

"Jesus, man," Yiorgos breathed from ahead. He stared at the side of the craft, rubbing his jaw in a gesture that looked like sympathy pain. "When you said you broke a seal, I didn't—I mean, have you seen this?"

I joined him. Sure enough, there was a gash. I saw where a combination of hard impacts and torque had torn the outer shell enough to strain and rupture the inner hull.

"Yeah," the staff sergeant agreed. Her fists were on her hips and she shook her head. "This thing looks like it went ten rounds with Bruno Somerset." Though I didn't follow boxing, I knew the heavyweight's reputation for mangling people's faces. "Everything is warped and misaligned. The inner hull and outer hull detached from each other in at least a dozen places. The twisted axle alone makes it unsalvageable. Craziest thing was that even with all that damage it only broke open in one place, which was partially covered by dirt. The twist jammed the middle bulkhead so it couldn't close, which meant it was more than just the front compartment's atmo leaking when you started venting."

"Damn," was all I said. I should have appreciated more of the science behind it, but I was on a mission, too focused on the tree to see the forest, or whatever the expression is. "Let's get inside."

"Right," Clancy said, shifting immediately from scientific awe to practical. She led us toward a ladder. "The top hatch is the best way in."

"Wait, there's a top hatch?" I was only acquainted with the rear hatch.

"Yeah, we disabled them for obvious reasons during first scenario. Ironically, that one is less damaged than the aft."

Yiorgos found this made sense. "Sort of like how a doorway is the sturdiest part of the structure during an earthquake."

I didn't pause to make observations. I started up the ladder to the roof of the Arteevee and to the hatch. It was obvious now that I was able to study the full design of the machine, not to mention it was already open.

I dropped inside and felt confused and a little detached. Much of the interior had been sprayed with fast-drying foam and probably radiation scrubbers, making it look like someone had graffitied a lab.

Yiorgos dropped into the vehicle a moment later and got to work.

I spent some time feeling around the walls and remembering the sensations. The emergency compartments were all open and the supplies had been removed. The cadet steering interface was gone, but, otherwise, all the pieces were where we had left them.

"Hey, Lidstrom," Yiorgos said from under the dash, "I don't think you're gonna find anything here, man."

"What? But you just got started."

"Yeah, I know. Come down here and check this out."

He sounded confident, so I laid on my back and joined him.

Yiorgos had his wrist light on. It shone bright enough that I needed a moment to adjust. Once I was able to focus he said, "See, where I'm pointin?"

I have to admit I didn't see or notice much. Which is why I had asked Yiorgos in the first place.

"I mean, man, this is—" He grunted, shifted his shoulders, and checked his wrist, redirecting the light. He jabbed at a processor, a switchboard from which the panel had been removed. It looked burnt and charred with a white residue. "This is basically the comm brain of the vehicle. Every external signal is filtered through here before it goes into the internal computers. Something disrupted this;

I would guess in the realm of a high-rad or rapidly modulating EMP. I mean, they lost your signal, right? Well, maybe the explosion triggered some—"

"It was before the explosion," I snapped.

Yiorgos didn't argue or take my attitude to heart. "Okay. Either way, the external cams would be processed through here. So, you won't have any clean records of anything."

Part of me wanted to play into the conspiracy angle, but a louder part of me didn't accept that. "Come on, isn't there some kind of black box or—"

"Well, yeah, but it also takes in processed information." Yiorgos traced a couple of lines and checked his wrist screen to cross-reference the schematics. "Here," he said pointing to an empty section. The box had already been removed, doubtless yanked and analyzed by the powers-that-be.

I noticed one set of dials next to the same section, and I asked, "What's that one?"

"Um…" He checked the wrist again. "Unless I'm wrong, that's an atomic chronometer."

I made a face at his word choice. "Couldn't you just say clock?"

"Well, it's not a clock exactly. Clocks tell you what time it thinks you're at. Chronometers tell you how much time has elapsed according to particle physics." I was already nodding politely and waving him ahead. He tried to clarify. "It's like location versus duration—"

"I get it," I broke in. Frustrated, I started to crawl out from under the console. "Okay, so no black box, but is there anything else?"

Yiorgos didn't reply. At first, it was a welcome reprieve while I checked out more of the interior. But when he went more than a couple minutes without babbling something new I ducked my head under the console again.

"Yiorgos?"

His face was scrunched up in one of those classic "thinker" expressions, the kind that appear on old marble busts and the imitation 3-D-printed ones. Except for the unibrow, he had the likeness of an immortalized ancient Greek philosopher.

"Yo? What's going on?"

"What time do you have?"

I glanced at my wrist. "I have 12:42. Which means we only have like five minutes to—"

He muttered to himself, "Right. Me too."

"Yiorgos, talk to me. What did you find?"

"Well, the chronometer is off—"

"What?" I ducked back under the panel without gauging distance or direction and rammed my shoulder into his arm. Yiorgos didn't budge. "You're sure?"

"Well, I mean, how sure is sure? But from what I can see it's about…fourteen minutes behind. Oh, check this; it's *exactly* fourteen minutes. I'm tracking a lag of 840 seconds with very minimal change and holding steady."

I squinted to see what he was looking at but the readings made no sense to me. I remembered only a little of my atomic minute conversion tables, but my brain was already busy rationalizing. "What if the reader's off? What if it got scrambled with the other stuff."

"Um, I don't think that's it." His bushy brow tightened. "These use Teek technology to track the particles directly; it's not something you can knock out with EMPs. It's the same kind the orbital stations use—even the Mons base…" Yiorgos shook his head, either annoyed or frustrated by the puzzle he felt he should be able to solve but couldn't work out.

"So, they should read the same then." In a very Human way, I double-checked my wrist, which would have been synced with the base's chronometer. "Are they tamper-proof?"

"Well, nothing's totally tamper-proof, but you can't just hit pause or switch them off without a lot of work. I just can't work out why anyone would take the time to change it and put it back."

"So, what does that mean?"

"Uh—" I don't think Yiorgos had expected to shift from observations to making his own theory. "Well, the first things that come to mind that might screw up an atomic clock—short of detonating or melting it—are moving it really fast or getting enough violent radiation to change the chemical composition."

"We all cleared the rad-checks, so there couldn't have been any extreme radiation."

"Right, and I can't imagine you were approaching relativistic speeds."

That was almost laughable. No matter how much I gunned Kesiel's supercharged engines, I couldn't ever go fast enough to create a noticeable particle change.

"Okay, but where does that leave us?"

Yiorgos opened his mouth and closed it again. I couldn't think of anything either.

From outside, Clancy called, "Hey, Greenies, wrap it up in there. You've got two minutes before I yank you out."

Yiorgos raised his joined eyebrows at me and I gave him a small shake of the head, tacitly saying that we wouldn't tell Staff Sergeant Clancy. Not yet at least.

* * * * *

Chapter Thirty-Nine:
Paul Newman

1300 Day 5

For the second time in as many days, I "came to"—a Human term for achieving awareness—feeling peaceful and jovial, with no direct sensation that anything was amiss. I had apparently already dressed and arrived at the counter of the medical area. A small-group training had begun in the adjoining room and two of the Human cadets were looking at me, so I waved at them, which precipitated whispering.

"If you'll just give your acknowledgment here you can be on your way," the medic said.

I then noticed he was presenting a tablet to me. There was information I had not read and a space for me to sign.

"Acknowledgment..." I repeated, my voice sounding slow to me. "What am I acknowledging?"

"Wow, that is some memory trick," he mused aloud, then said, with no apparent rudeness, "I've just gone through your vitals and determined you're good to go. Here's the preliminary report, but Doctor Goodall will follow up with you once she's gone through the Avowol's data more thoroughly."

"It's already done?" I asked, but as I spoke the words, I dimly recalled being placed in water..."Did it go well?"

"Yes." The medic was surprised at my question and laughed. "Yes, very well, and everything checks out that you're fine moving forward."

I wished to know more but I was not sure what quantifiable information would be most beneficial for me. I asked myself, "What would Lidstrom do," in order to assess a Human interpretation of the situation, which produced my query: "How many times have we had this conversation?"

"Well, it hasn't been exactly the same each time, but we've had a few repeated items. That's okay; it's totally normal for Teek after meeting with an Avowol."

He said it with enough authority that I deemed the answer acceptable. In retrospect, I did wonder how much expertise or experience this Transnat medic stationed on Mars really had.

Still, I was happy, soothed, and my previous troubles were too distant to present worry.

I made my way to my quarters feeling oddly lighter and considered removing the flexible boots so my feet could better grip the floor. I waved at the tree as I went by and nearly missed Arrksh crouching before it.

I noted a playful atmosphere as I returned to the cadet dorms. I found Lidstrom in one of the public areas and I asked him if he would teach me a Human game, but when he indicated he was busy, I resolved to find a recreational challenge on my own.

I was about to log into the flight simulator when a neighbor Teek informed me that Ella had been asking if I had concluded my medical checkup and returned. Reminded of my task, I thanked the messenger and proceeded back to my own cluster and pod to find my *jiki*.

When Ella asked about my visit with the doctor, I indicated a clear reading of all vital statistics and a formal stamp from a medic on my wrist. She appeared excited by the information, and I was grateful. I did not know if she was most relieved that I was in good health, eager to commune once again, or intrigued by my encounter with the Avowol.

She put out her hands and primed her antennae, while giving me space to do the same. We each buzzed and adjusted until we reached the same frequency. Then we communed.

It is difficult to explain to Humans, but when we meditate, we do not exactly "share thoughts." It is not as if she receives my complete inner monologue or every sensation I've experienced in the last day. Rather, it is a way of accounting for, recognizing, and rationalizing experiences in order to properly reset and prepare for a new day. It is a mode of shared memory, yes, but just the broadest strokes; the events and data that need to be preserved and then passed to the queen.

This process is intrinsically important for a hive. Without it, most Teek workers begin to dissociate, eventually losing their ability to permanently retain any memory. Without some form of shared medi- tation, Teek will inevitably go insane, unable to distinguish daytime imaginings from accurate depictions of reality, messages from drones or queens, or out-of-context sense memories. While losing a pocket of memory during a mental download or upload, to use the Human analog, was common, and daytime imaginings were part of what made workers sentient, my previous night's subconscious wanderings were entirely new to both of us. I had just managed to forget them, until our communing reminded me.

Ella could not miss my errant subconscious manifestations; she reached my dream immediately.

Releasing my hands and disconnecting our antennae, she shrieked, "Paul!"

"*Jiki*," I said, realizing what I had not told her.

"Paul, did you dream?"

"I do not know for certain." I realized my statement was technically accurate but nonetheless misleading. I am sure my eye color shifted, and I am sure Ella saw.

"I am dismayed by how much you are becoming like a Human," she stated quickly, but with a little less volume.

I did not know if she was referring to my poor attempt at deception or the dream itself.

"We must not commune," she said. She stepped back and her wings twitched nervously. "You might have an altered brain or have acquired a psychic affliction which is transmittable. What did the doctor—" she began, then chittered in frustration when she realized the question was wrong. "Why did the doctor not—" Wrong again. Finally, "Why did you not tell the doctor?"

"Jane Goodall was not available," I said, feeling my own error as surely as I would a crack in my plating. "I was pronounced healthy by their measurements and an Avowol."

"Those do not matter," Ella said firmly. "They are not Jyikj'tch'tyeek. We cannot trust them to diagnose or prioritize your health or my health or the hive's."

I struggled with this idea. I did not wish to accept her judgment, but I also could not find voice to argue.

"*Jiki*, if you have a communicable psychic ailment, you cannot return to the hive. And neither can I." She turned away for a moment, facing a blank wall in order to think through her next steps. "You must see the doctor again. Demand to be examined by Doctor Jane Goodall, or at least another Teek. You must tell them everything about the dream and anything else you can remember."

I watched her and realized I had never seen Ella's chromae so violet. She was clearly terrified, while I was more numb than I ought to have been.

* * * * *

Chapter Forty:
Kesiel

1400 Day 5

Such plans had I had for these hands
And many more crucial demands
That I cannot keep them in hands

The wheelchair I had requested upon release from the infirmary was not strictly necessary. My legs remained functional and my tail would hardly have been employed for balance on such a low gravity planet. Thanks to the generally competent doctors and the P'rukktah plasma working through my glands, I was fully healed in actuality if not appearances. I moaned about my legs being sore and sluggish and my hands needing more of the soothing balm, but not so much to demand another night's stay, so I asked if it would be too much trouble to send me out on wheels and treads. Doctor Koba, who smelled of fear and insecurity whenever she attempted to examine me, was eager to oblige any requested equipment if it would help me heal faster and prevent an interstellar incident. I had, after all, taken care to remind her of the three injured Tsanghar who swallowed their tongues on the trip in.

You might wonder why I had asked for such a device if I was perfectly mobile and healed. This "medical scooter" apparatus, which I straddled and leaned my chest against, was an opportunity. I would see who sneered, who sighed, and who sympathized at my injured state. Naturally, I would be most suspicious of the fake sympathizers, but even those still showed some derision behind their eyes. Some sentiments were because I was allowed rest with the tacit agreement that I would be newly placed on a squad when they were reassigned, whereas my sisters in scale and my non-special spiritual siblings had to work hard at irregular hours to maintain their standing in the Initiative.

As they could fake sympathy, I could fake injury, far better than poor Lidstrom. I made sad or pained eyes at any indifferent Tsangharee but offered a well-planned smile to those who looked to challenge me. All the while, my hands were still loosely wrapped and saturated with the Human's attempt at a soothing balm. Ideally, I would use more of Arrksh's natural remedy to aid in the healing process. Dulling the pain would actually do more harm than good while the new skin grew strong.

I did happen to catch Arrksh's eye as I made my way toward my room. She was in the soil in front of the Uua, passively leading some Belbehan in a moving prayer that was beautiful to watch but sickly with mammalian sentimentality. I gave the P'rukktah a subtle sign with a squeeze of my translucent eyelids, akin to the Human wink. Arrksh paused a little to receive it, clearly disrupting the Belbehan's attempts to follow, but I don't know if she understood me, so I proceeded onward.

The passage from the Nexus to the cadet rooms held a giddy sensation of foreboding for me. I passed cadets and the occasional staff along the way, but none were idly looking in my direction; they were between destinations with goals in mind. The clusters of open gathering space and milling areas outside the quarters, however, were rife with restless and nervous cadets, who appeared to me as students eager for a brief study break, even if only to gawk at a poor lizard.

I arrived at my side of the dormitories smoothly and quickly, even navigating the scooter around small clusters of Teek. Once at my own room, however, I paused.

I found a notification on the panel, a waiting message, to be unlocked by my swiped wrist. I opened the message rather than the door. This notice directed me to one of the study rooms a short distance away, an invitation to join an unnamed student or group.

I maneuvered my scooter to the end of the cluster and activated the sliding door. Who was waiting for me in that space but a patchy, orange-faced near-kin? She had a scar on her neck and an off smile on her face. Two other sisters were behind her, one whose name I knew, the other I only recognized by sight. All three had swallowed their tongues.

"Welcome safely, sister," Liesarn said in our common language, her voice scratchy and unbecoming of a clean-habitat Tsanghar. She beckoned, while the other two crowded forward. "Come in!"

I worked my way over the threshold, noting as I did, that the door had already begun to slide closed behind me. I affected a melodramatic melancholy.

"You wished to see me, sister?"

"Yes!" she said in a low voice but with high excitement. The other two echoed her in a similar tone and a manner that reminded me of a Teek drone, incapable of independent thought.

"Yes…" I agreed but noted their positions in the room.

"We must discuss," Liesarn said, closing the distance between us by another two steps—and I noted that the room was not particularly big, not large enough for a long-shinned lady such as herself to need more than a few good strides. "And here there is no recording to capture us."

I leapt. I did not need to hear more, did not need to know what machinations Liesarn had set for me in this place. I was upon her, my feet pinning her clawed arms at the elbows. I'd already flung off one hand wrap toward one of her stooges. The other hand I pressed into Liesarn's open mouth.

"*Sister!*" I hissed. "I am not as fragile as you hope!"

Liesarn made a strained sound, and one of the others asked, "Sister?" Either of me or both of us I didn't know. If they all attacked me, I could not hope to contend for long, but I had clearly maintained the surprise.

"Wait!" Liesarn rasped, shock in her eyes, working her mouth around my bandage and its bitter balm. "Sister Kesiel, you are mistaken!"

"Yes?" I asked. She tried to speak again, but I grabbed her under the chin, pinching off one of her throat muscles and stifling a yelp. I curled forward, my body rolling like a snake, but the fins on my head stood upright. I was in range to lick at her ear when I whispered, "Careful, sister; be very sure of what you say next. As you thumb my scales, I shall thumb that hole in your neck, and, due to my modified hands, I will not give you the courtesy of a swift, sharp slice."

I eased my hold but did not fully release my grip.

"Kesiel!" she squeaked.

I expected her to beg for her freedom or speak some excuse or even give an admission of sabotage. Instead, her voice was measured, with no hint of smile and full seriousness. "We are all in danger."

The door behind me slid open, and I whipped around, yanking Liesarn with me by her head.

Filling the bulk of the space, I saw the partially silhouetted form of a P'rukktah female and heard her say, "Kesiel!"

I turned back to Liesarn and demanded, "In danger? Of what? Tell me sister and do your best. *Lie* to me."

I expected Arrksh to grab hold of me and pull me off Liesarn. I had begun to wonder if there was any chance Liesarn could be guilty of anything. I did not expect her answer.

"Hridan!"

That made me let go, scramble up to my feet, and collide with my scooter.

Liesarn began picking herself up with the assistance of the others.

I accepted the aid of Arrksh as I came to my feet. My hands stung terribly, but I did not show it. My flesh fluttered with my rapid heartbeat, but I kept my feet on the floor.

"Tell me, sister, what do you mean, *hridan*?" The question was genuine, but I had already suspected the answer.

When Liesarn next spoke, so much fear showed on her face and sounded in her voice, I was concerned the poor creature might expire, but she was resolute in sharing her message.

"The Humans!" she said, in a tense whisper, ready to slash at any unwanted ears, whether or not they understood our language. "The Humans; they endanger us all. They try to transport *hridan*! They hold them here; they use them on the lower moon."

"*Hridanee* are space legend, sister," I told her, using the impossibly uncommon plural for the spectral superstition. I could not hope to convince her, for I did not manage to convince myself. I too had seen a light. Mine was blue, unlike the stories of unlucky starfarers, but I had seen the light, heard my own voice shouted back at me, and lost all sense of time and space during the encounter. It had all the markings of *hridan*, which I had been reluctant to acknowledge.

"No, sister," she said. "*Hridan* is here and present on this planet. And it is the Humans who hide it."

I turned to Arrksh, who mutely and numbly offered no objection. Somehow, I took her silence as agreement with Liesarn.

"For what purpose?" I wondered.

"For a Human purpose. A weapon, an advantage. If they can harness it, it will be truly destructive, and if they cannot..." She wheezed. This was not a forced dramatic gesture, but a closing of the airways in fear. Perhaps she was about to swallow her tongue again. "The last time they could not contain *hridan* they destroyed a planet."

I had heard of the outcome of the Syedi-Teek offensive, the Human battle that ended the war and saved the Teek at the cost of a hiveworld, as had everyone. But that, like this space ghost we called *hridan,* might have been nothing but rumor, exaggeration, and a good story. A part of me wished to run as far away from this revelation as possible, the part that I later learned Humans referred to as the lizard brain. But I held there to hear more.

One of the other Tsanghar, thus far silent, even when I attacked her moonkin, said, "You saw it too."

It was perhaps the least barbed accusation I'd ever heard from my species, the least leveraged claim.

Every scale from snout to tail wished to protest, or at the very least equivocate, and I am indeed a master equivocator when occasion calls for it. This, however, called for frank acknowledgment. "Yes."

"What of the P'rukktah?" asked the other orange-face, hunched and shifting back and forth, ready to attack or retreat, possibly to attempt to blend with the opaque matte wall.

So far, this entire exchange was carried out in the Yavamee dialect of Tsanghar. By now I knew that Arrksh understood much more than she could say, especially if her translator was filling in any of the gaps. Arrksh did not move, but there was someone to vouch for her.

"I trust!" came the scratched voice of Liesarn.

"I trust," I agreed.

Finally, Arrksh nodded and confirmed, "Trust."

* * * * *

Chapter Forty-One:
Lidstrom

1500 Day 5

I felt an eerie excitement all through the morning and into the afternoon. When Yiorgos' squad was called away for some more boring VR safety training, I was left to my own devices, which meant a lot of time for me to stew.

I took another run at the Rock Hopper, but I was so distracted that I only got worse instead of better. I wondered what it would be like to slow down the rocks and thereby up my reaction time, which I'm pretty sure was the opposite of what had happened with the Arteevee's clock. If something had slowed it, then, in theory, time on the outside would have appeared *faster*. This was why I didn't mess with relativity.

According to everything I knew about other spacefaring races, the rat-beebees probably had more experience with relativistic time dilation than anyone, but experience did not necessarily mean expertise. Paul Newman was likely a more knowledgeable person, but I knew that anything I told him might get shared with a drone and then with the hive-mind-network, however that worked out here. I would not say I was suspicious of Kesiel or Arrksh, but neither did I trust them. Maybe it was based on my observations—Kesiel's creepiness, even compared to other Tsanghar, and Arrksh's cageyness.

Maybe I was just being a closed-minded ape-man from Terra who still called the Belbehan rat-beebees. But even ape-men learned how to educate themselves, so I popped on the Source and started doing research.

You would be amazed by how disorienting it is to be cut off from the Net you're used to and placed instead on the Source. Originally called the Cooperative Interstellar Resource Database, and later renamed by Transnat pilots who didn't want to call it CIRD, the Source was a vast encyclopedia of everything the Human-Teek Alliance thought reasonable to make public to all their people: the collective species' science, mathematics, history, and literature, though there was very little of literary note from the Teek. Apparently, it was growing every day thanks to researchers in the field, and it was projected to double its information every year once the Initiative started exploring more deliberately.

Needless to say, the Source was intimidatingly large, and, unlike the Terran Net, or the "Web" if you asked the dinosaurs, it had many unhelpful chat forums or user tags saying who liked which article for what reason. Searching was difficult. You could go down a dozen different rabbit holes in a matter of minutes but have no idea if you were getting any closer to what you sought, and I was looking for "whatever could screw up the reader in an atomic clock."

Paul Newman found me in one of the study rooms and asked me to teach him to play a Human game. He had been told that chess and strip poker were both long-standing and highly popular concepts. I went cold and told him I was busy. I resumed my research in my quarters, where the only intruders would be Humans. The worst part is, I didn't even feel bad for blowing him off. I was so focused on my search that the idea of Paul Newman playing strip poker didn't make me laugh.

Time dilation provided about a million hits, almost all of which were either about fast travel or dead-end theories never tested in this universe. I shouldn't have been surprised that I couldn't access much on weapons that could slow time. If they did exist, all of the research was classified. Pretty much everything that had led to our alliance with the Teek was kept under close watch and not made available to other species or, apparently, even well-meaning Humans. The authorities in charge had published whatever they could about various conflicts between other species, including every recent dispute between the P'rukktah and Tsangharee, and other species I'd never heard of—who apparently didn't make the cut to join the Initiative.

Is it any wonder I ended up surfing through myths and legends?

Random tales of lost time and unexplainable phenomena across the stars populated my screen, and it mostly got me nowhere. There were a lot of Belbehan cases, but every one had an asterix saying that Belbeh were likely to have forgotten or misinterpreted reports that had been passed between a dozen people before being written down. There was a similar note on a Tsangharee superstition, a bad luck spirit called *Hree-Dahn*, or however they pronounced it. These reported space encounters may have been a cover-up for sabotage and murder. Where the P'rukktah were concerned, I felt like I couldn't find any interesting or weird phenomena that they hadn't already conquered.

I was starting to do a deep dive on the Avowol—no pun intended—when Yiorgos returned. I was so entranced that I must have leapt three feet in the air at the interruption, which is easier on Mars, but still not fun. My particular emotional cocktail was equal parts on edge and staring at a giant, benign, brain-invading jellyfish big enough to require the giant tank in the med wing.

I didn't give him long to settle in before I swiveled my desk chair to face him. "Hey, how would you view the surface? Like without taking an Arteevee."

Yiogros had half lain down, but popped back up. "Um—Okay, the easiest is the live feed itself. That's like from the base, cameras and scanners. Some of that is available footage for cadets, but it doesn't see very far."

"And if you wanted to look out past what the base cameras could catch."

"Then we're talking drones. Not like the Teek variety, but somewhere between the covert and overt spy tech. But they're rough to fly here. Can't exactly hover in .08 atmos, or at least not easily. And, in theory, cadets can't take those out."

"Sure. But we wouldn't take a drone out for something that's already happened."

He leaned forward and pressed his hands together. "You want to see your accident again, don't you?"

I tried to act casual but assumed I'd fail. "Yeah. What's wrong with that?"

"Well, rationally, nothing, I guess. It's just not really practical or doable."

"Why not? I thought everything was being recorded."

"Well, sure, on Earth, but we're on Mars with only a tiny fraction of the surveillance tech available. Look, in order for you to see the accident, someone would need a camera pointing in that direction at the time it happened *and* be recording, which they would've expected your Arteevee to do."

Unfortunately, every camera on the craft had fritzed out just before the explosion. I didn't need to remind Yiorgos of that.

I chewed on my lip for a moment and asked, "What about satellite feeds?"

"Um, sure, if you know how to access one and control it, I suppose you could see a lot, but that's way beyond practical on both counts."

"Both?"

"Yeah." He was nodding but not looking at me while seemingly running calculations in his head. "Not really something I can access or something that has a high likelihood of having been pointed in the right direction and recording while in the right point in orbit at the right time."

"Shit." I weigh each idea for a moment. "All right, let's revisit door number two."

"What?"

"We use a drone."

Yiorgos furrowed his untrimmed brow. "But you won't see the accident."

I shrugged that off. "I know. But I at least want to see the site. Maybe I'll find something."

"Man…" If I had to guess, Yiorgos was stuck between wanting to join me on my puzzle and telling me to give it a rest. "What do you think you'll see that no one else did?"

I stood and spread my arms. "I don't know! I really don't. But what if there is something out there? Some weird anomaly that just takes one of us to spot. Or even something that's being covered up. There could be anything—I mean, we are on an alien planet."

"Yeah, a planet that Humankind has been walking on for over ten years and studying for far longer. We've got like forty bases spread over the surface. If there was something to find—"

"No, I know, I hear you." And I did. I understood the chances were remote and that I was pressing against some pretty sturdy walls of logic and probability. But there was just too much that had happened. Too much that didn't quite fit. I had thought the desire to fly, to control an ultra-fast craft in three-dimensions, was the most important thing in the world to me, but the sensation in my gut and the pulling, tingling at the base of my neck were almost as unignorable. "I know I don't have much to go on, but we've barely scratched the surface of this planet or all the things that could be out in space. Even you said the chronometer was weird. Even if it turns out to be just a mundane glitch, don't you at least want to see, to verify as much as you can?" As I asked it, I felt a pang of something like guilt: Paul Newman would want to know, too. But I pressed Yiorgos. "Can you help me?"

Yiorgos pursed his lips from side to side while he considered. Luckily, intrigue won out. "Sure."

The process of procuring a drone and logging into it was much faster and less difficult than I anticipated. Of course, Yiorgos was doing all the work to patch in from the relative comfort of our quarters, using my access code on my cadet console; I was merely pacing behind him.

Rivers beeped at the door, and I let her in to provide the other component my Greek comm tech had asked for.

"Got it," she said, holding up a small data chip with a universal dock—or rather "standard among Human tech" as opposed to truly universal.

"Thank you," Yiorgos said, taking the chip and plugging it into the console.

"What is that?" I asked.

"It's permission," Yiorgos said.

"It's an LT's access code," Rivers clarified.

"What?"

Yiorgos took it in stride. "Yeah, the instructor, Lieutenant Chandan. He's been off base pretty much since we arrived. Someone copied his access one of the times a guest lecturer had to sign in to one of his classes." While he spoke, he kept his fingers moving, working through the academy system and checking out the drone. His voice was a dry monotone, his focus on his task. "A few of us have been trading the decryption node back and forth. Not to do anything bad, though."

"And we checked," Rivers said. "He doesn't have any early access to squad assignments or any way of anonymously influencing who gets paired with whom."

"Yeah, that's a weirdly guarded part of the academy…And done." Yiorgos played up the final keystroke. I think he was performing for Rivers more than me. He was wearing a big, goofy grin when he announced, "We have a drone."

"Skilled." I clapped him on the shoulder. "Can you pull up its video feed?"

"Already done," he said, and the screen populated with the drone's camera. "You wanna do the honors, pilot?"

We swapped chairs, and I guided the drone up and out of its charging station outside the base. It took me a bit to get my bearings, to accept that it wasn't dealing with normal propulsion physics and took a surprisingly soft touch, either that or the keyboard interface we were using was not optimal. Once I got oriented, however, I could use the pre-programmed commands to pick a direction and let the tech do the rest. It kind of took the fun out of learning a new machine, but made for much lower risk. I located the garages and the shuttle hangars and followed them into the open over the red-orange planet, along the ridge.

The view was awe inspiring, even with a grid overlay and viewed through a non-optimal computer screen. I traced our path, seeing the tracks of the other Arteevees, how far they got before they had to stop. Our closest competitor had managed maybe five hundred meters. We had gone over five kilometers.

"Damn, L!" Rivers remarked. "You really are the 'naut."

"Seriously skilled," Yiorgos agreed.

The little drone continued forward. I wanted it to scan for anomalies and do the kind of things they could work out in science fiction, but all I could do was scan within known parameters. Radiation, magnetism, heat, sound—not that there was much to be heard in such a thin atmosphere, no matter how hard Humans had been working to seed it.

My skin began to prickle as I arrived at the crash site. I saw drag marks, lift marks, detonation marks, all over the pockmarked surface of the planet. Nothing unusual stood out, at least not what I was looking for.

"You covered a lot of ground," Rivers said, in case I hadn't caught her earlier compliment.

"Yeah, I just—" I didn't really know what else to say. I found myself hoping for a blue light and a banshee's wail, but all I got was silence and stillness. I set the drone to hover and started checking the maps, desperately scanning to see if I'd missed something. "What about…What about this?" I pointed to an area ahead, marked with a symbol and a tiny picture from space.

"That's a defunct solar panel station," Yiorgos said. He started to work through the other nearby blips. "That's a portable lab that was dropped and left there years ago. There's a storage facility…a signal array, and on the far side of the caldera is an emergency landing facility. A skeleton crew runs it. The biggest base in Mons is the Olympus Mons Academy."

He would know; he was a data guy. With other mini bases and buildings all over the area, it was even less likely that something could have been missed.

"All right." I had been preparing my "what if" and was about to make a fool of myself when my wrist chimed.

I went to tap the alert, but it wasn't going to wait for me. A robotic voice said, "Cadet Lidstrom, please report to Commander Claude Poissonier immediately. A wrist beacon will guide you."

I regarded Yiorgos and Rivers, who seemed more worried on my behalf than I was. Rivers abruptly yanked Lieutenant Chandan's copied code from the console, and said, "I'm going to step away for a minute."

She exited, leaving Yiorgos, myself, and a glowing arrow on my wrist device, like a VR-game objective marker but far less fun.

Yiorgos looked like he was about to ask how I was doing. I didn't want to entertain the question, so I shook my finger at him and did my best Spacegirl Stella stance and voice: "And *that*, kids, is why you never steal an officer's access codes to use on your individual console."

* * * * *

Chapter Forty-Two:
Lidstrom

1700 Day 5

"O kay, let's sort this out."

He sounded frustrated but somewhat sympathetic. It was like what a grandfather would say just before he sits you on his knee and gives you some much needed wisdom. The tradeoff is that you might have to sit through a really long "when I was your age" lecture.

But I wasn't going to pass up the chance to get some closure or to meet with the commander, even if I received a reprimand for taking out a drone. His posture told me he wasn't going to hold the door open for long.

I entered his office a little sheepishly and tried to survey everything without obviously staring at his personal effects. He didn't have the usual accolades on display, even though I was sure he'd been involved in dozens, if not hundreds, of projects during the journey toward an interstellar Human race. There were two plaques: one was for his graduation from university with honors and distinction, the other with his list of promotions, including effective field rank. I recognized the symbols, locations, dates: a seal from the Metz-Dubrov Lunar Base, a patch with a scorpion in a Saturn-ring from in the middle of the W-Wars. Beyond those, there was very little that spoke about him in a professional or personal capacity. A few permanent, non-moving pictures were framed and mounted on the walls, including celebrity shots I didn't recognize and, weirdly, an autographed spatula. My eye was drawn to a shot of a much younger Claude Poissonier in one of the early dress uniforms of the Transnat Space Program, standing under a cherry-blossom trellis next to a tall, regal-looking man in a tux. I realized it was a wedding photo and the tuxedoed gent was his husband, or maybe ex-husband. The commander was not wearing a ring.

"Sit down," he said. I obeyed.

While I ogled his walls, the commander cut straight to the point and pulled up some images on the mounted monitor screen. He rotated it toward me so I too could see the feed. It was camera footage of an overturned Arteevee on the surface of Mars.

"That's it!" I exclaimed, louder than I should have within four hard walls. "The flipped Arteevee!"

"I know. That's why I'm showing it to you."

My chest got cold, like just before the floor drops out from under you. "So, you knew? The whole time, you knew there was another Arteevee and you kept trying to tell me that—"

"Mm. No," he said, barely shaking his head. "Cadet, this is *your* Arteevee from the vantage point of the rescue vehicle. Their footage survived the incident." He reached around and pointed one determined finger with the skill of someone used to walking people through both virtual and actual models of incomprehensible technology. "You can see where you hit the oxygen tank. Here you can see some debris. There's where you blew the tire off. But there's only one Arteevee."

I stared, dumbfounded. I had to deliberately close my mouth, but that didn't stop my stomach from plummeting or my head from spinning. "But it—" I was breathless, so I inhaled and tried again. "But that's—that's exactly what I saw *before* we got there. That's what it looked like. It was—I mean, I'm sure."

"That's the thing. In retrospect, you think you were sure. But you're working off a memory created while suffering from extreme exposure, not to mention minor head trauma, high adrenaline, and any other mix of factors. Lidstrom, I believed from the moment you said it that you had a memory of a flipped Arteevee that was true and real to you. I do, and there are aspects of the accident and recovery that we didn't anticipate and can't quite explain. But you have to ask yourself, what is more likely? That there is some grand conspiracy to cover up a second rolled Arteevee that no one wants you to know about, *or* that a good pilot in a high-stakes situation dreamed of what he was experiencing while losing pressure and oxygen?"

He stared at me for a long moment, leaning onto his desk, his fingers steepled in front of him. He shrugged, then turned his hands palm up. "At this point, it's Occam's Razor. Which, I admit, rarely works in the realm of propulsion systems or interspecies communication, but…" He gave an exasperated but sympathetic chuckle; Commander Claude was truly leaving it to me.

Which scenario made more sense? With some reluctance, I had to agree. "Got it, sir."

"Good. I've got a class to teach, so if there's nothing else, you are dismissed, Cadet."

I swallowed and pushed down my pride with the large lump in my throat. I was about to leave, but something needled at my mind as I stood. On one hand, I could have maintained some grace and dignity if I didn't poke the issue further, but just before I waved the door open, I paused. Who knew if I'd ever have another opportunity like this one?

"What couldn't you explain?"

"Say again?"

The question stuck in my throat; I knew I had to phrase it right. I turned back to squarely face the commander. "You said there were things about the accident you couldn't have predicted and couldn't explain. Like what?"

He chuckled, and it could have been wry or rueful, but he paused when he noticed I was resolute. "It's not exactly classified, but we still don't know the different ways Teek and Tsanghar minds send signals or how those signals might interfere with others while sleeping." His phrasing was technical, as if he was trying to say exactly the right thing to avoid any statements that might sound bigoted about different alien species. But I didn't care about that part. I had a feeling there was something more.

"I suppose," he went on, without me prompting him, "the other part is more philosophy than science. I—um—" He cleared his throat and assumed a practiced poise. "I was concerned, based on how long it took to reach you, that we would get there in time. Frankly, we were very, *very* fortunate that the damage from surface exposure was as mild as it was."

I kept my reaction low. I savored the full breath I got to take, knowing how close I'd come to death. "Why are you telling me this?"

"Because when I was in your boots, I'd rather have known than not. Officially, there was an accident and the I.I. safety precautions and quick response worked to bring all of you back. Unofficially, and more realistically, the five of you got out of the hangar before we thought anyone would, faster than the trials we'd run, and farther along in the mission than our response teams could adequately respond to in a timely manner, and we nearly lost you because of it."

My mouth was dry and my heart was beating fast. "How long did it take to reach us?"

"Just under fifteen minutes," the commander said, shaking his head. "Which would be some of the longest I've experienced."

"So, about the same time lost on the chronometer…" I whispered.

"What?" he asked sharply.

I realized that I should have kept that one a secret, but then I decided I wasn't investing in a conspiracy mindset, so I told him. "The atomic clock in the Arteevee was off by about fifteen minutes. 840 seconds actually. It looked like it stopped. Do you know why it would do that?"

Commander Claude twitched a little, then started nodding slowly. "I would assume something's gone wrong with the reader. But, um, yeah, maybe the force of the explosion jostled something it shouldn't have. I'll have someone look into it during repairs. Thank you for letting me know, Cadet."

I nodded. "Sir."

"You're a sharp kid, Lidstrom. You're back to classes and cadet duties tomorrow. Don't lose your head."

I grinned. "No, sir."

"Good. Now, get out of here."

I did as I was told, feeling a little more settled if not actually good about the accident.

I had to make a choice: either I could stay frustrated and fixated on an accident in the past, or I could focus on the future. Just a few minutes earlier, I would have read into and analyzed everything the commander said, or didn't say, as possible evidence of something fishy and underhanded. But he was right, and it was better for me to move forward.

Though I wasn't really a spiritual person, I wanted some kind of symbolic gesture of closure, and I knew about the tree-worship rituals people liked to do. I'd heard various people say to give your troubles to a higher power, so I made my way across the Nexus to the alien tree. I placed my palm on the bark and thought about everything I'd experienced, everything I was worrying about, and I tried to let it go.

I told myself I was ready to turn things around and dive into the rest of my academy training, clearheaded. The universe had other plans for me, in the form of an organic roadblock literally just around the corner.

"Lidstrom!" came the voice of the sweet, sneaking, scary lizard. She was drumming her nubby, newly healed fingers together and staring down at me from her full height and, of course, showing all her teeth, but this time I didn't interpret it as a smile.

If that wasn't enough, she was flanked by Arrksh. Arrksh didn't have to extend her neck to look intimidating, she just stood. Her outer tusks appeared longer and sharper to me.

"We need words with you," Kesiel continued, and I wasn't about to correct her use of idioms.

"Okay, yeah. What is it?"

"Something that requires privacy," she said and indicated a direction with an open hand.

Arrksh closed the distance between us with one step, pretty much blocking any consideration of retreat.

"Sure," I said and followed them to parts unknown.

* * * * *

Chapter Forty-Three:
Paul Newman

1700 Day 5

I sat nervously waiting for Jane Goodall. With each passing minute, my nascent thrumming grew louder and less manageable. I stood, a more natural state for Teek workers than sitting, and began pacing.

My choppy, marching movements attracted strange looks from the cadets and staff moving through the front office of the infirmary. I did not mind; after all, none of them were Teek. I was struck by the curious intent of the word patient. Perhaps Humans were expressing a hope that people waiting for their doctors would be patient patients; perhaps it was intended ironically.

When Jane Goodall arrived, it was not through the office—that is to say, she did not utilize the front door or the door from the classroom space. Though I had been told that she was out and not busy, she emerged from the back hallway that led toward the rooms we had woken up in, where Shin still slept. It was also one of the routes to the Avowol's tank and a number of small examination and evaluation labs. However, I did not know enough about the layout of the base to ascertain other entrances or anticipate Jane Goodall's sudden presence.

She took long strides and spoke quickly, abandoning the Human words and instead using Teek. "*Come.*"

I followed.

She led me to an examination room where she promptly closed the door, shut out the lights, and disabled the wall console. Before I could ask any questions, she picked up a handheld electrode tool and pulsed my wrist device. My screen, vitals monitor, and clock shut off. I was too surprised to protest.

"Take off your wrist device and give it to me," she ordered. I didn't know what she planned to do, but I complied. Then she pulsed her own device, similar to mine but a little larger, perhaps a previous generation of the tech. She removed it, exchanged it for mine and said, "Put this on."

"Why?" I asked, though I still followed her directive.

"There is little time to explain," she said. "I do not know how long we have." She turned away, opened a cabinet, and took out yet another device, which I interpreted as a scanning system with a miniature computer interface.

Though she was turned away, I tried to gain her attention, "Doctor Jane Goodall, I need to speak with you. Ella and I are concerned about my sleep and our meditation. Even though I was cleared—"

"Did you dream?" she asked.

I thrummed a nervous response, which must have been a confirmation.

Two of her four hands worked at the scanning device, while the other two began to undo her lab coat. "I suspected as much. I first began to worry when you scrambled that drone."

I grew cold with apprehension. In fact, I was so nervous that I suggested an option which could get me removed from the I.I. "Perhaps I was merely not compatible with off-hive drones."

Irritated, she clicked out my real name, the designation as Mother initially gave it. "Paul, it *wasn't* off-hive. I would know; I brought it from home." She glanced at me and read my cognitive shock, then spoke the point clearly and plainly once more. "That drone is your hive-kin—*our* hive-kin. It was spawned and imprinted by Mother, the hive queen the humans know as Bertha, and I brought it with me prior to the Initiative. It should have been able to interface with you perfectly, but it could not process your encounter on the surface of Mars."

I wanted to be terrified, awed, upset, and happy to reconnect with family, all at once, but I had neither the time nor the ability for that in my agitated state. "Why did you not tell me?"

"About being hive-kin? It wasn't important. About the drone or your encounter? I had to be certain, so I sent you to the Avowol. But I may have made a mistake in doing so." She finished removing her lab coat and handed it to me. "The Avowol's report was marked as confidential, to be read by me alone. Unfortunately, it was opened by someone with I.I. clearance of commander or higher. I do not know who saw it or who they may have relayed the data to, but someone is looking to..." She searched for the Human words, then reverted to Teek to say, "*Cover it up.*"

I felt strong foreboding from that comment but did not manage to express this before she said, "I have received covert orders to freeze you into deep hibernation again."

Perhaps she did not need to freeze me, given how cold my core felt at this revelation. I wondered if Lidstrom would appreciate that joke or if it would even translate to Human psyches. Either way, it would not be difficult to read my terror from my purple eyes.

"But I am not going to freeze you, *jik'tze*. Your task is too important. First duty may depend on you."

I warmed instantly. All of my shoulder joints primed, prepared for what pitiful combat I could attempt, but ready to defend my queen and hive.

"What threatens my hive?" I asked.

Her chromae shuddered a flash of orange then went green then gray. She was more practiced than I at showing neutral, but I could tell she was working against many shifting emotions. "That is difficult to explain. I do not believe what you encountered arrived by accident. Rather, I have seen evidence of a secret project run by a group of Humans, concealed from the rest of the alliance. You and your squad came in contact with a piece of that project. I ask that you trust me when I say you are in danger, but that you must act. First, put on my coat. With my wrist, coat, and rank stripes, anyone but kin will think you are me."

I did so but was worried. "What about you?"

"I will be fine," she said. "Second, you must take this scanner. It was meant for radiation detection in living systems, but it will work to find the anomaly. Search for radiation traces that do not belong and then concentrate on them. I believe your hind-brain will direct you."

I looked at the device in my hands. I had no fear of using the scanning systems, but I did not know exactly what I should be looking for or what to do when I found it.

"Shall I enlist Ella's aid—"

"No!" she said loudly, and I did not believe any of the infirmary space was soundproof. "It has to be you. You and no other Teek. Do you understand?"

I clicked my mandibles, curious.

Jane Goodall grasped my shoulders with her upper arms and placed her other hands on my thorax. I noticed she kept her antennae pointing up and away from mine. "Paul Newman, imprinted with linguistic skills and empathy, who loves Human and cultural discovery. You survived first encounter. If you knew what I know, you would not have, so I cannot tell you more. I cannot commune with you because you have to encounter again."

She released her grip and pointed to my wrist. "I have uploaded a base schematic. It will show you ways to exit the infirmary and medical labs without going through the front entrance. But I will not know where you have gone."

Though she wished to hurry me from the room, I halted her with a necessary question. "What must I do when I encounter again? What is *Third* step?"

She appeared very distant; her eyes gray once again.

"Ask it what it wants."

* * * * *

Chapter Forty-Four:
This Fine Crew

Kesiel is neither rough nor gentle with the Human; she directs and does not give him the option to redirect.

Though we progress generally in the direction of the hangars, Lidstrom asks, "Where are we going?"

"On an investigation," Kesiel says. I hear both their own words and my translator's slightly delayed interpretation. I listen closely; that is what I am here for.

Lidstrom makes another comment whose words are unimportant. I pick up on his nervousness.

Kesiel responds, "We are going to see our Arteevee and you are going to take us."

"What?"

"Yes! You were there today, let in by other Humans," Kesiel says. "Now, extend the courtesy, *please.*"

Lidstrom looks surprised. His expression seems to ask how Kesiel knew. He does not suspect how observant I have been or that I told her.

"But wait, it was sent in for repairs!" he protests and tries to halt and turn around.

His small frame runs into mine. I do not make any move to hurt him; I do not need to.

"Okay, hey, you wanna see for yourselves? Fine. There are probably logs or something." Mumbling, he adds, "Maybe Clancy can tell you."

We arrive at the closed door. Kesiel tells Lidstrom to open it.

"I can't," he says, flatly but with annoyance. Kesiel glances at me and I give no indication—after all, I have sensed no deception. "Look, what are you looking for? I mean, Commander Claude just showed me—"

"No other Humans!" Kesiel hisses, probably louder than is necessary.

I scan the corridor. Even with my less-evolved eyes, I can pick out two cameras that will see us in their arcs. Fortunately, the only visible people are still a great distance away toward the Nexus and the tree. Nearby, there is a door without a keypad whose label is written in Human and Teek, which I cannot read. It is a dark, metal door, the same one Gordon emerged from the night before.

Lidstrom still appears legitimately confused by Kesiel's outburst, and he has not responded.

In Human, I say, "This way. Safe."

I am not sure if it is the right word, but Kesiel takes my meaning.

This new door is also locked, but with far less care. From appearances, the opaque slab has a keyable latch.

"The janitor's closet? Really?" Lidstrom asks after reading the markings. Kesiel has figured her way through the physical lock before his comment is translated to me.

This time, Kesiel actually shoves the Human bodily into the space. He reacts quickly so he does not stumble on entry, but he does not exert enough main force to resist.

I close the door behind us while the lights come up. The room is bigger than I would have expected, with a much higher ceiling and a range of tools and chemicals available, primarily for cleaning. I stare up the ladder, which accesses a raised walkway. I begin looking at the various symbols and labels on all of the cupboards, but I notice Lidstrom is backing unsteadily toward a wall of tools.

"Okay, you're really starting to freak me out now," Lidstrom says.

"You tell first!" Kesiel says, more upset than I have seen her before. "There is much to freak about, Lidstrom. You Humans are toying with *hridan*!"

"I don't know what that is!" he exclaims, his intensity rising to match hers.

Kesiel looks to me. Lidstrom appears to be truthful.

I switch on my translator to produce Human words and ask, "Do you know what our team found on the surface?"

He puts up his hands. "No, I get it now; there was no second Arteevee. I just misremembered because we hit an O2 tank, but there was no sabotage."

To Kesiel I say, "He does not know."

"Really?" Kesiel softens her posture a little and approaches the small Human from one side. "What about the blue light, Lidstrom?"

"I don't know, Kesiel. But you seem to. Why don't you tell me?"

I appreciate his show of defiance. After all, he cannot hope to physically contend with one of us, let alone both, but still he commands respect, most importantly his own.

"*Hmm*mm," Kesiel muses. She softens further and smiles. "It seems the Humans too are divided, even those on this base. Factions, houses, and however Humans separate themselves. Perhaps mere ideologies or a matter of rank.

"Lidstrom!" She announces his name sharply. "I believe we may have had a psychic encounter on the surface with an alien entity we know by different names. A rarely sighted spectre, an enigma that baffles science, we call *hridan*."

Lidstrom shakes his head. "But that's just a legend. Like your version of a space boogeyman."

"*Yeeeessss…*" The higher notes of her voice tax my acute ears. "You Humans call it double-u."

"Double-u," repeats Lidstrom, then lifts his brows and his eyes dart in all directions. "Like Wayne—codename Wayne?"

"Mm! You are familiar," Kesiel says. "Then do you know what your Humans are trying to do with the entity?"

His lips move as he mumbles to himself, but he truly does not know. His youth and inexperience are plainer now than ever, but his ignorance of his people's plans may keep him a friend more than a foe.

In silence, with my other senses more readily available, I notice a dull sensation that I must have been smelling the whole time, but only now became aware of. First, I look up the ladder, toward the walkway, most likely connected with the observation rooms above the garages, but the scent is not coming from there. This aroma is local. It is somewhat Human and yet something else as well. It does not seem to be any of the tools. No it seems to come from one of the storage units.

With each step forward I become more certain.

* * *

Kesiel

S uddenly, Lidstrom shifted his focus. "Arrksh, what are you staring at?"

But Arrksh didn't answer. She merely stood before one of the cold storage units, fixated on the temperature gauge. She reached forward and put one palm against the surface, letting the condensation wrap around her fingers and vapors billow away to escape her breath.

She inhaled deeply through the nose. Recognizing the intent, I joined in, sniffing the air, entirely aware that Arrksh had far better olfactory senses than me. But I too smelled something strange.

"Mmm," I said. "Careful. The entity may reside within."

"No," Arrksh said in the common Human. She snapped the latch open by force. If you do not have a key, sometimes you can pick the lock and sometimes you have to destroy it.

She pulled open the door and revealed a nearly empty refrigerator, dark within. However, as my eyes adjusted, I saw a zippered bag. It was nearly two meters in length and capable of housing a somewhat scrunched Tsanghar form.

"Death," Arrksh said in Human, in that low, growling manner she has, which sounds all the more frightening.

Lidstrom pushed off of the wall and took a leaping step to her side.

"Is that a body bag?"

Whether or not Arrksh noticed the question, she answered it by unzipping the encasement. A cold, stiff, wan Human face rested on the other side.

"Shit!" Lidstrom said. "Why in hell would they have a corpse in a maintenance closet?"

"Mmm. Humans are indeed divided if they would kill their own."

"What are you—" Lidstrom began asking, but Arrksh was faster. She produced the proverbial bloodied dagger by reaching into the bag and extracting an arm, the dead man's arm, an altogether different set of colors from the standard flesh. Blue and white lines, wrinkled and dried. Two of the fingers were too shriveled to function even if there was a beating heart to sustain them, channels of veins along the skin were scabbed where they burst from pressure and constriction.

Arrksh utilized her translator and told us, "No. They did not murder. Just hid."

"Who is it?" I wondered.

"It's Chandan," Lidstrom said, quietly at first, then louder. "Lieutenant Nick Chandan. The missing instructor."

Arrksh checked the other arm but did not find a wrist device on either. There was no formal tag or label on his flightsuit, but the face did look familiar from stills and possibly in passing.

"Did you know him?" I asked.

"No, I—" he faltered. "I knew no one had seen him for days. I recognize his face." Lieutenant Chandan and his thin upper lip fur, his strained expression, even in death. In addition, Arrksh turned over one forearm and revealed a mark printed in ink that could withstand shedding. A nine-sided star with an animal silhouette and Human lettering inside.

"TSF," Lidstrom said, "Transnat Space Force."

"What is that marking?" I asked, pointing at the curving black outline.

"It's a scorpion," Lidstrom replied. "It's for the Transnats who crewed alongside the Teek during the war. Chandan was a veteran." I could not tell if this was observation or confirmation.

Arrksh didn't care about the man's identity. She was investigating the warped fingers of the dead man.

"What could have done that?" Lidstrom asked, swallowing nervously.

Arrksh said a word into the translator, but nothing was produced in Human. She tried again, and again, no output. Turning off the translator, she finally said what I was already thinking, in her growling voice, "Wayne. Hree-dahn."

"The question is, what are the Humans trying to do with it?" I asked.

"*That's* the question?" Lidstrom countered in an almost mocking tone.

I decided to counter his counter. "You're right! That question is easily answered by what Humans always do. They are trying to make an advantage out of it: a weapon or a new ship design to exert control over explored space. The *real* question should be how far have they come?"

Lidstrom stared at me, incredulous. "What are you talking about?"

"It is the nature!" I hissed. I scurried forward on all four limbs and rose up before him, a lick away from his hairless face. "The Teek build knowledge, the Belbehan multiply, the P'rukktah endure, the Tsangharee adapt, and the Humans destroy! You and your military kind follow your instinct, your conditioning and tradition—as do we! It was this tradition that brought you to the Teek and why the Teek allied with you in this war that you applaud. You are the only people who could destroy their enemy because it is your nature."

"Now wait just a minute! Humans can't be summed up in one word or one ideal. Look, even if it's true, that's not all of us, and that's not what we're doing here. We're here to learn and explore. Besides, most of us don't even know what happened in the war! It's classified."

I read in his eyes the offense I had brought him. I was…touched by how passionate and genuine this Human could be about his people's non-military virtues. Having nothing to say, I did not respond.

Lidstrom tried. "Look, I don't know what you know, or think you know, about us or what's going on here, but something's not right. Whatever they're hiding—" he pointed at the corpse, "—seems like the kind of thing where they don't want loose ends. Now, the way I see it, if there's a cover-up for what happened on the surface, we're all witnesses. So, it doesn't really matter that I'm a Human, you're a Tsanghar, you're a P'rukktah, or that Paul's a Teek, we're all in this together, so we might as well work together."

"Ah, a truce!" I remarked.

Lidstrom looked disappointed by my suggestion. "No. A partnership. Cooperation. I mean, we were chosen as a squad, weren't we? So, let's be a squad."

"I applaud you, Lidstrom!" I said, emitting a squeal of approval. "You have a flair for the dramatic."

"Trust," Arrksh said.

"Trust," Lidstrom agreed. "So, the most important question is what do we do now?"

We were not left wondering for long.

All three of us startled when Lidstrom's wrist device beeped an alert. An unnuanced robot voice said, "Cadet Lidstrom, report immediately to the infirmary."

Lidstrom's eyes widened, but his lips stayed shut. He looked to me, then Arrksh, then at the dead body we just discovered. I do not know if there is any precedent for literal emotion sharing between species, but I believe we all had a dose of the same foreboding.

"May I suggest, Lidstrom," I said, "that the first thing we do is *not* follow that directive."

"Yeah," he said, a little shaky. "I think you may be right…"

I put out my hand. "Here, give me your device."

He appeared to understand that I was taking away any means of tracking him and started to undo his wristband. "Where are you going to take it?"

"Away from you. Arrksh?"

Arrksh hesitated. "Translator," she said, in Human, reminding us that her translator's settings and functions largely routed through her device. She removed her device and placed it in the refrigerated storage unit, so anyone who came looking for her would find the dead body. The translator earpiece and microphone were still attached and at the ready, I assumed in a manner that would try to translate Human words to her, even if she did not wish to have a running program translating her words to us.

I knew where I planned to take the wrist devices, given my greater speed and ability to quickly climb, but I had to ask them, "Where will you go?"

Lidstrom glanced to either side, but saw nothing because it was a closed room.

Arrksh, on the other hand, pointed straight up the ladder, and said, "Hangar four." She immediately began climbing.

"Right," Lidstrom said. "Meet us there."

He stood at the base of the ladder and gave me a smile.

"You are very interesting, Lidstrom," I observed. "You just accept where Arrksh is leading?"

He shrugged and started up the ladder. "That's what trust is, Kesiel. Or maybe my faith in *tessenda* is growing."

Though his syntax was somewhat off, I appreciated his remark. Some open-mindedness was a small expectation, given the risk I was taking on his behalf. I assumed it was only a matter of time before a similar infirmary order would be issued for me.

* * *

Paul Newman

I only ever knew about the war academically, and even then only in a limited way. I later learned why that saved me. As a worker unit intended to learn, explore, and connect with all kinds of species, I was never imprinted with fear of the enemy in the same way my hive-kin were. I knew the enemy had been a threat to the preservation of the hive and the species as a whole, and I knew the Humans had been essential in defeating them. But I had never seen one or seen anyone else's memories of them. I did not even have a name for it, just a concept taught by an information drone, a Teek word meaning "without walls."

I tried to put it out of my fore-brain. After all, I had to be Doctor Jane Goodall and I had to make good use of the tools I'd been given. The wrist unit identified me as a lieutenant-equivalent and the scanner showed me radiation anomalies. I needed both to complete my mission.

I was not surprised when the scanner led me toward the garages and hangars, past the Nexus and the Uua. I wondered if I were looking at the readings correctly, I stopped doubting when I entered the hangar. The peculiar pockets of minimal radiation were much starker in this room, consistent with an entity that absorbs more radiation than it puts out.

The path led me directly to a locker in the small shuttle's hangar. Like most lockers, this one had a keypad which could be accessed by someone with the right code or someone with the right identification. I was neither, but I had planned for this.

I let the scanner hang slack from its shoulder strap and got to work with Jane Goodall's wrist device.

I heard the door behind me and rapid footsteps before I could enter the command. I looked over one shoulder, expecting—for reasons I cannot explain—Lidstrom. Instead, a woman in a TSF maintenance uniform and curled, orange hair had run close to me before halting. I believe I had met her before, when she was assisting in the transportation of a dead Human body. The woman was named Burke, and I now had suspicions about the body.

"Hey, you!" she yelled, her feet speeding up.

My fingers moved rapidly to compensate.

"Hey!" she said again, then I heard a telling *click* of a sidearm's safety being disabled. I had not before known a click to be ominous, but I was beginning to appreciate perspectives like Kesiel's, which granted sentient emotions to objects and actions. She said, "Turn slowly."

I obeyed, but I kept my hands ready.

Burke "recognized" me, too. "Doctor Jane-Two!" She sounded almost relieved that it was me. Her respiration was rapid, and I sensed perspiration on her brow, but she lowered the weapon. "Wh—What are you doing here?"

Had I felt more confident in the role, I might have come up with a feasible misdirect without my eyes turning bright green. Instead, I held up one finger to request pause, then completed my order on the wrist. "I am issuing a medical directive to the base."

Shortly after I said so, I was satisfied to hear the sounds of alarms and announcements: "Breech Alert. Head to the nearest sealed safe zone."

Burke did not understand my tactic, which is no fault of hers; I did not explain it. Her fingers tensed around her weapon to demonstrate her confusion.

Some locks had to be overridden strategically, using measures already in place, but I had to employ them in the right order. Now, I had to make sure that I would not be shot before I could open the locker of hangar four.

* * *

Kesiel

I moved quite rapidly through the base, in a "lizard-like" manner that was considered consistent and therefore acceptable. The corridor where I emerged was largely empty, with no one paying me much or any attention. The closest person was a four-armed Teek in a white laboratory coat far behind me and already facing and walking in the opposite direction. Naturally, my path away from the transportation wing would take me through the

North Nexus and the garden of the Uua. The Nexus-that-connects-us, once a pleasant arrival in my view, now a chokepoint. I had meant to go past it, to one of the gymnasiums and the mess hall, both places where a personal wrist device would be reasonable to locate but the number of people difficult to sort through.

It seems I was a little late in getting started, however, for my own device alerted me before I even entered that great dome space. In the same robotic voice it said, "Cadet Kesiel, report immediately to the infirmary." First in Human, then repeated in poorly approximated Tsanghar, which requires far more inflection than the computerized version allows.

My hands, feet, and tail adjusted quickly. I banked for one of the walls and started up it at a rapid pace. The low gravity was to my advantage, as were my clawless fingers and uncovered toes. I squeezed into the high corner until I reached the end of the hallway, then traversed the concave walls of the Nexus, partially hidden by the hanging flags and non-sentient flora around the edge.

I will not say that it was an easy ascent, many of the panels were what Humans exaggeratingly called frictionless, and once I reached them the triangular supports of the dome were far apart. My newly healed flesh had an easier time creating suction, but it was also far more tender, and I was not able to pull my weight along without pain. The leaps and upside-down portions were somewhat perilous, for a fall from this distance would be damaging, possibly fatal, if I did not land correctly, even on Mars-Human. But the true engineer knows the workings of her own body as the most essential complex machine, and my body carried me near the center of the dome, avoiding the transparent panels and keeping me successfully out of sight.

I saw the payout of my instincts. Three sure-footed Humans entered the space. One was in an I.I. uniform and had a shiny brown head: Gordon. The other two were base staff, security guards, one of whom toted a large foam gun used for short distance suppression—the mere sight of which scared the Belbehan sitting around the Uua.

I was almost directly above the Uua's trunk, which rose more than halfway to the ceiling. The militant Humans were just outside the soil plot. Gordon looked at a handheld screen. I could not hear what he said, but I imagined he was tracking Lidstrom's wrist, which I currently held in my mouth.

I looped an elbow and my tail around the beam, freeing my feet for angling and one arm for reaching. I took Lidstrom's device and extended my arm as far as I could. This may sound strange to a Human, but I breathed a silent prayer to the Goddess, though I know Her influence could not stretch beyond my home star system. Then I dropped Lidstrom's tracker so it could fall onto the Uua, in the soft top section of the trunk. I was undoing my own device to repeat the drop when I slipped!

My tail and feet clenched the beam instinctively, even though both arms fell free and I pitched forward. Overcoming the instinct to screech or hum was difficult, and I had to place both free hands over my mouth. Fortunately, even for their time in space, Humans still think in two dimensions and did not look up.

They were starting to stomp into the tree's soil, telling the Belbehan to scurry away. By the time I regained my handholds I managed to successfully free my own wrist unit and drop it just as another alert arrived surprising everyone.

"Breech Alert. Head to the nearest sealed safe zone."

This was broadcast over every speaker, first in Human, then in Teek, Tsanghar, Belbehan, and finally P'rukktah.

"What the hell is going on?" Gordon demanded loudly and clearly, though ten meters and a tree lay between us.

I agreed with his disbelief. I sensed no change in pressure nor even a wind. While the Belbehan scrambled and the few others in the Nexus quickly departed, I remained a moment to calculate, as did my would-be captors.

The alerts continued to sound, meaning there would be more distraction to anyone listening for me. The directives told them to go to safe zones, closed areas like our individual quarters or some of the airlocked classrooms. We had certainly drilled the safety standards enough for me to know. No one would want to go to the North Nexus on an occasion like this.

I began climbing back the way I'd come, taking less care for safety and aiming instead for speed. If they were looking for me or Lidstrom and were focused on the tree, they might miss me entirely.

I did not look back when I heard Gordon call out, "Hey! Tsanghar!" After all, I knew it was directed at me.

Fearing the foam suppression guns or the stunner, I let go of the wall, hoping I was close enough to the ground and the gravity was low enough for me to fall uninjured. I took the landing well, crumpling my legs and turning it into a roll, which invited only a very survivable level of pain to my hip. I was surprised that I heard no fire behind me, but only a confused muffled protest.

I looked and beheld a sight few have witnessed. The Uua had woken.

The great tree had reached up with a root and wrapped with a branch. The security man with the foam gun had been pressed into the bark, another had been turned upside down and dangled between the limbs, where he futilely commanded, "Let go!"

Gordon, who had spotted me, was the closest to the edge, but several roots had stretched out and taken hold, pinning him to the ground. The screened tablet lay before him, propelled by the momentum of his fall.

"Kesiel!" he called.

I was impressed he remembered my name. In place of a salutation, I collected his tablet.

"Kesiel, wait!" he pleaded. "What you're dealing with is dangerous! It's dangerous!"

The man was not eloquent while trapped by the mobile tree roots. I admired his volume and courage in the face of plant-based peril, though I believed the Uua had no intention to permanently damage or consume them.

I raced away from the scene, hearing the repeated alert of a breach, and I regretted that I could not thank the Uua in its own tongue. Although, I was comforted by the fact that the Uua did not have a tongue and, I believed, knew quite a bit more than it let on.

* * *

Paul Newman

Ensign Burke did not react well to my alarm. In fact, it seemed to frighten her.

She pointed the gun at the door of the hangar, which remained closed.

She lifted a hand to her head and yelled, "God! Stop! Stop screaming!"

Though it was said in my direction, the imperative was not given to me but the locker behind me. I turned, lifted my wrist, and drew up the interface to open the locker door.

"Wait! Jane, don't!" Burke struggled to keep her head up and her eyes open, but still she pointed the gun at me, at my legs, which was better than my head, but much harder to heal than my torso.

"Why not?" I asked. "What is inside this locker?"

"It's—" She shook her head. "It's dangerous. God, don't you hear it screaming?"

I was aware of the sound, but it was distant. Perhaps the entity did not intend the phantom noise to assault my brain. It appeared it was targeting Burke. Still, I was curious, I wished to investigate, even during her distress. "Do you see the blue light?"

"What?"

"The blue light of the entity," I clarified.

Burke opened her eyes. She strained and grunted. "Jane, you don't know what's going on. You have no idea what you're messing with! Now step away from the locker, or I will shoot you."

"No," I said, and somehow, I did not thrum. "I too have a duty, Ensign Burke."

Until this point, she did not seem to see *me*. She saw a four-armed arthromorph of a lieutenant-equivalent wearing a doctor's coat. Now, she saw *Paul Newman*. She sneered and snarled, "Christ, you're not Jane-Two! You're that nosey bug cadet, who—" She pointed the gun at my head. "Give me a reason why I shouldn't drop you right now."

I attempted to think of a good reason, but one did not immediately occur. I had noticed, however, one figure behind the glass of the observation window. This gave me some confidence in completing my mission, if not surviving. My wrist device was at the ready and I needed to open the locker door. After all, the station alarm was still ringing, and the emergency alert I had given allowed medical personnel extensive override abilities, which should extend to most doors and lockers. It was better I act while I could. Hopefully, my squad could determine what to do next.

I used Jane Goodall's ID to override the lock, and Burke fired the gun.

What I saw next was certainly the greatest marvel I had ever witnessed. I just hoped I would live to remember it.

* * *

Lidstrom

Arrksh got the compression hatch open just a moment too late. I heard the gunshot from behind the window, and I was powerless to stop it from our vantage point, a mere five meters above them.

Arrksh skipped the ladder, content to leap the distance on Mars, unsheathing a red, bejeweled dagger mid-flight.

But the air around the gunwoman shimmered, shuddered, then slowed, almost as if someone had put a bubble around her. It was not a freeze, just a delay, and a short one at that. Paul Newman, unaffected by the bubble, pitched to one side and out of the way of the delayed bullet.

Arrksh slowed as she got closer to Ensign Burke, then they both resumed normal speed and passage of time. Before Burke could manage to re-aim and take another shot, Arrksh demonstrated a chilling form of surgical precision by putting the dagger point through the woman's trigger finger.

A quick spray of blood, a rapid disarming move, and a massive elbow to the jaw ended the fight before I could get down the ladder.

While Arrksh pinned the knocked-out Burke, I rushed to Paul.

"Are you okay?"

He picked himself up and responded in an exceptionally Paul Newman way. "Yes, Cadet Lidstrom, I am fine. I feel obligated to let you know that I am not Lieutenant Doctor Jane 'Jane-Two' Goodall, but your squadmate, Paul Newman. I merely used her ID to open this door."

"Right. Thanks, Paul," I said, stifling a laugh, which I realized was entirely inappropriate. "I'm just relieved. Is Ensign Burke—" I began, but Arrksh was still holding her down in case the Human should stir.

"Yes," Arrksh said.

"Cadet Lidstrom," Paul said. "I must apologize for endangering you, but I am glad I do not need to continue alone." His eyes were a pale blue—fear, hesitation, and maybe a bit of wonder. A matching sliver of blue light shone out from the wall.

I felt the hair on the back of my neck prickle, aware of static electricity and another presence.

I turned to the unlocked storage locker and pulled the door open. I didn't need to shield my eyes from the blue light because it was much dimmer this time. I felt no urge to cover my ears, only to help remove it from its cell.

A loop of pliable copper wire sat at the entrance, connected to a battery. This, I perceived as a gate, an electric fence, but I didn't take any precaution when lifting it out. The coil provided only a minor tingle along my skin. The next step was a cage holding in the blue. The blue wanted to escape, but it was too small, too spent, too weak, and the faraday cage, while not perfect, was clearly enough.

"Shit," I said. The light made no reply.

Arrksh stood. She looked ready to retreat.

Paul did not move. He could not even blink.

The silence was interrupted by Kesiel's arrival. She rushed through the door, bootless and grasping a tablet under one arm. None of us were surprised by her entrance, not even Paul, who couldn't have known she was on her way. Kesiel didn't react to Paul, either.

I dragged the cage out of the locker. It was heavy, even on Mars. It would have been unliftable back on Terra. It sparked where metal dragged against metal, much more than it should have at the speed I was moving.

I swallowed some fear and knelt next to the cage. The blue light came from a small orb, no bigger than my fist, floating in the center of the enclosure, as if it were suspended on all sides. The cage itself was less than a meter cubed, like a medium dog's crate, with openings in the middle big enough for Arrksh to reach her arm through, but where the entity couldn't pass.

"So, this is it…" I said, then realizing I was talking to the little light, I adjusted. "You're what we came here for. You're what we've been wondering about this whole time, and you're just…" I reached into the cage. The light shrank away. "It's okay. I'm not going to hurt you." To be honest, I wasn't sure if I could.

The air around it felt cold and electric. There was a magnetic draw, as if it were a ball of static electricity without needing any solid matter to stop it from dispersing.

My fingers tingled as I approached.

"Lidstrom!" Kesiel whispered, high and frightened. "Careful."

But I was somehow sure of what I was doing. "You're not going to hurt me either."

I made contact.

My fingers felt like they'd been dipped in ice water, and soon the chill ran up my arm, into my shoulder and neck, until the signal reached my brain.... and I saw.

It came in flashes, jolts. Images were omnidirectional, hard to interpret, and not exactly seen by eyes. The information was flooding, hard to pick apart at first, as if every kind of signal was absorbed at once. Then, I caught glimpses I could make out. A lab under the surface of Mars, the faraday cage, the faces and minds and voices of Humans. I recognized Chandan, one of the people experimenting on the seed.

Then something else, something hard to explain. The entity had reached out in all directions, searching for something or someone—no, *called* by someone. Because it had found something familiar. It had woken it up and passed a signal through me.

A whale song on Phobos, felt through the rock. In my memory, along with the Rock Hopper scenario, a question about flipping a six-wheeled Red Terrain Vehicle, a sense of, again, wonder. Projections, signals, cries for help—a mental image for the Human, a suggestion to the Teek's hind-brain, a clue from a lizard speech, and the words, *"Free me!"*

An explosion! Decompression and waves of dust, breaking connection and concentration but only temporarily. Partially held by and anchored to the cage, reaching out, creating a bubble, an umbrella, drawing every bit of energy available, and trying to slow the loss of air. The air could not be slowed without being blocked by physical matter and there was no way to manipulate that much matter that quickly. So, instead, all matter had to be slowed.

I withdrew my hand with a gasp. My fingers were somewhat numb and chilled, and now sporting odd bruising patterns.

"I was—We were—" I slowly turned to see Arrksh at my side. She caught me as I stumbled, a little disoriented. "That's what saved us on the surface."

"Lidstrom!" Kesiel said, jerking me alert with her best nails-on-chalkboard tone. "The *hridan* is what endangered us, leading us along a wrong vector."

"Yeah, but…" I didn't know how to explain it. There were pieces I didn't understand, that felt like inconsistencies or gaps. I had trouble pinning down exactly what the entity had done, but I was pretty sure I knew why. "Here," I said. "You try."

Kesiel glanced at the door. "We have little time, Lidstrom."

"It will only take a second." Somehow, I knew that to be true as well.

Kesiel moved forward to stand across from me. Arrksh likewise readied herself to reach into the cage between us. Finally, Paul finished the square.

All four of us found an opening in the bars. I nodded and we connected.

* * *

Paul Newman

It did take less than a second for the narrative to play through, for all of us to experience through the being's consciousness. The images and sounds filtered through my hind-brain like a drone's message, except I was fully conscious for the exchange.

I did not shut down into hibernation this time. I did not lose any memory.

When I withdrew, I was the most lucid out of the four of us, but it did not take them long to steady themselves. Like Kesiel, I was aware of the door and knew it was only a matter of time before someone came after us.

Still, I had asked the being what it wanted and I had a clear answer which made a great deal of sense to me, and it was becoming even more crucial that we assist sooner than later.

I told the others, "We must bring it to Phobos where it can connect with its other half." Yes, there was another: a second part of a binary mind which had sent a signal into space.

"*Yee*esss, Paul Newman," Kesiel said. "We even have a shuttle for the errand." She gestured at the short-range shuttle docked in the hangar.

Arrksh responded by picking up the cage and walking it to the rear of the craft.

"We have to move quickly," Lidstrom said, "before anyone in the academy alerts the Phobos docking base."

"One of them is choking on a tree," Kesiel said, and did not offer any further explanation to ground the expression. "The other is this rather limp Human." Kesiel knelt to remove the Human's wrist device. To free up both her hands, she extended the tablet in my direction. "Make use of this," she told me. "It was used by Lieutenant Gordon."

I began to work the tablet. If Jane Goodall's authorization could navigate through a security obstacle, perhaps Human Gordon's could open a shuttle. Behind me, I heard Kesiel asking Lidstrom, "Help escort this Human to the locker." She assured him there would be enough oxygen.

The progression went quickly. Arrksh grabbed every emergency supply we might need and Kesiel did a quick check of the shuttle. I did not question her ability to manually disable the clamps.

Gordon's authorization was not hard to find in the tablet, which was then easy to point at the shuttle.

The only delay came from Lidstrom, who halted me during the loading. "Wait, Paul," he said, his hand on my arm, "are you absolutely certain—"

I interrupted him saying, "I presented the plan, Cadet Lidstrom."

"No, wait. Just like that? Paul, I need to know that you're really sure about this. This isn't just some random specimen we're ferrying or breaking the rules for. This is your enemy, isn't it? Code name Wayne. This is the thing Teek nightmares are made of; what keeps the little blind larva awake at night."

"Actually, Cadet Lidstrom, the larva would have no—"

"Paul, accept the idiom. Really. I mean, I know it saved us, and I'm in favor of helping in return, but my people weren't terrorized by them. How can you be okay with something that could be, and has been, your biggest threat?"

I gave it due consideration, accompanied by the continued sounds of alert and Kesiel's humming. I regarded the cage Arrksh had placed in the back of the small shuttle. Lidstrom did not err in his commentary on the Waynes, whose terrifying power had initially led to the Human-Teek Alliance. I suppose if I had been more like my endoskeletal companions, I would have felt a personal ire against the entity. I saw, however, not an enemy combatant but a seedling. It was an enigma who had done us no harm and had even protected the four of us after we'd followed its untranslatable distress signal into danger.

One truth kept resurfacing for me, and I did my best to explain it. "First duty is to protect my hive, it is true. But first duty to my hive does not require me to hate all beings who might be connected to a former enemy." Facing the makeshift faraday cage, I said, "This being is not an enemy of mine. So, I would offer aid."

Lidstrom smiled and nodded. Not the fast Human nod of agreement or awkwardness, but the thoughtful slow nod of camaraderie. "Good. I'm glad to hear it."

"Very well reasoned, Paul," Kesiel said, climbing into the shuttle. "After all, if the *hridan* had chosen to make an enemy of Mars, the only way to escape the danger would be to get off the planet."

The tiny creature's blue light continued to wane, giving new credence to the Human code name. "Off-planet is where its salvation lies, Cadet Kesiel." I felt far more trepidation in asking the favor than risking my own safety. "Cadet Lidstrom," I said, "can you fly us there?"

* * *

Lidstrom

I stole my first aircraft at the tender age of fifteen. Here I was, about to reprise the act and raise the bet before I'd even polished off the half-decade. Shuttlecraft, check; skilled pilot, I was willing to bet on myself; likelihood of a future in space...well, probably not with the I.I. after this.

The other three were staring at me, waiting for me to answer Paul's question.

"Okay," I said. But that wasn't good enough. I knew something was missing. I clapped my hands together and rubbed them aggressively, warming up my fingers that had chilled with nervousness while feeling a heat in my core, the kind of heat that should turn into a rousing speech.

But I didn't know what to say. I'd never been very adept at giving speeches in school. I could read them off with gusto but making up and delivering something moving was a new kind of challenge. Everyone was waiting, our precious little time ticking away, to hear the next words out of my mouth, I realized two very important things: One, that my future as a space pilot could hinge on our success, and two, that I was the only native English speaker, which meant any errors could be written off as poorly translated idioms.

"Okay," I began again, more exuberantly, "we're gonna do something." I waved them in, inviting them to cluster closer. "It's a very Human thing, but I think you'll like it. We're going to put our hands together, all four of us, at the same time."

Kesiel was by my side in a second, clearly ready. The other two proceeded together while Kesiel asked, "Palm up or down?"

"Down," I said.

"No crushing or bloodsharing, I presume." Once again, Kesiel.

I tried not to turn green over what could have been a very reasonable suggestion from another culture. "No, just stack them."

"I am ready," Paul said, putting his upper right hand out first, his eyes an electric red, excited. "This sounds exciting."

I placed my hand on top of Paul's, aware of the exoskeletal structure and the surprisingly comfortable cartilage at the joints.

Kesiel joined on top of mine, the suction of her thumb gripping the back of my wrist, the unscaled palm cold and rubbery to the touch.

Arrksh must have missed the memo. She went palm up on the bottom of the stack, under Paul's clawed hand. But her furry fingers were so long, she managed to wrap all the way up to Kesiel.

It was such an excellent moment and image that I found myself thinking it should be on the cover of a magazine or whatever advertisements the fully realized I.I. would send out. We wouldn't be around to see it, but I found myself bolstered by the thought of this cooperative future.

"Let's do this," I said and extracted my hand. I turned toward the shuttle and noticed the other three had not moved.

Bit of a moment-breaker, but it had to be said. "You guys can let go now." At least I didn't laugh.

* * *

The shuttle had a five-person cabin with two extra fold-down seats and a storage area in the rear. Like the Arteevee, it was segmented, to be sealed off and separated in the event of a breach. The foremost section was a single seat, front and center, more like a fighter cockpit than what you'd usually find in a shuttle. It was almost identical to the simulator.

Paul was doing everything he could to authorize our launch without running it by anyone, while Kesiel continued system checks. Arrksh attended to our guest in the cage.

"Cadet Lidstrom," Paul said, "I am sorry to say that you will not have autopilot enabled for takeoff."

I exhaled in grateful relief, having expected that to go far worse. "That's fine, Paul. You've unlocked all the doors. I can walk through them."

Kesiel hummed in amusement; I couldn't tell you why.

"Cadet Lidstrom!" came an angry voice, but not from within the shuttle. This one was piped in through the hangar speakers. I raised my eyes from the controls and looked up to the observation window, where I saw Staff Sergeant Clancy. "Get out of that shuttle immediately!"

I shook my head and yelled back, "I can't do that, Sarge."

I gestured to Kesiel, who sealed us in.

Even without the go-ahead, Paul was on the comm, and said, "Connecting you to control tower four."

He sounded completely friendly and matter of fact about it, as if there was nothing strange about hijacking a shuttle *and* opening a channel to a higher-up.

The green light seemed to surprise Clancy as well because she paused before speaking over the comm. "Lidstrom…I don't suppose you'll tell me what the hell you're doing?"

While I tried to come up with a good response, Kesiel slipped in beside me, put one of her declawed hands on my shoulder and almost licked my ear as she whispered, "We have engines online."

I cleared my throat and said, "I have to do this, Sarge."

The switches were second-nature to my fingers, the system very user-friendly. The steady whine became whirring as I pressed us into a stable hover. Behind me, the entity glowed a little brighter, very briefly, and I wondered if Clancy noticed or could even see it from her vantage point.

She looked sternly at me, separated by two panes of spaceworthy glass, years of experience, and the crazy decision I was making.

Leaning forward she pressed the comm again. "Lidstrom, can you safely fly that rig?"

A sidelong glance showed that Paul was as bewildered as I was. Kesiel, meanwhile, looked amused.

"Affirmative, Sarge," I said. "Thanks."

"Don't you dare thank me, Cadet. You just keep your squad safe. Clancy, out." Before she left, the sergeant gave me a quick nod.

I didn't know what she already knew or what she had found out. Maybe it was as simple as a gut feeling; maybe it was a covert order. Either way, I felt sure she wasn't going to try to blow us out of the sky...or I was as sure as I could be about anything we were about to do.

I eased into lift, followed the open hangar door into the secondary chamber, which would lift like an elevator before opening to space. While we moved, the airlocks auto sealed and transitioned. I left the shuttle in static hover. I took my hands off the controls to check on the others.

Kesiel had strapped into the fold-down seat where she could access more floor space and the cage. Arrksh stood, holding a brace with one hand, while she continued to ensure that life support was up to code.

To the Teek right behind me, I asked, "Paul, can you set up a signal jammer so Mons can't tell Phobos we're coming?"

Paul looked at me. I don't know if the hard Teek exoskeleton can really show incredulous, but Paul was there. "Lidstrom, this shuttle does not have nearly enough power for that."

"Okay, think outside the box, Paul. What can you do?"

He mused while I pulled up a trajectory map to intercept Phobos.

"I can try to overwhelm their systems with static and signals that seem like distress signals."

I thought it over. As far as I knew, that *was* jamming, but I had to admit it was not my wheelhouse. "Good. I trust you, Paul." I felt more than heard the decompression outside the craft as we exited into the open and the bright sun, small though it was.

"Either way, *someone's* gonna notice us," I said. "I can't guarantee a smooth journey."

"Indeed no, Lidstrom," Kesiel agreed, "but it is wonderfully exciting."

There was a pulse of blue light and a strange wave of encouragement. I couldn't even guess what the entity knew or thought, but as of that moment, it was the fifth member of our squad.

I throttled up and readied the range thrusters for full takeoff.

"All right. Hang on." And we left.

The surface of Mars fell away: the underwhelming atmosphere, strange nearby horizons, and everything. The illusion of flat land melted and rounded away. Surface stations and installations came into view, then grew too small to focus on. Soon, Mars looked like a whole planet, so red against the black of space that it appeared too real for Human eyes, practically CG. Olympus Mons itself was breathtaking, especially near sunset. In the distance, the far distance, I saw a large ship in low orbit, probably running its own training, to complete the picture.

"I've been waiting for this my whole life…" I whispered, as soon as I remembered to inhale again.

Not gonna lie, I wondered if it would be my last chance to see everything like this. Strangely, I didn't fear for my life, but a part of me knew I was putting the academy in my rearview for good. I had just traded any potential future to fly a *Command*-class ship for one jump in a shuttle with a dangerous creature made of light. I gave myself the luxury of one sigh, one long exhale of self-pity. The grief would have to wait until later.

I couldn't see Phobos yet, but I knew the fast-moving satellite would be clearing the horizon soon.

Both the shuttle's upward propulsion and distant planetary gravity began to wane. I had a knee-jerk desire to tell the passengers how and where to vomit if they had to, but I personally felt fine and had no idea what Kesiel or Arrksh could handle.

Kesiel grabbed a bit of my attention by saying, "Lidstrom! Here we are, propelling around this red planet toward a station. But once we arrive, have you thought through the next step?"

I wasn't sure if she thought we should wing it or was hoping for a bullet-point plan. I erred on the side of both. "Well, the landing should be easy enough. We're not big enough to jack into one of the exterior tubes for the liners."

I'd been a fanboy of Transnat programs and space installations long enough to know the layout. I had had a complete playset of Phobos as a kid, and not just a virtual space, but the scale model physical kind. It was an earlier version, but the early installation and the main hangar probably wouldn't have changed much—or so I hoped.

"We'll just fly to the main hangar bay. Hopefully, they'll see an academy ship and just let us through."

* * * * *

Chapter Forty-Five: Lidstrom

Phobos Station: Main Hangar

T hey did not let us through.

The docking authority transmitted over our comm. "Please stand by to identify yourselves with either your TSF or I.I. designation."

The main hangar door, a hybrid shielded gateway embedded in the moon remained closed, held together by more red tape.

We hovered in queue beside a small mix of other vessels who had no idea how bad their timing was, all of us waiting for the gate to be opened once we were cleared or detained. Paul waited obediently, but to say what? We couldn't exactly ID ourselves as cadets, and we weren't sure if the stolen credentials we currently had would still be accepted. Plus, the longer we waited the more likely someone would get through Paul's signal jams and remote hijack the shuttle controls altogether.

I had no idea who on Mons Station might have known of our roughshod plan and who they in turn might have contacted. For all I knew, they already had time to send up a warning, and the Phobos hangar crew was just waiting to confirm it.

"Do we release it here?" Kesiel asked, indicating the cage. "Let it out through open space to try to find its kin?"

Looking at the Wayne, I couldn't imagine it would be up to the challenge or that it could get through on its own without being intercepted. But the people on the station might see or hear what we were carrying and consider it a dangerous contagion, which would trigger strict protocols, as inevitable and annoying as the drills we had run for the I.I.

So, I grabbed the microphone, and played a hunch. "Code W! I repeat, Code W. There has been a breach on Phobos base; you have evacuation orders. Begin evacuation immediately."

My hands were steady but by heart was a jackhammer as I closed the comm.

"That was very impressive, Cadet Lidstrom," Paul commended. "But are we not looking to dock?"

"Right you are, Paul. And when they go out, I go in."

Kesiel hummed. "Lidstrom! That is risky. You may not have more than a few meters' wiggle room if you try to do this."

I didn't like the waiting. It discouraged me enough anyway. I responded to Kesiel by quoting one of the most poignant lines I knew. "'It's not impossible. I used to bullseye womp rats in my T-16 back home. They're not more than a couple of meters.'"

"But Lidstrom, I did not say it was impossible."

"No, you did not," I agreed, my fingers gripping the throttle tighter as the Phobos hangar door began to open. Fast response time. They must have trained in the drills too.

I wasn't looking to wait or waste any time, so I told my squad "Hang on!" as I picked the first window available.

Only two craft were aloft and ready to exit toward me, both small shuttles like ours, and I could dart between them. No sooner had I crossed the threshold of the bay doors than I saw why they had left so much distance between them. A much larger, non-reg freighter of Belbehan make was rising to fill the space between them. I got close enough to read the fear in the pilot's whiskers before I pulled up toward the ceiling.

Many people describe their life flashing before their eyes at times like this. I only saw the highlights. I saw that Detroit hopper, the object of my first joyride, which landed me on either a juvie or junior TSF track. I saw the jet I took around the Metz-Dubrov Lunar Base, still on a tether, with instructors' training wheels. And I saw the Rock Hopper Race and the Arteevee Run on Mars' surface, complete with flipping over in slow motion and the soft, guiding blue light of the entity.

The Wayne had little juice left to guide me this time, but I was ready.

Unlike my first flight, I managed this maneuver without a scratch, but I left behind a lot of confused ships that didn't know how to react to our arriving vessel. Fortunately, Phobos was not a military installation—just like the I.I. was not a military operation—which meant that whatever list of visitors, I.I. reps, Transnat crews, and Phobos Station staff would have no organized response to the one shuttle that didn't get the memo for a Code-W evacuation.

Several comms tried to tell me I was "Going the wrong way" or that there was an "Emergency evac!" or something in Belbeh with the occasional burst of nearly Human-sounding words. I was too busy looking for an easy-to-reach landing pad that would be able to maneuver us safely into the station, and too nervous to know what I would say.

I finally located one and as soon as I touched down an automatic bubble formed around the shuttle, which filled with air and pressurize. In that moment, I was thrilled for automation, but it didn't mean we would get into the base through the hatch, if it even opened.

My concentration was cut off by a shriek from the rear of our shuttle. I covered my ears and I realized the ringing was in my brain, bypassing my eardrums.

I looked back and saw Arrksh had rigged the cage like a backpack, heavy and unwieldy, but manageable by a large female P'rukktah against Phobos' gravity. She ground her jaw against the entity's scream.

She understood, though, that Wayne was not angry with her, and we weren't scared of Wayne. Wayne had felt the presence of its counterpart, close by and more tightly caged than it was.

"I am trying to issue an order from Lieutenant Doctor Jane Goodall's ID," Paul said, "but there is no response."

"Crap." I should've have guessed that Jane-Two's access would be frozen.

"Try another!" Kesiel said. "Lieutenant Gordon!"

Paul clicked at the touchscreen for a moment, and I had a sinking feeling even before he said, "I am sorry, it does not work."

I started pulling up any system interface I could and tried to figure out if there was another way in other than through our hatch, possibly a different hatch in a different bubble, possibly using the EVA suits Arrksh had brought.

"Burke," Arrksh suggested. I had totally forgotten about her and she was possibly the only person who might not have been found or reported yet.

Paul made quick work of the task with Ensign Burke's access. I don't know what he entered or which keystroke did the trick, but soon Paul said, "Done."

I confirmed from the cockpit that we had access to the catch on the platform. Hoping to impress upon them the need to take advantage of this short-term chaos, I said, "We gotta move!"

"Yes…" hissed Kesiel, "but there is one problem."

"That we don't know where we're going?" I guessed. "Actually, I've got a pretty good idea of the station layout, and I think I know where they had the tank before. If we're wrong, then maybe Wayne will tell us."

I realized I didn't sound anywhere near as assured as I wanted it to be.

Kesiel picked up on my low confidence. She hummed, at first it seemed like it was to herself, until it turned into, "I *see*. I may have erred in saying one problem, but I had another in mind. What about station staff and security?"

"Hopefully they're all scattered trying to evac after I gave the Code W."

Paul, seemingly emotionless, replied, "Or, Cadet Lidstrom, some of them may be on higher alert. After all, those who know they have a Wayne may be more wary of other Waynes."

"Shit…"

"Hrm!" The sound came from Arrksh. She furrowed her thick brow. I realized it was an attempt to work through the language barrier. Her translator was set up to receive and interpret to her, but without a connected wrist device to enable the speaking portions, she had to muddle through some guesswork; it was an unfortunate downside of hyper-efficient modern interfaces.

Once she had our attention, Arrksh gestured with a thumb toward the cargo on her back, then mimed a sort of umbrella with her arms. Two words pretty much summed it up: "Time bubble."

* * * * *

Chapter Forty-Six:
This Fine Crew

Arrksh

I hear the entity, not just in my mind but through my highest ear, in pitches beyond what Tsangharee, Humans, and Teek can interpret. She is screaming. She is crying. Though I am not an expert on her anatomy, I believe she is dying. Whether this is the result of prolonged separation or of recent overtaxation on her system, I do not know. I assume some combination of both, with other factors of which we are ignorant.

Though it pains me to press her further, I do not believe we can succeed in our endeavor without this Wayne's assistance.

The creature is curious. It seems to take in heat without producing any; it seems to absorb some forms of radiation and put out blue wavelengths of visible light, with the occasional electric or telepathic wave. I do not have any basis in temporal mechanics in order to determine how it approaches changes in time, and yet twice she has demonstrated the ability to put forth fields of temporal affectation, not unlike how the Tsanghar bubble fields can trap oxygen and atmospheric pressure.

The light is less intense now than it was when we left, far weaker than it was when Gordon closed it in the locker, and nothing compared to our encounter with it on the surface.

I have had no occasion to study the anatomy, if it has anatomy, but I know it is alive. I know it can take and manipulate many forms of energy; I wonder if it can feed on mine.

I do not check with the others before I open the cage—not just reach through the interfering bars, but break the field altogether. This alone inspires a brighter glow. It also elicits calls of "Careful!" and "Wait!" from my squad, but I do not think we can afford to slow down. I cannot find where to turn off the power source for the electromagnetic parts of the cage, and Kesiel has not moved in quickly enough to assist. I rip through three wires with the Belbeh blade, to account for redundancies, as these are more like veins than major arteries.

The wires spark for the last time and part, the entity swells a little in size, and floats closer to the bars. I do not know how to translate the concepts into Human, so I say nothing. Kesiel is at my side holding a handlamp and some amount of cable of her own.

I reach both my hands into the space and pick up the entity. It is amebous, indistinct in shape and adjustable in size, appearing liquid-like, it is difficult to tell where it begins. However, as I come further into contact, waves and thresholds seem to pass into my skin, electrifying and freezing my fingers, painful but not yet damaging.

At this proximity, I concentrate and ask it for assistance, to accelerate our relative time so we may pass through the base. I use what mental images I can. I fear I will not succeed.

Suddenly, a claw surrounds my forearm. Far below my own, I catch Paul Newman's eyes.

"Cadet Arrksh," he says, "I believe I can do it. We are…similar. Let me carry it." His chest vibrates and his chromae continue to turn more and more violet. "You might need to carry me."

Paul reaches out and takes the small blue light, then begins toning like a drone. His eyes change to pure white. I delicately cradle Paul Newman, as he does the entity.

I notice something else, something strange. Sound shifts, then filters, then delays. Kesiel's giant flapping heart has slowed, Lidstrom's heaving lungs stretch out his breaths until the field envelops them, too.

The entity has sped us. We are now accelerating through time faster than the world around us.

Within our bubble, Lidstrom says, "Let's go."

We go.

* * *

Kesiel

The occasion called for a concerto, possibly with overlapping voices, one for each of us—that is five, including Wayne. Paul maintained a low tone, so I supplied the high, singing with the measure of my footfalls, wishing I had a throat-harp and a recording device. Perhaps our own mental records were more fitting.

It was a beautiful tapestry of movement through the hatch and down the corridors, with confused light fixtures struggling to maintain consistent power through our temporal distortion. Paul Newman, all rictus and rigor, contained the pulsing light between all four of his armored hands, which occasionally sparked off bits of lightning. Arrksh carried Paul and Lidstrom navigated for us. I would speed ahead, sometimes out of the bubble, then back in, confusing the hapless station security as I defied what they knew of physics.

Every transition into the field pressed me like a full flop on still water, as parts of my body moved faster or slower than I would have ordinarily expected them to. But I was elastic enough to survive. My tail could withstand far more crimping and kinking than the average endoskeletal spine.

Lidstrom's directions led us through the underpassages, until we exploded out onto the main floor. Here, there was even more chaos to wade through as traders of all walks and species clamored for more information about this cryptic alert going through Phobos Station. I found the return to the station to be a charming symmetry, and, once again, I was paving the way for my large, fur-faced friend who was ministering to a patient in distress.

The plentiful Belbehan reacted faster than any of the other bystanders, wishing to get as far from the super-speedy lizard as they could. Screams of fear and anger rose up every time I emerged to shove someone out of the way of our bubble. We did not want *hri-dan*-Wayne to overexert on the unimportant.

The pace became more difficult when station security opened fire. They used foam guns to try to halt us, called out orders that, to our ears, were too slow to understand, but they attempted to close the distance, compensate for where they believed we would be. I estimated the bubble moved somewhere between three and five times faster than they, though without strict consistency. I also found that I was bleeding at a faster and faster rate from the eyes, nose, and ears, the most common places for pressure bleeding in Tsangharee, and I held my skin constricted, rather than letting it balloon to spare me some discomfort. It looked like Lidstrom was developing bruises, Arrksh merely clenched against the temporal vector forces, her brow and neck filling with fluid to go taut against it. Paul rattled.

Our hopeful assailants switched from foam guns to stunners, but try as they might, they could not calculate how to aim with enough lead for the bubble and the fact that time would pass normally outside of it. I imagined firing an arrow into a still liquid with a terrifying index of refraction, which grotesquely stretched the creatures underneath. Human stunners are notoriously inefficient on non-Humans and Teek stunners are very difficult to focus precisely. A cable net, however, could spread our path and halt us, so when I saw one surefooted TSF unit steadying to aim the net shooter I screamed, "Faster!"

Arrksh repeated this to Paul, who jerked and contorted, in response. The blue *hridanic* being glowed brighter and the world around us slowed further. The net that should have moved over a hundred meters per second was cut down to a tenth of that. We veered left as a unit, Lidstrom close on my tail. Arrksh had to duck as the net entered our bubble and began to speed up. A terrible crackling sound issued as the electrified cable net split and popped under the strain of temporal variation.

"That one!" Lidstrom called, indicating a stairwell, which I was only too eager to race through. We slipped through a bulkhead between levels, and I had to wonder if they didn't know where we were going or if no one had thought we would get this far. I was beginning to muse that perhaps whoever was orchestrating this covert study of the *hridan* did not have as much authority as I worried they might.

The bulkhead slammed closed behind us. Even with the time distortion it was loud, hard, and fast.

We were well into the rock of the moon now, into rough passages like those where I had been taken after my arrival. That had been only a few days before and again my actions were preventing interstellar conflict which others scarcely understood. Lidstrom appeared to know where we were going, though, so, by extension, so did I. The rhythm of his thoughts played in unrehearsed harmony to mine.

I twisted and juked into the next hallway, expecting to find people planted there, waiting to stop us, but it was empty.

"We're close," Lidstrom gasped, indicating something on the wall, pieces he recognized. I felt as if I saw a handprint on the rock, present and important in the Human's memory, along with the rush of a simulated flight, just down the hall, opposite from our destination.

During the moment's pause, I realized I was practically throat-whistling in fatigue. Arrksh showed no signs of wear, but Paul Newman was actively seizing in her arms.

Lidstrom surged through this open space to a set of double doors. He shoved them open. There were several Humans in a tall room surrounding a large cylindrical tank with a transparency a short climb up one side.

Then, still slowed, one of the Humans triggered a switch on the tank. This created a shriek and a white-orange light…and completely dispelled our bubble. Our *hridan* stopped glowing. The one in the tank grew dimmer.

"That's far enough," said a scratchy Human voice with a strange lilt and a woman with gray hair and a mechanical arm blocked our path.

* * *

Lidstrom

A dmiral Victoria Hass didn't look angry or worried, just stern.

She wore a movable face plate, which she had lifted for our benefit—maybe for mine. The lead over-jacket was evidence that she, personally, was getting her hands dirty, I realized, in more ways than one. It was hard not to respect the conviction of the woman: a hero who lost much of an arm, who returned from the war and helped bring the Initiative into being, and who, even now, had the guts to support a dangerous experiment. I would have bet anything she thought it was for the right reasons.

"Mister Lidstrom," she said, nodding toward me. Then, "Cadet Kesiel. *Kirshka* Arrksh." The final one came with a sneer. "And Paul Newman."

Paul groaned and the pale, baseball-sized orb barely hovered between his hands. Several of his fingers had split and were bleeding the dark arthropod blood.

"I commend the effort, and your initiative," she said, sounding too stoic to read as insincere, but not genuine either. "It stops now. What we are working on is too important."

I noticed that the four other people in the room were Human, none of them wore an I.I. jacket or patch.

"No!" Kesiel called, before spitting out some lower Tsanghar phrases and then, in English, "You are betraying!"

Hass' lips formed a tight, patronizing smile. "I am protecting."

"What are you trying to do?" I asked.

"That's classified." She glanced between us, then magnanimously said, "I know that you were acting under the guidance of the entity; you were manipulated. We chose to keep them apart because it is too dangerous to bring them together. But if you stand down now, we will take the specimen away to a secure location and you will be reinstated. It is not too late."

My tongue was dry, and my throat cold. I understood the offer; I already knew what it meant to get a second chance to fly, and I wasn't sure I could afford a third. The thought of piloting that *Command*-class ship into the unknown was everything I had worked for. I also knew something, somehow, that she didn't.

Behind me, Arrksh made a very low sound that reminded me of purring, until it lifted into a snarl. I saw her lips draw back to accentuate her tusks. Then she whispered, "No trust."

And I believed Arrksh.

Two Humans were approaching with a portable cage, ready to take the entity from Paul's suffering hands.

"Wait!" I said, stepping forward. "Admiral, with respect, what do the Teek say?"

"What?" she asked, scowl lines creasing her cheeks.

The cage-carriers halted.

"The Teek," I said again. "Did the queens approve? Did the I.I. and Transnats give the go? Or is it just you?"

That's when I saw her expression change. She was appalled, disgusted by me or by us. There was hate and bile and things I could hardly define. There were too many factors for me to understand what was going on at an interstellar scale, but I felt assured I was in the right place, on the right side of the room when she yelled, "Take them, now!"

I prepared to block the ones with the cage. Kesiel sang a declaration that might as well have been a bugle's battle call.

Paul Newman said to Arrksh, "Throw me." To Wayne he said, "Take everything you need."

Arrksh wound up while the entity drew on Paul. The Teek chattered but held on, and the time bubble came into being once more, smaller than before but more intense. I felt as if every organ and tissue rippled when the field hit me, and then again when it suddenly withdrew, following Paul as he sailed through the air, moving at the wrong speed—too fast in the personal bubble and emitting cracking sounds as it went by.

But Paul reached the tank before anyone could react. With the force of his arrival, the moving combination of Paul and the entity slammed into one Human and sent him careening out of the way until he hit a wall a few meters back.

With great effort, Paul maintained his balance and grip on the top of the tank as the temporal field faded. Unobstructed, Paul pressed Wayne into the tank. The pale blue and orange lights merged until they formed an all-encompassing white.

I felt...well, a lot of pain, from the time distortions and now a blinding light that I couldn't block by closing my eyes. I also felt the most intense wave of gratitude, just before a pulse shut down my muscles and dropped me to the floor. I heard everyone else collapsing around me. When the light abated, I saw that the only one still standing, probably out of stubbornness, was Arrksh, but even she looked like she'd rather be on the surface of Mars in a leaking Arteevee. Still, she hovered over the limp form of the admiral, just in case.

The newly merged pair of glowing entities emerged from the tank, passing right through the side and whatever containment the admiral and her team had attempted to use. Though I couldn't move and was a few heartbeats away from passing out, I felt a strange degree of peace and hope. I couldn't tell you if this newfound grace was mine or if it came from Arrksh, Kesiel, Paul, or the now-complete foreign being. I am certain that the entity spoke to all four of us, borrowing Kesiel's voice to say, "A truce."

The room was enveloped again in white light, and I finally blacked out.

* * * * *

Chapter Forty-Seven: Lidstrom

I don't remember dreaming, but I had the distinct impression a lot of time had passed. For one, I was in an entirely new location with smooth interior corners and soft color gradients on the walls. It certainly wasn't the Olympus Mons infirmary or like anything I'd seen in Phobos Station.

For another, I *felt* different. And I don't mean the bruised ribs sensation, which can only be met with so many painkillers. No, somewhere deep in my emotional core, I felt calm and assured.

When Arrksh approached, a little too close with her massive arms and tusks not far behind them, I said a pleasant, "Good morning."

"Actually," her translator told me, "it is mid-afternoon planetside."

Arrksh looked entirely unhurt, unfazed. Her fur was smooth and full and had the kind of sheen you associate with a really well-groomed collie.

But she had said *planetside*.

"Where is this?" I asked.

Before Arrksh could answer, a Teek approached waving her aside.

"Excuse me, Cadet," said the four-armed Teek. I might have mistaken her for Paul in appearance, but she had a different voice and a distinctly different smell. Arrksh stepped back, clearing space for my ranking doctor, Lieutenant Jane Goodall. She looked a little worse for wear, but I would have a hard time explaining how or why.

"Excellent," she said, after a moment's examination. "Please lift your left arm and bend at the elbow."

I did so, only then noticing the wrap around my arm, too flexible to be a cast, but clearly of alien make. My elbow felt swollen and filled with fluid, but it was less painful to bend that I thought it would be. "What happened? Did I break it?"

"No, you have strong bones and joints," Jane-Two said. "You suffered massive contusions and tore the muscle tissue, most likely while passing through the distortion field. You will heal well."

She asked me more questions and performed more mini-examinations, some of which felt routine, others which were a bit weird but acceptable. Through it all, Arrksh continued to observe without reaction and I found it comforting that I wasn't in handcuffs, or whatever they would use after everything we'd done.

Jane-Two was not to be interrupted and did not respond when I asked her what happened after I lost consciousness. So I turned to Arrksh, and repeated my question. "What happened with Wayne? Is everyone okay?"

Arrksh opened her mouth to reply, but Jane-Two cut her off. "Arrksh, go get Kesiel."

It was very calm for an order, but Cadet Arrksh followed it without question or hesitation. I didn't see any security personnel in the hallways when Arrksh exited the small room, which was more good news, unless we were already in some kind of prison colony orbiting Jupiter or something.

"No distractions," Jane-Two said as she continued her examination.

* * *

"Lidstrom!" Kesiel sang upon seeing me. She was leaning forward on a scooter, the appropriately ergonomic lizard version of a wheelchair, with Arrksh pushing. "You look beautiful for a Human!"

I chuckled. I was barely two steps outside my room and into the curving corridor and really not expecting that kind of a greeting.

"Thank you, Kesiel," I responded, but had trouble reciprocating the sentiment as I noticed both her wrists and ankles were in immobilizing casts. "Are you okay?"

"Wonderful!" she said, "No soft tissue damage and my bones are re-knitting themselves. It was indeed a thrilling adventure."

Was. As though she too expected us all to be punished and ejected.

Jane-Two was behind me and now said, "This way."

"Are you taking us to Paul?" I asked, but received no response from Jane-Two. I surmised that, if we were on a prison station, she might be a prisoner, too, given that she had helped Paul. I had yet to see any other personnel, though, and the interior of this space, whatever it was, was pristine, with the kind of aesthetics that Kesiel could write poetry about.

But every negative suspicion I had evaporated the moment the doctor activated the transparency and I saw Mars below us. It was maybe 500 kilometers away; we were in a very low orbit. The ship was using artificial gravity that must have been close to Earth standard, smoother than the Phobos Station's grav and able to overcome Mars at this distance.

Kesiel voiced it before I found my tongue. "Lidstrom! Are we on your *Command*-class ship?"

"That is correct, Cadet Kesiel," Jane-Two replied. "We could not bring you back to the academy just yet, and this vessel was already compromised."

I didn't hear any emotional inflection or see her chromae change color, so I wasn't sure what to make of the statement.

"All four of you need to be briefed before any decision is finalized."

At once, the three of us started asking about the fourth.

I said, "So Paul's all right?"

Kesiel asked mildly, "Yeeesss, where is our friend, Doctor?"

And Arrksh said simply, "Paul Newman."

This caused a chromae shift. Jane-Two's eyes warmed to orange. She spread her antennae in a gesture I was beginning to associate with a smile. "Paul Newman is still recovering. He suffered more damage than the rest of you, but he will be pleased to see you once he has finished resting." Which was as much as we would get for now. Jane-Two indicated a direction from the window and therefore deeper into the center of the ship, saying, "This way."

Kesiel began muttering excitedly to herself in Tsanghar, cataloguing as much as she could about the interior design. She abruptly stopped when she saw another Human, this one clearly security, in front of a closed door, a heavy, circular hatch with no label or window.

"Lieutenant," he said, giving Jane-Two a quick salute before stepping aside.

Jane-Two scanned her wrist and let us inside. The entryway looked almost like a vault, and certainly a different ship. It was coated in wire mesh and had asymmetrical warning tags posted on them. I didn't have to read them to know that there was high potential of electric shock. My skin tingled as I walked through the six or so meters of the charged hallway. Arrksh's hair stood on end, in a manner that was ridiculous enough that I was afraid to comment. We finally reached an interior door where Jane-Two paused.

"This is as far as I go," she said. "Come out when you're ready."

I couldn't help but wonder if we'd gone back a step, if we'd really accomplished anything. This had all the markings of another, more elaborate cage for Wayne. Could they be doing worse experiments, and where did we fit in? Maybe this would become a cage for us as well and Jane-Two was just trying to trick us into it.

I was still wondering when Arrksh stepped forward and pushed Kesiel's scooter into the door, opening it. The innermost door did not lock or even latch; it just provided a barrier. But barriers were strange things to the Wayne, so I had to assume that there was some kind of energy contained in that doorway as well.

"Apparently," Jane-Two began, looking at the bright light around the edge of the door, "the entity came straight to this ship after leaving Phobos Station. The consensus is that someone planted a suggestion."

I had no idea if Jane-Two was implying it was me. Then again, she had no way to know that this ship had been my final thought as I defied the admiral, did she?

"Lidstrom!" Kesiel called, beckoning me to follow. So I did.

The light inside was bright to the point that it had the illusion of substance. My eyes never adjusted to it, but they did manage to accept it without pain. Once I found some focus, I noticed the two pieces of the being which together formed the white light. One was just this side of orange and the other leaned toward blue. A binary pair, like twin suns, orbiting each other and, for lack of a better word, dancing.

The light had already framed Kesiel and Arrksh, creating bizarre halos. I felt it reach out to me and do the same. I had both a familiar and alien sensation of receiving an embrace, of gratitude, of the word "truce," more felt than spoken.

I wouldn't have been able to tell you how I knew, but I was convinced the entity was not being held here, that it could leave on its own accord if it desired. And it was happy.

I'm not sure there is any way to truly quantify that emotion.

* * * * *

Chapter Forty-Eight:
Paul Newman

The Starship Endeavor

The ship was extensive and, from what I could see, expertly suited for any and all tasks. From the medical lab I had been patched up and woken in, to the null-space communication center I had been escorted to, I could understand how this vessel would be the ultimate in collaboration between species. I was also saddened that I may have jeopardized my chance to be a part of that.

I stood in the dark chamber, focusing on the transmission interface, waiting for the signal to emerge, meditating on the connection in order to prevent lag due to time dilation. The ship made a connection across the many Human light-years and found me in a similar communication chamber on an orbital station around another planet.

I knew the technology emulated sight and sound, but I was sorely missing smell more than even her presence in my hind-brain. My queen's eyes appeared sympathetic. Perhaps she was aware of my distress and capable of feeling me far more than I could feel her.

"*Jaiku* Paul Newman," said Mother. "I am pleased to see you."

"Eminence," I responded. I did not know what I could or should say to her, so I waited.

"I have been told much of what has happened in the Initiative by my older daughter Jane Goodall as well as by the new Initiative directors, about the presence of the enemy."

"Yes, Eminence."

"*Jaiku*, I am immensely proud of what you have accomplished."

I thrummed in response. I felt joy, but I tempered it.

"Some other queens are skeptical and wish to halt alliances with Humans. However, I see you have saved our alliance and prevented renewed war with the enemy."

"Thank you, Eminence," I said.

"You are tasked to continue your work. You shall know them not as enemy but as friend. And you shall continue in the Initiative."

"I—" I hesitated to speak, knowing I should not object to a directive from my queen; I would not have been able to if I could feel her command mentally. But I was too far away not to voice the concern. "Eminence," I said, my tone despondent and quiet, "I fear I cannot. I fear I will be asked to leave the Initiative, if not for conduct, then capability." Though she already knew and could plainly see me, I presented my lower right arm to her. Or rather, I presented the bandaged stub where the forearm had shattered and the hand rendered unrecoverable. "I only have three hands," I whined. I wished for the Human capacity for tears, to purge negative toxins and the internal pressures of despair.

"*Jaiku*," she said softly, "most of the other cadets only have two. Paul Newman, you are my three-handed son, and I am proud of you." Her eyes were a wash of warm colors, her voice unwavering in its certainty and sharper in command than I had ever heard. "You will persevere. Prove yourself and remain in the Initiative. This is your queen's directive."

I buzzed enough that my voice was barely audible. "Yes, Eminence."

* * * * *

Chapter Forty-Nine:
Lidstrom

The door to the captain's office was open. I had been personally summoned; still, I had trouble interrupting the man who sat staring out his window at the glorious view of our solar system. His slumped posture showed strain, but I didn't sense anger or even real fatigue. The hair was still that shade of pink, made lighter under the wash of light from the ship's wall panels.

I knocked against the frame of the door, and asked, "Sir?"

Craning back to look at me, he said, "Lidstrom. Come in. Shut the door behind you." I did so and heard him mutter, "One of these days all those doors will be automatic."

Claude Poissonier half-swiveled his chair then stood. He adjusted his sleeveless I.I. jacket out of habit and I noticed he was not wearing any rank patch. Maybe there were too few people on the ship to warrant it.

I shut the door behind me and stood in front of the desk.

"Come on. Join me in a drink. You could use one, and I'll keep you company."

I didn't protest.

The ice sounded different in the ship's gravity, and I wasn't sure if the liquor's vapor was stronger or if I was just more aware of it. He handed me the glass with little ceremony and half-raised his before sipping.

I followed suit, swallowing the cool but burning liquid. I didn't have much experience sorting through the bitter, sweet, and smokey notes, so I just said, "This is good."

The commander gave a scoffing laugh, not derisive, but clearly with more authority. "No, it's not. It's comped. Seriously, one of the major Earthside investors in the I.I. owns this distillery. I've been given many bottles as gifts." He gestured toward the window, glass in hand. "See, that's the problem with anything like this. Any effort big enough needs to have investors and shareholders and decision-makers. It needs bureaucracy to make it run and that same bureaucracy means infighting and red tape and really selfish decisions, which also holds it back."

He looked at me. I nodded. *What else was I supposed to do?*

"You know, that was a really brave thing you and your friends did. Maybe a little foolish. Maybe very foolish."

"Thank you, sir."

"And it leaves us in a difficult position for a number of reasons."

"Yes, sir," I repeated, a little quieter, my head a little lower. My brain was busy recalling the contract I'd signed when I'd first arrived, just a handful of days ago. That, and I was trying to figure out how I would explain to my parents that I'd been ejected from the I.I. still a Green Cadet.

"You know what's funny?" He took another sip, as if to give me a chance to answer. "We don't even have terms for this kind of breach of secrecy. I remember when we still talked about things in terms of 'national security,' then it was 'transnational,' and now— what?—'system-wide' security. They actually argued about it—the bureaucrats, that is." He pointed vaguely overhead. "Took up way more of the meeting than it should have."

They had already met and decided; my fate was sealed.

"Do you know what we concluded? We determined that the secret venture and then what happened on Phobos impacts far more than just our home system or the Human race. That it needs to be considered by every sentient people who could be impacted, including the P'rukktah and the Tsangharee. Even the Belbehan or the Avowols were potentially endangered by one underground effort by a covert group of Human-first officers and enlisteds. And it was uncovered by four cadets. *Green Cadets*, not even sworn in yet. Do you appreciate the irony? *I* appreciate the irony."

He set his glass on the desk, polymer on polymer giving an unsatisfying clink. Then he folded his arms and faced me squarely. "So then, what do we do with *you?*"

It didn't sound like a rhetorical question, so I tried to respond, even if I wasn't feeling brave enough to answer directly. "Sir, I'm sorry I messed things up. I-I understand if I'm out of the program."

The commander raised his eyebrows at me. "That was one of the suggestions. I mean, we do have the shuttle theft. But we also have the log in which you stated your reasons why and the help and clearance of Lieutenant Jane Goodall, as well as Staff Sergeant Clancy."

I almost corrected him, but I got the strong impression I shouldn't.

"There's also the fact that it's the four of you. Four different species, which means four different homes and people to report to. Four people with sensitive information. Also, four of the best we have in the Initiative, if you ask any other cadets here, and in the most diverse squad who, I might add, was already blown up once because of the hidden operation. Then there's me. *I'm* not willing to wash you out for sticking to your guns and overturning a conspiracy. And thanks to that wonderful bureaucracy I mentioned, I'm not an assistant administrator of the Initiative anymore."

I reacted before I could stop it. "Shit! I'm sorry, sir, did they fire you or—"

He waved a hand and shook his head. "At ease, Cadet. They moved me into a different role; there was a vacancy." He was referring to the admiral—likely former Admiral Victoria Hass, who was to have been assigned to this ship. "They named me captain of the first integrated *Command*-class ship, which will become a training ship for cadets like you."

A short laugh escaped me before I could keep it contained. It was at least four parts relief and one part amusement, but the commander didn't seem to appreciate either his new position or my reaction. I quickly wiped the grin from my face and took another sip of my drink. "Thank you, sir—I mean, Captain."

"Mm-hmm." He looked thoughtful and tilted his head to one side. "Well, I'm not your captain yet. There are still some terms that need to be discussed."

I nodded frantically. "Okay. Yes," I said, demonstrating I was likely willing to sign anything to get on this ship and his crew.

"Right. Well, this will go for you, as well as Arrksh and Kesiel, and Paul Newman if he decides he wants to stay on." He turned to a console and swiped a document onto the desk's interface screen.

I sat to give it a better read, and he said, "We're having each of you agree to a non-disclosure concerning any fellow cadets or officers, apart from me and a handful of others who will be working with you. You don't have to lie or come up with any cover story, just say 'I'm under orders not to discuss.'"

I was stunned by how easy it was. "That's it?"

"No, that's just the beginning. Look, we want all four of you on this ship while we sort out the next steps. You're not going to be able to leave anytime soon or have free contact with anyone outside. You'll all receive a note in your file for disciplinary action just in case anyone with the rank sergeant or higher takes a look, and we're not going to reintegrate you with the other cadets until we're sure. Lidstrom, I don't want you to take any of this lightly. There were some major risks you took. Now, there isn't really a good case for throwing you all out. On one hand, every shred of evidence that might work against you is classified. On another, you were technically following orders. A member of your squad received a specific directive from Lieutenant Jane-Two and followed it. *But* you still have work to do to prove yourselves reliable enough to serve in this crew."

"Yes, sir. I'm prepared to do what I need to do."

"I hoped you'd say that. I thought you would. There's one more major logistical item we need to address and I'm hoping you'll agree to it before we tell any of the others."

"Sir?"

"Well, we don't know enough about the Waynes to just accept that they're on the ship. We're doing what we can to take protective measures, but the truth is that no one knows how long they're going to stay here or what they plan to do. I am told that you are partially responsible for their arrival."

I wasn't sure if I should smile or frown in response. I resisted a shrug.

"As such, you're going to be partially responsible for their caretaking. At least one of you will be on-call to respond to the entity at any time for the foreseeable future. We don't know how or why, but it's made a connection with you, and we may need to use that."

I nodded. It was an honor, but a very heavy, intimidating honor. "Why can't—Sir, why not someone with more...experience. I mean, we're not exactly qualified."

"True." He agreed so nonchalantly, I had trouble seeing it as a dig. He sighed and looked out the window. "I've been with the Transnat Space Program for a long time. Longer than you've been alive, I imagine. During the Teek campaign, I was involved—during the war and then the relief effort afterward—and I was read in for much of the classified pieces at the time. But I was building and testing engines. I never flew with any of the missions or the cleanup crews, so I never experienced a Wayne firsthand like the admiral, but I'd heard the stories. A lot of people who saw them, what they could do to planets and ships, are still afraid of them, not only as an enemy but as a species. But you, Kesiel, Arrksh, even Paul Newman, you never really did. You found a seedling when you still had open minds, and while it was small and insentient enough to have no notions about you.

"You see, there's a great temptation to want to group 'others' into clusters, to make them easier to sort. And not just out of malice. We say nice but restrictive things about the Teek, and we believe we understand them better if we put them into one group. The Tsangharee and P'rukktah are easier to think of as rivals or even as being at war with each other, but their relationship is so much more nuanced and complicated than that. Humans aren't united in every decision or even in a common language or national identity, why should anyone else be? I mean, the Tsangharee spread over a dozen moons before they left their solar system, and, in that time, they adapted and evolved many languages and cultures. The Belbehan have more deities than I can count and they're just as capable of tolerating these differences as they are of persecuting them.

"So why not the Waynes? Why can't they have their differences, too?" He didn't seem to be looking for an answer. "Can you still feel it? Are you mentally connected to it?"

I didn't know how I could test it, but it was a good question. So, I closed my eyes for a moment and tried to think through my experiences. I tried to remember everything from touching the rock wall of Phobos to the accident and then the actual interactions with the blue light which was now white.

"Nothing," I said, shaking my head. "I can't feel Wayne now." I supposed it had to do with the insulation between me and it, but I couldn't be certain.

"That's probably a good thing." He chewed his lip for a moment, then added, "And we probably shouldn't call it Wayne. We need to come up with a new name."

"What's in a name?" I asked, thinking of the CG show I'd watched growing up.

"Shakespeare," he said with a nod.

I felt my ears heat up. "No, I was quoting *Spacegirl Stella*. Did she steal that from Shakespeare?"

"Probably. But there is something important in the name, largely because people know Wayne. That was the name of the enemy; still is for a lot of people.

"Oh!" he exclaimed suddenly. "Why not Wallace? Let's call it Wallace."

I had no issue with the name.

Silence hung in the air for a while. It had been a while since there had been so much calm, with no emergencies to deal with or Kesiel to hum in the background.

"Is there anything else, Cadet?" he asked. "I think I've said everything I need to for now, but if you have questions, speak freely."

I realized I still had questions about a lot of things. Regarding my future as a cadet and crewman, I was wary but optimistic and very willing to put in the work, including the risk of being around our extra unplanned squadmate residing in a chamber at the rear of the ship.

"Sir, what happened to the admiral? What was she trying to do?"

"Well, that's a little tricky. I will say you don't need to worry about her right now. She's in custody. Even former TSF admirals have to answer for plans that could threaten interstellar alliances. As for her plan—" He blew out a heavy breath. "Would you accept classified? No. No, you wouldn't, but you don't have a choice. Let's say research and let you extrapolate from there. More importantly, research for what she called 'Human interests,' without the approval of the I.I., the Transnats, or any of the cooperating hives."

The commander rubbed his jaw and cheek, and I could tell from his eyes that he hadn't slept in a while. He was doubtless dealing with a mountain of paperwork, and he clearly didn't want the role of captain, but he was less likely to fall into the Human-first mentality that had gotten the admiral. No, this was a man who favored integration and thought that awkward conversations and vulnerability were worth having in order to achieve greater understanding.

I voiced a hunch: "Sir, did you choose our squad?"

His smile gave him away even though he tried to modestly side-step it. "I put in some recommendations. Given everything that happened, I'd say I did pretty well."

"Yeah, but you had no idea we'd started to connect with the entity. How did you know to put us together?"

He leaned back and drummed his fingers. "I think I picked the four of you for the same reason the entity did. You were each curious, a little outside the box, and you didn't seem to want to kill each other."

"Thank you, sir."

"You're welcome. You're a damn fine pilot, son. Good instincts, strong skills, and you showed up everyone else on the simulator."

"Thanks." Then I remembered and had to correct him. "Not everyone though, not quite. Another anonymous login overshot my score while we were in the infirmary."

"Oh, right…that." He chuckled to himself. "Listen, Lidstrom, I have a confession to make. I had an officer go in as a guest to beat your score."

"What?" I was too surprised and relieved to be angry, because that meant I was still the best of the cadets. "Why? And who?"

"Well, I felt it was a good idea to deflate your ego a little and take a bit of a target off you." I couldn't disagree with him there. At the time, it had been easy to assume sabotage. "As for who, you'll have a chance to meet her, assuming you stay on."

He stood. "Lidstrom, I don't want you to read into this as a formal enlistment—like I said, there's still some bureaucracy to sort through—but I'd like to shake your hand and welcome you to the ship."

I graciously accepted. "Thank you, Captain."

* * *

I was eager to see the now-conscious Paul, but, really, I was excited about everything.

It's hard to explain exactly what it felt like to be on the ship, but this is what I managed to say to Paul: "I've dreamed about flying a ship like this my whole life. I'm not in the pilot's seat yet, but I'm on the ship. It's real. I can reach out and touch it. In English—in Human, we say a goal is 'within arm's reach' or 'close enough to touch.'" I gestured at the walls. "Well, here I am. It's real, and nothing is going to stop me."

"I understand, Darren Lidstrom," he replied. "I have a dream of being part of Humankind, and I can reach out and touch you." He extended his hands. I accepted it and shook the primary right hand, though he used both lefts to secure the hold. The stub of the fourth arm completed the gesture only as a phantom limb.

"I think you're doing a great job," I told him, both as my squadmate and my friend. I was impressed with myself and how much I had learned in such a short time by partnering with all the non-Humans I was told to avoid.

"Lidstrom, I have a question for you, as a Human."

I suppressed a laugh. "What is it, Paul?"

"Do you think that this last week's experience could be long literature? I am contemplating writing the first Teek novel in the Human style."

"I mean, I guess…" I admired his ambition, but I had to admit that the prospect baffled me a little bit. "Paul, I feel like I only know a fraction of what actually happened, and a bunch of it is classified. How would you even know where to begin?"

He raised a finger, stopping me before I could continue. "Perhaps you could tell me what you experienced and help me fill in some of my gaps."

"Sure." I could only imagine what it would be like trying to squeeze any testimony from Arrksh or preventing Kesiel from singing a million-word saga, but I was more than willing to swap stories with Paul, especially since I could then keep him company through his recovery.

* * *

When Staff Sergeant Clancy arrived on the ship, I wanted to address her as a relative rather than a sergeant. I maintained my composure, of course, but I did smile when she told me, "At ease, Hotshot."

Clancy and a couple other officers in the know were charged with more cleanup than they wanted, but it was good to have all our things returned to us from Mons, few though they were. I was even more relieved to see she also had a smooth dark suitcase for Paul.

She escorted us to our new rooms where we'd been paired up for the time being. Kesiel and Arrksh were dropped off first. Paul and I were next door.

She issued me my newly calibrated wrist device, now set up to access the necessary parts of the Starship *Endeavor*. When I reactivated it I laughed out loud at my on-ship ID.

It figured I was I.I. 1; E-84.

Clancy asked, "What? Did we spell your name wrong, or are you just stuck on the fact that everything is labeled I.I. 1?"

I shook my head. "It's, uh...it's hard to explain."

Clancy folded her arms casually across her chest and leaned one shoulder into the wall space. "Try me."

I shrugged and gave a small laugh. "*Tessenda*," I told her of Kesiel's poetry of convergence, the idea that connections and patterns guided things everywhere and can be seen by those willing to look. I was E-84, if for no other reason other than consistency, and to me, it was a sure sign that I belonged.

Clancy, on the other hand, just looked confused.

* * * * *

Chapter Fifty: Arrksh

The ship is extensive, but the walls and space of the rooms are small. The proximity to the squad is always close; the proximity of the entity cannot even be heard directly outside of its tank unless I listen very carefully.

The sense of family is stronger.

Paul Newman joins us on the foredeck, entreats sympathy in a gesture with a missing arm. We all support in our own way. Lidstrom offers an embrace, after which Paul Newman asks if he has squeezed appropriately for a hug. Kesiel offers to cook and eat in celebration and does not clarify whether or not she means the disconnected hand—she knows the hand was largely destroyed, and I know that Tsangharee do not like to waste food. I commend Paul for his bravery.

I assist Kesiel's healing process, using practices not documented by Human or Teek scientists while Doctor Jane turns a blind eye. Lidstrom helps me with my Human, and Paul Newman helps me to understand more of the history and politics of the Teek. The squad will remain isolated from the other cadets on the planet, but each of us is rarely alone for long periods of time.

So quickly, each *I* forms into *we*.

We regard Mars together. We visit the entity in shifts. We answer questions, submit to examinations, and then, eventually, resume training.

I am listening to my language lessons one evening when I receive a message which has been approved from the outside. It is the envoy, Elder Saerpstra, my kin, expressing equal parts concern and ire over my recent ordeal. She asks if, given my experiences among Humans and potential station among our people, I should want to come home.

I examine my small quarters, the smooth rounded corners, the simple modular bed, and the desk space. I note the second bed, of very different design, contoured for a side-lying lizard, my roommate who would soon be finishing her evening's physical therapy.

I try my tongue at the language I have been learning and record, "Gratitude, Elder, but no. I am a part of this fine crew."

* * * * *

Epilogue:
Shin

I opened my eyes and regretted the decision immediately. Never before had I felt so hungover. I've had the shit kicked out of me in kickboxing enough times to learn some really good lessons, but this was a whole new level of sore.

"Hey," a voice said. I tried to find it with my eyes, but they had trouble focusing. "Can you hear me? Sorry about the pain. We couldn't put you on a higher dose without risking you staying in a coma."

A coma? Shit. I couldn't remember enough of what had happened, but the spinning sensation was still really strong. The word sabotage was in my brain, the last thought bookmarked before I'd been taken down.

"Green Cadet Helen Shin," the voice said again. "If you can hear me, please indicate. If you cannot speak, two blinks will do."

My voice came out in a controlled croak. "I hear you."

"Good. Cadet, my name is Staff Sergeant Genevieve Ramirez." She started to come into focus. Completely bald and whiter than I would have figured for someone named Ramirez. "Do you know where you are?"

"Mars," I said. I licked my lips. My mouth felt dry, but my lips weren't cracked. "Mons Academy. I.I."

"Good. Cadet, you probably feel disoriented, and you're on an intense muscle relaxer, so it will be hard to move. You will make a full recovery, though."

This statement hardly comforted me. How badly had I been injured? I wanted to close my eyes, but Genevieve Ramirez was still staring at me. She was trying to determine...something. My expression? My temperament? My sanity? I didn't know how much I could show through the layers of gauze on my forehead, but I decided to project resoluteness, which was only a slight frown away from defiant.

"Cadet," she said, slowly and carefully, "will you uphold the safety and progress of Humanity as your highest mandate?"

"Of course," I said, without hesitation. Was it a trick question? Didn't matter, so I doubled down. "Yes, Sergeant."

"Good." This time the sergeant didn't smile. She matched my serious and added deadly. "The admiral is out of commission but she has a very important mission for you."

* * * * *

About Mike Jack Stoumbos

Mike Jack Stoumbos is an fiction author, disguised as a believably normal high school teacher, living with his wife and their parrot. THIS FINE CREW is his debut space opera series, and is probably the natural result of a lifelong love of series featuring the word "Star." Mike Jack is also a 1st-place winner of the Writers of the Future Contest (Winter 2021), and has had his short fiction published in a number of anthologies, including STREET MAGIC, HOLD YOUR FIRE, GALACTIC STEW from Zombies Need Brains, and DRAGON WRITERS alongside Brandon Sanderson. In addition to writing fiction, Mike Jack has published academic/informational articles, stageplays, and lovably geeky parody lyrics. You can find him online at MikeJackStoumbos.com or @MJStoumbos on Twitter, as well as on several karaoke stages.

* * * * *

The following is an

Excerpt from Book One of the Lunar Free State:

The Moon and Beyond

John E. Siers

Available from Theogony Books

eBook, Audio, and Paperback

Excerpt from "The Moon and Beyond:"

"So, what have we got?" The chief had no patience for inter-agency squabbles.

The FBI man turned to him with a scowl. "We've got some abandoned buildings, a lot of abandoned stuff—none of which has anything to do with spaceships—and about a hundred and sixty scientists, maintenance people, and dependents left behind, all of whom claim they knew nothing at all about what was really going on until today. Oh, yeah, and we have some stripped computer hardware with all memory and processor sections removed. I mean physically taken out, not a chip left, nothing for the techies to work with. And not a scrap of paper around that will give us any more information…at least, not that we've found so far. My people are still looking."

"What about that underground complex on the other side of the hill?"

"That place is wiped out. It looks like somebody set off a *nuke* in there. The concrete walls are partly fused! The floor is still too hot to walk on. Our people say they aren't sure how you could even *do* something like that. They're working on it, but I doubt they're going to find anything."

"What about our man inside, the guy who set up the computer tap?"

"Not a trace, chief," one of the NSA men said. "Either he managed to keep his cover and stayed with them, or they're holding him prisoner, or else…" The agent shrugged.

"You think they terminated him?" The chief lifted an eyebrow. "A bunch of rocket scientists?"

"Wouldn't put it past them. Look at what Homeland Security ran into. Those motion-sensing chain guns are *nasty*, and the area between the inner and outer perimeter fence is mined! Of course, they posted warning signs, even marked the fire zones for the guns. Nobody would have gotten hurt if the troops had taken the signs seriously."

435

The Homeland Security colonel favored the NSA man with an icy look. "That's bullshit. How did we know they weren't bluffing? You'd feel pretty stupid if we'd played it safe and then found out there were no defenses, just a bunch of signs!"

"Forget it!" snarled the chief. "Their whole purpose was to delay us, and it worked. What about the Air Force?"

"It might as well have been a UFO sighting as far as they're concerned. Two of their F-25s went after that spaceship, or whatever it was we saw leaving. The damned thing went straight up, over eighty thousand meters per minute, they say. That's nearly Mach Two, in a *vertical climb*. No aircraft in *anybody's* arsenal can sustain a climb like that. Thirty seconds after they picked it up, it was well above their service ceiling and still accelerating. Ordinary ground radar couldn't find it, but NORAD *thinks* they might have caught a short glimpse with one of their satellite-watch systems, a hundred miles up and still going."

"So where did they go?"

"Well, chief, if we believe what those leftover scientists are telling us, I guess they went to the Moon."

* * * * *

Get "The Moon and Beyond" here:
https://www.amazon.com/dp/B097QMN7PJ.

Find out more about John E. Siers at:
https://chriskennedypublishing.com.

* * * * *

The following is an

Excerpt from Book One of Abner Fortis, ISMC:

Cherry Drop

P.A. Piatt

Available from Theogony Books

eBook, Audio, and Paperback

Excerpt from "Cherry Drop:"

"Here they come!"

A low, throbbing buzz rose from the trees and the undergrowth shook. Thousands of bugs exploded out of the jungle, and Fortis' breath caught in his throat. The insects tumbled over each other in a rolling, skittering mass that engulfed everything in its path.

The Space Marines didn't need an order to open fire. Rifles cracked and the grenade launcher thumped over and over as they tried to stem the tide of bugs. Grenades tore holes in the ranks of the bugs and well-aimed rifle fire dropped many more. Still, the bugs advanced.

Hawkins' voice boomed in Fortis' ear. "LT, fall back behind the fighting position, clear the way for the heavy weapons."

Fortis looked over his shoulder and saw the fighting holes bristling with Marines who couldn't fire for fear of hitting their own comrades. He thumped Thorsen on the shoulder.

"Fall back!" he ordered. "Take up positions behind the fighting holes."

Thorsen stopped firing and moved among the other Marines, relaying Fortis' order. One by one, the Marines stopped firing and made for the rear. As the gunfire slacked off, the bugs closed ranks and continued forward.

After the last Marine had fallen back, Fortis motioned to Thorsen.

"Let's go!"

Thorsen turned and let out a blood-chilling scream. A bug had approached unnoticed and buried its stinger deep in Thorsen's calf. The stricken Marine fell to the ground and began to convulse as the neurotoxin entered his bloodstream.

439

"Holy shit!" Fortis drew his kukri, ran over, and chopped at the insect stinger. The injured bug made a high-pitched shrieking noise, which Fortis cut short with another stroke of his knife.

Viscous, black goo oozed from the hole in Thorsen's armor and his convulsions ceased.

"Get the hell out of there!"

Hawkins was shouting in his ear, and Abner looked up. The line of bugs was ten meters away. For a split second he almost turned and ran, but the urge vanished as quickly as it appeared. He grabbed Thorsen under the arms and dragged the injured Marine along with him, pursued by the inexorable tide of gaping pincers and dripping stingers.

Fortis pulled Thorsen as fast as he could, straining with all his might against the substantial Pada-Pada gravity. Thorsen convulsed and slipped from Abner's grip and the young officer fell backward. When he sat up, he saw the bugs were almost on them.

* * * * *

Get "Cherry Drop" now at:
https://www.amazon.com/dp/B09B14VBK2

Find out more about P.A. Piatt at:
https://chriskennedypublishing.com

* * * * *

The following is an

Excerpt from Book One of Murphy's Lawless:

Shakes

Mike Massa

Available from Beyond Terra Press

eBook and Paperback

Excerpt from "Shakes:"

"My name is Volo of the House Zobulakos," the SpinDog announced haughtily. Harry watched as his slender ally found his feet and made a show of brushing imaginary dust from his shoulder where the lance had rested.

Volo was defiant even in the face of drawn weapons; Harry had to give him points for style.

"I am here representing the esteemed friend to all Sarmatchani, my father, Arko Primus Heraklis Zobulakos. This is a mission of great importance. What honorless prole names my brother a liar and interferes with the will of the Primus? Tell me, that I might inform your chief of this insolence."

Harry tensed as two of the newcomers surged forward in angry reaction to the word "honorless," but the tall man interposed his lance, barring their way.

"Father!" the shorter one objected, throwing back her hood, revealing a sharp featured young woman. She'd drawn her blade and balefully eyed the SpinDog. "Let me teach this arrogant weakling about honor!"

"Nay, Stella," the broad-shouldered man said grimly. "Even my daughter must cleave to the law. This is a clan matter. And as to the stripling's question…

"I, hight Yannis al-Caoimhip ex-huscarlo, Patrisero of the Herdbane, First among the Sarmatchani," he went on, fixing his eyes first on Volo and then each of the Terrans. "I name Stabilo of the Sky People a liar, a cheat, and a coward. I call his people to account. Blood or treasure. At dawn tomorrow either will suffice."

443

Harry didn't say a word but heard a deep sigh from Rodriguez. These were the allies he'd been sent to find, all right. Just like every other joint operation with indigs, it was SNAFU.

Murphy's Law was in still in effect.

* * * * *

Get "Shakes" now at: https://www.amazon.com/dp/B0861F23KH

Find out more about Myrphy's Lawless and Beyond Terra Press at: https://chriskennedypublishing.com/imprints-authors/beyond-terra-press/

* * * * *